THE
PRIMAL
YOKE

THE PRIMAL YOKE

A Novel by
Tom Lea
WITH DRAWINGS BY THE AUTHOR

LITTLE, BROWN AND COMPANY
BOSTON · TORONTO

THAT OLE DEVIL CALLED LOVE
Words and music by Allan Roberts and Doris Fisher

© Copyright MCMXLIV, MCMXLV by PICKWICK MUSIC CORPORATION,
322 West 48th Street, New York 36, N.Y.
Reprinted by Permission   All Rights Reserved

to
my companions
those present in body
those present in spirit
at a lunch we had one time
in Craig

The wise man delights in water.
The Good man delights in mountains.
For the wise move, but the Good stay still.
The wise are happy; but the Good, secure.

The Analects, Book VI, 21

THE
PRIMAL
YOKE

He sprang from the gritty iron of the Pullman car step and caught his balance upon the dim whiteness that covered the ground. His feet felt the snow. His pounding heart felt it.

Turning in the dark to look along the side of the train,

3

by the light of the bulbs over the station platform he could make out the painted letters: GREEN JUNCTION, ELEVATION 6779, UNION PACIFIC. He could see a lone baggageman wheeling a truck, and two trainmen with their lanterns. He could see no one else. The parking space by the platform was empty.

He stood for a moment trying to tell himself that he had not expected anyone to meet him. It was 0450 in the morning watch — like hell. It was four-fifty A.M., Wyoming Civilian Time, it was ten minutes to five in the morning. And Silvertip was twenty-six miles away with ice on the road.

Maybe they hadn't gotten the wire.

Shove off with that, he told himself. They got it.

He had expected them at the station. He had imagined many times how they would be there waiting for him when he finally got back. He stood looking for them in the dark.

"Kind of a hard hour, for people —" the Pullman porter said, looking too. "— Oh, thank you, Sergeant."

He put his glove back on and stood alone on the snow with his suitcase. The closing slam of the vestibule door over the car steps knocked loose a luminous cloud of powdery frost. The train began to move. It rolled away leaving him and he looked across the empty tracks at the familiar town.

It had not changed. The lightless business blocks of Green Junction slept in the night quiet, rimmed and laced with the paleness of the snow. Higher than the rest a rounded patch of paleness on the Fontenelle County Courthouse showed vague against the sky.

Two blocks up the street from the station platform a single neon sign blinked a recurrent flash, pumping a little squirt of hot scarlet into the big bloodless dark of the world. The sign said *Covered Wagon,* with EATS that

4

ticked on and off, then on again. He started for it, with his suitcase in his hand.

The cold came reaching through him. At each breath he drew, frost stiffened the hairs inside his nostrils. The soles of his shoes crackled grainy on the ice-crusted snow; in the winter silence his footfalls seemed to speak.

They made the solitary sound of his welcome home.

The swinging heft of the suitcase brought a stitch through his right side. He strode disregarding it for half a block. Then he stopped, hunching up his right shoulder, and he changed over, to carry the weight with his other hand.

At the edge of light where the neon ruddied the sidewalk he slipped on ice and nearly sprawled. Irked with himself, with his lubberly footing, with the unrelieved twinge in his side, he shoved open the café door and stepped in, scowling.

The pair of coffee drinkers sitting sleepy at the counter, and the waitress leaning on the pass-through shelf opening to the kitchen, turned casually to look, then stared like gawks, totally unprepared for a scowling night-borne military apparition in a formidable forest-green service overcoat with bright red chevrons on the sleeve.

He stamped muck from his well-shined low quarter shoes, chose the table closest to the hissing radiator, pushed his suitcase against the wall, took off his gloves, cap and overcoat, hung them on a rack, and sat down.

The flat light flooding from overhead disclosed a pallor, a yellowish cast of tan unlike any color ever evoked by Wyoming winter, on his face. It was a young but tense and thin-fleshed face, with straight mouth and gray eyes uncommonly sharp under the sandy brows and close-cropped sandy hair.

The uniform was of the same green wool as the coat and

5

cap on the rack. Highly polished leather belted the trim, square-pocketed blouse. The upper sleeve was marked with three red-bordered chevrons. Two precisely horizontal lines of crisply colored ribbons, some encrusted with small bronze stars, were ranged above the square flap of the left breast pocket; beneath the ribbons were pinned the silver glints of Expert badges and pendant bars. At the shoulder there was sewn an insignia shaped like a diamond. Its blue field carried five white stars disposed to enfigure the Southern Cross, and a tall blood-red numeral 1 bearing a word in white: Guadalcanal.

The abstruse emblems on display, the buttons, badges, bits of colored cloth, were a history in hieroglyphs of the taut face. They brought a strange report, of battle smokes and alien oceans, to the peaceable inland ignorance of the Covered Wagon Café.

"I couldn't make it out," the waitress said, "until now." She handed him the breakfast card. "I bet you are a Marine. I bet you just came in on Number Nine."

"It's hard to make out, you think?"

"That color suit, it's a different kind. Like some other army not ours. It dawned on me when I saw there — Guada'canal. Seems like about a million years ago, reading stuff like Guada'canal."

"Give me the orange juice, and three boiled eggs — four minutes — and some toast and coffee. No butter on the toast."

"Gee. Coffee now?"

"It might help."

She came back with the cup from the coffee urn behind the counter. "First time I ever did serve anybody in a Marine suit. You seen a lot, I can tell."

"You wouldn't give me a snow job."

"What's that mean?"

6

"It means you wouldn't kid me."

"Okay, Mister Snowman. You didn't see a thing." She walked away with her heels hitting hard on the linoleum.

He drank the rancid coffee, staring at the front window, idly pronouncing to himself the reversed letters on the plate glass, nogaW derevoC.

Outside there was not a hint of daylight yet.

"About a snow job," he said to her when she came bringing the breakfast, "there's one I want to see. The one out there."

"Huh?"

"Real snow. All over the ground. Deep."

"Who's kidding who now? Maybe it's sugar, out there." She found not the slightest sign of the levity she looked for in the gray eyes. "It's real snow, God knows, and it's been there since November. Looky. Where'd you come from anyhow? How come you're in Green Junction?"

"I'm nearly home."

Her eyes came open wider as she looked at him. "Wait a minute. You're from Silvertip?"

He nodded.

"Then you're the Spurling brother, the other one. You're the one had the picture in the Cheyenne and Casper papers, the war medal. Say now! *Hey* Claude!" she called to one of the coffee drinkers at the counter, who turned on his stool, "you know who this is? It's the Spurling —"

"I be dogged," the man said, coming to the table. He wore a cap with plaid earflaps and he had a long nose. "I know your daddy. I'm C. M. Nagle. Shake, will you?"

"My name is Hank Spurling."

"I haven't seen that old daddy of yours for some time. I kind of forgot, or I would of guessed who you was. Are you just now getting back? Or are you still in?"

"Paid off. I'm back."

"Your folks come to meet you? Where are they?"

"I guess they couldn't make it."

"Danged shame, ain't it? Why couldn't they? How long since they seen you?"

"Four years."

"You mean you couldn't hook no leave in all that time? What's the matter? Couldn't you work it?"

"I had a leave. In Melbourne, Australia."

"You was at the end of the line, wasn't you? You know, your daddy and me, we worked together awhile over at the Rackland Dam during the war. That's where I knew him. In 'forty-three and 'forty-four. Ingo Spurling, that son of a gun. He'd git high and he'd bust his buttons telling about how his boy, or his boys, was winning the war. It liked to knocked the daylights out of him when the lieutenant he talked about got killed over in Europe. That was your brother, wasn't it? You the only one left, eh?"

"I still have one brother."

"Say, all them ribbons. I do recognize a Purple Heart, don't I? Where'd you git nicked? Was it bad?"

"You can knock off the quiz program. I'm not on it."

"How's that? What'd you say?"

"I said — I got a quiz program myself. What times does the Elk Park mail stage leave for Silvertip?"

"Well. You are kind of far behind now, ain't you, son? If you want to know, that thing don't never leave. Not any more, it don't. These days it's like a Greyhound bus."

"Okay, Mac. It's a honey boat. Just so it leaves, these days. You know what time it leaves?"

"Nope. You know why I don't?"

"Nope."

"I got my own car."

"You be careful with it — coxs'n."

"I ain't sure what you're calling me —"

8

The other coffee drinker at the counter had risen to his feet. "That northbound bus comes through at six-fifty if the ice isn't too bad," he said. He saw Spurling's eyes. "Come on now, Claude. Quit chewing the rag. We got twenty minutes to ride to work."

C. M. Nagle paid for his coffee at the cash register, jerked on his mackinaw and pulled down his plaid earflaps. Holding the street door half open, ready to use, he stood for a moment like a ruffled hen with a long bill and he managed to form another question, as if laying an egg. "Why do you fellers come out of the Army so uncivil?"

"Army —" Hank Spurling said, watching the door go shut. "The Army so uncivil." He turned to the waitress. "That yardbird's chum said six-fifty. Did he mean morning or evening?"

"He meant morning."

"Could you tell me where the bus stops — these days?"

"Over by the Gulf station, across from the courthouse. Like some more coffee?"

While she was pouring it four new customers came into the Covered Wagon and sat down to order at the counter, talking among themselves.

Hank Spurling sat alone, in his own silence, eating boiled egg and toast. Daylight showed through the window.

A beaded film of steam on the plate glass withheld all detail of street and sky outside; only a principal fact penetrated the fogged pane. Day had come. It was a day beyond any measure Hank Spurling could give it. It was not arriving, and neither was he, the way he had imagined it. But here it was.

He got up from his chair and went to his overcoat. From one of its pockets he pulled the curve-stemmed brier pipe and tobacco pouch he had bought at Aiea Naval Hospital. Back at his table he loaded the pipe, tamped it, lit it, and

9

sat waiting, watching the black hands on the white face of the clock over the cash register.

At six thirty-eight he put on his coat and cap and paid for his breakfast. Half a dozen customers paused in their eating, to look.

"I decided you just want to be left alone," the waitress said, making change. "Come back and see us."

"Sure."

He picked up his suitcase and walked out into the gray light on the silent snow-banked street. The coming of day brought a rising temperature and a lowering sky. As he walked toward the courthouse a hush in the air foretold a new fall of snow. The bus with its headlights burning and its tire chains clinking hauled to a stop on the strewn cinders by the service station at ten past seven.

A chill had pierced to Hank Spurling's bones by the time he climbed aboard. He paid the driver a dollar-ten fare, stowed the suitcase and took a seat toward the back of the bus, alone, where he sat gathering warmth to himself with hands in pockets and coat collar turned high. He clenched his jaws to keep his teeth from chattering.

The bus door flapped shut. The engine with a blue stink of exhaust went grinding into gear and the bus lumbered up the street, out the highway past the last house of Green Junction, climbed the slow grade to the rimrock and rolled into the winter emptiness of the Fontenelle Plateau.

A vault of cloud reached down to enclose the sweep of whiteness upon the ghostly plain. In the west stood the far wraiths of the Kainah Hills. In the east and to the north stood only sky mist of oncoming storm that swallowed the build of the world.

The Silvertip road forked from the main highway; the bus turned into the narrower, snow-plowed track. It followed curves of low hills that flattened away into the

10

valley of the frozen Freefolk River. A twisting hazed line of gray willow marked the course of the stream. Upon the wan flatness of the valley's floor, a few thin lines of winter-bare cottonwoods stood lonely. The bus moved by half-buried fences and ragged hayricks capped with white, to the dozen houses and sheds at the hamlet of Cottonwood, where the first flakes tumbled as precursors from the gray-ness overhead.

Hank Spurling sat the jolting bus seat, nearly home.

Beyond fields and the bend of the Freefolk, the road be-gan a climb into the flank of the ascending valley. Upon the near slope of an overlooking ridge stood the blue-black rich darkness of spruce dusted with pale tracery of new falling snow. Hank Spurling looked up at it with all his being centered in the vivid act of seeing.

What he looked for most, he could not see. Through the whitening whirl of snowflakes outside the window of the crawling bus, he looked for a jag of peaks, a loom of high granite and snowy ice, the Cloudrock Mountains. He could not see them in the shroud of storm. They had a shape he had dreamed of seeing in bloody holes on coral islands.

2

"Ingo." Em Spurling shook him by the arm. "Ingo, if I wasn't so brokenhearted, I'd be mad. Wake up!"

Lying fully dressed on a battered leather couch, Ingo Spurling opened his eyes. The light globe hanging from the ceiling was lit; it beamed down into his face and made him squint. He looked up at his wife. "I'm awake," he said.

"Ingo. He's surely on the bus — he must be on it. It's a quarter to seven. Breakfast's on the table. I haven't closed my eyes — but there's no use — talking about it. When I think of Haven getting in on that train in the night and nobody to meet him —"

"It might be that he caught a ride. With somebody coming this way. He might be — getting here already." Ingo Spurling sat up, coughed, rubbed at the sting in his eyes. The taint of the whiskey still on his breath fumed with the rotten taste in his mouth; the smell of coffee coming from the kitchen stove made him faintly sick. "We better get over to town, Em," he said, with his hand pressing his forehead. "We're afoot —"

"I know," Em Spurling said, not trusting her tongue to say more.

It was snowing hard when they came out the back door. Ingo Spurling felt the cold invade his reluctant lungs. He squared his shoulders, balling his chapped fists in the side pockets of his red mackinaw. He was wearing the special-occasion hat that usually hung in state on the polished antelope prong by the parlor door. It was a very big roll-brimmed, peak-crowned pearl-gray "Beldon" Stetson and it collected a cap of snow like the overhanging eaves on a tall house. His wife had a home-knitted blue muffler tied over her head and under her chin, with the ends tucked into the buttoned collar of her coat, and her high galoshes were buckled up tight. She walked behind Ingo. His booted feet printed tracks for her to follow through the drifts on the path across the feed yard, to the swing gate and the byroad that led through bleak whiteness a cold mile to Silvertip.

Less than a hundred yards beyond the gate they came to the ice-needled runt willows and box elders where the tracks

13

of the road made a sharp turn to meet the plank bridge over Plew Creek. Nosed down the slope of the bank at the near side of the planking, careened with a front wheel out of sight in rough ice at the edge of the stream, sat a 1940 Ford pickup truck.

There was an air of desolation in its useless tilt off the road; the fallen snow that caked it made it more forlorn. It sat reproachfully in silence, with the grooves of its mistaken, side-slipped skid marks visible yet, a doleful monument to error, an error by Ingo Spurling.

They looked at it.

"I've made that turn a million times," Ingo said. "Practice makes perfect. Kind of funny."

"Funny? You call that funny?"

"Never mind. Not real funny. I only missed the whole bridge —" He walked to the edge of the ice, bent down and felt at the top of the submerged wheel, and came back to the planking where Em waited. "The wheel's bent, I guess. Maybe the axle." He shook his head. "It's a job for a tow truck."

"It's a bill — but let's hurry. Don't talk about it. Even to think about anything else with Haven coming home —"

They trudged the road in the quiet of the falling snow, to town.

There were only dimmed stirrings of early morning life and warmth, a few lights in windows, one moving car, an occasional bundled-up walker blurred with snowflakes, on Silvertip's main stem when the Spurlings came around the corner and tramped a sidewalk mantled in clean white to the covered porchway with the peeled log columns in front of the Rodemacher Mercantile Co.

Max Rodemacher, hearing them stamp their feet at the sill, peered through his horn-rimmed glasses and came surprised out of the Post Office cage by the hardware counter.

14

"Did he get in all right? Where is that boy? You brought him by so we could see him?"

For a moment neither Spurling answered. "We didn't get to Green Junction," Em said. "The bus hasn't come yet, has it?"

"You — what happened?"

"The pickup," Ingo said. "The old Jessie slid off the road. Back of the house, before crossing Plew Creek. Put us afoot in the middle of the night. Em's mad."

"I'm heartsick," Em said. *"Has* the bus come yet, Max?"

"No. It's only ten after eight. Is Hank on the bus? How'd he let you know?"

"He didn't. But he must be on it."

"Well. You walk into town?"

"We wanted to meet Haven. Ingo, please keep a good eye on the street out there."

"Em," Max Rodemacher said, "weather like this, you know how the bus is. Maybe late, maybe not. When it comes, we can't miss it. We won't miss that boy, either. How bad is the pickup, Ingo?"

"It needs a little lifting back on the road —" He knew Max was standing close trying to smell his breath. "Nothing else, to amount to much."

"Lucky it was near the house, not halfway to Junction," Max said, looking at Em Spurling. He started back to the Post Office cage, to tie up the mail sack.

"I ought to go to Piggott's and see Tom about a tow," Ingo said, "before this storm buries old Jessie — Why, howdy, Rowdey!"

Rowdey Bustleton came in from the street and closed the door, scuffing his feet. "Greetings, Ingo. Oh —" he tipped his snow-speckled hat — "good morning, Mrs. Spurling. Ingo, did that boy get home? He here?"

"We expect him on the bus —" Ingo began.

15

"It's coming now —"

"There it is!" Em Spurling said, starting for the door. Ingo looked and started too.

They saw him standing tall and different in his uniform, facing the step, waiting for the bus to stop and the door to open. They had formed a certain picture of what they would see, remembering the nineteen-year-old boy that went away. To both of them, the picture was instantly, poignantly wrong. Their second son Haven stood there, alive, back in Silvertip from the other side of the world: he was a stranger thin and tall, a man with a look they did not know.

He saw them come hurrying, his mother first, out into the flying snowflakes, with their faces turned toward him.

He saw them as they actually looked, his mother and father in that instant, before his memories of them and their meanings to him and his expectations for them overlapped and blurred the clear image in the eye with the less measurable and less clear images in the heart.

He saw in that moment that his mother with her flushed, round face framed in a rough winter muffler was a stout and patient woman grown older now with the good humor gone from where it once had lived in the creases at the corners of her mouth.

He saw in that moment that his father's formerly handsome face under the sporty sweep of a big rodeo hat was the face of a not quite impressive man grown older with the colorful flair and the confident assurance that had once been his charm now the intimation of his weakness.

In that moment before the bus door opened, before images in his heart obscured images in his eyes, doubt touched for a flicking instant at Hank Spurling's battle-born dream of the mountains, the impregnable fortress of the good life waiting yet in the Cloudrocks.

16

It had sufficed to bring him home. He was home. The door came open and he stepped out with a bear hug for his folks.

"Oh Haven — oh goodness, Haven. Here you are," his mother said with her arms reaching up around him.

"Well — Mother —" he kissed her. He felt his father's hand on his shoulder. He saw his face. "And Dad —"

"You — doggone —" his father said, hugging — "rascal."

"Let me get my suitcase off." The bus driver handed it to him. "You whistled me up some snow, didn't you? Didn't you, Mother?"

"Oh Haven. Tell me did you think we were awful? Not being there in the night?"

"Look, I just took the first train I could grab, out of Dago, then Los Angeles. I never asked what time it got to Junction till after the ticket was bought. Couldn't have been a worse time, I knew it when I telegraphed."

"You knew we would be there. We started out. The car went off the road."

"Whereabouts? Bad?"

"Not bad, Hank. Right close to the house, lucky."

"It was bad not being there to bring you home, Haven. But you're here! Aren't you? You look so — fine. In the uniform and all —"

Max Rodemacher and Rowdey Bustleton were both waiting, grinning, under the cover of the porchway.

"Welcome back," Rodemacher said, gripping Hank's hand. "Such a long time! I wouldn't know you, so changed. Come on in the store!"

"These folks are a leetle glad to see you, son. I'm Rowdey Bustleton." He shook Hank's hand. "Maybe you're a leetle glad yourself."

17

"Looks good, all right. This is the first snow I seen since March, 1942."

"Think of that," his mother said. "Do you notice the cold, Haven?"

"It's what I been waiting to notice."

Max Rodemacher was bringing Alf Klein and old Bill Clancy from the storeroom to shake Hank Spurling's hand.

"He looks like he's been there and back, don't he?" Ingo called out. "Show us the rest of that uniform, Hank. Take off your coat."

Hank Spurling frowned, then checked himself, looking at his father. In wordless constraint he unbuttoned the overcoat, pulled it off, put it on a counter.

"A regular old campaign soldier," his father said.

Trapped in discomfort, with eyes upon him, he groped for words — anything — to fend off remarks like his father's. "This leather belt here, in the Corps we call it a Peter Bain. It's extra, not issue. This winter service uniform, I haven't had it on since Melbourne. In 1943." Still groping, trying to keep talking, with eyes still upon him, he reached into a pocket. "Something maybe interesting — Jap flag, not a fake. And this thing, kind of unusual."

"What is it?"

"What the Shamboes call Belt of a Thousand Stitches. All those little dots —" he pointed to them, embroidered red on the rich yellow silk — "every one was sewed by a different friend back in Japan. Japs wore these for luck."

"How'd you get it?"

"This particular Jap wasn't lucky."

"Where was he?"

"He was on Peleliu."

"Did you kill him, Hank?"

"A Marine killed him."

"When the Air Force dropped that Bomb," said old

18

Bill Clancy, "was when they really got down to business killing them Japanese boogers."

"Say Hank," his father said. "Tell us about the ribbons on your chest."

"They're issued with the uniform. All but the Good Conduct."

"Now wait a minute, son."

He looked at his father. "There's nothing to tell."

"A Navy Cross is something to tell," his father said. "It's the equivalent of a Distinguished Service Cross. Isn't it? In my day that was something to tell."

"Ingo," Em Spurling said, "we want to get home before long. It's snowing bad and if it keeps up we —"

"Em," Ingo Spurling said, "I'm just proud of him. *Proud, that's all!* If you want to get home — Hank, you and your mother wait here. I'll get Tom Piggott's truck and we'll ride out to the house. I got to get the Ford going again — we're afoot until I do. Unless you want to saddle old Hemlock."

"Ingo," Rowdey Bustleton said, "you're a bird. We get a good man back from the wars and you want to carry him home on a tow truck. I'm going to take Mrs. Spurling and the sergeant in my car, and I'm inviting you to go along. I'll bring you back to town to get Tom Piggott. My car's in front of my place down the street. Wait here." He went out the door.

"It's kind of him," Em said.

"He's a dandy fellow," Ingo said. "He's got the Cloudrock Bar."

"Dad, you mentioned old Hemlock. How is he?"

"Eating his head off. On a pension and don't know it."

"Did you keep any of the others?"

"Two of the old pack string. Kind of for sentiment. Kind of for use. Big Agnes. She's so mean I love her. And Sonny

19

because your brother Rut was the one that broke him."

"I remember when he did. Rut. It — well, speaking of pack strings. You ought to have worked the pack horse I liberated on Okinawa. About hip pocket high at the withers and he had an action like Old Lightning at Cheyenne. I think I wrote you. I wish I had a picture of —"

"Rut wrote about riding a farm horse in Normandy. It was one of those froggy half-blood Percherons. I could just imagine it. You know, Hank, I knew a lot of that country Rut fought in. I knew it in 1918 and 1919. I could see it all before me."

"I guess you could."

"Rut got a battlefield commission as a second lieutenant. He was a fighting son of a gun. Good at it. Good at everything."

"I know. What do you hear from Fenno?"

"Fenwick is coming home at Easter," Em said. "He's just fine. I wrote you about his skiing, and his water colors."

"You going to be skiing again now pretty soon, Hank?" Alf Klein asked.

"About tomorrow — trying, anyway."

"All set for a ride, folks," Bustleton called from the door.

"Em." As she started away Max Rodemacher touched her sleeve. "With this storm it's going to be slow here at the store. I won't need you. I want you to take tomorrow off too. That's with pay like today, understand? Get in some visiting with that boy."

"I do thank you, Max," she said.

Out by the curb, Bustleton had opened the trunk for the suitcase. "Taxi!" he said. "You want to ride back there with your mother? Ingo, you get in with me."

The falling snow veiled all but the nearest foreground as

20

the car moved through the whiteness. It was not until they had come over the bridge, past the old pickup, past the brush along Plew Creek, that Hank saw the house. He saw beyond the fence, dim in the swirl of snowflakes, the pitch of the roof, then the dimmer shape of the sagging barn farther on. Coming closer, he saw the stone chimney at the gable end of the peeled-log house, with the snow stuck along the lines of mortar in the chinks. There was the woodpile. There was the blue spruce growing in the yard, the tree that he and Rut had loaded in a pannier and brought down from the mountain when they were boys. There were all the old elk horns, from so many hunts, sticking up out of the snow, lining the front walk to the snow-huddled porch.

Over all things visible loomed an invisible presence of great mountains hidden in the quiet fall of whiteness from the grayness overhead.

"Better not try to get any farther, Rowdey," Ingo said. "You're liable to get hung up. You can turn around here." He opened the door and got out. "Hank, we'll take you in the front way! Like company."

"Mr. Bustleton," Em said, "come in for coffee and some cake. I baked a cake for Haven."

"Thank you, Mrs. Spurling, I'd like to. But I think I better get back before I need a snowplow. So had Ingo, if he wants to get that truck out."

"Then you come again," Em said. "You were very good to bring us out here. I'm grateful."

"We're all grateful." Hank had his suitcase out of the trunk. "Let me put this in the house, Dad, and I'll go back with you to help."

"Nope," Ingo said. "You're home. I'm going to walk in the house with you. Then I'm going back with Rowdey and you're going to stay here and let your mother enjoy your company."

Hank Spurling walked past the blue spruce tree, by the line of elk horns, with his mother and father. They came up on the porch. Then he saw the service flag hanging inside the window. There was a gold star, hand cut and hand sewn, and a blue star below. It was hanging in the window that looked out at the Cloudrock Mountains.

"There was something about leaving it up till you got back," Ingo Spurling said. He turned the knob and pushed the front door open. "You're home."

Hank saw that his father was crying.

"Throw a chunk on the fire, Hank. See you later."

He stood on the doorsill watching his father hurry through the snow to the gray shape of the car. It drove away. Hank Spurling stepped into the house where he lived.

Without turning his eyes to his mother's face, he closed the door, put down the suitcase, crossed the room to the wood box by the hearth.

"I'll fix the fire," he said.

He found a stick of fat pitch. With it he poked down to the red coals beneath the ashes in the fireplace. He put the stick on the coals and from it leaped a smoking small tongue of flame. When he had nourished the blaze with carefully laid new wood, he straightened up and looked at his mother. She had taken off her galoshes, coat and muffler. She had blown her nose.

"It's hard to believe you're here," she said.

"I made it. It took a while."

"You get warm, Haven, by the fire. How would a cup of coffee and a piece of my orange white cake taste?"

"It would taste like being home. Let me put the coffee to warming."

"No, I want you to please stay there by the fire, till I'm

22

ready." She turned and walked not to the kitchen but to the bedroom and she closed the door.

Hank took off his overcoat, threw it on a chair, over his snow-damped cap and its metallic dark emblem of Globe and Fouled Anchor.

With his back turned to the warmth of the crackling fire, he stood in quietness looking at the familiar room, at the mounted elk head with its great antlers touching the ceiling, at the old picture of Cloudrock Peak at Sunrise, at Rut's stuffed and varnished golden trout that had weighed nine pounds at Sky Lake, at the green curtains, the faded rug, the pine table with the magazines, the scuffed chairs, the old couch. Nothing was different, except the rectangle of flag hanging in the middle of the front window, except the end-table placed now against the side wall, except some pictures grouped on the wall above that table.

On the table top he could see there was a scrapbook. By it stood a black leather box opened to display the bronze shape of a Navy Cross. Another small open box on the table held the eaglehead insignia of the 101st Airborne Division to which were pinned a pair of second lieutenant's bars. On the wall above were two framed hand-tinted studio photographs, one of smiling Private Rutherford Spurling in uniform at Fort Benning, Georgia, one of unsmiling Private Haven Spurling at Parris Island, South Carolina. An official citation, an official letter, a few war news-photographers' glossy prints with typewritten captions glued below them, were ranged around the tinted portraits. It was a votive shrine devoted to two sons absent in war, one dead, one alive.

He was looking at the opposite wall, at the old photograph of his father and Hemlock winning the *skijor* at Pinedale, at the new water color in the homemade frame, of a skier in a nearly perpendicular *schuss* on powder snow,

23

signed Fen Spurling, when his mother opened the door and came from the bedroom.

"I want to tell you why I went in there," she said quietly. "I have been down on my knees in gratefulness to God. The psalmist said, 'I will give thanks unto thee, O Lord, with my whole heart.' And he said again, 'Be strong, and he shall establish your heart, all ye that put your trust in the Lord.' I hope you are giving Him thinks, Haven. I hope that I can get to Junction for church next Sunday and that you will be there with me. Now — I'll make some better coffee and cut that cake."

He walked into the kitchen with her.

"So that's the new stove —"

"It makes such a difference! It's butane."

"You think I can keep busy around here now with no more short wood to cut?"

"I expect there'll be things for you to do." She put the coffee pot on the lighted burner, and looked at him. "Tell me, Haven, because I just have to know. How do you really feel? Are you all right?"

"Pretty good. The docs all told me it would take some time."

"We never did know exactly from your letters, where the bullet went in and what it did to you."

"I wrote you. I was gut-shot by a little hard-nosed twenty-five-caliber Jap slug. It hit me here in the right side, on the edge of the low rib. I never knew exactly what all it did. It took three operations and eight months in hospitals. The bullet hole never did look like much. It was what it did inside."

"I won't keep bothering you, asking you about it. I just have to know the main things. It's all healed now?"

"Sure."

"Can you eat all right? You're thin."

24

"Mainly grease and too much fried stuff I have to watch yet."

"Will you tell me the things to fix for you so that you'll get the proper diet?"

"No diet. You forget it and fix anything. I'll watch it myself. I'll be eating right. Starting with this cake."

"Just one more question, Haven, I know it bothers you. Does it ever hurt you now? Do you have pain?"

"No. A catch in my middle, occasionally. Nothing to worry about. I have to work the kinks out myself. It's a matter of getting back into condition."

"And the doctors do say you're healed? I want to know that."

"Would you believe it better if you had it in writing?" He unbuttoned a shirt pocket, pulled out a paper. "This is pretty official." He unfolded it. "It's dated day before yesterday, '11th day of March, 1946.' Ahem. 'Honorable Discharge, Semper Fidelis' it says here, for 'Haven Spurling, a sergeant.' You know the fellow? On the back, right here, it says, 'Is physically qualified for discharge. Requires neither treatment nor hospitalization. I certify that this is the actual print of the right index finger of the man herein mentioned.' Signed by Medical Officer 'Marvin Otwell Commander (MC) U.S.N.R.' How's that?"

"That's grand, Haven. Can I kiss you on the forehead?"

"You can if you'll tell me about yourself."

"Here's some cake. I think the coffee's about ready."

"You're having some with me, aren't you?"

"I'll take a taste."

"It's better than ever," he said with his mouth full. "Remember the time — it was Big Agnes that blew up and slipped the pack with the birthday cake you were sending up to Rut, at Corner Lake. Orange icing, like this. We ate every crumb, pine needles and all."

They sat at the kitchen table. Outside the snowflakes floated down.

"I wish we could get you to quit your job at the store and take it easy."

"No you don't. I like to be seeing people every day, away from this house. Since last fall with Fenwick off at college and with you in a hospital so far away on the Hawaiian Islands — I would have gone crazy, not working. The money too. It's not much, but useful —"

"Listen. In this pocket I got all my pay I saved and my mustering-out money to help any way it can. Cash. Eleven hundred and eighty bucks. This year when summer comes — there won't be Rut — but there will be Dad and me and Fenno and we'll be booking dudes on pack trips again into those Cloudrocks. Like old times."

"I know how you loved it up there." Her eyes fastened to his. "You remember the frazzling hard job it is, tending to city people in the mountains? Look at it honestly, Haven. Can you work like that now, with horses and all, after what that bullet did to you?"

"Don't worry about it. There's something else on your mind. It's Dad. He's not doing so good?"

"This is the second winter he hasn't even tried to start his trap line."

"He must be doing something. Isn't he?"

"Oh, since New Year he helps the Fentons and Lars Rovelstad feed their stock, when he feels like it."

"I've seen him be the workingest man in Wyoming, when he feels like it. He's drinking? Huh?"

"Son, there was no earthly good writing it in letters. And there's no use going into it now, the minute you get here. When all I want to say is — how happy this day should be. With you home."

"With me home we better go into it. He always did drink

26

some. Not too bad. With guests in the mountains, and all. He could handle it."

"Nobody can handle it. All my life I have despised the sure evil of drink. It has got the upper hand on your father."

"He's just going through hard times. He'll be all right."

"I ought to pray with greater faith, I know that."

"He's got to be all right. It's so good, what he's got. You know the old letterhead? 'Ingo Spurling, Outfitter and Guide' with the picture of the trout, 'Silvertip, Wyoming.' I would prop it up where I could see it and look at it, laying in those hospital sacks, wishing."

"Haven, we don't set our hearts too high on the change-ables. Things change, people change. About your father, I think he's just about lost the way he used to have with people who knew him, that jaunty, that lovable way —"

"But he hasn't lost the main thing. Because he can't lose that. It was him taught us the mountains! He feels about them. The way I do. The way Rut did. The way Fenno will."

"Let me tell you, Haven. Some of it you know. Some you don't. The first summer you boys were in the service, it was 1942, your father booked just one paying party of fisher-men, from the East, and he had to quit after that. People wouldn't come to Silvertip, it was too hard. There was the gasoline rationing and the tire rationing and the priorities and we had the food rationing and scarcities and everything. People couldn't feel right anyway taking big pack trips fish-ing and hunting with a war going on. Don't you forget it's a luxury, 'roughing it' the way prominent people do. The war killed the guiding and outfitting business dead."

"And now it'll come back. Better than ever."

"I don't know if your father will. I hate to say — it al-most seems he's old now. After you and Rutherford went

27

away, he would ride and ride up in the mountains. Over the divide. Sometimes he'd take skinny little Fenwick, but mostly he would camp alone. Like old Mr. Claunch. Way up there. I don't think Ingo found pleasure in it. He would come home drinking. He would talk and talk and talk about Rutherford — and you — being in the war. And about the First World War. I found out later he went over to Casper with his old Army papers and tried to enlist and they wouldn't take him.

"Then he got a job with the Reclamation down at Rackland Dam. It was so expensive buying feed and so hard to take the right care of stock that he sold the horses, all but the three. He would say it was like selling off a part of his life. Maybe it was. He worked a night shift at the dam, a guard at the power plant, and he'd come home weekends, looking for letters from you boys overseas. We were so worried. I worked at the store and those were such lonesome days for poor Fenwick, for all of us, but Fenwick was so young.

"When the message came from the War Department about Rutherford, it struck your father down, it seemed to cut him away from everything else that was dear to him. He grieved. He quit work. He drank and he talked about losing Rutherford and he wouldn't try to get his mind on anything else. We all know that he was always partial to Rutherford.

"And there was something else, Haven, I better tell you the whole thing, now we're at it. Your father's quit talking about it but he's not over it yet. About your brother's service life insurance policy. It was made payable to me alone. I know Rutherford fixed it that way simply because he knew I would take care of the money with some thought of the future. He knew how Ingo has always been, bless his heart, with a dollar in his pocket — such a spender. When the

28

check came I took it myself and went down alone to Mr. Gus Sprigg at the bank in Junction and I told him about it. He put it safe in my name.

"I never saw anybody take on like your father, about such a thing. It was so senseless, so mistaken, so ugly, mixed up with grieving and drinking. He'd say that his oldest son, that he had so much deep faith in, hadn't shown confidence in his own father. He'd blame me for it, and keep talking about it. He'd say that I had gone behind his back with Rutherford, that I was trying to be foxy — he'd use that word — with money that wasn't mine — he'd say worse things than that — it was about unbearable. It didn't change what I knew Rutherford wanted me to do. I did buy that new stove — maybe that was selfish. I did use a little over two thousand of the money to pay off this place. After all these years it's ours. It's Rutherford's gift to this family. Losing his life — oh Haven I — hope I — understand your father yet. I love him, so many ways. I hope he will take a hold of himself. One thing I know. To me — your getting back — is a kind of salvation."

Hank Spurling sat for a long time in silence.

He traced with his coffee spoon the pattern of the oil cloth on the table. "About Dad," he said finally, with his mother looking at him, "God knows. About old Rut, he was like Dad said this morning, 'good at everything.' So are you."

"Fenwick writes that so many veterans are starting to the University on that GI Bill. Have you thought of going back to Laramie?"

"A freshman again? I'm too far along the track. To be going back to a school."

"Education is valuable."

"Depends on what kind you want and what you use it for. Are my old skis still around some place?"

29

"I'm sorry, Fenwick took them. And broke one of them in a race."

"I was going to buy new ones. Good ones. The best. Does Dad have any skis at all?"

"He used yours. He hasn't skied for a long, long time."

"I wonder how he's doing with the truck. Maybe I ought to con that operation."

Outside the window, snowflakes no longer floated down. A newly risen wind carried them at flurrying slants. The wind's sound stirred at the notched log corners of the house.

"Are my boots or any of my old clothes still around handy?"

"Fenwick grew into your size and —"

"Like I used to grow into Rut's — I ought to know that. And I forget this uniform don't have to stay policed any more. These are old clothes that I got on. The cruise is over. All over. At Dago I shipped my sea bag by Railway Express to Green Junction and I want to ride down there soon and pick it up. It's got good boondockers and dungarees and a field jacket with a liner and some other gear I lawyered off the Corps, for the mountains. I think I'll walk back to the creek — see if Dad's there yet."

He got up from the table and went into the parlor. "How do you like the new suitcase? I bought it at Dago." He opened it. "A swabbie watch cap ought to work good in Wyoming." He rolled the bottom of the navy blue wool stocking cap and pulled it down tight on his head. Before he put on his overcoat, he threw a heavy log on the fire.

"Haven, I wish you had boots, or high shoes. Maybe you ought not to go out."

"I'm going out. And take a look."

The falling flakes were small and fast. They struck biting at his face when he peered toward the invisible mountains. He rolled the watch cap down over his ears, then turned,

30

with the wind and the slant of the snow at his back, and he made his way to the creek.

The pickup was gone. He judged from the fill of new snow in the tracks that it had been gone for quite a while. He could read where the tow truck had backed around, he could see the set of footprints made in fastening the cable to the pickup and how it had been pulled out. He saw how the tow truck had churned around to the forward end of the pickup and had lifted its front wheels from the ground and had hauled it away. He enjoyed himself, reading exactly what happened by marks left in snow. It was a kind of reading he had not practiced for years.

The wind was cold. Standing on the bridge, with his hands in his coat's side pockets, he mused at snow patterns tufted on the ice-gripped sedge below him, he savored his own presence alone on Plew Creek, centered in a tiny circle of visible world bound in by a slanting veil of snowflakes falling.

A figure came dim from the emptiness of the slanting veil. Hank saw the caked red mackinaw, the big pale hat, moving against the wind-driven bite of the tumbling snow.

"What are you doing out here?" His father's voice was hoarse.

"I'm taking a look."

"I'm surprised Em let you git away. She's been bending your ear. No doubt."

"How's the old Ford?"

"Right front spindle's bent. And a wheel."

"That's not so bad."

"Fixed by tomorrow. We won't have no use for it tomorrow. Road's already drifted shut."

"This wind."

"I went by Rowdey's — to warm up some. Then I figured, I better hit the road now, before I have to thrash my

31

way. I got to thinking I put no hay down for the horses this morning. Say Hank. I bought me a package at Rowdey's, to cache in the barn. I got it right here. A little something for cheer, and such as that. You're invited."

"I don't use the stuff."

"You don't? Well, well now. And what kind of a old soldier are you?"

"You — *you* want to know — I'll tell you what kind! In this belly I got a slug of something else and I got it in combat not conversation —"

The words came slow and they slugged Ingo Spurling. He said "Oh" when they hit. "Oh."

Hank started for the house. His father caught up with him and came alongside.

"Hank —"

"Skip it. I'm sorry."

"Hank. You mean you haven't really got well? From that bullet?"

"Forget any bullet. I feel all right. I'm nearly home."

"What do you mean, nearly home?"

"I mean I will be all the way home when I can see those mountains." He raised his arm to point into the driving snowfall. "You remember them? I guess they're there. I haven't seen them yet."

3

He glanced out the window and saw them there, waiting. They stood in a stabbing glitter of snow glare and a high shine of morning sun. Along the south faces of lower slopes frosty patches of yellowed sage, of gray stone, of brown earth showed how the last days of March were touching now at winter's white.

"You ought to wait," his mother said, "until Fenwick gets here for Easter. You could both go up there together." She got up from the breakfast table and carried her dish to the sink.

"Too long to wait, I've waited two solid weeks, I've waited long enough," Hank said. "And I'll be going with Fenno. When he gets here with skis. That's the only thing I'm sorry about today is no skis."

"Bound and determined, aren't you? If you'd wait until old Mr. Claunch comes by he'd know what all's in the cabin now and what you'd really need to carry."

"She's right," Ingo Spurling said. "Old Merlin's got the trap line going some place up there. Now the weather's so good he ought to be by here any time."

"My pack's all made and I'm going," Hank said. "Today is just right to go."

Ingo Spurling drank the last of his coffee. "I'd go with you myself. But like I say, I told Lars — I told him I'd be at his place. He's feeding three hundred head. We can move hay, weather like this."

"Haven. How long do you plan to stay up there alone? We ought to know exactly."

"Well now — you might get out the search party for the missing dude if I'm not back in about three days. You both been sounding like I was going up Ezekiel Glacier clear to Cloudrock Peak. It's only to the cabin I'm going. For a look."

"Hank, I'm saying you aren't climatized yet. You're not used to it, with a pack."

"This'll start me pretty good, getting used to it. I can't help thinking about a look at the old lake again, all wintered in up there. And I can't find the snowshoes — the beavertail shoes, Dad, not those murdering wide bearpaws. You mind telling me where they are?"

34

"Unless Fenny's messed with them, the saddle shed. The wall with the traps."

"Ingo, it's time we got started for work," Em Spurling said. "It's time I did, anyhow. Leave those dishes, Haven. I'll wash them tonight."

"Not this stack, you won't. I'll bet you on that."

"Before you leave, Hank, could you knock the ice out of the trough and throw down a few bales for the horses?"

"I planned to."

Walking with his mother and father outside to the pick-up he said to them, "See you about Thursday. Maybe sooner."

"You take care of yourself, Haven." His mother looked down from the truck cab, "Don't try anything foolish. You be careful."

His father climbed in behind the steering wheel, fastened the door shut with a loop of baling wire, turned the ignition key and pulled the choke. "If Merlin Claunch shows up I'm going to tell him there's a Marine up there poaching off his line —"

"Make it ex-Marine. And tell him I'm armed — armed for mice. That's mountain mice —"

The Ford started with a sputter and jerk. Hank waved as it went out the gate. Then he turned and looked again at the mountains.

Blue Gap Ridge rising steep along the edge of the valley's floor towered like a humped and buttressed wall so close at hand it blocked from view the great heights of the Cloud-rocks at the heart of the range farther back; yet the jagged tops of four lesser peaks stood high enough and near enough behind Blue Gap's timbered crestline to show tall stone and naked snow against the sky.

He went to the saddle shed for snowshoes.

The sun was an hour higher when he finished all his

chores. Then he changed to the thick sweat shirt, he pulled on the long-legged socks and over them laced the oiled new boots.

The pack was already cinched into the thong-patched old Trapper Nelson frame; he lashed the zipper jacket and the cumbersome snowshoes high on the pack's wrapped back. Whistling to himself through his front teeth, he stuffed his pipe and tobacco in a pocket, buckled around his belly the cartridge belt with the sheathed Marine knife, put on the watch cap, adjusted the new snow goggles on the roll of the knitted wool over his forehead. With the pack propped upright on a chair, he backed to its bulkiness stooping, ran his arms under the leather shoulder straps and straightened up snugging the weight to his back. Fitting his footing and his balance to the backpull riding his shoulders, he picked up his carbine. Then he was ready and he started from the house. The kitchen door as he closed it banged against the snowshoes hanging on his back.

A strap needed a hitch to the next notch; a lump poking at the small of his back needed smoothing. Beyond the feedlot fence he stopped twice to fix everything right. Then he headed out, over thin snow on the open flat, straight across the haying field toward the curve of Plew Creek upstream where it issued from its mountain ravine.

He judged there must be sixty pounds upon his back. He felt them. He felt them more than he thought he would. Moving in a steady jog, the muscles of his body then the workings of his mind began to fasten tight, too tight, to the test of the load he carried, the test of the hike ahead. Pronging aches spread from his strap-clamped shoulders to the stiffened side muscles of his outthrust neck. The load got heavier. He was sweating hard when he came scraping through brush and deeper snow to the creek. Cautious of his balance with the load, stepping a slow way from stone to

36

stone over mushy ice, slopping through ice water ankle deep, he crossed the stream.

The sound of its trickling water made a first note of spring.

He came to the far face of the creek's steepening ravine and reached as a kind of first goal the piled stones of the cairn that pointed the trail up Quaker Ridge, where Spurling clients began their guided climbs on horseback into summer mountains. He put down his pack, leaning it carefully against the stones, and stood in the stillness for a long breather.

Up the mottled whiteness of the sunny slope beyond the speckles of sage at the edge of the timber stood the bare-limbed aspen groves, the "quakers" that gave the ridge its name. He peered up, far up, facing into the glare, marking the climb. It was all before him.

He began it before he had cooled too much, moving uphill with a mountaineer's swaying gait, as Rut had taught him — it seemed so long ago. Avoiding high lift of foot, at each step he advanced with a kind of built-in momentum derived from a slight sway of the whole body across the supporting leg: in a swing like a pendulum the slightly bent loose leg was carried up and forward by the body's sway. The lifted foot coming down heel flat, firm to the rise of the ground, left the downhill leg ready for its turn to be carried with the alternate sway of the next upward swinging mountaineer's step, higher. He knew how. He had pace. He had balance. Conditioned muscle and sustained wind he had not.

He tried to disregard what he lacked.

Fixing his mind on former walk-ups and former times, doggedly plodding he denied himself any pause to rest, to breathe. The kink of pain came pulling at the pit of his stomach. Progress up the rise became a gasping punish-

37

ment. He stopped a moment, angry, the pack biting at his shoulders. Then an unreasoning desire, a frenzy to prove his fitness for the mountains, grabbed him and drove him stumbling up muddy patches of slippery incline, across infirm pockets of snow, to the spine of the ridge and into the aspens — where the frenzy came to its collapse. Reeling dizzy and ready to fall he had to drop the load from his back, he had to grant his lungs their bursting desire to heave unhampered.

It was a witless performance. In the silence broken only by the sound of his racking breath, he was ashamed — and he was glad the performance was private. He wiped at the itching sweat on his face. He looked up the ridge, where it merged with the forested backbone of Blue Gap's crest. It was a long way up.

The sun, unlike Hank Spurling, had climbed now to the top of the sky.

He had to rest, leaning with his back against the trunk of an aspen tree, waiting for the catch in his belly to ease. His lungs began to find the air they wanted. The cold-hot prickles from the numbness at the back of his neck, out across the tops of his stiff shoulders, began to go away. The pulsing tingle began to leave the trembled muscles of his motionless legs. Casual objects casting images in his eyes as he rested began to register in his mind.

He saw the dark scars on the pale smoothness of the up-reaching aspen trunks around him. The scars were records of old wounds, marks of old events in growth, patterned bumps and furrows healed dry, crisp, black. On a satiny bole not five paces from where he leaned, his gaze came upon a scar that faced him from uphill. It confronted him suddenly. Two black and well-shaped arcs, vividly drawn by some accident of growth, joined to define the eyelids

38

around a big smooth eyeball and a knobbed black iris of eye.

From the gray column of the living wood the eye stared at Hank Spurling. In the noon brilliance of the snow, in the solitude of the mountainside, he stared back. It seemed the occult eye of the mountain.

And Semper Fi to you, his mind replied to the stare of the eye. What am I up here for? To prove I'm in shape? Like I was when I last made this trip? Okay, I agree with you, Eye. I am a cockeyed knocked-up Wyoming asiatic if that is what I am trying to prove.

What is it you have to prove? Anything?

I am just glad I am back.

You do not have to prove it. Enjoy it.

I can tell you something I probably would not have the nerve to tell anybody, Eye. What I'm doing is what you might be able to call a — a pilgrimage.

Good. It is not a punishment. It is a pleasure.

I know. I was born up there. At Haven Lake.

You were a long way from Haven Lake. Out with the coconuts. Now you are back. Why don't you quit proving anything? Why don't you enjoy your walk? You are not trying to secure that ridge up there. It is already secured. You are not packing ammo now for a rifle platoon. Today there is no hurry.

Do me a favor, Eye. Do not tell a soul I stood around hearing from any oddball scar on a quaker tree. People would put me with you and the squirrels.

He looked around.

He saw his tracks marking untracked snow to where he stood. He saw how high he had come above the valley's floor. He saw Plew Creek far below. He saw his house. He saw Silvertip beyond, and State Road 241, and the winding

Freefolk River. All very tiny. The Kainah Hills looked crystal clean at the far side of the glitter of the valley so far beneath him. And his sweat was drying cold now.

He stood flexing the ache in the muscles of his back and shoulders — feeling the mountain world. It was above any flatland. It had a kind of air, it even had a sound to its silence, that was different.

He ate a hand's scoop of snow, and another, washing out his mouth and wetting his gullet. He relashed the snowshoes higher and tighter to the pack. Then he lifted the weight settling it very carefully, evenly on his shoulders, took the carbine from where it leaned against the tree, and moved up the ridge challenging neither the slope nor himself. He stopped often to rest.

The way led into heavy timber. High above the aspens of Quaker Ridge the steep slants jammed with lodgepole pine stood exactly as he remembered. Resiny yellow blaze marks led through a labyrinth choked with deadfall. In it gaunt pine trunks arose straight, tapering, pointing bare and branchless like monster arrows to the needly crowns that half hid the sky. When breeze touched at their tops the trees faintly swayed, creaking and grating against propped deadfall leaning askew in the gray maze. Footsteps crunching the shadowed snow intruded upon a haunted stillness. As a boy he had thought the lodgepole slope might be the place where the goblins lived.

There was still an unnamed relief in breaking free of the eerie wood, to the brightness of the open sky on the granite edge of a mountain meadow far up in Blue Gap's back. He felt relief and he felt nearly bushed; he put down his load in sunlight on dry mother rock where the snow had melted. Sitting there, with his breath returned, it seemed the right place to eat before going on.

He reached over and untied a string on the top of his

pack, loosening his jacket enough to get at the side pocket and pull out the lump of his lunch. It was in a wax paper bakery bread wrapper circled by a rubber band. Inside was a cheese sandwich, a hard-boiled egg, a Hershey bar and an orange.

He ate the sandwich first, swallowing its dryness wishing he had put more mayonnaise with the cheese. When he had peeled the crackled shell from the egg, on its moist slickness he poured salt out of a little folded squib he had made from newsprint; when the egg was half gone he poured more salt on its yellow interior. The Hershey he ate square by square, melting each on his tongue and against the roof of his mouth, tasting, taking his time. The orange, with the clean tang of the peel on his fingers, was dessert; the tart juice was drink.

Done, he wiped his fingers on his pants and wadded the paper and eggshell and orange peel into a tight ball, dropped it in a rock crack and poked it out of sight for keeps with a broken stick. Then he eased back on the rock with his hands clasped behind his neck. His stomach did not ache. He looked up at the unspecked blue of the sky and the pitch of the slope at the far end of the meadow. It was fir country, spruce country. High country.

He went by the frozen bog in the deer-tracked meadow and climbed zigzag beyond it, watching blaze marks along an incline and over its brow, through a stand of venerable fir.

Lofty trees led him toward the final slope of his climb, up a steepness where snow was thigh deep between half-buried boulders. He began to think of putting on the snowshoes. Postponing their use as long as possible, he managed to flounder on, pausing often, mapping a way, to sunnier ground and firmer footing. Scraping past low branches of whitebark pines and around a weather-maimed clump of

41

runted spruce, he made for the notch on the stone spine of Blue Gap's crest.

With hammering heart he came up between the trees into the notch and he looked over the other side seeing all the great peaks of the Cloudrock Mountains.

They stood revealed in an aerial radiance above the snow slopes and slashed ravines at their feet. Their heights had a luminous pallor, of sheer stone and flinty ice, ribbed with angled shadows of a vivid blue. They were quiet.

The load was off his back, dropped to an edge of rock between the trees. He sat holding the carbine, filling his lungs with breath, filling his eyes with the shapes before him. He traveled them, out to their distance. He named them, to possess them again with his mind.

Through a V formed in the foreground by the north shoulder of Chuckbox Mountain and the south face of the Gun Cliffs he peered into the gouge of an ancient glacier's weathered trough. It was flanked on the one hand by the jags of the Moosetooth Ridges and Anvil Peak, on the other hand by the black stone of the Quill Bluffs and the shining crest of Rampart Mountain. At the far end of the trough he could see the white lip of Moraine Pass. He could see beyond it, into the awesome cirque, Ezekiel Basin, bound in by the rock face of Mount Felix, the Steeple crags, the wedge and hump of West Shoulder Mountain. The hump's side bore the fractured dazzle of the Ezekiel Glacier. Over the glacier's head towered a highest wall of ice-veined and fissured granite. It led whitening to the sharp-edged pinnacle tall against the sky, Cloudrock Peak.

The Cloudrock Mountains, he thought, were not just exactly the way he dreamed them. They were better. And they had requirements. All the lakes, the streams, the trails, the camps snowed under, eight months of the year without a living soul. A Cloudrock winter was like a big white door,

42

locked. If you knew enough about it, if you really wanted to, bad enough, you could pick the lock from the outside sometimes, like today, and you could walk in the door. It could slam shut and lock you behind it. Lock you beneath it, stiff. But the Cloudrock Mountains were another thing very different when all the lakes were blue, when you saw the sunlight sparkle on the grass and smelled spruce in the rain. A thousand rocky streams were running unfished and you knew where the big trout would be. Then the requirements were different. Then there wasn't any lock. There wasn't any door, it was melted, almost. You came up into the high country in summer like living in the first morning the world was made.

It was quite a while yet, until summer.

The westering sun straight at his back had lost all warmth. The puff of breeze coming over the ridge carried a chill. He got up and put on his jacket. He zipped it all the way to his chin. Then he put on the snowshoes, he had to. The snows on Blue Gap's northeast side stayed shady all winter.

He found the pack straps riding a little better on his jacketed shoulders, but the platters lashed under his boots were a misery, a muscle-pulling woe in his ankles first and then in his calves and thighs. The springy, bent-kneed balance downhill under the pack load's weight, and the nice measurement of the body's sway that went with a minimum lift of foot to carry the inner edge of one snowshoe neatly above and beyond the inner edge of the other, without straddle-gaiting — after so long without practice, the effort demanded his will, it demanded all his tired attention, all his body. He went with his jaw clamped hard in a grin against each step's encumbrance; his comfort was in having his wind, on a down grade. Breath rolled smoking from between his teeth.

The deep accumulation of old snow on the shaded slope was fine-grained and loose, pocked with fallen needles and cones under the trees. Most of the trail's blaze marks were buried; he saw none above his knees. In summertime the blazes were eye-level high.

Out ahead, before the face of Chuckbox Mountain angled in to hide the heights beyond, the blues on the peaks took a tinge of violet.

He worked the snowshoes without being able to hurry, stopping often to stand for a moment to ease his legs, down a winding dip that flattened to easier ground along a nearly smooth shelf with deep drifts and in deepening shade. The shelf's side was girded by an outcrop of granite. Below, the trail took twisting traverses on a final slope into the oblong bottom of a rough big mountain bowl.

It held Haven Lake.

He looked out and down to see it, between the trees. He recognized it only because he knew exactly where it was. The summer greens of the lake's steep timber rim were blurred somber, almost black, against the snow. The lake's living summer blue was locked under a dead flatness of empty white.

He made the turn of the last traverse in a lambent dusk that robbed the dimension of depth from the tangle of trees and the tilt of snow. High in the twilight above the far side of the lake, glow from an invisible west ruddied the top of Chuckbox Mountain and faded.

He lugged his pack and all his pains in a laborious snow-shoe trudge down the hump of a familiar hillock. Past the site of the old horse corral, its poles tumbled under the drifts, he got to the foot of the cove, to the mounded shape of the snowbound log cabin under the firs on the edge of Haven Lake.

He slipped off the pack, leaned it and the carbine against

44

the cornice of snow curved pale over the edge of the cabin's roof. On the bare log just below the roof's edge he could see the old horseshoe tacked over the door top. He stood looking down at it, before he conquered his aching soreness enough to bend over and unbind the snowshoes from his feet. For the first time all day he felt alone. A sundown wind stirred the fir boughs. Thin cloud wisped the gloaming sky in the north.

He had to kick, scoop, shove and stomp the snow away from the buried door. It was fastened shut by the same old slide bar, held home to its hole in the jamb by twists of rusty wire; he undid the wire and slid back the ice-flecked bar. A stiff push forced the door open, scraping snow.

Stumbling tired he brought his carbine, then his pack, then the snowshoes through the low doorway and down the log step to the dirt floor. The black shadow had a musty mouse-nest smell, with a stale hint of rancid fat on pelts, of fetid scent on steel traps. From the blue snow glow outside the rectangle of open door, a ghost of light touched into the cabin's dark.

At the far end of the room his eyes, straining, found the obscure shapes of the comfort he hoped for: the little iron cook stove on stilts, under its column of stovepipe. He stepped toward it. A mouse, or a rat, scurried rustling paper somewhere in the dark.

He fumbled off a snow-caked glove, from his pocket pulled a match, scratched it on the stove top. Against the wall by the stove there was a stack of chopped wood, even a fuzz-stick and a mouse-scattered pile of dry spruce twigs. The match's flame caught a glint on the cupboard shelf. It was the chimney of a kerosene lamp. He lit another match. Inside the murky glass of the lamp's bowl there was yellowish oil. A gray wick curled down into it. He was glad.

He was grateful, to old Merlin Claunch.

In the last paleness of dusk he floundered half numb around the outside of the cabin, found the stovepipe sticking up outside the wall flue, pulled the frozen wad of gunnysack from the stovepipe's plugged mouth.

Shivering, by tawny faint lamplight, he got a fire going in the stove. He took the bucket and dishpan from where he found them sitting upside down on the trestle table, went out the door with them, packed them tight and topped them high with snow and brought them to the stove top over the popping fire.

While water heated he unlashed his pack and sorted his gear. He leaned his short-helved pack ax against the wall by the clutter of old wooden pelt frames and traps; his groceries he placed carefully on the cupboard shelf; everything else he put at the end of the table by his carbine and cartridge belt. On the bare bunk frame built into the corner he spread down his canvas pack cover, his blankets, his quilt. For a pillow at the head he made a roll of his extra sweat shirt and longjohns.

In a fog of half dizzy fatigue and of heat from the stove, he got himself some supper. He had two cups of beef tea made with bouillon cubes and scalding water, then a can of heated spaghetti in tomato sauce dumped out in a big smoking pile on his tin plate. He ate it all, cutting it to mouthfuls with his spoon. To finish off, he dissolved a pack of lemon Jello in a steamy cup of water and drank it hot.

He was too dead tired to light his pipe. Firewood and lamp oil were too fine to waste.

In the pitch-black quiet the open damper on the stove door showed a dull orange dot. He lay stretched flat in his clothes, with boots off but with watch cap on, rolled in his covers, anchored in a weariness deeper than snow on the Cloudrocks. The mice rustled their nest under the cupboard. The iron in the stove clicked, cooling in the dark.

46

That was the last he remembered except that he ached, that he was happy, that he was bygod not counting on any changeables. The Cloudrock Mountains were just like they always were.

4

Robert Kendall Royston was privately amused by the size and the decor of his new office. It was a gift from the Board of Directors, Royston Machine Corporation, and there was not much he could do about it, without seeming ungrateful: it had been readied, and waiting expectantly for him, upon his return to private industry after service in the war. It was evident that his new lair had been too assiduously dreamed up, in richly executive tones of brown and tan and bronze, by some very expensive interior decorator. The big thing was the shape and position of the new executive desk — clearly resembling, Royston thought, a citadel built to command every approach. From the silent far door across the menace of the silent thick carpet a storming party had to advance without cover right into the loom of executive firepower zeroed in. Royston's amusement stemmed from his knowledge concerning citadels. They were an antique piece of silliness, with or without modern decor. There were no impregnable positions.

Alone at his mahogany and leather emplacement, Royston surveyed the cushioned terrain and turned to glance again at the drapery-flanked window. It was tall, of clear plate glass, twenty-seven floors above Michigan Boulevard. Its view revealed nothing now but a gray blank of March mid-afternoon fog outside. He turned his eyes from it, looked at his wrist watch, put on his reading glasses and took up the brief that had been deposited upon the great expanse of desk top a few moments before by Director Personnel, Sage Tool Division.

There was a situation to be ironed out in the Sage plant office management; there were some facts to catch up on, some details to get straight, before steps were taken; these were the facts, the details — and Royston's strict attention wandered from typewritten words and figures in the opened folder before him. Other matters kept caroming into his mind.

A discreet buzz from a muffled buzzer interrupted the silence.

There were three phones not far from his right elbow. He picked up the one nearest. "Yes?" he spoke.

The voice of Miss Agnes Meadows, at her desk outside Royston's office door, sounded crisp and at the same time soothing, as if Miss Meadows were always aware of alternate solutions to any difficulty. "Long distance for you, Colonel."

"Who is it? Hulette Bent at Crawford?"

49

"The call comes from Reno, Nevada. Your daughter Dorothy."

"God," Royston said. "Put her on."

He picked up another phone and waited.

"How are you, Daddy Boy?"

"Hello, Dot —"

"Darling, I'm calling to let you know, the decree's granted! Uncork the wine — little Dottie's free as the breeze."

"Maybe aspirin ought to be uncorked —"

"Daddy Boy, don't be a bear! Aren't you glad for me?"

"Of course I'm glad. Seriously. Did those people out there Able & Ott handle it well?"

"So sweet — and *so* legal!"

"What does your mother say? Is she there with you?"

"Heavens, she's in Honoruru. Didn't you know?"

"What? — What's she doing in Honolulu?"

"Visiting. With old Aunt Crash."

"Oh."

"Daddy Boy, you don't sound very rejoiceful. About me. Aren't you glad? About it being done? And so easy this time! Aren't you glad?"

"I'm glad and I want you to come to Lake Forest. I want you to spend some time now here with me."

"I'm taking an apartment, it's in New York, it's a doll. The Chili Fessendens let me have it till summer, they're going to Rio."

"Dot. Listen. You are twenty-six years old. You have a divorce again. Now be intelligent, you understand? If for no other reason than as a favor to your father. Be intelligent, will you?"

"Doll *Baby!* People in New York are terribly intelligent."

"I want to see you. My thought is to — to see you happy."

50

"I'm frightfully happy today. Here are kisses!"

"I'll expect you here, Dot. I'll meet you. Let me know when."

"Celebration, jubilation. Bye, Daddy."

The instant he put down the phone the buzzer sounded.

"Colonel," Miss Meadows's voice said, "Mr. Bent at Crawford has been holding on."

"Get him," Royston said, changing phones. "Hello?"

"Huley Bent, Colonel."

"Anything definite?"

"Couldn't be more clarified, Colonel. We've gone around and around. Since ten this morning. As far as they are concerned, it stays a flat-footed eighteen and a half cents."

"Then we've got a walkout."

There was silence at the other end.

"Huley? You there?"

"God knows I'm here."

"I said we'll shut down."

"Colonel. The labor boys, as you know, put the prod pole to the sore place every time. I want to say this again: a shutdown at Crawford will cut our delivery of RM12 heavy hydraulic presses for every damned one of the big reconversion patterns ready to go next month at South Bend. Furthermore, the building trades won't be crossing any picket line. All construction on Crawford Annex comes to a damned dead stop and there goes our schedule for components on the new powered headstocks and toolslides they're screaming for down at Moline. Furthermore, a shutdown is a futile fight at this time. Look at steel, at GM, at GE — they just fought the battle of eighteen and a half cents. We can't fight CPA now, we can't stem an already acc —"

"Huley —"

"— Yes."

"I'll say something again, myself. I've said it to you. I've said it to the Board. I've said it loud to Civilian Production Administration. We are not in a quarrel with an eighteen and a half cent per hour wage jump as such. What we're in, is a fight to keep a United States dollar worth something. It better be a clobbering fight or the whole economy's on the road to hell. Everybody's heard me enough on the subject of a postwar inflationary spiral. In early phases of inflation if there are enough delaying tactics they may in combination act as a kind of control or cushion tactic. With steel so short — what better time for RMC to put in a lick? In the big picture, and that's the one we've got to see, beyond our production noses, RMC maintains a policy: we *fight* increasing price levels. If we can't win, we can delay. To help a possible win on the long haul. I hate a strike worse than you do, Huley. But that's what we've got. Here it goes again. With the blood pressure. And the bargainers and the negotiators. The arbitrators. That scramble of alphabets, those vacillators down in Washington. The Crawford situation is your baby. But you call on me at any hour and I will be anywhere, any time you say whenever you think I can help. We've got fog here, socked in and no flying, but the public relations will get there for the press tomorrow. Have Miss Meadows put you on the line to Mullins now. And I'll call you in the morning. Anything else?"

"Nothing else."

When Royston put down the phone he found himself standing tensed on his feet. He paced over to the plate glass, lit a cigarette, looked out into the fog. It was a blue nothingness now in the wane of afternoon.

Blurred rumble of invisible traffic on invisible pavements, dimmed growl from the city's throat at the tired end of a working day came up to Royston, entered vaguely into his mind. The rumble and growl mixed in the blue nothingness

52

with Hulette Bent telling the delegates, with news going through clusters of people in front of Union Hall on the corner of Main Street and Third in Crawford in the rain.

They mixed with Dottie in noise and neon, frightfully happy.

As he stood alone with himself at the window, Royston's mind in the blue nothingness came to an image of Crash Gleaves's lanai in the morning sun on Oahu, with Cynthia managing to make suntan look icy, but his mind moved away from it with armed watchmen walking through dim aisles in the Crawford, the metal dead, nothing moving in the silence.

His mind tangled at RM12 assemblies for imageless — a sudden single gray image of a soaring gull curved close by the window in the fog outside and then curved away alone and silent into the nothingness again. Hydraulic presses fell away supplanted by a vividness of wheeling gulls Royston would never forget, gulls not silent or alone, gulls with remembered cries over the rocking Lobnitz piers at the Mulberry A, off Omaha Beach, the evening the storm brewed, many gulls crying like white ghosts against the purple sky, crying the ruin to come, the Omaha Beach gulls crying, flying the worst Channel gale in forty years —

He did not hear Miss Meadows when she opened the far door. She did not see him until she had looked beyond his desk. Then she saw his tweed back; cigarette smoke wreathed above his white hair. He was standing stone still, looking out the tall window into the mist. His shoulders sagged. Miss Meadows rapped on the opened door before stepping in.

"Colonel, if you're not busy —" she offered. "Letters are ready now. I have them here."

"Oh," Royston said. "Very well." He turned away from the window. "Put the Pittsburgh Metallurgical one on top.

I want to be sure we said it right. We may have to take another shot at it." He walked to his desk. "Anybody or anything else written in the book for today?"

"No, sir, that's all. Except Mr. Mullins who wants to know if you want to see him before he leaves for Crawford."

"No. Tell him to see Hulette Bent." Royston sat down, put on his glasses and picked up a pen. Miss Meadows started for the door. "And call Ernest at the house, please," Royston said. "Tell him I won't be out there, I'm spending the night in town. Tell him I won't need any car either."

He read the letter to Pittsburgh twice, decided it was in order now with everything at Crawford so contingent, put his signature to it. Then he read and signed the rest of the stack. Before he pressed the button to summon Miss Meadows he made another decision. He looked at his watch and reached for the phone with the direct outside line. From memory he dialed a number.

"Miss Bren, please?"

He waited, then she answered.

"Hester. This is Robert."

"Robert, how are you?"

"I'm wondering, at this late hour. If you might spare a little food and drink. To a weary man."

"Please do not wonder! Simply come!" The faintest accent of Vienna gave charm to the low timbre of Hester Bren's voice. "How nice, Robert! And we must also talk again of the portrait — I want to tell you now about a painter!"

"Good. When do you want me? Seven?"

"Come as it pleases you."

"I'll be up there."

When he walked alone through the lobby door at street level and came out upon the sidewalk he bought an eve-

54

ning *News* in a kind of absent-minded reflex, without any desire for news of any kind. He tucked the paper under his overcoated arm and waited in the half light at the curb, looking for an empty cab in the steady grind of traffic up the Boulevard.

The fog let fall a raw drizzle that slicked the pavements with a coat of shine. It took him a while to hail a taxi; when he got in and sat on its dark back seat, over wheels whishing in the wet, water droplets on the rattling windows were crusts of gems changing colors and sparkles with the moving lights.

Beyond the Drake at a stop light on the Parkway's edge the cabman managed a left turn out of the traffic into a street where lights were decorous and few. Past another turn and a street lamp that made shining topaz of droplets on the window, the taxi stopped. Stepping out, Royston paid the fare and the car drove away leaving him alone by the dark trunk of a winter-bare tree. It stood in a strip of turf between curb and sidewalk in front of an old-style two-story town house with a modest narrow front of stone. Its entrance lamp was lighted.

In the side street's quietness Royston could hear long-drawn dismal honks from a remote foghorn somewhere out on the Lake. He walked up the stone steps and pressed the bell; the servant Ana opened the thick door and he went in.

Ana was taking his overcoat and hat when Hester Bren came downstairs in the hallway. Her severely plain black dress smartly fitted her carefully preserved figure. The big pearl beads at her neck made the proper accent for her pale skin, her red mouth, her straight dark hair combed smoothly back to a smoothly rounded coil at the nape of her neck. "I heard the bell," she said. She kissed Royston on the mouth, holding lightly to both his hands, and led him into a

55

small and pleasant room lined with books. Under the light of the big parchment-shaded lamp at the end of the library's table sat a tray readied to provide drinks.

"Rest yourself, Robert," she said. "Is this a martini evening?"

"It is indeed."

"Good." She busied herself with the pouring of a potion over ice cubes in a slender glass pitcher, and she stirred it well with ice rattling.

"Nearly three long weeks, Robert. Since I have made you a drink. I am sure you have been very busy, very preoccupied."

"I'm trying to relearn the bearfight business. And moving around at it. To Crawford. Then to Pittsburgh and to Moline. And this week to Crawford again."

"It has been going well, I hope."

"Hester, this will go better." He took the stemmed glass she proffered him. "Skoal," they toasted smiling, and drank.

Royston settled back in his chair and took another satisfactory sip from his glass. "Oh-h-h-h —" he raised his voice without a warning and went into a burlesque basso singsong, off key:

"Oh-h-h-h —
My liver and my lights,
And my reins and my heart,
They're troublin' me,
Are a-painin' me —"

"Robert!"

Royston grinned. "That's a song. Can't you tell?"

"Simply ghastly!"

"It's what old Muldoon, the hardrock tool sharpener, used to sing coming out of the Coney Island Saloon. In Sanskrit. When I was a boy. It came to me hearing a fog-

56

horn going, outside just now. It seemed like old Muldoon. Bellowing up the hill. That was nearly fifty years ago —

> 'They're troublin' me,
> *Are* a-painin' me.'

Old Muldoon's reins and heart — they're your own fault, Hester. Putting Sanskrit in my mind, with that mention of the picture I want for my office. God, it needs it. It needs something calculated to help kill off the increasing chill of the damned interior decorator that's ensconced me up there. I feel like a carefully chosen piece of toned mahogany myself —"

"But Robert. Listen now. Let me tell you something curious. Today simply by chance I confronted a painter who has *been* to your Sanskrit, New Mexico."

"A crumbling ghost since 1896. If he's really been to the forgotten and unsung birthplace of R. K. Royston, your man's either a relic or a sheepherder!"

"He told me that he once painted a landscape, with ruined mining shafts in a canyon, where Sanskrit had been, and I believe him."

"My God. Who is this bird? He gets around."

"His name is Mr. Cosmo Flynn."

"With a name like that, I don't know whether to believe him or not. Can he paint? And are there any dregs in that martini pitcher?"

"Certainly — here. And about Mr. Flynn — I did not know his work before — but he paints rather well indeed. He lived in New Mexico for a time. That explains of course his knowledge of the ancient Sanskrit — the place, not the language, eh? He is not identified with the coterie of Santa Fe and Taos, however, he works mainly in the East. Recently he has been out to Indianapolis, doing portraits for a

57

family there. By chance, he came into the gallery this morning, carrying reproductions to show his work. I was rather impressed. You see, Robert, the portrait you want of your father demands a certain kind of a painter. I have not known where to find him. You wish a portrait which is in essence rather an illustration, a work not so much for a good portraitist as for a good illustrator."

"What I want is a good-sized good painting of Father, outdoors. In a mountain sunlight. The way he looked when he was superintendent of the Sanskrit Mine — with maybe the mill and the winding road showing in the canyon."

"And you must have it well done. It must have quality. In the course of my pleasant interview with Mr. Cosmo Flynn, I wanted his response to those photographs you brought me. I showed them to him. — Another martini, Robert?"

"Thank you, I will. Please go on with Cosmo. What did he say?"

"He was interested. He looked longest at the photograph taken at the big wagon, the one of your father with the straight-brimmed hat and the leather puttees. He asked for a magnifying glass. He may very well be the painter you want."

"If you think so, Hester, you tell him he's hired. But I want to meet him first."

"That would be absolutely necessary."

"I want to tell him about the liver and the lights at my new office. They need cheer."

"De dinner is serve, Modom," Ana said from the doorway.

"When he got old," Royston said, "my father used to go off by himself, at our old Superior plant in California, and work with mine installation problems at his old drafting table. It was his medicine. He loved it. He kept a hand in the

58

engineering — and what a hand he had — till the day he died. Working alone, he got so he'd talk the problem and the figures to himself, out loud. One time one of our foremen asked him, 'Mr. Royston, I'd like to know why in the world it is I hear you so often in there talking to yourself.' Father blinked at him and said, 'I'll tell you why. I like to talk to an intelligent man and I like to hear an intelligent man talk!' You know, Hester, as the years go by I keep on seeing my father as the one member of my family who dealt well with everybody. That included himself."

Hester Bren smiled, looking at Royston. "Other members of your family — I'm not acquainted with them. But that father of yours had a son Robert, who bears resemblance."

"I'm not talking to myself — yet."

"And there is something else. In dealing with everybody I believe the son Robert deals last of all with himself, for himself." She touched her hand to his shoulder. "A very extraordinary man — and don't argue. Because a very ordinary roast leg of lamb is waiting. I wish, Robert, you had given Ana and me more notice this evening. So we could treat you better."

"You always mistreat me terribly — and don't argue. Let's eat." They went through the door, into the dining room, to the candle-lighted table.

Hester Bren's voice made a pleasant sound of small talk as they ate. Observing Royston across the table, she kept the talk small, about trivial events of her working day at the Uhdy Galleries, about old Herr Uhdy in New York, about Ana's joke with the grocer on Division Street, about an alleged Cranach bought from an alleged Polish count by a neighbor of Royston's in Lake Forest. Perceiving Royston's mind in motion with a deepening preoccupation of its own, Hester Bren arranged her words to require no reply.

Royston forked the last piece of roast lamb left on his plate, and dipped it in the sauce. "I wonder if our artist Cosmo," Royston said, "has been around Taos lately. Do you suppose he's met Isabel and her René out there?"

"I think he has not been in New Mexico for some time."

"Maybe his soul isn't given to much vibrating. With music of the spheres. Or what Isabel calls 'the Pueblo cosmology.' "

"Artists are all sorts, Robert." Hester Bren smiled. "Do you have recent news of your Isabel and René Marecaux?"

"They're back from Cuernavaca. They're in Taos again."

"Marecaux has talent, Juilliard people say."

"Having a composer for a son-in-law — wouldn't it be interesting if he would compose something? Isabel writes that René has plans. He proposes — not composes — the writing of, and I quote, 'a symphonic suite starkly titled: *Desert.*' The title is tentative, perhaps too representational, according to Isabel. So, I suspect, may be the suite. Formerly, I believe it was a something for bassoons and strings.

"Hester, there's a world — just one of the worlds — I know nothing about. Quite a world. — And in a personal way I have to be grateful for it whether I personally think it may be phony or not. It appears to have given Isabel some kind of a handhold for living. I hope it lasts. What an aggressive little highbrow my daughter Isabel is — and I don't understand her as a highbrow. Yet as a person, I think I do —

"She grew up with the handicap of that polio leg, and with that older sister of hers sparkling all over the place. I can see where Isabel was forced to a refuge; she found it in books, in arts with the capital A. Yet somewhere along that line Isabel faced — with an honesty I admire — the fact that she had no talent herself. That was something,

60

wasn't it? Her recourse was to become an understander and a partisan of those who did have talent, or thought they had. She still chose her own ground for her own battle. Being a torch bearer for the Higher Things, for an *avant-garde,* I think was Isabel's style of proving something, of competing for attention with her gorgeous whing-dinging sister Dottie. I give Isabel credit.

"At the same time I can't neglect to notice another factor involved. The fact that Isabel is not exactly a penniless devotee does not exactly decrease her popularity in circles of genius. Does it? But if she hadn't married this René, it would have been some other fellow up there in the thin air. Anyway. She's got some kind of a world now, whether I can measure it or not — *and* I wish to God that her sister Dorothy — would find something we could call a world to live in! Hester, she is worrying hell out of me. Dot's got everything on earth an attractive female ought to have. Everything but judgment."

Hester Bren never asked Robert Royston to say more than he volunteered to tell her. Looking at him, she said nothing now.

"I suppose it must be in the paper that Dot's Nevada divorce was granted today," Royston said. "The bo's'n's mate didn't reply to the proceedings. He didn't ask for anything either. He must be a strapping sort of sailor man. With the fleet in the Far East somewhere. And that's finished."

Royston had always maintained, for no logical reason he could fathom within himself, a somehow moral reluctance to talk of his wife Cynthia with Hester Bren. "I had hoped," Royston said, "some of Dot's family from San Francisco would be staying with her in Reno while she was there. Now I'm trying to get Dot to come stay with me here for a while. On the phone this afternoon, she said she's taking an apartment in New York. She's an attractive woman and she knows it too well. It's her trouble with life."

Hester Bren saw that Royston expected a reply. "I think," she improvised, "a very attractive woman must attract a very good man. Robert — may I offer you more to eat?"

"Thank you, no. I've talked too much family."

"You ate little. We have fruits for a dessert. And we have some cheese."

"None, thank you. Just coffee."

"With a cognac? The imports are coming better now. I found a good Courvoisier last week. Ana will bring coffee to the library. That will be more comfortable."

In the library chair, with the brandy pony warm in his hand, Royston found himself without comfort.

He lit Hester Bren's cigarette, and lit one for himself. They sat in the warm light, in silence.

"I'm old, Hester."

"That is nonsense."

"Old."

"Have you been well, Robert?"

"I'm always well. Well enough. To keep getting older."

"Tomorrow, you ought —"

"Tomorrow? Tomorrow, in all probability there will be about twenty-one hundred and eighty people off their jobs — good jobs. Owing to strong personal convictions, maintained by myself. And by next month, as a result, there could be twenty thousand people not at their work, good work."

"I'm not following you well."

"Many people aren't. RMC has a strike situation on its hands at Crawford."

"Your world in that office, Robert — I am not prepared to help you with it by understanding it even a little. There is too much to understand! I suppose few people —"

62

"A lot of people ought to understand one particular thing now. You saw the big inflation time in the Reich after the first war. Didn't you, Hester?"

"I lived through it."

"That's an extreme example but I happened to see the start of it myself and it's what I'm talking about. In another degree, another set of conditions, we can go on letting wage levels and price levels climb and climb again while the economy tries wrenching itself back into a peacetime production for a damned uncertain and mortgaged peace — and we can wake up in an inflationary ruination of our own. So many elements involved. People, both in government and out, that know about it and care about it — now's their time to be responsible about it."

Royston ground out his cigarette in an ash tray.

"You call it my world. If it is a world, I could hardly call it mine." Royston spoke with his eyes fastened to the wall of books across the room. "Anyway, it's a head-breaking big scrounge. Trying to know the right thing. Trying to do the right thing. — That goes in everybody's world, doesn't it? Lately, only lately, I get moments when I wonder why I'm back in my particular scrounge. That must be a bad symptom, for an old-time scrounger. Yet, looking straight at whatever life I've got now, I haven't many aggressive reasons to go on scrounging for the Royston Machine Corporation. It certainly lived without me during those twenty-two months I spent in the Army. It may be I should have come back and asked for a few 'retirement benefits' myself. A well-behaving old chairman of a board. Let a man in his prime, somebody like Huley Bent, take on the grizzlies. With his own butcher knife."

"One thing is wrong with that, dear Robert. You don't believe it."

"Don't I? Why don't I? When I started out, it was ap-

63

proximately a thousand years ago — I was a technical man. My father and I designed and built machines. About five hundred years ago, I think it must have been, I got separated from the machines. I got involved with the men making the machines and the money the machines made. I quit working a slipstick and started working a pushbutton. When I was the bushy young engineer out of Stanford, traveling with a whole hatful of futures from Kaslo to Chuquicamata, I was involved with equations that were workable, metals that were predictable, and the performance of machines that behaved only according to logic. How sensible, how delightful, and I got sidetracked forever. With grim mankind. I got sidetracked with R. K. Royston. A querimonious man. An old man. Now in need of another brandy."

"While he has that brandy, may I say something?" Hester Bren smiled, lighting another cigarette. "May I express a point of view? Since a spring day eleven years ago next month, I have been acquainted with Mr. Robert Kendall Royston. He often talks a great deal, and he talks very well — usually. The privilege of my acquaintance with him, however, is such that I am able positively to inform him that he is not old. It does not become him to say or to feel that he is —"

"Then what's the matter with him?"

"He knows perfectly well! Robert — how long has it been since you have taken any rest or relief from daily responsibility, from difficult work, from military duty, from dangers in a war, from worry, from tension, from all else? How long? You! Returning to business in the same week you put away the uniform. In the three months since — I have seen you but a few times and each time I see you I must tell you I wonder what you expect of yourself. What *do* you?"

64

"Dear Hester, chew me out, loud and clear! Make it sound as if I do labor mightily — it's music! Remember again those pains of service I suffered in a second world war — that bird colonel, AUS, on his detached duty from that very, very high level staff, in his service of supply, experiencing danger and privation daily. He was in direst peril, more than once, of smothering under tons of paper. It was gruesome." Royston touched with his little finger at the tiny colored oblong of the DSC button in his tweed lapel — and he faintly lifted his brandy glass. "I did have a better war, about seven hundred years ago. — And you know — there's one thing I haven't taken the time to do since coming back here in December. And I ought to do it. I ought to write my old sergeant in that old war.

"Hester. If I could have gotten sprung right after V-J last summer, maybe I wouldn't have come back here raising the general hell at the Royston Machine Corporation general offices quite so quick. I could have thumbed some kind of a ride to Silvertip, Wyoming. I could have climbed on a horse named Hemlock and I could have ridden up to Sky Lake with Ingo Jingo Spurling. And caught a fish. — Time and again I have thought standing in the noise how quiet it was that moment in the Cloudrock Mountains. Oh I wonder how deep, how lonesome the snow is tonight, covering the cabin at Haven Lake."

"I know how you loved it up there," said Hester Bren.

"Who was that old Greek, that old giant wrestler, that renewed himself with the earth?"

"Antaeus?"

"That's the man. If he'd kept his feet on the ground, Hercules would never have throttled him."

5

There was a boding peculiarity of silence in the angled sunlight, a queerly snow-dazzled loneliness in the air, as the afternoon wore away.

Hank Spurling stacked a dozen hard-gotten armloads of chopped firewood against the wall near the stove. Stiff with fatigues he felt to the marrow of his bones, pressing a wet-gloved hand at the ache in the small of his back, sweating, he stepped out again into the cold in front of the cabin door. He looked again, perfunctorily, across the snowbank where his tracks plowed a trampled pathway to the level flat of the lake. He noticed, at one of the holes he had drilled in the ice there, that the signal stick was raised, waggling. He hurried to it.

Picking up the cross-stick, he felt the old happy tug and quiver of a line in his hand. He had just horsed the brookie, a dandy two-pounder, almost, up through the hole — when the ice began a shudder under him and a rumble came shaking the air.

Scared, he jerked up quick. The trout dropped out upon the ice, flopping and flashing in sunlight. Hank Spurling stood as if impaled, with the rumble booming louder.

He thanked God he saw it where he did.

Above and beyond the crestline, over the near ridge of Chuckbox Mountain's cragged south shoulder, a spreading cloud of smoky snow dust churned boiling into the sky. The long-drawn pounding of the air, the tremor of the ice and of the earth under the ice, faded rolling like thunder when a stir of sound from across the lake became a sharp flaw of wind sucking a queer sigh and sudden sway through the tops of the timber. Powdery cloud above the ridge hazed, climbing the blue. Quietness hovered, troubled, while air and earth settled to themselves again. Hank Spurling stared up at the unchanged height of Chuckbox Mountain unmoving in the sun.

Then he remembered. He looked down at the trout with the hook and glob of bacon caught in its jaw. Grains of ice were forming along the slick red-dotted gray-green side, along the shine of orange belly. He squatted, pulled his knife and cleaned his fish.

The queerness that came with the afternoon did not quite leave. It hung in the air.

He had baited the hook again with some of the fish offal, he had reset the line down the hole in the ice, he had checked the lines in the other two holes, he had climbed up through the snowbank, a few paces from the cabin, with his supper in his hand, when he saw more meat.

It gave an almost imperceivable flick near the foot of a sapling spruce thirty feet away; shadowed white on shadowy white, it was betrayed by three dark dots, the black tip of a laid-back ear, two round eyes looking. A snowshoe hare, too big to be anything but an old buck, sat hunched dead still, watching a man carry a fish.

I am going to get you, Hank thought.

The hare hopped then. It went up the slope slowly, into the firs. Hank moved to the cabin.

He cautiously tied his cleaned fish to a cord dangling down from a nail on a rafter inside. He got his snowshoes and carbine. Standing outside the door he fastened the snowshoe bindings to his boots, he pushed the door shut and bolted it. He threw a load into the chamber of his carbine, uncocked the hammer to safety, and started for the tracks.

The four prints, the two long hind feet, the two round forefeet half as big, were as easy to follow in the snow as a line of repeated letters across white paper. He had not walked seventy yards, slow on his snowshoes, into the clearing of the old horse pen, when he saw his quarry — and lost it when it flashed into a thicket of brown chokeberry before he could shoot. Angling around the brush clump, ready, he found the tracks leading from covert. The hare had slipped away.

Then he saw it suddenly, across a hollow in the slope, by

the snowbanked butt end of a big fallen pine. He pulled up cocking and squeezed smooth as the sights came lining.

The shot cracked.

It carried a *thwack* of hurtling slug through flesh. It brought a quick pitiful scream from the hare, a mortal scrabble and spasm of white fur spattering red on white snow — and the hit, the cry, the blood in the gun smell ripped a buried corridor of Sergeant Spurling's brain. Dead Vogle sprang dying again knocked with the scream in the crackle *thwack* his torn flesh *splat* red wet on the burn-splintered rocks by Spurling's unwipable face the stitching thump of the 7 mm. *slubslubslubslub* coming yet coming back — trembling with the gun terrible in his hands, with the hare jerking on the snow, Spurling felt black gorge rise reeling.

Vomit poured up his throat out his mouth upon the snow. Standing retched, with his sore belly heaved, with bitter water welled in his eyes, he leaned over the vomit of the war. On clean snow, it smoked more than hare's blood.

"Huu-u-ohh-h! Spurrr-ling!"

Caught with it sick and dizzy, he felt the queer new sound in the queer air bring hackles rising on his neck. He jerked up. He jerked around, darting his eyes, trying to clear them, trying to see. Then he saw.

The burly figure moved with a slow rolling gait like an old bear walking upright in the snow. Merlin Claunch on his snowshoes, with his shaggy pack on his back, waved his rifle coming down the hill through the spruce.

The dark eyes were small in the massive face. The face was ruddy bronze creased with big wrinkles. The storm-burned lips went set by habit in a half grin which was a part of an outdoor squint rather than a part of an interior smile. As it came closer the grin got wider.

69

Hank Spurling tried to scrape his snowshoes over the place in the snow where he had been sick.

"Young Haven!" Merlin Claunch said.

"Well —" the word scraped his burned throat — he had to cough and swallow — "Mr. Claunch!" They shook hands.

"Heerd your shot. Then I seen. I thought I'd hail then, let you know." The dark eyes looked hard into Hank Spurling's face. "Long, long, long time! Since I seen you."

"Long time."

"*Glad* to see you. *Yeh!* — You sick, Haven?"

"No I'm not sick."

Claunch looked over, casually, at the dead hare on the snow. "See you got something for stew pot. How you find the cabin?"

"Good shape, Mr. Claunch. Got here at dark, last night. It looked plenty good."

Claunch squinted at the shadows reaching across the lake. "I made some fair time," he said. His raised his eyes, measuring sunlight on the face of Chuckbox Mountain high above. The squint became an evident grin. "You been knocking slides loose up there, Haven?"

"God. I was pulling a brookie out when the ice commenced to shake and wobble. I thought it had me —"

"I was coming this side the dip below top of Blue Gap when I heerd it tear loose. I seen the snow cloud rise. About where it looked like, must of mashed a hole through bottom at Rainbow Lake and clumb up the far side, huh?"

"I was close enough, to feel the wind it made — I always heard about the wind a big slide brings. Now I know."

"My advice, don't be there, a slide like that. Don't be there, at no slide. *Fuh!* Be glad it was not the Gun Cliffs — I been having the luck by them little caves there with nice fox this winter, Haven."

Claunch trudged over to the hare, stooped easily with

70

his pack, picked up the limp body by a hind foot. "Gut shot," he said, flopping it. *"Big* old buck you killed. Near four pound." He started down the slope.

"I can carry that —" Hank called, forcing himself.

"You can clean that. For supper. While we git the big hotel to going. Sky's got some wind tonight, and colder."

Down the cove and past the cabin, Hank took the bloody hare behind a thick Douglas fir, safely out of sight. It was necessary to look at what was in his hand. He gagged. It was necessary for self-respect to overrule aversion. He drew his knife and made himself begin.

He made his cold-fingered hands perform, cutting and pulling. Intent at their work, his hands then found themselves at nothing more than the ordinary chore of skinning and dressing a rabbit for a stew. His senses following the commonplace labor of his hands trailed back into common sureties of the commonplace. The commonplace smoke rising now from the cabin's stovepipe, where Merlin Claunch had remade the fire, seemed a surety not merely against cold but against a boding loneliness that earlier possessed the afternoon's air.

In bitter cold Hank spent the last hour of daylight tearing dead branches from where they hung low on spruce trunks, breaking the pieces to size, carrying the wood inside where Claunch had the stew, the coffee, the pan bread going on the little stove. He had even put prunes to soak. "Your fish will go good with flapjacks, breakfast," he said. "You might hook another by then. Glad you found the crowbar to drill them holes." From his unloaded pack, along with what he brought to eat, and the brown paper and bottle of scent for setting his traps, he pulled two stumpy candles and an old vinegar bottle full of coal oil for the lamp.

They had light. They had warmth, they had coffee, and they finally had supper when the stew was done enough, with both of them sitting on the rickety bench at the old trestle table near the stove.

They each carried a pipe; they each loaded and lit their pipes when their eating was done.

"Never seen you with a pipe before, Haven."

"I got me this, something to do, sitting around a recreation hall, a hospital I was in."

Wind gusts hummed in the stovepipe, tapping at the closed damper, and the fire popped.

"I used to sit there puffing this thing, thinking about Wyoming. God, it don't seem possible! I'm here, in Wyoming. On Haven Lake. These old Cloudrocks, they don't change, do they? You don't change either, Mr. Claunch."

"There's changes. And more coming. Always is. Looking back, I seen you changing aplenty." Claunch took long burbling pulls on his corncob. "I know who I am with, setting here with you. It was me went to git the doctor the night you was born."

"I know it."

"I got him here, too. Your daddy waiting with the water buckets boiling and little Rutherford owl-eye skeered. Your mother was laying over there in that corner," he pointed into the shadow, "right there. It was a different bunk then.

"You come along in middle July, there was still snow patches — I give that doc a wild Blackfoot horseback ride, in the dark! It was a hard summer, Nineteen and twenty-two.

"I given your daddy and mother this place to live, when Ingo got laid off dude wrangling at Plunkett Blakely's Diamond Slash. Not much of a roof, but some kind of a roof, over their heads. I moved over onto Upper Plew and made camp. *Huh!* I taken a shine to Ingo Spurling the year he come to Wyoming, bringing your mother. That is the best woman ever I knew. They ain't many good women."

72

He found another match in his pocket and worked a while at lighting his pipe.

"Mr. Claunch," Hank said. "I guess you must know as well as anybody how it was at the house when they got the word about Rut. That's a year and a half ago! I wish to God that Dad would get straightened up. It's about time."

"Ingo thought the world of that oldest boy of his. Still does. When Ingo comes back to the mountains, he'll be all right."

"He won't even listen! It's like talking to a post when I ask him what we're going to do about outfitting again. Christ, I know about Rut, he was a damn good man and he was the best brother a man could have, but Dad acts like it's no use thinking about anything without Rut here! Sometimes he acts like he's pretty glad I'm back and sometimes he acts like he resents having me around the house. Mother claims it's booze got him. I don't think so. Maybe I will, but I don't yet. He acts to me, Mr. Claunch, like a man that hasn't got his nerve back, after being punched around all of a sudden. And then getting kind of proud of the beating he's took, instead of getting some nerve back, and doing something. Mother working, and him down the street, sitting on his duff in the Cloudrock Bar —"

"Say Haven —" Claunch said, quietly, "yesterday afternoon Ingo come by my place on Longstick. He'd been to Rovelstad's trucking feed. He quit early to come see me. Ast me when I figured to run my line again. I told him sometime next few days, if weather held good. He said you was up here by yourself. Told me he didn't think much of the idy you being up here alone. In case anything happened. He had me scratching my head! I said, Haven's all right, Rut and him was good mountain boys from the start. What's the matter? He said, well Merlin I think I will go up there tomorrow if you ain't. I said, well I can go up tomor-

73

row, we can both go tomorrow, I'd like to have you, and take some traps, you ain't been up there in a long time, I told him. He said I know it, but there is no use both us going. Hank might get the idy we might be worried about him, both of us going. I said Ingo, he has been in those mountains before, he knows what they are. Ingo says, Merlin you haven't seen him since he got back. He ain't well yet from being wounded and he's bull-headed as hell, heavy-packing up there by himself. — See, Haven?"

Merlin Claunch rose ponderously to the stove, and shoved into it the heaviest sticks he could find.

"Haven. I seen you was sick when I come down the hill this afternoon. It don't pay to be in mountains wintertime sick by yourself. It don't pay to think you can work much — these mountains — anytime — you ain't well. You know that. I seen you fiddle with that stew on your plate — look at it. What I want to know is, how sick you be, *huh?*"

Hank had to grin.

"I don't think I'm very sick — I don't think I'm sick at all. I think it takes time —" The grin was gone. "I know damn well it takes patience. I came up here as soon as I could, on a — a kind of a start I am making. I don't want to just look at these mountains. I want to be in them. I admit I thought I was going to break apart this morning when I tried to crawl out, after that pack yesterday. I limbered myself up, putting those holes in the ice. Working the kinks out, it's the beginning anybody makes, getting back in shape —"

"You was puking your head off when I come down the hill. You was green as a gourd. Like you seen a ghost. What about that? *Huh?*"

"I'll tell you about that. I'll tell you the exact truth. I wasn't expecting anything like it — how could I? I got sick when I knocked over that rabbit and it squalled. Now I real-

74

ize. It was the first time I used a gun at all, for anything, since last May. May twelfth."

When Claunch finally spoke, he turned to look Hank in the face. "I never had to kill nobody. I never have been further than Thompson Falls, Montana. I have killed bear. I have stood up to a bear. In a cave. But I never killed no man. You seen the ocean — and them Japs — you seen everything else — over there. I guess you git tired, telling of it."

"I don't go for trying to tell very much, to anybody. The main reason, it's hard to tell much, Mr. Claunch."

"You ain't your daddy! Telling about that motorcycle and all them French women and the wine over there the first war."

"He must have had quite a war," Hank said. He filled his pipe from the tobacco can on the table, and lit up. "I guess I got in the wrong war, Mr. Claunch. But I sure as hell got back to the right place afterwards. I'm just about as far from coconuts and as near to spruce as I can get."

Claunch's old corncob burbled.

"I seen a real coconut with the shell on," he said, "one time in a store at Junction. I never seen a coconut growing."

"I damn sure wish I could say the same."

The wind roared pulling at flame in the stovepipe. The wind shook the cabin's shadowy door.

"It ain't bad, fixed on a cake, Haven."

"What's that?"

"Coconut."

"Oh — coconut," Hank said. "I guess if I did start in, about the Marine Corps, it would take all night."

"Funny thing, we got exactly all night till me and you start with a bag of traps for Gun Cliffs. Seems like there has to be an all night before morning comes."

75

The face of Merlin Claunch in the lamplight looked as craggy as the face of Cloudrock Peak. It looked as good.

"When I enlisted at Laramie," Hank Spurling said, "there happened to be a crowd-up shipping recruits. For some reason, instead of going to Dago where boots from western states usually got sent, our bunch got orders to Parris Island. It was how I happened to wind up in the Seventh Marines and the First Division, the Old Corps —

"I was in good condition to begin with and it wasn't the physical part bothered me, it was the discipline, getting used to it and the senseless stuff the DIs give us to do. The training made us into Marines all right. But I'd say any time that Parris Island was a hole. I remember getting there on that bus, about sundown, a cloudy Sunday. I never had been out of Wyoming before.

"It was late in May, a Saturday noon, when we got through being boots and we got a spiel, You are United States Marines, Semper Fi, My Boys, and we went ashore first liberty. I was wearing khakis with a sharp crease and my brand-new Expert Rifleman badge. I just stood around.

"I had made Expert that week. That was what kept me at Parris. There was an instructor shortage and I could handle a piece pretty well. Orders put me on the range helping an old sea-daddy five-stripe sergeant instruct new boots how to hit something with the M-1.

"While I was still a boot, we kept getting scoop about how the First Marine Division was shipping out. First and Fifth Marines, Seventh Marines, all to the Pacific, hush hush. I could picture those coconut trees and little grass shacks. When I got assigned to rifle instruction I began to picture myself spending my whole cruise teaching city skinheads to squeeze off at a paper target in South Carolina with a war going on. That August, I qualified Expert with pistol.

76

"When orders did come — *bing!* We proceeded by railway transportation to San Francisco, California, destination question mark. I was a replacement headed for a rifle platoon in the First Battalion, Seventh Marines. But I didn't know that. Not till I got to Guadalcanal. Somebody raised the finger, somebody hit a few typewriter keys spelling name and serial number. There I went.

"I got ashore on the night of 30 October during an air raid, coming in on a Higgins boat, from the AKA that had brought us and some 155 mm. artillery. I had my first battle, and it was with myself as well as Japs, under old Chesty Puller, a fighting man is he, on the stinking jungle east bank of the Metapona River six miles from Lunga Point, first week in November. Things were very bad, Mr. Claunch.

"We were just replacements and had a kind of what-in-hell-is-going-to-happen look in the middle of what seemed like crazy desperate people.

"When I first saw those hills of Guadalcanal humped up above the ocean coming in on that ship I felt someway relieved that now I was going to do what I had been training for and hoping for, not knowing, exactly. Before long I would be lining up my sights on live targets, and not like elk or antelope either. God knows I wasn't thinking at that time about a snowshoe rabbit! I was quite a Marine. I wanted to know what it would be like and what I would be like and I kept pretty well away from the idea that I could be a live target too. They always told us, you want to overlook the dark side if you are going to keep the spirit that will bring you out on top.

"They didn't mention the odds.

"When you do have the target that you have wondered about, then you realize: this kind of shooting is the gambling game. You are your own stake. You can be nervous if

77

you think about it. So you just do it and try not to think about it. Part of it is training and part of it is luck, trying to keep from losing that stake you put up. You keep putting it up, you have to. When you get to be the gambler of that kind, no wonder you seem crazy.

"You learned quick, on the Canal. It was quick or ignorance forever. You felt like an old-timer in practically no time and then time went so slow. After a while, it was nearly impossible to overlook the dark side.

"Because the Canal seemed to last so long, being stuck there I mean, most all Marines grew whiskers, big mustaches, maybe pointed goatees. You'd see all different shaped mustaches and sometimes we would try to shape them with candle wax. Twirl them. There seemed to be a pride having a wide mustache. I figure now that it was connected someway with what might seem to others the crazy part of being an old-timer. Nobody that was dead went on growing whiskers.

"They pulled us off the Canal aboard USS *Republic*. At Espiritu Santo, we called it code name Buttons, I was sent aboard hospital ship *Solace* with malaria and they shipped a bunch of us to Mobile Hospital Four, Auckland, New Zealand. Talk about sick! I was. The fever and the shakes lasted for more than a month. I was hoping for a chance to see what they call the New Zealand Alps because at school in Laramie I had read about the New Zealand Alpine Club and Mount Cook. But those mountains were way down on South Island. I never got there, I was shipped back to my battalion at a camp outside of Sydney. We went by train to Melbourne.

"Melbourne was like heaven.

"Up to then I never had more than a few beers in my whole life. Booze never give me much. But in Melbourne you would stay with your bunch and sometimes you would

78

get a snoot full. There was a cheap whiskey we called 'ko-rye-oh' and it was murder the next morning. The hell-raisers we referred to them as Flinders Street commandos and the Aussie girls they were called Sheilas. Marines got mixed up thick with Aussies and Dinky Die and all that, but a good deal of that old Melbourne stud talk was smoke. You listened to a lot of lying about what the Aussies called 'tubes.' Mr. Claunch, if the real truth was known, I never laid but two girls during the Pacific war. One at Melbourne. One in Honolulu, a little Chink waitress, last December.

"The division went to Cape Sudest, New Guinea, in October of 1943. Supposed to be readying for a landing operation. It was air raids at Sudest, plenty.

"The first one we had was at night. We had just listened to a honey tongue lecture saying the Japanese didn't know where the First Marine Division was at, and also that we had complete control of the air. Then I heard that old familiar *whish-rattle* sound of falling bombs in the air. You always imagined it was coming right for you! I jumped for the cover of the river bank in the dark, and splashed my dumb self smack into the muddy Samboga River while the bombs hit down the beach. Those bombings began to put us back in the groove.

"We embarked for the Cape Gloucester assault Christmas morning. We didn't know what we would be up against. We spent Christmas Day sitting on a hot iron deck, with our gear, imagining. We spent all that night, imagining. I didn't have to swim in, I got tossed ashore by a wave, and there was not a shooting Jap when we hit. Real shooting started later.

"There was one goofy thing. A Zero comes diving out of the sun strafing the beach. I hit the deck and the second I knew the plane had gone past me I looked up and there

79

— *close* I mean — was that dirty red orange ball on that wing, pulling up in a bank away from our ships' AA. And here is a comical incident, Mr. Claunch. During whole seconds I had this beautiful target in sight and in range — my mind slipped a cog back to Guadalcanal. There I was armed with a BAR. I forgot that now I was armed with the M-1 — and me a has-been instructor of it! I quick drew back the operating handle which on the BAR would load the weapon but on the M-1 it extracted the round from the chamber! Then I realized my mistake and it was too late. The Zero was behind the trees. I never can to this day forget that chance I had or the way that Japanese pilot looked sitting in that sleek plane.

"In that jungle on Gloucester you never had a chance to get dry. My God it rained. Your skin turned fishbelly white from the wet, all wrinkled like a sponge, and your feet got sores. I had mine wrapped in crummy bandages all the time we were on Hill 660, and after.

"Here's something I have to tell about. I first noticed it on the Canal and then it came back really strong at Gloucester. I had the feeling of a shell bursting at my feet which would blow my head off. I expected this to happen. Like waiting for something you know has to happen. I imagined the hot piece of metal come through my flesh. I expected time and again to have it hit.

"Why I was not exactly afraid, when I thought I had to be hit, I believe is due to the fact that I kept my mind on something else even more. And that was keeping my eye and keeping my trigger finger tense for those little Japanese-uniformed men you might see move in the jungle. You could not see those Japs, hardly ever. To do any good of course you got to have a target and in the jungle you were nearly desperate for one. If you thought you caught movement, you'd let fly. I've seen tommygunners just hold and empty a full drum, at nothing. The jungle gets alive as a person when your enemy is in it.

"On trails in any jungle there are openings where the brush is thinner. Those are the likely places to expect a sniper's shot. One thing you go hoping is true: if it's hard to spot a sniper, it is usually hard for him to spot you. If you cross thin patches fast, you give him less time to line up his sights. On long patrols you get so edged up and finally so bushed, you don't care. Then a burst — the leaves and grass crackling pushed with slugs — you sure care again quick!

"At Borgen Bay on Gloucester a number of Marines were killed by falling trees. Big ones would get rain-rotted and weak, and artillery fire and bombs shook and loosened them and they would just topple without warning. I nearly got it one night when the platoon was pulled back next to Batt. CP. A tree crashed down ten feet from my poncho shelter. I had just started to doze — after it was over, it must have taken me a full minute to register the close shave. Those falling trees, and the typhus rats, and cold chow most of the time — we once ate K9 rations, dog food out of the cans — and rain and mud and Japs. One time my buddy Vogle, he was from Milwaukee, dug a nice hole for the night and the first time Vogle jumped in I could see him dancing around trying to step on a big rat or kick it out, with the bombers nearly overhead. Things like that seem crazy funny at the time, like the land crab that took a chunk out of One Brew Dodd's ass the first night on Peleliu.

"We got off New Britain in April. We were supposed to be going back to rest in Melbourne. They shipped us, all beat up, to Pavuvu. One of the godforsaken Russell Islands about sixty miles from Guadalcanal. We had to build our own 'rest camp' at Pavuvu, in more mud. The rats there

81

would bite a hole in your face while you slept in your sack.

"At Pavuvu we went asiatic. We cursed the Corps and the day we were born. At Pavuvu I spent my twenty-second birthday. At Pavuvu I got a bitter hate for coconut trees. I tried not to think of Wyoming. It was on another planet.

"I had made corporal at Melbourne. I made sergeant at Pavuvu on 5 August, 1944. We were getting lots of replacements and now I was one of the old men of the platoon. And then we started to train for another landing. Jesus.

"On the rehearsals, they were always fouled up, we used beaches over on the old Canal. Our bunch came in about a hundred and fifty yards from a beached Japanese transport ship, bombed, gutted, rusting for nearly two years. Standing on that beach, just old-timers understood. Myself, I didn't care for any look at Henderson Field, or anything else. It was changed but it brought back a feeling that the word Guadalcanal still brings back. Mr. Claunch, it looks better in white letters on the Division shoulder patch than it ever did in real life.

"We shoved off in convoy from Ironbottom Sound on 8 September, 1944, for the assault on Peleliu. D Day was the fifteenth of September.

"To begin with, coming in over the reef our amtrac took a hit. Killed the coxswain, stalled the vehicle, and those of us that were left went over the side fifty yards from the beach. In direct lane of enemy fire.

"It was too shallow to swim, too deep to wade. The bottom was uneven slippery niggerhead coral. Trying to run, your knees got gripped by the water, holding you like in slow motion. It was a flounder toward the beach with the fire whapping the air, knocking dirty water with smoke and concussion. Nine of us got in, I made the count, to the sand bank and line of smashed trees about twenty

82

feet beyond tidemark. Marines were flopped flat in the sand, the dead and wounded and plenty just hugging the deck too damn scared to get up and make a run for it.

"We caught pure hell making our way to the lieutenant and the rest of the platoon. We knew it would be to the right, up Orange Beach Three, like our briefing said. I hoped the lieutenant had luck and would be there and he was. Under fire like that, the only way you do it is to say to yourself what the hell here goes nothing and you go. You make it or you don't.

"By the time of the tank battle late that afternoon north of us on the airstrip where the Fifth Marines were slugging, we were entrenched in broken trees and coral at a forward position not three hundred yards from the beach at our backs. That was our total penetration for D Day. That night came the counterattack like we all dreaded — the Japs are very sneaky and plenty good at night.

"Those flares would float down throwing that sickly light. The enemy would yammer coming. You could hear them with the machine guns pounding, and our 105s blasting at our backs. A few Japs got through and had to be killed body contact. There were three waves, then the attack fizzled out.

"Nobody had much time to notice any weather the first day, they were too busy. Next morning when the grind began we felt what we were in for, besides Japs. The sun and that hot rock was fierce. Seven degrees from the Equator. It cooked you and did something to you inside, in your brains.

"The only thing good at all was the air power. We had it *all*, for a change. What a sight. Strafing out ahead of the perimeter with tracers and rockets and laying in bomb after bomb after bomb with explosions that made the whole island jump punishing the Japs that had dished us the grief

83

so long. Then our cruisers and BBs out beyond the reef would slam their big stuff. It was like what we took at Guadal, only the Japs were getting it now.

"But those Peleliu Japs, they were good troops, the way they fought. Five long days, five long nights, we would advance a little and hold, advance and hold, with the tanks blasting and the flame throwers burning at the blockhouses and strong points, and there always seemed to be another tougher one yet. That whole sonofabitching island was only eleven thousand yards long and thirty-three hundred yards across at the widest place. Taking the south end of it was the Seventh's battle objective. We did it. We got chewed up doing it. Then the command had word for us.

"Over at the high ridge on the island's other side, we called it Bloody Nose, old Chesty Puller was now commanding the First Marines. They had it. When the First was finally pulled after eight days, it had over sixty percent casualties, dead and wounded. For instance, out of the nine rifle platoons in their First Battalion, which was nearly five hundred men, there was seventy-four poor ragged bastards left. And Bloody Nose was not secured. Between four and five thousand Japs were holed up in a hard-to-believe system of rock caves. They were fixed with artillery emplacements, armor doors, ammo, rice and everything else. Those caves had to be grubbed out, one by one. The Seventh was sent in to relieve the First. We took up where they left off.

"The First Battalion, Seventh, moved on 20 September to north points of the high ground, to try to crack it from a new angle. That afternoon when my browned-off platoon dragged up, what a — I don't know what you'd call it —

"It wasn't death, exactly. There were no dead in sight. Just dead silence and knocked-out tanks. Nothing moved. The rising ground led up to Jap territory where not a

84

branch stirred in the breeze. There wasn't any branches left. And little if any breeze. Only bare coral rock and dust. You could see no enemy but you knew eyes, slant-eyes, were somewhere, watching.

"It was the third day up there in the broken rock when they pulled my platoon back and around, to move for another position. To get there, they told us to go up a side gulch that led into the main ridge. Two days before, a unit of the Second Battalion had already cleaned up this gulch, moving behind tanks, and they had burned out the Jap bunker cut high in the steep rock at the head of the gulch. We were supposed to move up past it, over the hogback and onto the ridge, to reinforce the pocket C Company was holding.

"The gulch was secured, we were told. We walked into it. With no tank.

"Either through tunnels or else by sneaking up at night, Japs had got back to their smashed bunker. They let us get into that gulch good. Clear in. Then they turned on the juice. Seven-millimeter squirting all over rattling with the whump of one of those big mortars. It was terrible in that bare rock. Many were dead and I could hear wounded crying.

"My buddy Vogle and me had hit the deck right by each other in the boulders. I squinted up from behind our little piece of rock and in the racket I sounded off — Vogie, the bunker! And I saw him rise up pointing the bazooka at the black hole up in the bluff.

"A machine gun got him. It stitched him, knocking, across the middle. After all the time he put in the Pacific. He fell, part of him, on me. I couldn't stand it. Then I raised up and I started.

"When you honest to God don't care is when they don't hit. I remember like flame stood around edges of every-

85

thing, wavy fire I thought and I swear I could hear like I was with the queer noise Vogle made, the sound he gave when he died. I think I ran bent over, crossing the gully toward the black hole in the bluff.

"Then it got steep, and rough. I had to grab, mainly at roots and stems of brush. Finally there was a rotten kind of steep pitch where I had to use a couple of cling holds scrambling like a fool, but by now I was getting some fire support from the platoon and by this time the Japs had lost me because I was getting too close under. They started to pitch out grenades but they were blind. The things would fall past me and pop off in the rocks below. I figured all that out later, when I looked down. At the time, I didn't know — nothing. I was out of my head. I didn't have any feeling in my hands. I knocked all the hide off and didn't know it.

"I hadn't rock climbed since Wyoming and this wasn't climbing, understand, it was about a Class Three fast scramble. But some of that firing — must have been about Class Six. The Overhanging Sand Dune Class. When I got up under a kind of crumbly coral knob a little to the side and a little under the black hole, I heard Jap yammering. I fumbled a grenade from my bag, jerked the pin, stood out balancing and lobbed it for the yammer. She blasted off sweet and smoky. White phosphorus. I scrambled farther around the knob to change position. No more yammer.

"I pulled and heaved another, and then another. By this time I was out to the side of and even with the rock lip in front of the black place. And then I was above it and I could begin to see behind the lip and nothing moved. I jumped over and then down, in behind the emplacement, and saw. I can't remember how, but I had my forty-five in my hand when I lit.

86

"Then I saw one not burned was still alive, laying there starting to roll his eyes and I started to blow his head off. Some kind of sense hit me. Wait a minute. Maybe this one can talk. What they want at the CP. One alive.

"So help me God I *kneeled* down and I deep-sixed him with the silliest punch ever thrown. Bare fist. I was afraid I would kill him with the pistol butt or my boondocker. I guess that was why.

"Just then the lieutenant, old Dinker, come jumping the rocks with his piece poked at me, his eyes about like saucers.

"Keep away from the back end of this joint, he yells, there's probably a tunnel, until the boys bring up the Flit.

"My little kayoed Jap was laying there with the stiff short fuzz growing out of his shavehead, it looked like the plush stuff that covers seats in a movie house. The bodies and machine guns and the mortar were mixed with rock dust and burns. That first grenade of mine, it just lucked.

"Lieutenant Rackley, his Marine nickname was Dinker and we were on Gloucester together, stood there and give his head a shake. Spurling, Dinker says, you crazy bastard. If you and me get out of this one, I want to watch them pin on you the goddamned fattest goddamned medal this lousy Corps puts out.

"By this time, what was left of the platoon is coming up. Everybody wanted to kill my little Jap. Later Dinker managed to send him back with an intelligence detail and the CP got him safe and he talked, all right.

"We moved away while the bunker was secured for keeps. With a charge at the back end that blew the whole thing to hell. That was when a sniper bullet came pinging from someplace and caught One Brew Dodd in the fleshy part of the arm. He sat down bleeding like a pig. Jokers were

87

calling me the mountain goat from Wyoming. By that time I had shakes and dry heaves. It didn't leave me. I saw the corpsmen carry Vogle and the others away.

"We went for sixteen days, and nights. It is a nightmare to me yet, without no end. There was still a pocket of Japs left when we were finally pulled out to Beach Purple. That was 6 October. Eighteen of us left in the platoon and Lieutenant Dinker Rackley didn't make it.

"There was a moonface ensign in real clean khakis standing by the gangway with the Marines coming aboard from the beach. Hey, the ensign sounds off, you got any souvenirs to trade? A Marine stops and looks him up and down and finally says, Listen swabbie boy. I happened to bring my ass off that beach. That is my souvenir from Peleliu.

"I can tell you how Peleliu was: Pavuvu looked like Home Sweet Home the day we got back.

"It was 29 October and there was our band on the dock and when it started in to play 'California Here I Come,' the boys went crazy. Trucks were waiting there to haul us to the same camps we had left. For a rest and no more battling. Our mail was waiting for us.

"That was the day I got the letter from Mother saying Rut was gone. Killed making a paratroop jump in Holland. On 17 September, that was D plus 2 at Peleliu.

"I wasn't asiatic any more, I was cracked up. Nearly every day they gave us close-order drills. We would cover off very sharp and slap that piece doing the manual and then step out with the cadence and the band playing. Everybody together. While we were doing it everybody was together then, not thinking.

"Green stateside replacements were bringing the division back to strength. Some of the old-timers, call them plain survivors, had thirty-one months of Pacific duty. I had twenty-four myself. Men began shipping home. My orders

88

were on the way. One day I got the word I was going to take a front and center.

"When it came, there were four of us, one officer and three men, in front of the whole Seventh, facing the new division commander, Major General del Valle, and the brass — some from Pearl. General del Valle would read a citation into the PA mike, then pin on the medal, then give that man's hand a shake. I'm proud, sure, I'm human. And I'm not kidding myself either. It was two things. I went nuts, out of my head. And my number wasn't up.

"I never had actually seen a Navy Cross medal until I got back to my tent and took it off and looked at it. A little box with my name, and the blue and white ribbon, and a copy of the citation all came with it. It was from beyond the grave someway, I did not want it around. I mailed it to Dad and Mother that day. Insured for twenty-five dollars. Why I picked twenty-five, I don't know yet.

"Some of the green boots in camp began to get on our nerves. The Fighting Gyrenes, going to show the world. One night I couldn't take any more. I blew my top. I grabbed this new character from Texas, he was a loud-mouth Red Cross Canteen commando, and I got him by the windpipe. I pulled him down and when he was wheezing nice and loud and his eyes began to wall, I told him, Brave aren't you, you brave chickenshit Marine. Get this. There are not any brave Marines. There are not any left, you hear this? They are under the white crosses on islands you never saw.

"I was going to kill him. Giggo Bellini and One Brew Dodd pried me loose.

"I got hauled up to the carpet for a read-off from the captain. He did not bust me. I knew him when he was a second lieutenant at Guadalcanal, and now he looked like a thin old man.

89

"It was what torpedoed me.

"I thought everything came together all of a sudden then: about Rut dead, my own brother, and all the others and all that had happened since Guadalcanal, and that Navy Cross. I *asked* the captain if I could stay, not go stateside! I put in a request for continued duty with my unit. It was hard to think straight at that time. Maybe the Old Corps idea had me snowed. I would hate to think so. But all of a sudden I wasn't cracked up any more, I thought.

"I should have known that my luck was all used up.

"The last part of the war never has seemed real. After three beaches it may be you are punchy and don't know it and the fourth one isn't too clear.

"We sailed to rendezvous at Ulithi. I read later it was the biggest fleet ever to come together in the whole history of the world. I believe that. We were going to hit Okinawa, we were in a big army now. At our briefing about what the division had to do, we were shook. Behind our landing beach was reported a high sea wall. Ladders had been built for us: we were going to carry those ladders in, and scale that wall. I could see another Peleliu, only worse. I kept my mouth shut, but I knew.

"We landed on April Fool Day. And that is exactly what it was. We went ashore standing up. In the quiet. It was so unbelievable, walking up from the beach that I kept craning around expecting to get clipped from behind. By the fifth day we had pushed clean across the island to the other coast about ten miles away. It wasn't real. Neither was the climate. No coconuts — but *pine* trees, little umbrella pines! You couldn't believe it. It was about like bivouacking on training maneuvers, the whole month of April. I even had time to fool with a little Okinawa horse. We got up a pack string that would have made you laugh, and it car-

90

ried our gear. I hadn't even smelled a horse in three years.

"We moved south the first of May. Ten days later the Seventh Marines were in a position for a push against Dakeshi Ridge, north of Shuri Castle. The picnic was over. Our push didn't push — in a very few minutes we were in as hard a fighting as I have ever seen. Same old Shamboes.

"When it hit me, it did not feel like I had imagined it so long. It did not feel as bad when it happened.

"It was a sharp sting kind of a burn on my right side at the edge of my ribs. I was down. There was a little round torn hole in my dungaree just starting red. Getting wider red I saw, with something feeling warm and wet down the right side of my stomach, warm like a little kid feels when he's wet the sack.

"I couldn't get up. Then I knew I was hit bad. I began to drown in sweat. Things got all slow motion, all but the pain, getting worse, with the noise and fight like it was going far off and nothing I could do. Just sweat and the bellyache.

"The corpsmen made a scraping noise with the stretcher. They were squatting hunched way down, two of them. I could hear them. I remember them squeezing the syrette into my arm. When they moved me I think I passed out halfway: it still hurt. I remember being lashed to the outside of a Sherman tank and the godawful bumping and racket. And that's all, about Okinawa. About the First Battalion, Seventh Marines. I never saw them again.

"I wouldn't say I knew much about anything until I woke up in a white bed, at sea. I had to know where I was. A corpsman standing by the bed told me. I thought it was quite a thing, what he told me, it was important, it meant something. The name of the ship was the *Haven*. My own real name is Haven, named for Haven Lake, in Wyo-

91

ming, and here was a ship, same name. I was on it. It meant something.

"They took me to Fleet Hospital 111, a few miles up from Apra Harbor, Guam. It was made of Butler huts joined together. Inside it was just the bare iron. I was in one of the surgical wards with sixty beds, and we were Marines, swabbies and dogfaces all mixed in together. And sick. Outside the window the view was of bushes and coconut trees. The walks around the buildings were coral shell and you could hear the footsteps crunch when people walked, out there. A breeze would come in a little at night and it would carry the sound of the ocean from the beach which was about a half a mile.

"I was on Guam only a few days when the surgeons opened me up again, and I was in that hospital until the end of June. The thing I remember was at night hearing the B29s warm up in the distance and then take off right over our heads. On their way to Japan with a load for Tojo. I never minded the racket, when I would think what it was.

"One night we had a real rumpus. Scuttlebutt got around that there were two wounded Japs, prisoners, locked in the private room down at the end of the ward by the doctors' office. Don't ask me how he did it or where he got it, but a crazy Marine who could walk went out and got himself a grenade. A good one. In the midwatch this character tried to sneak down the ward and lay that egg into the Shamboes' room. A corpsman on watch caught him, but he had to holler for help. For a few seconds there was a big skirmish. It tickled everybody, we wished that yardbird had really done it. The Japs were really there. They got moved in a hurry.

"I got so I was walking a little, but I was keelhauled, I was about like a toothpick, yellow-colored. There was one

92

thing the docs kept looking at, looking at. In the lower end
of the big cut they had made in my stomach there was a
watery place that wouldn't heal. It wasn't infected, it just
stayed raw. They explained it. The watery stuff was juice
from a part of your guts called duct of Wirsung, on the
pancreas. It had a leak, inside. This juice was to digest
food with; here it was loose and trying to digest me. I was
shipped aboard an APA to the big Aiea Naval Hospital
at Pearl Harbor in July.

"Aiea had big-time doctors. One of the best of the best
was a USNR captain, named Gray. A surgeon. He asked
me all kinds of questions and put me 'under observation.'
That is almost worse than being under fire. Then he
opened me up again. It was on the day the bomb was
dropped on Hiroshima.

"By the time I could give a damn, the war with the Japs
was over. I remember a short dark-complected nurse trying to tell me about the Atomic Bomb. And Dugout Doug
on his way to Tokyo Bay to sign the papers on the war he
had won. I was glad the Japs were beat, but so was I.

"There was nothing to fight but yourself and the clock
and the calendar. Those hospital nightshirts and the swabbie bathrobe and the hospital smell of being sick and the
never-ending time, with no change. I would be awake when
the daylight would finally come and every morning I could
see the rain shower and the rainbow over the mountain outside the window up there, but I didn't believe in it. I
would get to feeling almost fair, then another flareup would
come. Some days I was hopeless. At the time it was taking
to get back to living or to die. Aiea wasn't either one. It
was in between.

"But I healed. In November finally I was getting liberty
to ride the bus to Honolulu, to walk in a civilian street, to
order up chow in a civilian restaurant and sit in a civilian

movie. I was like a timid country jake. With a war that was over still stuck in my craw. The day after Christmas I felt good enough to hike up Tantalus, all alone, through the big ferns and flowers up to where I had seen the rainbows, and look out over Pearl and Oahu and the ocean.

"I was released from Aiea on the twentieth of January with orders to report to Fleet Marine Force, Pearl Harbor. My cruise would be up in March — my stateside orders came through on the thirteenth of February. Two weeks later I was in Dago. Two weeks after that I was in Fontenelle County, Wyoming. And two weeks after that, it was taking me a long time, Mr. Claunch, to tell why I wanted to be at Haven Lake again and why I didn't want much rabbit for supper."

6

The sun shining through high and hazy cloud cast a steely light upon the gaunt street where State Road 241 bumped in from the valley of the Freefolk River and became, for three straggling village blocks, the thoroughfare of Silvertip. Along its muddy length windows were spattered and walls were stained with winter; sagging lumps of gray snow still sat in coves and corners of cold

95

shade. Yet an intimation of spring came down from the infinite space of Wyoming sky. A promise lived in the Saturday afternoon air. Ingo Spurling turned toward the curb, parked the old pickup and walked into the Cloudrock Bar.

"Greetings," he said. "Say Rowdey, will you cash my check from Lars?"

Rowdey Bustleton, shining a glass, shifted the toothpick in his mouth before he spoke. "Glad to. I even got a pen —"

Ingo Spurling's eyes, relieved from the raw light of infinity, focused to the amber glow of snugger spaces. His nostrils caught a rich and moisty redolence of old beer suds and bourbon. His ears found a hint of music in the whir and click from a slot machine.

"Rowdey," he said, with two tens and a five green in his hands, "I'd like some silver for this one."

When Rowdey handed him the hard money, one of the big round dollars had a glinty, unworn shine. It looked special; it spoke to Ingo. And he answered. He walked straight to the dollar machine, poked the shiny one into the slot, yanked the handle, looked away — and hit three oranges. Ten silver dollars spilled down banging sweetly into the cup and two rolled out on the floor.

"I had a feeling, just a pure feeling about it," Ingo grinned, walking to a bar stool and climbing on. He hefted the pleasant weight of the stack of iron men in his hand. "And I got another feeling," he added, "not to play it again." He placed the stack of dollars on the bar in front of him, pushed his wool cap far back on his head and smiled. "A shot of the red, Rowdey. Like I always say:

> 'Win without crowing,
> Lose without crying,
> And play the cards as they may fall.'

96

Old Senator Pycheley had that printed for his friends. He sent me one. I got the card yet. Senator Monroe Pycheley of Old Kaintuck. I used to take him clear up to Rampart Lake."

"Here's bourbon from Old Kaintuck," Rowdey said. "You want a leetle of anything on the side?"

"Yeah," Ingo said. "Pour me a bottle of that Wolters' Lager. My old uncle Barney O. Whetmer knew the man that made it, in Denver."

"Seen Fenny on the street last evening," Rowdey commented. "When'd he get in?"

Ingo glanced up at the rough mural scene of the Cloudrock Mountains painted on the plaster above the glassware behind the bar. The artist had signed it boldly: Fenwick Spurling. "He got here night before last." Ingo squinted at the anatomy of the moose painted by the lake in the right-hand corner. Except for the antlers, it wasn't much of a moose.

"Guess he was glad, seeing Hank again."

"Hank was the glad one. Fenny brought him those imported new skis and ski boots he got for him in Laramie. New type of bindings too. Hank sent him the money, he paid plenty. The boys were out all day yesterday on the north face of Plew Canyon. Hank's found out how rusty he is, new skis and all. Timing's way off like it naturally would be after four years. They went out again early this morning before I left the house. It's kind of got Hank's goat, those tricky boards giving him a fit now, and Fenny so cocky about himself —"

Ingo finished the bourbon and sipped the beer. "It's a skiing family. All my boys went to Wyoming U. on athaletic scholarships. First Rut — he was football halfback too — then Hank, now Fenny. I put Rut on a pair of homemade skis when he was six years old. I made them my-

97

self, we couldn't get any other kind. I taught him. Before going to the war he won the Intercollegiate Downhills — he won the Giant Slalom over at the Valley, on borrowed skis! The two younger boys I got, they can't touch Rut, the way he was. I was raised myself with old-time ski men and snowshoers, plenty of Hoovians and Canucks, back in Wisconsin. But racing skis now, and skiing, they're all changed, nearly everything is changed. I need another drink, Rowdey."

"That boy Hank's changed," Rowdey said, pouring, "since he got back. He's looking better."

"Claims he's better — and still thin as a rail. He's been up to Haven Lake twice now, running that trap line with Merlin Claunch. That's a pair. Old Merlin and Hank. Two unsociables. Teetotalers. Bet they don't say ten words to each other, up there." Ingo chased his whiskey with a gulp of beer. "Rowdey. You ought to see the pictures Fenny paints now. No, I don't mean that. He could daub better with axle grease when he was three. You can't even tell now which side is up. He brought some home to show his mother. He says it's art. If that's a college education, I'm glad I attended the school of experience. Even his mother hasn't got much to say, about art. You're lucky! You got him to paint the Cloudrocks for you before he learned art — though if you look at that moose —"

"It's not a bad picture, for a kid seventeen and never been out of Silvertip when he did it, or had a lesson in his life," Rowdey said. "I tell all my trade that. He might get famous some day. — Hello there, Chet!"

"Howdy, Rowdey," Chet Lanner said. He took the bar stool next to Ingo's.

"Chet, I'll buy you a drink," Ingo said.

"Don't mind if you do."

98

"How's things in the sunshine up on Shoulder Creek?" Rowdey inquired.

"Busy. Feeding calves. And come summertime, going to be real busy with something else. The dudes'll be swarming again, finally! All hungry for good trout fishing. After a long war. Mrs. Lanner is getting up our letter to our old mailing list, inviting everybody back to the Cloudrocks, the Sportsman's Wonderland. It's been a long dry spell for Shoulder Creek Lodge! — Here's how, Ingo!"

"Hmm," Ingo said, looking depressed and shoving a silver dollar to Rowdey.

"I just come from Junction," Lanner said. "Talking to the new man at the Forest Service office. Nice fellow. Getting my permit all lined up and seeing about everything to pack the paying campers into the Shoulder Creek drainage of the Wilderness Area. It can't miss now. Got me a deal going up at Elk Park for a new string of gentled horses. Buying quite a bit of new saddle equipment. Got my eye out now for some war surplus camp tents and inflatable life rafts for lake fishing. You ready to compete us, Ingo?"

"I never competed you, Chet. I took my own kind of clients into the mountains. Way in. And I always took good care of every one of them, every minute they were up there."

Lanner took it smiling. "You started to refitting yet?"

"Nope." Ingo tossed off his drink.

"Rowdey, bring us another, the same," Lanner said. "This one's on me, Ingo. Tell me something. If you don't mind. You planning on anything much, this summer?"

"I don't know," Ingo said. "Whether I am or not. Why?"

"I been giving it a thought, that Haven Lake and that Longstick country into Ezekiel Basin. If you don't plan to

99

use it. Matter of fact, I mentioned it to the Forest Service."
Chet Lanner's eyes were intent. His manner was as casually
good-humored as he could make it. "I can't find anybody
that seems to know why that old Haven Lake cabin is still
standing, it's in the Wilderness Area, it's against federal law
to maintain a permanent habitation in that area. There
can't be any private rights up there, by Act of Congress. If
you aren't planning to operate like you used to somebody
could set up a dandy summer tent camp there on Haven
Lake, improved. Plenty of room for everybody. Really make
something profitable of it —"

"Are you trying to fool with me, Chet?" Ingo Spurling's
face was flushed red. "Do I have to tell you — that cabin
was built by Merlin Claunch as a trapper's wintering shelter
before you were dry behind the ears? And before there
was any such of a thing as a law about a Cloudrock Wilderness Area. It was wilderness, plain. It still is, like the law
provides. That cabin has never been misused. Neither has
Haven Lake. And it ain't a permanent habitation as you
goddamn well know. It's my pack trip base camp for
parties I take into the high Cloudrocks and it's been that
way since I quit Plunkett Blakely and started my own
outfit in 1928! That cabin belongs to the mountains and
that country up there is a friendly agreement between me
and my friend Merlin Claunch. Nobody has ever questioned
our rights. We keep that country the way God made it.
Would you call that a right or would you call that a duty,
which? And I got the same legal right and the same kind of
Forest Service agreement to it, and to taking people up the
Plew and the Longstick and the Possibles Creek drainage
that you got further north in your own bailiwick!"

"Okay, Ingo. Take it easy. I just wanted to know if you
were interested. I just asked."

"And you found out. I don't take kindly to any cheap-

100

skate three-day tourist campers throwing tomato cans and box tops and cundrums in Haven Lake."

"Tell me how you take those big sheep bands that will be chewing through that country dunging it nice this summer. Old Gus Sprigg has got the grazing permits all fixed."

"I can't help that. I hate the sheep and the sheepmen of Wyoming but it's about like trying to fight the coming of frost, you can't do much. All you can do is be glad the Cloudrocks are big and high and hope you're dead before they change. I'll drink with you on that, Chet! You want another one?"

"No thanks."

A hay farmer from Cottonwood was on Lanner's stool and Ingo Spurling was sitting silent in the bar noise, fingering a nearly empty beer glass, when someone tapped him on the shoulder.

"Hey Dad," Fenwick Spurling said.

His dark hair was combed slick; his slacks and sports shirt and windbreaker were sharp. "Can I use the Ford? You got the key." He looked not at his father but at the mural behind the bar.

"Where'd you come from?" Ingo said. "Thought you were out on the slope."

"I came in. Can I have the key?"

"What you want with it? Where's Hank?"

"I wouldn't know where Hank is. I guess he's still trying to ski. The Marine Corps *rücklage*. He took a big flop on a goofed swing turn and when I laughed he got sore. Real sore. He must be war happy yet —"

"Hey Fenny!" Rowdey Bustleton said, mopping along the bar. "How's the picture look to you with the soft light on it?"

"That's quite a light."

"Adds something to the place, don't it?"

101

"Ug. Genius at work. Gimme a beer!"

"Get lost!"

"I'll come back when I'm twenty-one — Can I have the key, Pop?"

"Do your prowling afoot."

"I been afoot. I want to ride out to the Fenton place. See if Nick's going to the movies at Dwindle tonight."

"That all?"

"That's all, honest."

"Fenny. All right. You can have the Ford, one condition. You be at Rodemacher's before six and you take your mother home from the store when she's ready. You be there?"

"Absolutely."

"You be there." He handed him the key.

"Okay! I'll *be* there!" He had gotten almost to the door when he turned and came back. "I was by the post office. Nothing came. Just this thing for you. I forgot." He gave Ingo a letter, and went out the door.

Ingo put the white envelope on the bar and started to ask for another drink. Then he saw the engraved address and emblem on the envelope's upper left-hand corner. He saw the oval-shaped RMC trademark. "Well what do you know," he mumbled, "what do you know —"

Ingo Spurling blinked. He pocketed his silver, picked up the letter, got off the bar stool and walked over to the empty booth against the wall. He sat down at its table alone under a light. He tore the envelope open, unfolded the two handsomely typewritten pages. The fine white paper crackled in his hand. He read.

Dear Ingo:

I regret that I have not written you, or heard from you, in more than a year.

102

Your last letter — acknowledging receipt of the news photo I finally wrangled from that elusive AP photographer who took the picture of Rut in his battle gear at Welford Airdrome just before the takeoff for Holland — that letter caught up with me in Paris. The old trout on your letterhead brought a note of happier days to wartime Europe.

I returned from ETO in April of last year for paper duty in the Pentagon — to work on plans for certain phases of amphibious landings on Honshu. Two Bombs last August took care of that. I remained in the service in Washington, however, until December when I came back to Chicago and this office.

Since then a series of strikes and the general problems of retooling RMC to a peacetime civilian economy have demanded some strenuous attention. You may have noticed in the news last week that the government stepped on us ordering RMC to grant labor demands at this time "to expedite industrial reconversion to vital peacetime needs." So we gave everybody another raise, and quit arguing. The plants are booming. I see record employment and big expansion plans everywhere and I also see ultimate consequences, of wage inflation and price inflation, this country may have to face. And I wonder how long the peace will last under the strain of the Communist threat. Enough of trouble.

Many times, many places, I have thought of the mountains and the Spurlings.

I have wondered about Hank in the Marines. Your last letter said he came through the Peleliu landing, and decorated for gallantry. I presume he must have returned stateside on the rotation plan shortly after and that he is with you in the Cloudrocks enjoying the good life again. Fenny must be about ready for college and I wonder if you made him a skier like his brothers. I hope that Mrs. Spurling is

103

well. Give her my kindest regards. I am sure that you are deeply proud of the memory of your splendid son Rut, and are just as deeply grateful for the two splendid sons yet with you. They will be almost strangers to me when I see them, and not the little boys I remember best at their chores at so many camps, in the mountains.

One of the purposes of this letter is to send you a warning, Sergeant. If things can be shaped properly here, so that I can get away for a few weeks, I would like to come to the Cloudrocks for an old-time pack with you. I want to plan early and make my reservations with you early. I'm sure you'll have several parties anxious to be in the mountains with you this first postwar summer. So I'm putting in my chit now, trusting that you will have everything in shape for our best trip yet.

My mind has gone back often to that last trip in 1941, how we got clear up into that narrow pass you found, and how we could see, far down the other side of the divide, those three hidden lakes you said had golden trout. We didn't try to make it, the snow was too deep, the country too rough. Those lakes looked beautiful. Have you ever been back? Could we make it if we tried it later in the season, when there might not be so much snow? What if I came out the middle of August and stayed on into September as long as the weather held? Let me know. Meanwhile consider that I'm making reservations for a first-class pack beginning August 15 and extending to about September 15. When you firm this up, inform me what you want on deposit and a check will be forthcoming.

As you know, I like to make these trips without bringing any party of associates, business, poker or otherwise. My companionship in the Cloudrocks is of another kind. I like to go up there alone with the mountains and with the

Spurlings. This year it may be that we will have a guest or two for a part of the time.

I am anxious to have a recent acquaintance of mine, Mr. Cosmo Flynn, spend a few days in camp with me. Mr. Flynn is an artist and I want him to paint me that first view of the high Cloudrocks as we see it from the top of old Blue Gap Ridge. It is also possible that I may persuade my older daughter Dorothy to spend a few days with me on horseback and in camp. I would like to introduce her to those grand mountains. Her arrival at a camp in the rugged Cloudrocks is not too likely, but I mention it.

RMC has placed an order for a new DC-3 for use as a company plane. Delivery is anticipated before August, so transportation and the shipping of our camp and fishing gear ought to offer no logistical problems this year. I understand Green Junction is now on a scheduled airlines route, so I presume its landing field is a good deal better than it used to be.

Let me hear from you, with news of your family, and those Wyoming mountains, and your plans for the summer. Check with me on any scarcities of equipment your outfitting may encounter; maybe I can find for you what you want.

With warmest personal regards always, I am

Sincerely,

R. K. Royston

P.S. How is old Hemlock?

Ingo Spurling looked at the familiar scrawl of the signature. It went blurred. He pulled his bandana from his pocket and blew his nose. He wiped his eyes. He folded the letter back into its envelope. He buttoned it securely under the flap of his wool shirt pocket. He sat motionless, staring at his veined and tendoned hands quiet on the shiny yellow varnish of the empty table top.

The stools were all taken when he walked up to the bar again. "Rowdey — make it a double," Ingo said. "No beer."

Rowdey thrust his shoulder and elbow forward leaning over the bar toward Ingo and he lowered his voice asking, "Get some bad news of some kind?"

"No," Ingo said. He gulped the double slug, shook his head, put the glass down. Liquor was hot in his throat, hot in his stomach. All the drinks of the afternoon had taken hold. He lifted his booted foot to the brass rail and bellied the bar.

"Fill that double," Ingo said. Rowdey's eyes were inquiring. "Who I heard from," Ingo answered, "was my old captain. Of my old battery, St. Mihiel in 1918. This last war — he's a colonel. It was him saw Rut by luck on a street in London. And they had them a little visit. Ten days before Rut was killed in action at St. Odenrode, Holland. It was him went to Rut's grave, over there. He saw it."

"Oh." Looking Ingo in the face, Rowdey was somehow unprepared. "Yeah. I can see. How you feel."

"You can't. He is a damned good goddamned good man that's all! The man I am telling about. One summer that he was up in the mountains with me, it comes to me clear, it was ten years ago, he came out here to the mountains right after his only son, the only one he had, was drowned in a sailboat on Lake Michigan —" Tilting his glass drinking, Ingo spilled whiskey down his chin. He wiped at his chin with his sleeve. He pulled silver dollars out of his pocket, dropped them jangling loud on the bar. "Fill her up," he said.

"Ingo," Rowdey Bustleton said. "I believe you ought not to take any more."

106

"Trying to tell me how?"

"I'm not trying to tell you. I'm a friend of yours and I'm a friend of your family and I believe you are harming yourself and I ain't going to serve you any more."

"Friend huh? Well I had some friends in my day. Quality people." He had raised his voice.

Several places down the bar a friendly beer salesman from Cody, stranger to Silvertip's Saturday afternoon, nudged the man seated next to him; the man was deputy sheriff of Fontenelle County.

"Who's the red-faced old daddy giving Rowdey a time?"

"Used to be quite an outfitter — I wouldn't care to try him in the mountains now. Biting at the old iron bottle. Name's Spurling —"

Ingo Spurling heard him say it. He turned and glowered.

"Here's your two iron men, Ingo," Rowdey Bustleton said. "Put them in your pocket. Come back some other time."

"The hell with you," Ingo said, shoving away from the bar, starting for the door, in a caricature of wool-capped dignity. He halted by the deputy sheriff. "You talking about me?"

The officer turned on his stool and looked. "I was. Nothing I wouldn't say to your face, Mr. Spurling."

"You trying to throw that gun and badge around at people?"

"Not unless they need it."

"Well I don't need it."

"You need a little air, Mr. Spurling. You don't need any trouble at all, you just need fresh air. You're all right. Shall we go out for a little air?"

"To hell with your air, it's too damned fresh. I'll find my own." He walked with a surprising steadiness out the door. The air he found for himself outside was bracing.

107

He did not want to think, he tried not to think. But he thought he was glad he did not have the Ford to drive. He stood on the sidewalk with his feet planted against the whirl in his head, against thought.

Above the line of frame buildings across the street, out beyond the village of Silvertip, the thin sunlight of late afternoon touched at the long hump of Blue Gap Ridge. It stood like a darkly timbered wall. Over the spruce along its crest the snowy tops of Chuckbox and Gun Mountain, Anvil Peak and the highest of the Moosetooth Ridges showed against the sky. They stood like wan ghosts.

Alone with ghosts he started up the street trying not to think but thinking his name's Spurling biting at the old iron bottle I wouldn't care to try him in the mountains now and just as deeply grateful for the two splendid sons yet with you at so many camps in the mountains my companionship in the Cloudrocks is of another kind.

He came to the street's end, to the turn of the lane, to the mud ruts leading through the thaw to the gray willows of Plew Creek, home, with the long shadows of his walking legs moving like the opening and closing of scissors along the ground.

"Hi Dad," Hank said to him when he came in the kitchen door. "I didn't hear the truck when you drove up."

"Didn't drive up. Walked up."

Hank saw where his father had been. "Where's the truck?"

"Fenny's got it. Going to — to bring your mother."

Hank did not answer. He looked up from the ski he was waxing and watched his father go wordless through the door into the parlor, past the table, to the couch where he took off his cap, stretched out on his back with his hands clasped across his chest and closed his eyes.

Jesus Christ, Hank thought to himself. Happy Easter.

108

I guess only a woman like Mother could take it. And this does it, I am going to see Lanner or the Forest Service or even the Blakelys, or the Game and Fish if I have to walk to Cheyenne, about a job.

He wiped off his hands and went over to the stove, opened the oven door, slid out the elk roast and potatoes, poked them testing with a fork, spooned fat juice over them again, shoved the roaster back into the oven and turned the gas down low.

Before he finished with the coat of dark klister on both his skis, he could hear his father snoring in the parlor.

When he took his skis outside and leaned them carefully against the wall by his shiny new poles, near Fenno's, he noticed the three horses waiting by the feedlot fence. He went down through the opened barn, where the chickens were going to roost, and walked to the pasture gate to let the horses in.

"Hemlock, you yardbird —" He slapped the strong old bay saddle horse on the shoulder. Sounds, movements were welcome in the shadowy silence under the clouding sky. "That grass you found today — kind of thin? So was the snow I found. — Agnes, your figure is lousy and so's your face and Sonny's no better. Git along you reprobates!" He forked some hay for them.

The open barn door framed a lonesome sunset of smudged red and murky purple above the line of the Kainah Hills in the west. He heard the pickup rattle the planks over Plew Creek and watched the old truck come driving to the yard in the dusk.

"Hello, son!" Em Spurling called. She had a grocery sack in her arms when she got out. Fenny shut off the engine, undid the wire from the door handle on the other side of the cab, jumped out and sauntered into the house without a greeting.

109

"Anything more to bring in?" Hank asked. He took the sack from his mother.

"That's all," she said smiling. "Did you enjoy it today? Any bad falls? Fenwick says he doesn't think you are used to skis yet —"

"After I ran him off, I did a little more. Snow's getting soggy."

"It did feel like spring today! This evening now we'll have our family Easter dinner together and this whole Easter time would be so grand, Haven, if you would go to Junction with us for Easter service in the morning. The Rodemachers are going and they're taking me! Fenwick is going too. He's going to ride down with us and meet the Sprigg boy there and drive back to Laramie with him in his car later tomorrow. The Rodemachers have plenty of room and you're invited. We can all eat at the Covered Wagon down there after church and then drive home. Will you go? I wish we could persuade your father to go. Is he home?"

"He's home."

"Oh." They came in the kitchen door.

"Sleeping it off," Fenny said. "Drifted to birdland." With a jerk of his thumb he indicated the unlighted parlor. "Loaded again."

"Fenwick!" Tears came to Em Spurling's eyes. "Enough out of you!" She went over and closed the parlor door. "You guard your tongue! — O Haven! — Is the roast — about done?"

Dinner was a distressful family strain.

Ingo Spurling, awakened from his sleep, had gotten up and washed his stubbled face and brushed his sandy hair with a wet comb. Seated at table he was neither surly nor contrite. He seemed merely passive, stiffly withdrawn into himself; yet his very presence, with his silence and his

110

bloodshot eyes, flooded morbid cross-drifts of unresolved tension into the air.

The four very different Spurlings, with a ghost of a fifth Spurling hovering, constrainedly sat in silence eating because they were hungry, wishing in different ways and for different reasons and with different degrees of differing passions that the world were not as they found it at that dinner table that night under that strong electric light bulb over Em's lovingly mended white damask special-occasion tablecloth.

The raisin pie was eaten and there was more coffee in the cups and Em was thinking of hot water for the dishes when Ingo Spurling unbuttoned the flap on his shirt pocket. His face looked pale, tired, old. "I got a letter today," he said.

Hank was stuffing tobacco in his pipe. "Who from?"

"Excuse me now —" Fenny found his first chance to escape. "Mom." He started for his room. "Nick's coming any minute — got a car tonight —"

"From the captain."

"Royston?" Hank was looking at his father.

"Colonel, I should of said. He wrote."

"How is he?"

"See what you think." He handed Hank the letter. "Read it. Like you to read it too, Em."

Hank moved his chair close to his mother's, and opened the sheets from the envelope. They read Royston's letter. It took a while. Ingo unsteadily rolled a brown paper cigarette, lit it, watched them read.

When they came to the signature, Hank's eyes went straight to his father's face as if it were a part of the letter. "Well?"

Looking straight in Hank's face, Ingo said nothing.

"Why'n't you quit the boozing — and do it?"

111

"I quit drinking."

"Yeah? When was that?"

"This afternoon. When I walked out the Cloudrock Bar."

"O Ingo —" anguish choked Em's voice.

"Yeah. You quit. You can say that again —"

"I said it. You never hear me say it before, did you?"

"So you quit, huh? That's something to know. I wish I knew it."

"You heard me. Something else too. You ought to know. You ought to know it for sure. We haven't got no outfit. It starts with money."

Hank did not wait. Biting hard on the stem of his unlighted pipe, he got up from the table. He went to his room, jerked open the top drawer of the bureau, got the roll of bills from the bottom of the cigar box where he kept his old fly book and reel, and walked back to the table where his father and mother sat saying nothing.

"Here," Hank said. He put the money down in front of his father. "What I got left from a war. Eight hundred and ninety-five bucks for the pot. Royston's advance deposit ought to add up good too. To start with."

Ingo Spurling looked down at the money and looked up at his second son Haven. "You're all right, Hank. You're all right. But it's not enough. Not near. You know that. Even with a five hundred from Royston, if we ask. Myself, I got nothing but twenty-seven dollars and three horses and a pile of junk, rotten leather and canvas in a saddle shed that ain't been used for four years. I got no credit. Not in this house. Or any place else. And I ain't got ahold of any kind of pursestrings either —"

Em Spurling found her husband's eyes and her son's eyes upon her. Her own eyes looked at theirs, into theirs. She said nothing.

In the quiet outside an auto horn honked. It honked

112

again. Fenwick Spurling came pulling on his jacket and clattering toward the door.

"Wait a second —" Hank said. He grabbed his brother by the arm as he started past. "I got word for you —"

"Leggo — Nick and his date's waiting! What ya want?"

"I want to tell you you're hired out in the mountains this summer. We're going in business — and you're going to be there, Wrangler —"

The horn outside gave a long honk.

"That can wait — that's next summer — and wait a second, yourself! As I remember it up there, it's all work and no pay. Why don't you *wise* up?" He went out the door.

Hank lit his pipe.

"That Fenwick," Em said.

"I'll put the squirt into line," Hank said. "I have handled a few goldbricking boots. Cracking *wise.*"

"I've saddled a few ponies myself," Ingo said. "And in case you forgot, it ain't all sirup and bearcat gravy and such as that, pounding those mountains with dudes." He pressed his forehead with his hand. "Hank. I'm about as bad out of shape as you are. And I'm thirty years older. And we got no outfit. We got no saddle stock, we got no packstring. We got a Ford truck due for a collapse any day if not sooner. We got practically no saddles, no blankets, no bridles, no halters, hobbles, pack saddles, lash ropes, panniers, box panniers, utensils, tarps, tools, tents and we ain't got one of them service inflatable life rafts for high lake fishing either. What we got is just memories and no credit."

"We got six weeks till June," Hank said. "And we got to write the best of the old fly fishermen, the old list like Mr. Messmore and Governor Heawood and Mrs. Tynge and those Oklahoma Finucanes and people like that."

"We ain't even got any letter paper left."

"But the first thing you do," Hank said, "is write Colonel

113

R. K. Royston in Chicago. You can write him on a brown paper sack but you write him! And I'll mail it. Then we'll go out to the shed and see exactly what we've got and make a careful list. What we need. Including money."

"That old letter paper I had printed," Ingo said. He was rolling another cigarette, using Hank's pipe tobacco. "With the trout. If we had any, I'd add something. It would say at the top 'Ingo Spurling & Sons.' That's Rut too. With us. Did you know, Hank, when you come putting that pile of money on the table, it was — Rut?"

Em spoke. "We have Rutherford's gift to us," she said. "We still have it."

Hank looked at his mother. "You'd be willing to stake this outfit — partly."

"I'd be willing if you'd let me keep the books."

"You'd be keeping the books and the money both," Hank said. "Here —" he pushed the stack of bills to her hand.

"Here —" said Ingo. He pulled from his pocket two ten dollar bills and seven silver dollars and handed them all to his wife across the table.

"I pray it's the right thing," said Em Spurling. "Those mountains —" She shook her head. " 'This is God's hill, in which it pleaseth him to dwell —' "

114

7

An afternoon of mountain summer drew toward its close. Woodsmoke from a rekindled cookfire climbed thin, straight into the air, by the blue calm of Haven Lake. The smoke's tang blended with a balsam smell of forests warmed in a long day of sun. Midges and flies hummed the silence of lengthening shade.

115

Camp sounds, companions to woodsmoke and men, mildly touched at the quiet. Behind the cabin in the cove a camp ax chopped with a woody *clack, click, clack, crack.* Farther off between the trees a short-handled hammer drove horseshoe nails to a rasped hoof with a muffled *tock, tack, tacktack.*

Into the ease of the windless air came an alien sound.

An airplane engine's remote hum intruded upon the quiet. The hum grew and lost its blur, enlarged to a louder droning. Low over the rim of the bowl that held Haven Lake a slow single-engine plane appeared. It banked in a tight turn at the outlet end of the lake and came back over the water in a lowering churn of noise and with a waggle of wings. Circling again lower still it dropped an object that landed with a little skittered splash and stayed afloat not fifty yards from the shore of the cove where the cabin and its wisp of woodsmoke stood. Then the plane climbed. Turning away it went out of sight over the tops of the firs.

The air grew silent again.

Ingo Spurling had quit cleaning trout. He stood at the water's edge with his knife in his hand, peering at whatever it was that floated small and bobbling on the lake.

Fenwick Spurling had left the ax and the chopping block. He had untied the painter that moored the yellow life raft to the rock on the shore and he had grabbed up the oars to shove off.

Hank Spurling had tossed the hammer to the horseshoe box. He had unfastened his ragged apron of canvas, flung it over a cross pole, and he had started down the trail from the horse pen to the cabin.

Robert Royston had shut the lid of his tackle box and had risen from the shady log near the front of his pale gray nylon tent. He was limping slightly, in a pair of fleece-lined camp moccasins, toward Ingo Spurling and his wash-pan full of rainbows down at the water's edge.

A mile away Mr. Cosmo Flynn standing with wet feet in a tangle of brush at the inlet of Haven Lake examined the vacant end of his leader, cursed the loss of his last good No. 12 cowdung fly and wondered who the crazy pilot was.

"I'll git it!" Fenwick yelled. He was in the raft, with the aluminum-handled oars engaged in their grommet locks, and beginning to row.

Don't hurry, it's bad, Royston thought to himself.

Hank came to where his father stood with Royston. "I think Washing-Machine Charlie's found the Cloudrocks and me and that mare Mary Louise — we don't care for Condition Red."

"And *who* does?" Royston lit a cigarette. "Disturbing of the peace and quiet. Invasion of privacy. Committing a public nuisance, violating a sanctuary, rape of a virgin forest! The bastard ought to be dry-gulched."

"Nail him, Colonel!" Ingo said. "The puddlejumper's from Junction, I recognize it. Fellow's a crop duster over at the Rackland project."

"I think he's a vulture of ill tidings," Royston said.

"How's that?"

"Enterprising people at my office — that bush fly boy came up here to drop some kind of trouble from Chicago. Couldn't be anything else."

"Hey!" Fenwick hailed from out on the lake. "A bottle! Corked! With a *telah — gram!*"

"What's he hollering?"

"I don't know. But he's coming with it." They stood watching the rower's back as he pumped the yawing raft toward shore.

"For you, Colonel —" Fenwick called over his shoulder, coming close. "A telegram — in a bottle —"

117

"I've gotten all kinds of news in a bottle —" Royston said. "Thank you, Fenny —"

The yellow paper was rolled, held by a rubber band; the roll slipped easily from the uncorked bottle's neck. Royston straightened the dry envelope. The word "Undeliverable" was scrawled in pencil across the envelope's face. Its address window showed the words "Col RK Royston Care Ingo Spurling Silvertip Via Green Junction Wyo."

Royston tore open the message and read.

"What's it say?" Fenwick asked. He had not unshipped the oars or tied the painter and he came breathing hard. Hank scowled at him. Royston kept reading.

"No surprise — except for our delivery boy," Royston said finally. "Not trouble. Just disappointment. Wired from Chicago August twenty-second about the RMC plane we were planning to meet tomorrow. Anyway, we'll get our artist down the hill to Green Junction for his free ride back to Chicago. — Here, read it —"

NO COMMUNICATION HERE YET FROM YOUR DAUGHTER MRS DOROTHY ROYSTON HASKETT BUT PILOT EJ SOUCEK PLANNING FLIGHT AS PER YOUR PREVIOUS INSTRUCTION ARRIVAL GREEN JUNCTION MONDAY 26 AUGUST ETA 1800 MOUNTAIN STANDARD TIME WEATHER PERMITTING AND UNLESS WORD RECEIVED HERE TO CANCEL FLIGHT BEST WISHES PLEASANT VACATION GOOD FISHING

AGNES MEADOWS

"My private enterprising secretary," Royston said, "would have made a brilliant major of WACs. She probably had the Governor and the Wyoming State Police on the phone trying to explain to her why this thing was 'Undeliverable.' So she delivered it. And my daughter's not coming, I guess. I was pretty sure she wouldn't be." The wrin-

118

kle between his gray eyebrows deepened. "And I'm sorry she won't be." He looked up at the rock face of Chuckbox across the lake. "These hills are good medicine. When they're not getting buzzed by Manchurian aviators dropping bottles —"

Royston mashed his cigarette into the ground with the toe of his moccasin. "It's about the time," he said, "for cheer out of a better bottle, but I ought to wait for Fisherman Flynn. His last evening. He's been a good man, up here, hasn't he? — Hank, while your culinary father gilds those rainbows I caught, how about dragging a pile of wood to the old fire rock — let's sit in the open tonight and slay a firedrake or two."

With the going of the sun the temperature dropped and then the weather itself changed. A breeze with an edge stirred through the timber; spreading coils of cloud hid the stars. Haven Lake was as dark and empty as the sky. In the frosty pitch blackness the fire after supper made a gold harbor of warmth for the body and for the mind.

"Ingo, the thing that disillusions me," Royston said, "is the way this artist prefers fishing to painting. I thought artists were devoted to their work."

Cosmo Flynn rubbed at the stubble of whiskers on his chapped chin and he laughed. "This one paints in a studio with a steady north light where the fishing is not so good."

"I bring him up here," Royston went on, "to paint a large lot of very large mountains, and he makes a small lot of very small sketches. Then goes fishing!"

"If the colonel's giving you trouble, Cosmo," Ingo said, "you ask him who caught the old granddaddy cutthroat at Sky. Who did that?"

"Pure impossible luck," Royston said.

"I got up here, Colonel," Flynn said, "and had to fish to steady my nerves! You have to admit there's something

119

shaky about coming with a paint brush smack out of the Vale of Tears into the Vale of — of Eden Revisited. At timberline. It skins the eyeballs. The mist melting and the sun striking across those milky green lakes in the bare rock of Ezekiel Basin — you're alive in a poem, helpless! That glacier way up there and that granite piled up to a snow cornice in the sky — these Cloudrocks! They're not just an escape from the world, they're an escape from time. You ride up old. You ride away young. How do you paint that?"

"You have to make another trip with us," Ingo said.

Royston took a long sip at his tin cup. "Cosmo, these mountains have enlarged you. They have afforded the delights of perspective."

Hank Spurling walked from the darkness into the fire's light. A gust of wind whipped a sideward whirl of smoke and red sparks from the wavered flames.

"Join us, Hank!"

"Galley fire's secured. Dishes done, sourdough's working, smoking lamp's lit — and it looks like rain. Can I do anything for you gentlemen?"

"You can throw a chunk on the fire," Ingo said. "I feel like I'm about to sing 'Mormon Town.' "

"You do and I'll blast you again with 'My Liver and My Lights,' " Royston said.

Fenwick Spurling, with the light of a flashlamp bobbling in his hand, scuffed through the dark toward the figures by the fire. He eased himself down beside them and snapped off the flash. "Tent flaps all closed. My brother, Haven Simon Legree, believes it might rain —"

"Your brother's about right."

"Ingo," Royston said, "now the council's assembled, how's the plan now for sending Cosmo back to the Vale of Tears where he can quit fishing and paint me a picture?"

120

A lightning flicker lit the pointed black tops of the firs high above the fire.

"Hank will take him and get him to Junction in good shape," Ingo said. He turned to Fenwick. "We'll be stirring early, wanting horses early. Saddled, ready for packs, by the time breakfast's done —" Long thunder rumbled from the other side of Chuckbox. "Maybe you'll be going too, Colonel, do you figure?"

"I'd be going if I thought Dot would be on that plane. I'm convinced she won't be. So I'm going to do some loafing tomorrow and try to stay off this blister on my foot. Maybe fish from our raft, here on Haven."

"Fenny can row you. There's giants under those rocks by the outlet," Ingo said. "I'll be shaping up things around here so that when Hank gets back with the new grub on Tuesday we'll be fixed to take out for the high country whenever you say, Colonel. Hardway Pass and the goldens!"

"I never got to watch how you work, Mr. Flynn," Fenwick said, "except that sketch on Blue Gap."

"Be glad, Fenny," Flynn said. "It could warp your career. Watching me sweat."

"We're going to miss you, Mr. Flynn," Hank said, puffing his pipe. "Someday you have to see the Cloudrocks from up on the divide. Standing in snow. Looking down."

"Hank, just looking up," Flynn said, "was pretty good. I don't know where ten days went! And now they're gone. It's a long day down the mountain tomorrow — it's a sad day —"

The lightning quivered pale and brought thunder rattling.

"Colonel and me — we've had a good camp always," said Ingo Spurling. "Rain or shine." Royston reached over and supplied Ingo's tin cup with another half finger of

121

Demerara rum from the bottle Royston carried in his big jacket pocket. Ingo sipped and looked up at the pattern of firelight and shadow on an arching bough of fir. "The last night a man like Cosmo Flynn's in these mountains — I'd like to recite him a verse," Ingo said. "Back East when you're walking down a big city street in a crowd, you'll remember.

'O sing me a song of the bit and spur,
A song of the smiling plain;
Blow me the breeze from the mountain top,
And send me the Western rain.

O mine be the light of the Western stars,
My breath of the fir and pine,
Where youth and joy and love come back
Like a taste of rare old wine.' "

Ingo raised his cup. Firelight glinted on it. The firelight glinted on Royston's and Flynn's, who raised theirs. "So —" Ingo said,

" 'Here's to the song of the mountain stream,
To the dreams in Wyoming's sky,
And may I wake in the Cloudrocks,
Instead of heaven when I die!' "

The rain arrived quietly, touching cold on the sunburned hands and faces around the fire. Raindrops hissed hitting the fire. Then the wind came in a gust and the rain pelted. It seethed on the blackness of Haven Lake.

"The old Chinese," Flynn said, not wanting to move, "they painted grand mountains. They wrote of mountains. They knew mountains." He mused for a last moment at red dragons of fire glow dying in the rain. "They said a good man delights in mountains."

122

Flynn slept with the rain tapping on the canvas of his tent.

He awoke in gray light hearing Hank Spurling say, "Here's warm water, Mr. Flynn." The sooty bucket smoked, coming in through the dripping tent flaps. "The other water out here's chilly."

"Moisty saddle seat this morning — it'll keep you lively," Ingo grinned when Flynn came into the cabin for breakfast. "Looks like a damp ride —" Ingo worked the turner with a flourish lifting brown pancakes from the griddle to a waiting tin plate. "Eat 'em while they're smoking, and take plenty of ham." He spooned new puddles of sourdough batter onto the hot iron. "Hank! I haven't heard no sound of any horse bell yet —"

"He hasn't showed. I been out there."

"These are the mornings that try wranglers' souls," Royston said. He sat hunched over the oilcloth-covered table in the hard white light of the Coleman lantern, smoking his morning cigarette and drinking black coffee. "The cavvy drifted down country God knows where. The tracks washed out. The rain pouring and the belly hollow and the view damned dim. A morning like this, I hate to contemplate even my forthcoming trip to The Green Room in that cold and leaky bower of spruce."

"What I should've done," Hank scowled, "was go for the horses myself. With those hobbles, they're not far. The devils are just smart."

"What you could've done," Ingo said, "is to keep up more than one night horse. You'd have one now."

"Yeah. Send Joe College looking for the horses. Then go looking for Joe College."

It was after ten o'clock when they heard the horse bell jangle through the trees around the cove.

"Where in hell — you been?" Hank yelled, coming toward the corral. Horses were penned; Fenwick was afoot fastening the gate pole. His mount, a thin black gelding, stood jaded with head down, steaming wet.

"And where the hell's the rest of the string, Wrangler?"

"Screw you, Sergeant," Fenwick said.

His face looked gray; water dripped from it. His boots squished in the mud. His torn slicker rattled. "They were clear up in that rocky box on the Plew above Rainbow," he said. "And screw you."

"I'll fix you when I got time, Angel Face. Where the hell's the horse Flynn rides?"

"On Highway 80 going west."

"Never mind. Start moving. Put Flynn's saddle on Hemlock. Get the saddles for packs onto Sonny and Agnes and that Mary Louise and get them down to the cabin for loading and I mean goddam chopchop! Watch that breeching on Mary Louise and I want the good long lead ropes on the halters. I'll saddle Poker myself. Start moving. Them panniers and Flynn's stuff's been sitting there waiting three hours. And give me any lip now — I'll slap the piss out of you."

Stiffened pack covers ran with water droplets; gloves were sodden, fingers cold; stubborn wet lash ropes slipped, refusing tight hitches. Spurlings cursed. Big Agnes shied at a box pannier, slid, fell down in a puddle of water and a cascade of oaths, kicked a slop of mud into Hank's face.

Cosmo Flynn had a fiery slug of Demerara with Royston at the cabin door before he climbed on Hemlock. The saddle seat was colder and wetter than Ingo predicted. Flynn pulled down the dripping folds of his raincoat, turned its clammy collar up around his neck and waved good-bye; the drenched cavalcade started moving through the timber. Hank led the roped file of pack horses. Flynn rode the rear.

124

He turned in his saddle often, to look down for a last view of Haven Lake between the trees.

The pack horses put interval enough between the two riders to discourage conversation. They rode silent, hearing the thump and scrape of the hooves on the trail, the scuff and jounce of the swaying packs, the tap of raindrops on their hats. Their way led through tangles of gray-green thicket, up slanting carpets of grass and greener fern and beds of greenest kinnikinnik under dark shafts and somber-needled arches of great trees, across muddy slabs of mother rock, around tilted boulders shiny with rain. As the horses climbed the winding trace through the timber and came higher into the slopes and shelves of spruce toward the top of Blue Gap, the rain thinned. The mist thickened. The riders rode in a quietness of gray that made ghosts of all but the nearest trees and shrouded all distance.

They halted, with the horses breathing hard in the stony notch on the high crest of Blue Gap's ridge. Flynn's wet knees were aching stiff; one of his wet feet was asleep in the wet stirrup. He looked over and saw the wet rock where a week before he had spent the long day in the shine of the sun, with the sketching pad and the watercolor box and the august view of the Cloudrocks.

The view was a void of mist; the riders sat their horses, looking back.

"I could have used another look at the colonel's big landscape," Flynn called in the quiet.

Hank grinned back at him. "Stay with us. Don't go home. Like the Aussies, they used to say — 'tyke another shufti —' "

"Cobber, I'm tyking it! The grays now, the mysterious trees, what a painting —"

"Want to stand by? For a sketch?"

125

"I'll remember." Flynn pointed to his forehead. "It'll seem like a dream."

"How about lunch? You hungry?"

"Not especially."

"Then let's start down. Find a drier place." Hank turned his horse raising the lead rope and they moved on.

They ate their sandwiches at the foot of a granite ledge, near a spring above a boggy meadow on the mountainside. It held a pond where water-lilies bloomed. The horses stood quiet, their halter ropes tied to gnarled saplings; the men sat sheltered by an overhang of rock, looking down upon the pale gold and green of the lily pads and the rain-dimmed pines beyond.

"One of the things I keep noticing," Flynn said, "is the way you respond to the looks, to the constant visual delights, of these mountains. Most men born in them would take them for granted. I've watched you find drama in them as if you might be seeing them for the first time — the way I see them, all new, vivid."

"I like them," Hank said, chewing meat.

His old Marine poncho with its faded jungle mottle of forest greens and browns fell over his shoulders like an ancient hunter's cloak. An imaginary crayon in the working mind of artist Flynn followed the drape and turn of the poncho's archaic folds.

As Flynn sat eating, the imaginary crayon kept working. It moved constructing shapes to show the bone and tendon and grimed callous flesh of work-hardened hands. It described the worn foot-forms of the rock-punished boots, detailed the ripped welt and raveled stitching on one of the mud-crusted leather toes. The crayon working in Flynn's brain climbed the angled contour of the figure to its top. A sharp crimp of a hat's frayed brim, a crease in its stained crown, built a curve and thrust of interlocking line to meet

126

and marry perfectly the lean shape of the head with the bony cheek and jaw, the intent gray eyes — where Flynn's working mind lost the crayon. It wandered away with a sound of many names for high visages on old mountains. Jedediah Smith, Flynn thought. Old Peter Taugwalder before he was old. Ranald of Clanranald. Hungry Esau.

"Ever get tired of nursing dudes, Hank? They must burn you at times. Or amuse you."

"I hope it don't show, Mr. Flynn. I'm hired out to give people a good trip. That's my job." The gray eyes were turned straight at Flynn's face. "Up here's where you can see how different kinds of characters show up, uh? Including your own. I don't forget it takes some effort for indoors people. To ride horseback long hours, fairly high altitude, and live on the ground any weather without comforts like they're used to having every day. What I notice is how most people, if they aren't plain jerks or else sick, get paid for their effort. The mountains are what pays them. People say they come up here to fish. I think it's more. Being in a place like this can make a difference. People see a bigger thing. Than just the crowds and all the fancy stuff they have to deal with in their regular life."

Flynn had a smile on his face.

"This whole trip, I've heard you and your father say almost nothing about what must be a lot of other people you bring up here."

"We have others. We figure each trip is a private thing for the ones that make it. It's theirs." Hank's straight mouth shaped to a faint smile. "And Dad learned something about guests long ago. You see, when people come up here, the country looks nearly untouched. Clean. They like to think they're sort of discoverers. They kind of feel it belongs to them in a personal way; they found it. If they ask about others that have been up here, and that come up here, we

127

tell them. But they don't ask much. They like it better being the only ones, in their own minds."

"I'm going to ask, Hank. I'd like to know. How many, for instance, have been up here with Ingo Spurling & Sons this summer?"

"We handled four parties before you and the colonel got here. About thirteen — it was fourteen people altogether."

"On that discoverer feeling, I know what you mean, but something's wrong with the Flynn reflex. Somehow it doesn't bother me a bit to know another fellow had a martini on a peak in Darien before I did. I just don't want him leaving old olive pits around —"

"But you take Royston! Him cussing what he calls the 'Manchurians.' I don't know how he picked up the name for them but that's a word he's been using up here ever since I was a kid. A Manchurian is anybody and everybody with the green gall to show up in these mountains without Royston's personal invitation. He's a card. I guess he looks at so many people so much of the time that when he gets up here he likes to imagine he's got the world to himself. Some of the places we take him — he dern near does."

"I thought he was going to blow his main fuse when those sheep came baaing past Corner Lake."

"Every year that we've happened to meet a sheep band! Get up a Congressional Investigation by God! Of blank blankity blank privileged political sheepherders! Foul greed ruining public lands! Blankity blank Manchurians! I always like to hear him — I hate sheep worse than he does. The colonel's quite a fellow. And a friend. How did you get acquainted with him, Mr. Flynn?"

"Hank, I wish you'd quit mistering me. If the Cosmo throws you, make it plain Flynn, will you? I met Royston by accident. In my life the careful designs nearly always flop. The clicks look so accidental. Last spring I happened

128

to be in Chicago. I happened to walk into an art dealer's. And the woman in charge happened to be pleasant. I happened to be carrying some prints of my work in a brief-case and we got on so well that I showed her some of the stuff. It happened that she had a commission from Royston. She told me she thought I might be the painter for the job. It happened that I was.

"Her name was Miss Bren — very handsome! Very good friend of the colonel's if I am not mistaken. She arranged my introduction to him.

"I happened to deliver a pretty successful painting, based on Royston's memory and some old photos, of Royston's father. The portrait is hanging, as Royston told you, in his office. You ought to see his office! Dynastic Nonpareil High Executive, just to coin a Period. And since my painting's been there, the charming Miss Hester Bren of Uhdy Galleries has found me two more commissions in Chicago. I rented a temporary studio there. Royston asked me out to paint the Wyoming Cloudrocks. Since a foggy day last March, the affairs of Flynn — frankly, they've flourished."

"I can look back to last March, myself," Hank said. "Only it was a snowy day. I got back from the Pacific. And it was actually Royston — he kind of changed our luck. He was the first one to ask about a pack trip this summer. Dad and me, and my mother, we kind of started from there and we practically had to begin all over, after four years. We could do more if my brother Rut was here. Handle more. I'm disappointed Fenny hasn't worked out so good. He's not going to make any kind of man for this mountain work — not interested. You saw some of those pictures he did down at Laramie. What are they about? Is Fenny good at that work?"

"I don't know, Hank. With a painter, he keeps going, he works and he hopes. That school work of Fenny's is the

129

kind of post-Picasso stuff every kid tries to cut his teeth on these days. It's hard to judge its promise. If he's after serious painting — that's hungry. He might be that serious. I'm inclined to doubt it. Depends on the personal drive that he has, or that he finds, or that he loses, here —" Flynn poked at his own chest with his thumb. "Cleverness, or a flair, doesn't do the job. Fenny has talent. Natural facility."

"He acts like being up here is being in the brig."

"Maybe painting's an escape hatch too, Hank. One thing I'll have to tell you. I'm not going to do much worrying about Fenwick Spurling. He'll be there ready when there's a ride to catch."

"He's about to catch a boot in the butt, if you ask me."

Hank got up, walked over to the spring's clean flow, drank, and came back with a tin cup filled for Flynn.

While Flynn drank, Hank picked up the lunch sack, wax paper and bread crusts. He wadded them together in a tight ball, stuffed them under a rotten log and pounded them into the wet dirt with the toe of his boot. "I guess nobody ever ate here," he said. "Nobody since old Ezekiel Williams on his way to name his glacier. He had run out of martinis. Shall we mount the steeds?"

"And meet that flying machine from Chicago." Flynn stood up, flexed his knees, blew on his cold fingers and walked out into the patter of the rain. He hooked back his sleeve cuff and peered under its wet edge at his wrist watch. "Already five minutes to three. Wonder how the weather looks at Green Junction. For that flying machine."

"Up here it's hard to tell. Maybe the soup's in Cheyenne. Or maybe the sun's shining nice right now in Silvertip."

Down the slopes through the labyrinth of lodgepole pine, the rain thinned to a drizzle, then stopped.

Pale light cut through the gray above the trees. On the rocky spine of Quaker Ridge the cloud-mist shredded

130

suddenly and came melted apart. The disk of the sun stood over the remote blue of the far Kainah Hills. The riders rode down into sunlight through the aspens.

Spread out below, swaths of hazy light and shade reached across the greens and golds of the valley's floor; a shine of silver touched the turn of the Freefolk River. The village of Silvertip made a little pattern of square walls and pitched roofs catching sunlight. The Spurling place sat tiny in angled shade by Plew Creek's willows.

Flynn had unbuttoned his raincoat, pulled it off and folded it across the pommel of his saddle. "Say —" he called.

Hank reined around, stopping the horses.

"Even the old flat world —" Flynn pointed down — "looks beautiful."

"Flynn, that's because you're still seeing it from up here —"

When they had forded Plew Creek, the tired horses broke into an impatient trot, nearly home. As the riders came jogging through the haying field's high grass they saw Em Spurling. She stood waiting by the tall post of the opened feed yard gate and she waved to greet them.

"Hello, son!"

"Say, lady —" Hank spurred through the gate with the horses he was leading — "ain't I seen you from somewheres?" He swung to the ground and hugged her with one arm. "How's everything in the rest of Wyoming?" He scraped his stubbled chin against her cheek. She kissed him.

"My, my," she said. "Hello, Mr. Flynn! Did you get awfully wet? In that storm up there today?"

Flynn had his hat off. "I got awfully impressed up there, Mrs. Spurling! And happy — wet or dry!"

"You had a grand trip?"

131

"Couldn't be grander."

"At camp is — everybody fine?"

"They're in great shape. They send their best to you." Flynn got down from Hemlock and patted him on the sweaty shoulder. "And tomorrow — I'll be riding a bus — not a horse —"

"I thought surely Colonel would make the trip down with you today."

"Civilization doesn't beguile him, Mrs. Spurling."

"I just thought he'd want to be at Junction to meet her. It's her first time here."

Hank walked over from where he had shut the gate. *"What?"*

"His daughter, that Mrs. Haskett."

"She's not coming," Hank said. "Royston said she's not coming —"

"Haven! The Junction operator, she phoned a telegram to me at the store this morning early. From that Miss Meadows. That I talked to so much Saturday long distance. All those calls! About getting a telegram delivered to Colonel. Good lands, didn't that airplane pilot from Junction fly up and find the camp? He said he could —"

"He did — that's why Royston didn't ride down today. From that telegram he decided his daughter wasn't showing."

"The telegram this morning said definitely Mrs. Haskett would arrive on that plane, Haven. Arrive about six o'clock. That's not more than about twenty minutes from now. And nobody there to meet her and her expecting her father. I did phone and make reservations for her and Colonel's pilots, so they'd have a nice place to stay tonight, two rooms at the Fontenelle Motor Court there in Junction. Then I came home early from the store to wait for you. I thought you'd be down earlier and bring Colonel."

132

"Snafu!" Hank said. "Fubar —"

His mother frowned.

"Surprise at Haven Lake," Flynn said. "Gee whiz."

"Surprise all over," Hank said. "There blows the big trip, Ezekiel, Cloudrock Peak, those high goldens." He looked around at the horses, and shook his head. "Well. Mrs. Haskett. Lemme get these packs off and turn out the horses — Flynn, why don't you go with Mother to the house — you can relax, wash up a little. I'll get your gear into the truck, then we can shove off. Truck all right, Mother?"

"I changed a flat yesterday. You ought to run by Tom Piggott's to pick up the spare. It's fixed, by now. Mr. Flynn, there's hot coffee waiting in the house."

"Thank you, but I'll help Hank. Get these saddles off."

"I'll help too," Em said.

Flynn's wrist watch said a quarter past six when he put down the empty coffee cup and walked out the kitchen door with Hank and Em Spurling.

"Haven, I s'pose you're right, not to take the time, but I wish you'd clean up a little bit — that old elkhide shirt — and you have some black looks like mud in those awful whiskers. I don't know what that lady in Junction is going to think of the Spurling family, seeing you that way —"

"Maybe I can skeer her, Ma. Maybe I can skeer her plumb back to Chicago."

They walked past the camp-stained pile of Flynn's gear on the truck's open bed.

"Something I want to leave with you, Mrs. Spurling," Flynn said. He had already rummaged through his duffel, found the big Winsor & Newton water-color box. He picked it up, with the sable brushes rattling inside, and handed it to Em. "This is for Fenwick," he said. "He'll have time to use this when he gets down from the mountain. He'll know what it's for. You give it to him and tell him I wish him

133

luck. I wish I had something good to leave with each Spurling. You leave a lot with me — I'm taking it with me. You'll be getting a print, or something, I hope, of a painting I'm going to do of your mountains. Meanwhile, thanks. Wonderful people, wonderful mountains." He turned and climbed into the truck cab and got the door shut.

Em stood looking up at him, holding the black box. "This is wonderful of you, Mr. Flynn. And you'll come back and we'll be glad. That is what you're leaving with us all." She stood waving as they drove away.

Flynn sat bracing himself on the jolting seat.

"Flatlands feel different," he said. "They smell different. And I'm different already. I don't feel as tall."

It was hard to talk much in the truck's rattling clatter. They bumped along, swaying around the turns, peering through the specked windshield at the dips and climbs and twists of the corduroyed gravel along State Road 241 in the sundown light.

"Think of the world," Flynn said, "before there were wheels. Just feet. We been there for ten days! Now we're back. With the goddam wheels. Big wheels. Little wheels. All turning."

"Hope these stay turning. Nice and round. I didn't pick up the spare."

Flynn glanced at the intent profile of the mountain visage in the crimped hat: the archaic hunter could gun a banging truck.

"About this Mrs. Haskett," Hank said, "you didn't meet her? There in Chicago?"

"No. She's living in New York. In a different crowd, you might say!"

"Know anything about her?"

"Hardly. She's had a couple of husbands. Call it the leisure class — I can remember seeing her name in Win-

134

chell's column. You heard Royston — 'my attractive daughter Dottie' —"

"It's not sounding too good. Nothing like this — that I know of — ever came up, on one of our trips. When it's a man you're meeting cold, no problem. I'm just now thinking this woman really might balk. Me a stranger, to take her alone. Into mountains she never saw."

"She'll see your mother tomorrow morning. What are you worrying about?"

"The whole thing. Society women on pack trips — first thing, they carry about four ton of gear for the packs. Then they get headaches. When they get headaches, they get problems. When they get problems they get bossy. And when they get bossy — we got problems! It happens even when they're the fly-fishing sunburned outdoor dames with muscle, and ride horses. Problems in the mountains. We try to please. We hire out for it. But I wish the colonel was here to start this one off. She expects him. God knows what else, probably a Cadillac and Gene Autry with a guitar. Not me or this truck. And to hell with her. We'll shake her up, won't we, Flynn?"

"We'll scare the living beWinchell out of her. But be ye not dismayed, fair Haskett! Thy sire awaits on yon high eastern hill. And will he ever be surprised, honey."

Hank flipped on the car lights before they turned into the main highway six miles out of Green Junction. In the turn Flynn craned his neck looking back for a last sight of the Cloudrocks. They were only a long and low shape in the north, dull purple in the dusk. Their peaks were barely visible, floating pale as if disembodied from their bases, more like clouds than rocks. Flynn saluted them.

The truck's clatter seemed almost silenced on the highway's smooth asphalt. Hank shoved the gas pedal with his muddy boot.

135

"You must feed this old wagon with mountain vitamins, Hank."

"She got nearly a new engine in May."

The sign-marked ribbon of pavement eased curving to the downgrade over the dark edge of the Fontenelle rim-rock. Beyond Green Junction's evening lights an airport beacon showed its regular revolving flash.

Flynn glanced down to read the luminous hands on his watch. "After seven," he said.

The landing field was dark when they jolted through the cattleguard gate of the airport's barbed wire fence.

"There's that Manchurian the colonel had yesterday." Hank pointed. "Gone to roost."

They drove around the end of the hangar; on the shadowy apron under the beacon tower and lighted windsock sat a DC-3 parked for the night. The Royston Machine Corporation's oval trademark stood chastely painted above the line of windows on the plane's metal side.

They walked into the waiting room, blinking their eyes in the brightness of light. No one waited there but the young man in the crisp gray shirt and tie behind the ticket counter.

"Mr. Spurling — hello there, Mr. Flynn," he smiled at them, "looks like you had a real trip. I got your private plane people a taxi to town about thirty minutes ago. They waited, expecting you. I told them it stormed in the Cloudrocks today." He looked at Hank and Hank saw his eyebrows raise. "You're going to have a mighty attractive young lady at your fishing camp. Mr. Royston's daughter. Is Mr. R. K. Royston here with you this evening?"

"He's in the mountains."

"She was very definitely expecting him when she got off the plane."

"She was?" Hank said. "Where'd they go in town?"

136

"I told the pilots it was probably the Fontenelle again, where they stayed before. They were a little anxious to have you show up —"

"We better get moving. Much obliged for helping us."

"Don't mention it and don't forget I'm coming fishing with you and your father some day —"

At the Fontenelle Motor Court the No Vacancy sign was lit. Dusty automobiles crowded the parking spaces.

When Hank rang the office bell, the stout woman who came to the desk still chewing a bite of her supper said yes, the young lady and the two *nicely* dressed gentlemen had registered. They had come from the airport in a hired taxi. They had kept it waiting. They had gone over to town to eat now, she thought.

"We're in from the mountains," Hank said. "You remember Mr. Flynn of Chicago. Do you have a room for him tonight? He was here with Mr. R. K. Royston's party earlier this month."

"We're just absolutely full up this evening," the stout woman said. "Next Monday's Labor Day. All these tourists starting for home from the Park."

Hank turned to Flynn. "Cheer up. We'll eat too — things may look better." They went out the office door. "I'll take you back to Silvertip."

"I'm ready," Flynn said, scratching his chin. "This is unadulterated civilization. Crud on the concrete. Bugs under the lights. And to think where I was last night."

They angle-parked on the main street, with Flynn's gear still piled in the pickup, near the red sign that said EATS. When they got out of the truck they could hear the time switch ticking the sign on and off in a fluttering of moths. Flynn felt his boot sole mash a big beetle on the dirty sidewalk under the neon glow. He looked up at the scaly gold leaf lettering *Covered Wagon* on the plate glass; he saw the

137

potted rubber plants inside. Hank opened the smudged door and they smelled the deep-fry in the warm air.

"There's Soucek," Flynn said, "that table over by the wall. There they are —" He grinned as he walked toward them.

"Hi there, Soucek — Fink —" They had risen from their chairs. Flynn shook their hands.

"Mr. Cosmo Flynn with red whiskers!" Soucek said. "Don't tell me you caught all the fish!"

"Only a few left," Flynn said, thinking very little about trout, for his eyes were fastened to the face and seated figure of Mrs. Dorothy Royston Haskett. Flynn realized the colonel had miserably understated his daughter's sheer decorative qualities.

"Mrs. Haskett —" the pilot Soucek was saying, "may I present Mr. Flynn? Mr. Flynn, Mrs. Haskett —"

"Welcome to Wyoming," Mrs. Haskett smiled. "And where is Father? I want to welcome him too." The teeth were very white. The lips looked lovely, colored precisely with bright scarlet. The blue eyes were a startling darkness of blue, almost ultramarine, Flynn thought, but nearly violet.

"Your father decided you weren't coming," Flynn managed to say. "He's in the mountains. He'll be delight —"

"Holy Toledo," said Mrs. Haskett. "That terribly efficient secretariat was supposed to wire him this morning! That I would arrive. *Didn't* they?"

"They did. Your father isn't very easy to reach by wire. About six hours horseback from the nearest telephone. And there wasn't enough —"

"I suppose there are maps — enormous maps —" Mrs. Haskett said, with her penciled eyebrows arched at smiling Pilot Soucek. "How I ever madly conceived of leaving Sutton Place anyway, I was out of my *mind!* Isn't it the dreamy bit? Cow Corners after curfew with you three darling men."

"Four." Cosmo Flynn had pulled himself together and he had Hank Spurling by the sleeve. "Mrs. Haskett. This is Hank Spurling. His father and your father are camped this evening by a superb lake in the Cloudrock Mountains. Hank is right here. Tomorrow he will take you very surely, I'm sure very comfortably, to your father."

"Hello," she said. "I thought you were Daniel Boone. Just standing there."

Hank felt the sweat in his hand holding his hat. He stood looking down at the expensive tan of the flawless face, at the expensive short haircut with the richness of the brown curls carefully awry, at the expensive softness of the turtleneck sweater white against the toasty tan of the skin, the long fingernails the bright color of the mouth.

"The name," he said, looking straight at the amused eyes, "is Hank Spurling." Then he turned and shook hands with the two pilots.

"You eaten yet?" Fink asked.

"Not yet," Hank said.

"We're straight from the mountains," Flynn said. "As you can see. And I haven't found a place to stay yet, for tonight."

"You have now," Soucek said. "Fink's going to sleep in the berth on the plane tonight. Taking no chances with Wyoming badmen or Wyoming weather. There's twin beds in that stall of mine at the tourist court. One's yours, compliments RMC."

"I'll be grateful," Flynn said. "And I'll be unrecognizable — Mrs. Haskett — after certain ablutions."

"We mustn't lose you," she said. "Please sit down now. And tell me more."

"Flynn," Hank said. "Do that. I got chores at Silvertip. I'm going back. I'll drive by and leave all your stuff with the lady at the Fontenelle. And I'll see you all in the morning. What time you gentlemen taking off?"

"I wrote ten o'clock on the flight plan," Soucek said. "No later."

"I'll be waiting at the motor court by eight, and I'll see you." He looked down at Mrs. Haskett. "I'll have Colonel Royston's horse, he's a good one, ready to take you up the mountain tomorrow morning."

"Tomorrow morning — I think I'll have Colonel Royston's airplane, it's a dandy, take me back to a telephone."

"That's for you to decide. Mam."

"You're so right!" she said.

The waitress with another menu card stood at Hank's elbow.

"Hi Hank," she said quietly, "aren't you gonna eat?"

"Hi Inez," Mrs. Haskett heard Hank answer, "I'm getting back to Silvertip now."

"Hey you know the last time you set at this table?" Inez asked him. "You remember?"

"Yeah."

"It was that morning early when you got back. From the war. Remember?"

"Sort of. See you all in the morning." He put on his hat, cocking it to the side, as he turned away. They watched his back, clad in stained elkhide, go out the door.

"The name is not Daniel Boone," Mrs. Haskett said. "The name is Hank Spurling."

"You're so *right,* Mrs. Haskett!" Flynn said. "And you'd miss a great deal, if you missed riding up a mountain with him. You'd like it."

"Would I really? Tell me more. After we have these hash browns, men, might there be a local pub to crawl?"

140

8

Robert Royston glanced down at the peanut butter jar lid full of cigarette butts, at the jumbled cards of a lost game of solitaire on the oilcloth. He glanced over at the square of gray light beyond the end of the table and he could see the rain hit spattering the leaves of the pin cherry outside the little windowpane. The old cabin's heavy logs

141

and thick sod roof were impervious to the rain's murmur;
Royston was suddenly aware of the great quiet he sat in.
A faintest sigh from the teakettle on the stove made the only
sound in the silence.

Royston lit another cigarette, screwed the cap on the
fountain pen and looked down again at the sheets of notepaper from the tablet on the table in front of him. It was
not a bad letter, he thought. He started reading. It was a
damned sight better than solitaire.

Haven Lake
8/26

Dear Hester:

*Rainy day in the Cloudrocks. Maybe the first intimation
of summer's departure — and up here when summer departs, winter arrives rather promptly. Since last night a
murky wet blanket of cloud hangs low over the dripping
firs. Cold gray and not without gloom. I went out with a rod
about noon and found the local trout gloomy too, abstemious
toward every lure. I expect they will not rise again until the
heavens cease with tears. I sit now in the venerable cabin
built by the venerable hand of Claunch — the dirt roof
leaks a bit — and indite you a few lines from wilderness.*

*We sent Cosmo Flynn on his way down the mountain
this morning in the rain. One of the Spurling boys went with
him. They had a late start but they will doubtless greet the
RMC plane late this afternoon. By late tomorrow afternoon
Flynn will be lowering his flaps and touching down at dirty
Midway in Chicago again. I hope this has been a pleasant
trip for him.*

*The fellow did very little work up here. I asked him to
please go by and see you. He will doubtless give you a
highly colored account of mountain doin's. You will get it,
of course, long before you get this letter.*

142

I want to say it was good fun having Flynn in camp. He made a hand. While he was with us we packed to Sky Lake and rode on one day to the lower lip of the Ezekiel Basin, under the sheer faces of the high peaks. Flynn got an eyeful. Also, for a man claiming to know so little about fly fishing, he got trout. You must keep after the man now and see that we get some of what he saw, on canvas.

I had hoped that Dot might use the RMC plane scheduled today, and that I might get her out here to enjoy these mountains for a little while with me, and perhaps have an opportunity to renew our acquaintance with each other, after years. Before I left Chicago every arrangement was made — to the optimistic point of having Ernest pack a VL & A tent and camp gear duffel all ready for Dot at Lake Forest when she came on from New York, as planned. But Miss Meadows sent word — which I received yesterday via a message drop by a local aircraft to this camp, outrageous — that Dot had not been heard from. I conclude that the arrangements came to naught and that Dot remains somewhere on the Sound, or effete points North, at God knows what mischief of her own. I'm nevertheless determined to keep any and all worry at the minimum up here, and to take advantage of the medicine — while it lasts — that these heights and trout waters afford. I carefully follow your prescription, Doctor Bren.

From the realistic — I better say selfish — point of view, it may be just as well not to have Dot with me. The three Spurlings and I are about ready for a long pack into country very high and rough through an unmarked pass over the Divide down to remote lakes where golden trout are reputed to have been planted years ago and not revisited. Our horseback passage there will depend upon the condition of the year's snow pack and the weather we encounter, but we intend to make the try and we will probably be up in

143

*that grand bleak country until I come away from these
mountains next month to resume the old bearfight on the
lower plane.*

*The Cloudrocks are as fine as I remembered. I knew it
the moment I got back.*

*That moment comes at the edge of the high forests at the
top of the first ridge. You find another world. You may
have changed, but it has not. You do remember it as a different world when you are down in the flatlands, but you
never quite remember well enough. You climb to it. Into a
kind of newness. Nothing like it exists on the lower tables of
the earth. High on a mountain the gift of life itself seems
to attain altitude. You notice it most when you first come to
it — and then when you leave it. Meanwhile, you're in it.*

*It may interest you to hear that the Wyoming Spurlings
are forced to deal with what may be an artist in the family.
The youngest son Fenwick is a freshman at the state university, moreover a convert to the "modernist" school of
painting — a limner of what I believe you would call ab-
stracts. These endeavors have not improved his mountain
craft, or brought him much acclaim from father or brother.
Flynn was amused. Fenwick may be only a teen-ager at this
time, but he may also be the only Spurling flatlander. Hank,
the ex-Marine, is lean, tense, handsome without suspect-
ing it of himself, rather somber-minded, wholly devoted to
the Cloudrocks and the life his father showed him. I think
I have never seen a young man more strongly rooted to a
place or a way of living. He is a thoroughly good man up
here. His father shows the years but remains amazingly
wiry — my old sergeant Ingo is my devoted friend and still
the old dispenser of his own brand of warmhearted blarney.
I believe he drank a good deal after his son was killed in
the war, but the mountains are medicine. As he once
pointed out to me. And though Mrs. Spurling does not*

144

climb the Cloudrocks, perhaps it is she who holds all things together. Ingo Spurling is a fortunate man.

As ever yours,

R

Royston sealed the letter in an envelope, addressed it and stamped it with an airmail stamp from the wallet in his hip pocket. Another sheet of paper crowded with Royston's writing looked up at him from the tablet. He reread it, scowling.

Dear Rich:

Had a little difficulty sleeping on the ground at eleven thousand altitude last week and my mind naturally went over things at the office. I took off believing that matters as you and I surveyed them were in a fairly predictable shape. I've pondered a bit since. That appalling possibility which I mentioned and which we then briefly discussed may be only foolishly or unduly sticking in my mind out here. I'm mailing this to you at the Club for you to read and destroy: should any move on the part of HB become overt, wire me c/o Mrs. Ingo Spurling, telephone Rodemacher Merc. Co., Silvertip via Green Junction, Wyo., and just say "Return immediately, signed Richard Mullins." I left word at the office that I wanted no business communications while I'm on vacation. But you send me personal word if I need it. I could cut this trip and get back quick. The fishing is good.

Regards,

R K R

Royston squinted at the blue ink words and he shook his head. To write that, to mail that — even to think that — Royston said to himself, is pure damn fool — damn fool —

145

He crumpled the paper, got up from the table, lifted the stove lid and dropped the note to Mullins on the coals in the firebox. He was watching the ball of paper flare and burn when the cabin door squeaked wider open and Ingo Spurling came in. He hung his dripping hat on a nail. Royston picked up a couple of sticks of firewood from the pile by the wall, and shoved them into the stove.

"That tarp lean-to at the horsepen ain't waterproof, you might say," Ingo remarked. "But it's easier to stay wet than to lug them pack saddles down here where it's dry."

"Did you remember that cinch ring on that saddle of mine? It put that sore on Hemlock."

"Everything fixed. For high country. Including shoes on that brute Hank calls Pavuvu." Ingo stood with his damp backside to the warmth of the popping fire. "Everything fixed but the weather." He scratched his head and hesitated a moment before he added, "And Fenny."

Royston sat down again and took off his glasses. "What's the matter with Fenny?"

"Him and Hank have their little ins and outs up here," Ingo said. "Hank rides him I guess. Fenny ain't interested in being the mountain boy. He wants to leave camp, he just told me. Says he'd rather make a haying hand down at Silvertip. For the rest of the time before he goes back to Laramie."

"Haying hand? He *must* be unhappy! What'd you tell him?"

"I told him go ahead. Hope that's all right with you, Colonel. Actually we won't need him now. Your daughter isn't going to be here. Me and Hank'll be plenty to take care of everything — even better. With a smaller outfit, faster moving, in the rough country."

"You're the packer. When's Fenwick leaving us?"

"After Hank gets back. I wish he was back right now —

146

carrying in our meat bag! I have to warn you that tonight it's ham again — unless you want more fish —"

"We didn't earn much today. But maybe a little bourbon before supper would help the ham and us too," Royston said. "Incidentally, when Fenwick does go down the hill I have a letter here that he can mail."

"You'll be getting the mail yourself when Hank comes up."

"Not looking for any. That Dottie doesn't ever write, she telephones. It's her sister Isabel who writes. About once a year, that is."

Ingo rolled a cigarette, wondering vaguely if Royston got letters from Mrs. Royston. If he ever did, he said nothing about it; the colonel didn't mention his wife. Ingo let it go. He lit his cigarette and considered the prospect of bourbon before supper. Still considering it, he stepped over to the cupboard shelves to look for something to fix with ham.

It was still raining when Royston came back along the sticky mud from his tent to the cabin in the early twilight. He had put a flashlight in one of his jacket pockets. In another he carried an unopened bottle from the liquor box he kept in the back corner of his tent.

Chuckbox Mountain was a dim place lost in cloud. Haven Lake was the color of lead. Royston's breath smoked as he walked with his raincoat rattling in the solemn quietness of the cold rain. He was glad when he came down the wet steps into the cabin's lighted shelter, smelling woodsmoke and coffee.

Fenwick had come in from his chores. He sat near the stove, drinking a synthetic lemonade made with a yellow powder poured from a packet into a Mason jar of cold water. Ingo stood under the Coleman lantern's shine, chopping onion to put into the potatoes for supper. His eyes

147

were watering with the onion but he clearly observed the bulge of Royston's jacket pocket. Ingo carefully wiped his hands and set out upon the table a couple of clean tin cups, conveniently.

"Hear you're going down the hill," Royston said to Fenwick.

"Yes sir."

"We'll miss you. And you'll miss those goldens we're going to find."

"I guess I will." He glanced over at his father. "I'll be haying. If it don't rain."

"I don't know why able-bodied boys pray for rain at haying time," Ingo said. "Haying's fun. And there's so much of it."

"Fun in the sun, they call it," Fenwick said.

"And the pay's real good," Ingo said, starting to slice cheese.

"Okay Pop. Lay off, will you? I'm going haying at the Fentons', like I said. Just for fun and money."

Royston uncorked the whiskey. "The money and the fun are soon parted," he said.

"Starting with money, I could give that a whirl. For a change," Fenwick said.

"The invention of money was the devil's own deed," Royston said. "I guess it's too late now to do anything about it."

"Except make some," Fenwick said. There was an edge to his voice. "Make plenty."

"Oh," Royston said, lining up the cups.

"Like old Senator Pycheley," Ingo said. "He used to tell me with a kind of quavering to his voice like in a speech, 'Ingo, it takes a dollar here and there to light the dreary way.'"

"I guess you haven't heard, Pop," Fenwick said. "The

148

best things in life are free — ask Hank. He doesn't want any money. Oh no. He just wants to be in these mountains. Nature Boy. He's as bats as old Claunch. They stick around these mountains long enough, everybody gets batty. Everybody."

"I better stick around," Royston said. "Sorry you won't plan to, Fenny." Royston poured a good slug into each of the two cups before him. "Fish have done all right today. It's not been so good for men and horses."

"Colonel," Fenwick said, hesitating. "I'm not a horse. Would it be out of line if I asked for a drink of that?"

"I've been rude, Fenwick. I'm sorry I didn't offer —" Royston glanced at Ingo. Fenwick set another cup on the table and looked around at his father.

"If you're not a horse and you're not a boy, you must be a man. Suit yourself," Ingo said, reaching for his own cup.

"Some days are better than others," Royston said. "Here's how—"

Feeling his father's and the colonel's eyes turned at him and at the cup he held, Fenwick said, "Good, uh? Thanks, Colonel."

"A little's good," Royston said. "A lot is not good. Learn that."

"Yes sir." Fenwick displayed an advert hint of archness. "I know what you mean —"

Ingo stirred the potatoes with a loud sizzling. He turned from the stove, took another sip from his cup, and cleared his throat. "I haven't had a chance yet to really ask you, Colonel. I wondered, many's the time. During the war. You seen two wars over there. I thought of everything, and of Paris too, and such as that. Was it the same?"

"No," Royston said. "Paris was different. It was a different war. Hell, I was a different Royston."

"I tried to get in it. I went all the way to Casper. They wouldn't take me."

"They wouldn't take me either. So I found me a back door, upstairs. I sneaked in. I wanted to be there, like you did. And I found one thing about the Army you'd still recognize, Sergeant. You still don't tell them. They tell you."

Ingo grinned. "I thought with colonels, they —"

"I thought you'd remember corporals, captains, colonels. They just have a different man chewing them. Don't you remember?"

"My recollection, they ain't too many able to chew a colonel —"

"Don't need too many! Take an example. A general named Somervell in Washington spotted my brand-new eagles. He just pointed his solid brass finger. That was all he had to do. Whack! I had it."

"What was that?"

"Staff, Army Service Forces. High, high staff."

"Was that bad? Anyway you got in —"

"And it's damned vanity and delusion for me to bitch about not being with troops in the field. In a different war a man gets a different job. I didn't fire a shot. I was just an engineer worried sick, a production man worried stiff and a liaison man worried silly — most of the time worried over a little matter that gloried in the name of Mulberry. Haven't I told you about Mulberry? I must have."

"You never have."

"Then you better have another drink. Here. Fenwick, you want any more?"

"Fenny's had one," Ingo said, "and that's it."

"Well," Royston said, "at the particular time I'm talking about, this particular Mulberry was topmost top secret. It was so completely hush-hush that a big admiral cracked,

150

'What's this *Mulberry* stuff? What the hell kind of a ship is the soft fruit class?' He didn't know for a long time.

"Mulberry was the code name for something that had never been done in history. The Normandy invasion depended on it. It was enough to make any mere engineering genius jump out of his skin. Our invasion plan stated that our initial assaults would not be directed at any existing ports on the French coast. To handle the enormous amount of combat supply required immediately after the first landings, our ports were to be *made* — there at the beachheads. We were going to prefabricate the facilities, tow them into position, assemble them, put them into operation at the earliest possible moment on certain open Normandy beaches! That was Mulberry, Operation Mulberry.

"One little leak of information about purpose or position of Mulberry harbors could fatally tip our hand to the Nazi command. Mulberry couldn't be explained, but it had to be *built* — practically nobody knowing why.

"So there was the British Admiralty and the War Office and the Ministry of Supply and the Ministry of Labor. That whole lot were somehow supposed to get together to command, design, execute the fabrication of the secret components. Then there was the U. S. Navy. It was somehow supposed to oversee the work the British did, tow everything into position on D Day and then be responsible for the immediate assembly and operation of the two American harbors. They were the sailor boys all right but the U. S. Army with its neck totally out and totally dependent on nonexistent combat port facilities was supposed to stand around till D Day sucking its big military thumb.

"There were one hundred and fifty untried giant cellular caissons to be built of concrete and every one of them was as big as a five-story apartment house a block long. These had to be floated, towed across the Channel on precise

151

schedule and sunk into precise position as seawalls. There were seven and a half *miles* of heavy steel bridging to be made in eighty-foot sections we called Whales. Put together, they were to connect unloading piers with assault beaches. And those piers? When I first met them they were drawings on a designer's table in Scotland. They would have to sit in the water on spud legs behind the sea walls and hoist themselves by diesel electric winches up and down to stay level with unloading craft in the rise and fall of the twenty-one-foot Normandy tides.

"This is all God's truth, Sergeant Spurling. Don't look that way. Have a drink.

"Mulberry had the most equivocal cross-command ever perpetrated by red tape since the invention of war and paper. It had other things. Everything it needed, it didn't have. I became the inter-Service, inter-Allied low-rank liaison officer from the U. S. Army in that Mulberry insanity. I was totally frustrated. Mulberry changed the color of my hair — not to purple. To white. I don't think it could have been the Navy, I believe it was the God of Hosts, at long last sent a sulphuric man-eater to chew Mulberry into some kind of shape. That slugger never slept, he didn't have time, and he knocked apples off every brass applecart in the U.K. My job then was going around trying to polish the bruised apples. The bloody battle of Sassoon House and Grosvenor Square. My war.

"D-Morning off Utah Beach I was with the Deputy Task Group Commander of Operation Mulberry aboard Sub Chaser 1352 when tugs began to arrive with the stuff. Right place, right time, believe it or not. The peculiar thing is that our Mulberries did get planted. At Omaha Beach three full days ahead of the earliest possible completion schedule, that first day I watched nine thousand fat tons of supply for battle roll direct from deckloaded LSTs to

152

dumps on the beach! Those monster sea wall sections, those spud-legged piers, those floating roadways — they worked and they worked right. And a week later with the fight on the beach at critical issue I watched that remarkable unlucky dream named Mulberry get knocked to pieces by the goddamnest June storm any Channel man could remember."

"Whew," Fenwick remarked, in a kind of filler for the silence after the long monologue. He was feeling his drink. "Socko finish, uh?"

Royston looked over at the young face, not quite hiding his commiseration for it. "Socko funeral services and repairs began at about the same time. Our troops took Cherbourg six days later. We got harbors."

"Colonel," Ingo said. His empty cup was on the table. "I didn't know you actually was at Utah Beach D Day. That's where Rut was."

"Rut told me." Royston poured more whiskey into two cups on the table. "That time we ate together in London. D Day he was at St. Martin-de-Varreville. About three miles inland from Utah Beach. I was two thousand yards off the beach, not in there behind it. Rut's outfit made a drop in the moonlight, five hours before H Hour. Your boy was one of the first men to crack Fortress Europe. And make it stick."

"Yeah," Ingo said. "This grub's ready. Whenever you want it."

Royston did not look but he felt that Ingo Spurling's eyes weren't dry. "They're talking about the next war," Ingo said. "You think we'll see it?"

"It's coming," Royston said.

"They've got that Bomb for that one," Fenwick said. "And they haven't got me, the stoops. Not yet, they haven't!"

153

"I hope we don't have to use either one," Royston said.

Talk did not flourish during supper.

Fenwick was pouring the hot water into the loaded dishpan when Royston got up from the table and said, "Where's the dish towel? I haven't wiped any dishes in so long I need reorientation."

Fenwick looked surprised.

Ingo got up. "You don't do that, Colonel, I'll do it myself! You don't fool with dishes up here. I don't run a camp that way —"

Royston felt better on his feet, moving around. "I'm going to dry dishes. Get a production line moving, won't we, Fen?"

"Coming up!" Fenwick said, pouring more hot water into another pan. "Here's the rinse. Thanks, Colonel — watch that — it's hot!"

"Ruining the help," Ingo said.

"Ruining the dudes," Royston said. "I've been too penned up today. I should've been cutting willows and Indian-smoking some fish — if I'd thought of it. I've been thinking the old bullpopper of RMC doesn't move in popping quite the way he used to. Wonder if it's still raining."

Ingo put on his hat and walked out the dark doorway. When he came back in, his red flannel shirt was specked with wet. "Black as sin," he reported. "Changed to a kind of piddling sleet." He got out his cigarette papers and tobacco sack.

"Bet it's lovely tonight on Moraine Pass," Royston said.

"And those sss-so-and-so horses in the morning —" Fenwick thumped the skillet down into the gray suds. "Colonel," he said. "Something could I ask you? Would a Milo P. Royston be a relative of yours?"

The towel in Robert Royston's hand quit moving on the

154

biscuit pan. "My father's name was Milo P. Royston. That was my son's name too. Why?"

"Whew! The Milo P. Royston Foundation — it was on the bulletin board all spring, the library at school —"

"Fenny —" Ingo said. *"I* could have told you who Milo P. Royston was, any time. Where you been?"

"I been doped off," Fenwick said. He glanced at the Royston with the gray stubble of beard on his face and the dirty dish towel in his hand. "Your own father — founding something that big —"

"Father would have liked to," Royston said. "I established the trust. For the Foundation. As a memorial to my father and to my son."

"How strictly from ignorance can I get?" Fenwick shook his head. He squeezed the dish rag, came upon two knives in the bottom of the pan and devoted himself to rubbing the grease from their blades.

Royston hung all the dried cups on the hooks in the cupboard.

Ingo eyed them there, more or less abandoning hope concerning another bourbon.

"About the Milo P. Royston Foundation, Colonel," Fenwick finally decided to say. "I couldn't find where it had anything on that notice — well, like art, like for studying painting. Does it have anything like that? That a student could try for?"

"My daughter Isabel is interested in the arts. She's needled me about it. So has another person, a friend of mine in Chicago, who knows and cares a good deal about art. But you see there are half a dozen leading universities involved now and the foundation's work is done through those particular institutions. They have a policy to follow in that work. I suppose that my own fields of interest originally determined that. Maybe I should have been broader.

155

We do make funds available for many kinds of young scientists to develop themselves, their studies, their work in their chosen fields. We're also seriously interested in world economics. In studies of the political sciences — our destiny devolves from them! The foundation makes possible international exchange of scholars and maintains a liberal publication fund. I'll admit our grants don't touch much at the area of the creative arts."

"You lost me." Fenwick carefully smiled. "I just asked."

"Let me ask you something. I know you're working your way at Laramie. You get some sort of student aid?"

"I get tuition and some of the books, because I ski."

"Athaletic scholarship," Ingo put in. "Like Rut, like Hank —"

"And other expenses?" Royston asked. "How do you handle them?"

Fenwick cocked a soapy thumb and forefinger at the dish water. "Like this. Pearl diver, as they say. And mop and broom corps. And Sundays a filling station on Highway 30."

"How'd you happen to pick Wyoming University?"

"It wasn't anything about picking. I could ski and I was All-Conference Halfback Rutherford Spurling's brother. Also the brother of that other War Hero Haven Spurling. What else?"

"You getting what you want from your studies?"

"The art courses are corn. I found that out."

"You're thinking of some place that would offer more in that line?"

"How could I? How do I thumb the ride to where I ski and study real painting too?"

"I guess you make up your mind. What needs doing most, skiing or painting."

"Or eating. Look, Colonel. The way it is now — skiing's

156

the only real *class* I got! The only fun I get, those slopes. It's a bug!"

"And painting's no bug."

"I can't afford that bug. You have to paint steady and where's any time?" He wrung out the dish rag and hung it on a nail. "Besides. I never been in the door of a museum. I mean a real one. What do I know about it? At least I been through a slalom gate. I'm registering at old Wy-oh You the sixteenth of September. After a little haying on the Free-folk." The dish water was ready to dump. He poured the rinse water into the big pan, picked it up by its bent handles and, slopping a little, carried it out the door into the dark.

By the time he came back in carrying the empty dish pan and a bucket of fresh drinking water dipped from the lake, his father and the colonel were both seated at the table. Royston had lit a cigarette. The bottle of bourbon was on the oilcloth. So were two tin cups.

"Fen," Royston said.

"Yes sir."

"On that campus, you keep showing that class, you hear? I don't think the Royston Foundation at present has any large provision for advanced studies with skis. But it might have some other pertinent information. If it does, I'll see that it's sent to you."

"It's okay, Colonel — thanks for wiping the dishes." Fenwick looked over at the table. "Guess I'll call it a day, I feel kind of beat," he said, glancing again at the two elderly faces and their bottle. He felt a strong urge to make a crack, about getting their crummy wars all hashed over, but he resisted it. "Think I'll go for the mummy bag. If it's all right with you. Anything else, Pop?"

"Those horses, Fenny. Every one of them tomorrow morning."

"And tomorrow night, I'm in Silvertip, I hope to God —"
Fenwick went out the door with his flashlight.

Musing, Ingo said, "Funny thing, the three boys. In the real bad part of the depression when Em started at the Rodemachers and I was on WPA over at Dwindle, it was Rut and Hank took care of their baby brother a lot of the time. They half raised him. Then during the war with Em working and me down at the dam and the two boys away, Fenny was all by himself a lot of the time. He got different idys in his head. God knows what they are. Fenny don't know. He's growing up a different kind. He don't care a owl hoot for this up here. He don't think it's enough. And maybe in the long run he's right, Colonel. His mother wants Fenny to make something of himself, she says. Maybe she's right, too."

"You make something of yourself by pursuing your own abilities."

"I didn't end up with much."

"You chose, didn't you? You found the Cloudrocks. You found a kind of life to go with them. What do you mean by much? What kind of much? If you had to trade with me, for instance, would you?"

"I couldn't handle it and you couldn't stand it, Colonel. There's plenty of people have treated me like I was an old fool. And maybe I am, I don't know. But you never treated me like that. Never. I said I didn't end up with much. I didn't mean it the way it sounds. I want to tell you what I have. Now. I guess you know what I thought about Rut. From the time he was a baby and I rode him around with his little husky legs up here around my neck, I taught him everything I could. Everything I knew. He learned everything. Better than me. He had a real head on his shoulders. Maybe more important, he had a heart. He had a way with these mountains, he had a way with every soul he met. See-

158

ing that boy, I hoped — I hoped I had started on — on carving out a complete man. I hoped Rut was him. I thought he was, and he got killed. Hank was the one came back. What I'm saying is a man better watch out the way his life will treat him when his mind is too made up. I lost Rut and I got Hank. I almost didn't want him, when he got back. You see I didn't know. I never paid much attention to Hank. What he got, he got for himself. By himself. He was all right, but he didn't have Rut's shine. Hank came back. A grown man, about half sick and a noticeable look in them gray eyes of his. He had to teach me, the kind of a man he is. I know now. He's a good man. And this is what I want to tell you. I don't see Rut just the way I used to. I see Hank."

After a silence, Ingo Spurling went on. "Not ending up with much, I only meant the way I feel about what I done myself. That ain't much. God knows my wife Em's made enough allowances for me! But ending up with Hank? Him and me in these mountains? How could I end up better?"

Royston did not try to answer. "You want a night cap?" he finally asked.

"Yes sir."

"Pour it. I realized tonight how old we seem to somebody like Fenwick. How miserably ancient. We pity him because he is so young and he pities us because we are so old. We might be that old. Coming to an age where we think about and talk about what we end up with! As if we were actually ending up. I don't like that."

"A man can look way back," Ingo said. "And see how a little thing turned out big in his life later. You take that day some dude left a magazine in one of Plunk Blakely's leaky tents up on Longstick and I was looking at it, it was a new magazine called *Time,* the first one I ever saw. And there was your picture, a piece about my old captain that I had

159

in France, the head of a big company at Chicago. If I hadn't seen it, I wouldn't have wrote. About the Cloudrocks. And chances are, you probably wouldn't have ever come this way. It would have made a big difference, I mean with me it would have, anyway."

"That random element," Royston said. "Referred to, in some circles, as fate. You might not have written, and I certainly would not have answered as I did, if there hadn't been another random element. The time in St. Jean de Luz. Me standing there on the cobbles, with an MP parking his motorcycle ten feet away. He just happened to have the face of a buck sergeant by the name of Spurling. Out of my old battery. My God he gave me a wild ride past Pau, up the mountain trail to the little inn! Old Ingo Jingo Spurling."

"Remember the Spanish champagne we located? Remember those black-haired sisters when we'd come in from hunting?"

"Those damned chamois! Jumpy, weren't they? And that genuine chamois we got finally with the old liberated Mannlicher — some leave, we had."

"Some days! Those goat-legged Basque fellows, those climbing fools that took us into their mountains, they were the first genuine guides and outfitters I saw in my life! Here it is the Cloudrock Mountains in Wyoming only twenty-odd years and a few thousand tears later!"

The bottle stood empty on the table; Royston stood outside the cabin door, fumbling for the press-button on his flashlight, taking a dark bearing down the muddy trail toward his invisible tent. The chill in the air was very sharp. He looked up. Stars showed in a clearing sky above the blackness of the firs.

160

This Mrs. Haskett had thawed a little, Hank decided, on the rutty road from Junction. She was quite a deal, he thought. Someways. She was different, anyway, from what he had figured earlier that morning. A hint of her perfume, a clinging rich pleasantness, faintly spiced the air inside the battered truck cab.

"Here we are," Hank said. "Silvertip, Wyoming. A poke and plumb town."

"A what?" asked Mrs. Haskett.

"You poke your head out the window and you're plumb out of town."

"Oh stop —" she hunched her shoulders and she shuddered becomingly. He had to notice again the way she could put the sparkles in her eyes when she laughed, looking straight at him.

"On that airplane by now you'd be east of Casper. Out of danger. No mountains. Telephones behind every bush."

"It's another mistake," she sparkled. "It's my talent."

"This is the Rodemacher Mercantile Company on your right. If you don't mind, we'll go in there." He shut off the engine.

From the large leathery handbag in her smooth lap she produced a lipstick and a compact and she fixed her face, then with one of her long-fingered tan hands tapped and touched at curls above her ears. She stepped down from the truck with Hank at her arm and the sun catching dusky gold on her hair.

Inside the store Em Spurling came smiling expectantly from behind a counter. "It's so good," she began, "to meet a part of Colonel's family, and have you here —" a pang withered the cordiality her heart had prepared. An instinct alerted her. She felt an unreasoning guard rising against the young woman standing at Hank's side. "I hope you do know —" Em found herself saying, feeling the death of her own smile — "we're anxious to take care of you the very best we can, Miss Royst-*Hask*ett I mean —" the slip of her tongue increased Em's confusion.

Dorothy Royston Haskett's lack of warmth for instinctively protective mothers of males was also instinctive. She

162

turned her eyes at Hank and put the sparkles in them for Mrs. Spurling to see. "I'm bearing up in Father's absence," Mrs. Haskett said. "Don't you think?"

"Well —" Em said, trying to smooth over her son's self-conscious silence, "I'm sure with Haven looking like he did last night, you must be relieved. To see him a good deal more presentable this morning."

"Is his name really Haven? Last night he *was* a bit bushy. And so solemn. In that ghastly café."

"I — he came home saying he didn't know whether you were going into the mountains or not."

"Surprise!" She made her laughter musical. "I'm coming unglued. Or is the Old West getting through to me?"

"Mrs. Haskett's ridden horses," Hank said to his mother, very uncomfortably.

"As a child. California, France," she explained brightly to Em. "I rode a bit last spring. Near Reno. I stayed on a dude ranch waiting for my decree."

"We — have dependable horses," Em said. She hoped she was somehow countering an evil she was sure of. "Haven will see that you have a safe ride to your father." Em went on with her duty. "It's cold and sometimes damp up there, just camping. Haven and I spoke of it last night, about checking over what you're taking. Heavy clothes and shoes and women's little conveniences — just things you'll need. If there's anything you might have forgotten, I could try to provide it for you, here at the store, before packs are loaded."

"Jumping tunket," Mrs. Haskett said. "I just brought some jodhpurs. Sweaters. Travel things like I'm wearing. A cosmetic case. And this handbag, which I did think looked rather Western." She paused, arching her flawless eyebrows. "It didn't dawn at the time —" she smiled — "Er-

163

nest said I'd have everything I'd need when he put all those canvas things aboard the plane in Chicago. Enormously outdoorsy, he said. The old coot!"

"Who's Ernest?" Hank asked.

"Father's man," Mrs. Haskett said.

"I guess you got everything," Hank said. He turned to his mother. "Out on the truck. New Woods eiderdown bag, and air mattress. Some kind of wall tent never been broken out. And a loaded brand-new duffel with a fancy side zipper."

"A brand-new what?" asked Mrs. Haskett.

"Duffel."

"What's that?"

"Come on now! Don't tell me you don't know what a duffel is! Or that you don't know what's in that one out there!"

"I thought I was very clear. I don't know."

"Key-ryste."

"Haven, guard your tongue." Em looked at him.

Hank clamped his jaws. "A duffel is a bag," he said. "Suitcases don't pile good on a pack horse, you know."

"I didn't know that either."

"Okay. Everything goes in the duffel. I mean whatever clothes you take, and little stuff you need. And I think you better see what you're taking. It's not a dude ranch up there, mam. It's just country. You're going to be living on the ground."

"Sounds simply fascinating. In the pig's eye."

When he brought in the duffel bag and dropped it onto a counter, Mrs. Haskett had just been introduced to Max Rodemacher and old Bill Clancy. They were charmed, standing by; it annoyed Hank. His mother looked worried and Mrs. Haskett looked amused. "Klein's getting Dad's grub list together," Hank said, pointedly. "I got panniers here to try to save some time — I'll load on the truck and

164

get that meat bag packed at the locker —" he poked the duffel — "while you see what's in this thing, please."

Walking to the back of the grocery counter he heard Mrs. Haskett's voice. "Zip-*po!* Nothing like airing one's outdoors linens. If that's what these *are* —"

He came back sweaty from lugging and hoisting all the loads to the truck. And he came back edgy with the uncertainties of the day before him. His mind felt mussed.

"What'd you find?" he asked his mother.

"Everything but dear Admiral Byrd," said Mrs. Haskett.

"See you got a hat," Hank said, very dry.

"Bought it myself," Mrs. Haskett said. "Powder River, podner. Do look at these by-cracky shoes here! Ernest must've been shoplifting in Dogpatch."

"Do they fit you?"

"I'm advised by experts that they do. Sadly."

"Haven, this duffel had just about everything," Em said.

"The young lady is ready for the Cloudrocks," Max Rodemacher put in. "Very fine equipment."

"Jeepers," Mrs. Haskett said, lighting a cigarette. "It's touching, you know. I must ask Ernest how he got so nosy. Spying out the size for these long-handled Girl Scout drawers."

"Um," old Bill Clancy said. He thought she was rare.

Hank frowned.

"We ought to get started, Haven," Em said.

"I'm ready. Zip it up." He carried Mrs. Haskett's duffel, her cartons of just purchased cigarettes, matches, Kleenex, with a paper bag of other sundries, out to the truck; and he helped Mrs. Haskett, her new hat and her dangling handbag, and then his mother, up into the cab. "You drive," he said to his mother, "I'll ride behind where there's room." He swung himself up and flopped into the corner on the softness of the rolled sleeping bag, then braced his feet

165

against a heavy pannier when the old Ford began to jolt toward Plew Creek. Mrs. Haskett's matched air-travel luggage went scraping and sliding on the lurching iron of the truck bed.

Hank eased back. He gave his bones a little luxury of rest, the last they would get for themselves until this Mrs. Good-looking Haskett, this screwy dame, and three top-loaded pack brutes, had all been hauled into camp at Haven Lake that night.

At least the weather was good, he thought.

The five unsaddled horses stood in shade by the barn when the truck came to a stop at the feedlot gate. Hank stirred himself. It took four trips to bring Mrs. Haskett's assorted baggage into the house.

He found her standing in the parlor, somewhat cautiously examining Rut's old stuffed golden on the wall. "I'm going to make up the packs," he said. "Mother'll bear a hand here. If you're taking any stuff from these suitcases, would you mind sticking it all in your duffel? If you and Mother could get that ready first, I'll be back for it pretty soon, to load."

Her duffel bag was ready when he came back. Mrs. Haskett was changing to her riding clothes in Em's room. Em was in the kitchen preparing lunch.

"You'll want to eat here, won't you, Haven? It'll be noon," Em said.

"Yeah, let's feed her before we start out." He swung the bulged duffel to his shoulder. "No telling how slow this jobby'll be. Getting her up that hill —" He went out the door. His mother followed him outside.

"Haven. Wait a minute." He stopped and looked around at her. "I want to tell you," she said.

"Tell me what?"

"You mustn't let anybody like that bother you."

166

"Bother me — don't it raise a sweat every time we have to load a green dude to a saddle? When it happens to be a society dame — *bother* me?"

"Haven. You know what I'm talking about. That's all I'll say."

"And I'll say I wish Royston had come down here yesterday." He walked away with the weight on his shoulder, to the saddled horses by the fence.

Mrs. Haskett came into the kitchen feeling freshened, ready for a jaunt to the mountains. Her white broadcloth shirt with its open collar and long sleeves was crisply mannish; the cut of her tailored jodhpurs crisply denied there was anything at all mannish about Mrs. Haskett herself. Her presence carried the scent she had imparted to the Ford's front seat. Her boot toes glistened. She was gay.

"I do have on those long handles, Mrs. Spurling, the barn door is buttoned!" She put the sparkles in her eyes. "Golly."

Hank appeared, wearing now the elkhide shirt, the crimped hat, the mountain boots, and clean Levis. Out by the fence, a lash rope had just knocked the big scab from one of his sore knuckles; it was bleeding. He was not gay.

Seated with the Spurlings at the Spurlings' own kitchen table, it was Mrs. Haskett who seemed least ill at ease.

She could not greatly fancy the thick bologna and cheese sandwich on her plate but she ate the tuna fish and rye bread and the canned fruit cup and drank two glasses of iced tea and she talked. She asked about the other Spurlings and about Fenwick's art work on display in the parlor. She said that her own sister Isabel was without a doubt the world's ickiest painter but interested in music. Musicians that is. Mrs. Haskett volunteered the information that she herself usually preferred the less long-hair types in realms of art. For instance, she did know a quite outstanding trum-

167

pet player rather well, for a while. But his private life, she said, it was fantastic. It bugged her, it really did. Some of that far-out life among the cats.

Em Spurling sat wordless. Hank Spurling ate faster, aware of his mother's rigid face across the table. "If you'll excuse me," he said, "I better get everything set. I'll take these for you —" He stood and picked up Mrs. Haskett's new fleece-lined jacket and plastic raincoat. "These'll be on your saddle. Don't forget to put one of those candy bars there in your pocket. It might taste pretty good, later." He put one in his own pocket, and turned to his mother. "Any mail here for Colonel Royston?"

"Nothing. Fenwick got the only letter, and you have it, don't you? That girl, from over at Dwindle —"

"Dwindle," said Mrs. Haskett. "I can tell already. Your Fenwick's a little beaver."

Hank had his pack horses lined up loaded, he was putting a tighter hitch to the rope from Mary Louise's halter to Sonny's tail, when the two women came through the gate. Mrs. Haskett had a silk scarf around her neck. She had on that new cowpoke hat with the chin string. She had that large and leathery handbag dangling from her arm.

"This bay horse over here," Hank said, "you'll get along fine with him. Name's Hemlock."

"The poison Hemlock?"

"Poison? He's named for a tree. Named a long time. He's your father's mount. Let me take that bag you got there — Wouldn't it go in the duffel?"

"It goes with me."

It rattled.

"Anything liable to break?"

"Must you care, dear boy? It's what little girls are made of — everything nice, including toilet tissue. Just tie it *on*."

168

When it was tied on, he helped Mrs. Haskett into her saddle. "Ugh," she said, swinging up. "Hemlock's so high!"

"You'll limber," Hank said.

He glanced over at his mother; they were both relieved that Mrs. Haskett seemed to know what she was doing aboard a horse.

"These stirrups," Mrs. Haskett said.

"I know," Hank said. "Flynn was riding them. We'll fix the length."

When the stirrups were adjusted, Hank backed off for a view of Mrs. Haskett's seat in the saddle. "Feel right?"

"Dauntless Dottie! She rides again!"

Em stood by the opened gate. "Have a nice trip. I'm sure you will, Mrs. Haskett. With your father."

Hank had mounted, with the lead rope to the pack horses in his hand. He motioned to Mrs. Haskett. "Ride up here, alongside —" he called to her.

As he started out the gate past his mother she looked up at him and she said, "You must take good care of yourself, Haven. Bless you, son." He noticed she did not smile. Looking back across the grass of the haying field, he saw his mother standing still by the gate.

He nearly always felt a moment of relief, of liberation, when the packs were lashed and finally moving and the mountains were ahead. It was a good moment, and he tried to enjoy it now, for as long as he could make it last, in easy silence, before there was a horse or a pack or a word that would need to be dealt with again.

Riding in a silence that was not easy, into a terrain and an experience where horses and timber slopes and weather and muscles and uncounted unknowns were to become actualities, personally to be dealt with as inescapable and personal responsibilities, Dorothy Royston Haskett very privately felt a very real and sudden need for self-assurance. To try

169

to possess it she tried to make it something familiar and she tried to name it aloud now: when the horses came up the willow bank out of the splash of hooves across the cold water of Plew Creek, she called out, "This is *fun,* isn't it?"

Hank nodded.

"What is the neat pile of stones ahead there? Where first casualties are buried?"

"It's where the Forest Service marked the start of a trail. Goes clear to Ezekiel Basin."

"Do we go there?"

"We're taking a turnoff. To your father's camp on Haven Lake."

"What lake?"

"Haven Lake."

"I thought that's what you said. Any connection? Son?"

"Connection? Oh. I was born up there."

"Really! Must be like Father. On the subject of Sanskrit, New Mexico."

They rode in silence.

"How far up this mountain is Haven Lake?"

"It's up and then it's down. The other side."

"Holy satchel," she said.

He reined by the cairn at the foot of Quaker Ridge. "See that notch, the break in the trees, right against the sky? That's where we go over."

She peered into the silvery glare. "You think I'll make that?"

"A regular highway. You just follow it up easy, with me right behind you, hauling these elephants. Hemlock'll show the way. He's a mountain expert and he likes it out in front. So will you."

"Well then — but let me die with my boots on. And my sun glasses. If I can ever get the beastly knot around this bag untied —"

170

He chose to consider it purely accidental when her gloved fingers slowly brushed across the back of his hand as he reached out retying the handbag to the horn of her saddle. He reined carefully away lifting the rope that led touchy Big Agnes and the explodable string behind her. The packs looked all right. So did Mrs. Haskett in her sun glasses. They began the climbing zigzags up the slope.

A stir of breeze tempered the bright air.

The way led past gray sage into groves of aspen where leaves were turning gold from the season's first frost. Up the slant through the trees, under their canopies of old summer greens and new autumn yellows, the trail twisted higher and higher above the Freefolk valley's floor.

Dorothy Royston Haskett discovered an unexpected exhilaration, in leading the file up the ridge. Fun became real. In a pure pleasure with her horse's free stride and her own body's smooth motion with it high into the tall slope's clean color and clear air, she rode for unnoticed minutes outside any confining measure of time or space, self-centered but not solitary, oblivious of any need for any guide in the flowing benignity of the world; she forgot to look back down the trail. When she did, her guide Hank Spurling was not there.

He was gone, his horses were gone. She jerked rein in a flash of fright, alone in the midst of nothing she knew.

The way ahead was menacing, trackless; the way at her back was empty. It stayed empty. Pale aspen trunks with black runic marks stood still around her. She stood still. Strange leaves a color of flame quivered, whispering her fright in the quiet.

At last from beyond the leaves came a clack and slide of rock and she saw him ride into sight with the three packs in a jogging line behind him; he pulled to a halt a few paces from where she waited. It seemed to her maddeningly casual, after a personal crisis. Yet it seemed absurd to try

171

to tell him so, to tell him anything at all — now that it was over.

He looked up at her and he saw that Hemlock had started to carry her up a shortcut away from the marked trail.

"Did you think I was lost?" he said grinning.

She considered the grin deplorable. "I thought you — probably were," she limited herself to saying.

"Sonny's pack slipped. We had a little horse trouble. And bad language. Glad you kept going."

"Oh."

"You and that steed look plenty okay."

"Do we?"

"Moving right up —" his eyes checked Hemlock's shoes, his saddle cinch and blanket. "Doing real good. See where you been, away down there?"

"In reference to any damned scenery —" she decided not to limit herself — "I want mine with some attentive people in it!"

He had to spar for a moment with such bafflements as might be behind the rhinestone-rimmed sun glasses. "Uh, we're getting up toward timber," he said. "Out of the dust." He looked at her. "I'll take over the lead now if you don't mind."

"Mind? Let me say it's one of your better ideas."

He spurred past her, pulling the pack horses on the lead rope. "Up farther we'll take a break. There's a spot I got in mind."

She took her place at the end of the file, moving up the slope with Hemlock fretting, held to a jog at the rear, close behind the massive croup and switching tail and rocking high load of the mare Mary Louise.

They climbed to towering timber, into aromatic shade along steeps where the rider in the lead stopped often to let the laboring horses have their breath. The zigs and zags of the ride became increasingly featureless to the rider at the rear as she began to grow tired. Her seat felt the warmish hint of the saddle's chafe, her knees felt stiff, all of her felt dulled, when the trail broke from its upward slant through shadowy crowded pine into an abrupt brightness of open sky, and she saw the greens of a mountain meadow and water lilies in a pond. Above the pond's margin of grass stood a rise of crag rock and fir.

"Chickaree Spring," Hank said. "We'll take a rest."

"Why I ever engaged in this bit — I'll never know! I'm falling apart!" she said to him as he held the reins and helped her from the saddle.

"Ease your legs a little, you'll be raring to hit the top! It's not far now. It's right up there."

"Don't be cheerful. It's revolting!" Not watching where she pounded her numbed feet against the welcome ground, she stepped into an edge of grass-matted quag that muddied both her boots to the ankles.

"Oh hell," she said.

"Country livin'," Hank said.

She found herself laughing, a little out of control, and she took off the sun glasses and blinked, turning her eyes at him. "Country livin'," she said. "You can play that again." Her eyes were a very deepest blue in the reflected sunlight under the hat brim when she pointed to the handbag hanging at Hemlock's shoulder and said, "I need that tool chest."

Hank untied the saddle strings and handed her the bag.

"About country livin'," he said, hesitating, "you'd maybe like to sort of explore a little, yourself. I'll be here tying the horses and studying the Kainah Hills, over that way —"

"You're a country doll, aren't you? Incidentally —" she looked around — "there aren't any snakes or bears or things, are there, over thataway?"

173

He nearly grinned. "You're safe. No snakes, no bears, and no kidding!"

He had brought a tin cup from his saddle bags, and he was puffing on his lighted pipe, when she came picking her steps to where he stood in the shade by the spring's flow. He dipped the shiny cup down into the cold water and handed it up to her. After she drank she touched the damp scarlet corners of her freshly painted mouth and she said, "I might revive."

"Those pine needles over there would make a soft seat. You relax a little. Get the saddle kinks out." He walked over with her and they sat down.

"Trying not to be cheerful," he said, "you are more than halfway now to Haven Lake."

"That kind of cheer — I can use." She sighed and leaned back resting on one elbow. "If you haven't fetched me into the forest primeval, I'll eat it, lilies and all. It's crazy." She gazed out over the meadow. "Crazier all the time."

"I been thinking," Hank said. "You ever drink a beer?"

She turned amused, half inquiring, to see his face. "Is that the way your little mind goes around working?" She laughed. "Or is this a riddle?"

"I just asked. Since about the end of July there's been a couple of cans cooling in this spring. And I thought, if you enjoyed a brew —"

"Did I say forest primeval? Imagine: a chocolate bar, a can of beer and thou. I must say, I'd love a brew!"

Hank got to his feet. "We had a man up here, Mr. Finucane, last month — left two cans and on his way back down didn't want them. I been waiting for an occasion. To see if they're cold."

"You think they might be?"

She watched him kneel on the wet moss, pull up a sleeve, reach almost his arm's length under a fallen log in the water, and bring up the beer. "They're cold all right," he said, rolling down his sleeve. He drew the heavy knife from the sheath on his belt and punched two slits in each of the can tops. Foam oozed from the holes.

He handed her a can and, lifting his before he drank, said, "Here's to a fine trip in the Cloudrock Mountains."

"It's cheers with beers," she said. "Here's to that thoughtful Mr. Finucane. And of course, Mr. Haven Lake Spurling!"

They sat looking out over the blue pond in the green meadow.

The sun made it a different place, Hank thought, it was hard to believe how gray it looked yesterday in the rain with Flynn.

"I can't think when a beer seemed so jazzy," she said. "Pardon my burp."

"Last beer I had was last Christmas. A Chink restaurant in Honolulu." He struck a match and held it for her to light her cigarette.

"Last beer I had — must have been last Friday. A yawl on Long Island Sound."

"I figured from that suntan you been outdoors a lot. On a sailboat?"

"A sunlamp does a neater job. But I do like sailing — discounting certain obnoxious sailors, that is." She drew deep on her cigarette.

"Swab jockeys, we called them. In the Corps."

"They're all over, even in twelve-meter boats. As to the dear old Navy common variety, I must tell you I was married to one. Briefly. Chief Boatswain's Mate Bink Haskett, USN. The jolly dog. In the lobby of the St. Francis Hotel, that is, where I first viewed his darling face. The musclebound creep. He sailed off to the seven seas, I think it was. Turned out to be an excellent idea."

175

"I guess you're not raising a family, or anything."

"Family? No. Why?"

"I just wondered. Like keeping the name Haskett."

"After going around being a Mrs. Alton, then a Mrs. Haskett, it could seem silly, couldn't it? To go around being a sweet little old Miss Prudie Royston. Also, making with the Royston seems to kick a gong a bit at times. Expensive too, I've found. Question answered?"

"I guess so."

"You do really suppose Father has no inkling I'm on my way into this incredible performance?"

"That telegram was the last word he got. When his office hadn't heard from you, he figured you weren't coming."

"Actually, I couldn't decide. About leaving New York. Then I did decide. Unexpectedly. And do you know now I think I'm reviving slightly? I really am. This mountain brew, it must be loaded."

"It's just the mountains. They make you feel good."

"Is that what it is?"

"Must be." He was smiling. "You remember those snow peaks you saw when you were in the truck coming from Junction? When we get to the top of this ridge you are going to see them close, all of a sudden. Standing there. From then on, everything gets better. You'll see."

The beer, or the mountains, or Mrs. Haskett, something, he realized, did have punch and he said, "I'm thinking I'm sorry that you got upset."

"Upset? This whole bit's a bashy upset, if that's what you mean."

"Well, I meant down there on Quaker Ridge. Being all by yourself. In new country."

"Oh that."

"I guess it seemed to you like you weren't being taken

176

care of. I just wanted to mention it. It won't happen that way again."

"Not if I can help it —" she laughed. "While we're at this — I think I'll tell you. It was perfectly insane. Because I was frightened. You know how all those quaking aspen trees are, those marks on the white trunks? It could have been imagination, but one of those things seemed to be an eye. An old Egyptian sort of King Tut eye, black and spooky, really. Looking at me. It's what I remember about being there alone and now I've told you can you think of anything any more fantastic?"

For a moment before he said anything she was aware of his intent eyes on her face. "Those quakers," he said. "They show funny marks on their bark, sometimes, you get alone. I've noticed it, myself." His straight mouth smiled. "The old eye was looking at you, uh?"

"Loony," she said.

"Maybe we're all loony."

"You're so right!"

He got up and walked over to where she had tossed her cigarette. It lay smoking on the pine needles. "You have to be kind of careful," he said, "so this place won't burn up."

"Sorry." She watched him grind the butt down into damp dirt with his boot toe and then tamp the place smooth.

"I'll bury these beer cans," he said. "Then we ought to be about ready to ride."

"Bury them? Will they start a fire too?"

"No. They start a decent place to looking like jerks had a picnic."

"Bongo," she said. "You still remind me of Daniel Boone. What did you say the name of this place was?"

"Chickaree Spring."

"What's a chickaree?"

"You walked into that! A chickaree's a kind of little brownish squirrel that makes a lot of racket in the woods."

"Oh stop! The Adventures of Chicky Haskett. Or, A Town Squirrel — Horseback in The Rockies! How's that?"

"Sounds like a book all right. Hard to read."

"Easy to read! And real dirty, that part about having to get back up on a horse now —"

Again at the end of the climbing file she found herself oppressed by the stultifying mass of the mountainside, its matted timber and tedious stone. It sloped up interminably while the saddle lurched and trail rocks rattled and the sun at her back crept lower down the sky. Both her knees went painfully stiff with the stirrups' cramp. An ache twinged between her tensed shoulders. Her throat was dry and her temper was tattered — comfort and cool beer and good humor seemed immensely long past — as she rode through weather-dwarfed spruce up the last stony pitch to the ridge's top, not realizing where she had come. She noticed her guide was turned in his saddle, smiling at her. Fatuously, she thought.

She looked out quite suddenly past him into an aerial radiance of blue space and all the great peaks of the Cloudrock Mountains and she said, "My God!"

Hank dismounted, tied the horses, and walked up to where Mrs. Haskett sat the saddle. "Like to look for a while?" he asked. He was still smiling. He helped her down and they stood together on a big tilted rock by the trail.

"You didn't tell me!" she said. "Switzerland. No it's not, it's terribly different. Without a chalet anywhere, without a nice cow valley. Just wild!"

"Quiet, uh?"

"It's not for me! I mustn't lose you. Not for a moment. Scene me no scenery — look at that peak. I suppose lunatics with ropes get to the top of it."

178

"My brother Rut was one that climbed it. I never had the chance. But I will. I've been up that one to the right. Mount Felix."

"I'll take Manhattan, thank you. But look! Those are lakes! Blue, blue — so many —"

"The thing about them, the closer they are, the prettier they get. Big old trout, waiting for a fly —"

"Wait a minute! This Haven Lake bit — in the name of God don't tell me I still have that far to ride!"

"Nope! You can't see Haven from here. But I'll show you. See this nearest peak, with the flat top? That's Chuckbox Mountain. Haven is this side, right at the foot of it. Down there —" he pointed.

"Your poor mother. The pioneer bit. Imagine."

"She did all right. Or don't you think so?"

"Leftenant, it would beat the hell out of me! To coin a phrase. And another thing. There wouldn't by any chance be another spring around here, would there? I'm thirsty."

"Just sit there and relax." He jumped down from the rock.

"Don't *leave* me!"

"I'm not."

"I don't like it here alone."

He came back from his saddlebags with a worn little thermos bottle and he poured her a cup of lukewarm black coffee. "Emergency rations," he said. "We got everything. Including a tootsie-pop."

"Pop? Steady there, tootsie, steady —"

He laughed. "The name of this kind of candy sucker. Here. Try one. Tastes pretty good, riding along. Might keep you from getting so thirsty. That one's grape."

"Ugh."

"This view you're seeing right here is what Mr. Flynn is going to paint a picture of, for your father."

179

"Father's dear Mr. Flynn couldn't knock a barn with a bucket last night. He got stone."

"Got what?"

"Stone. Loaded! The snake. He was the one that kept ordering those stingers and saying this was such a good idea. The snake."

"Is this so bad?"

"Scenery by the ton and let's be grim now, darling. Would you tell me exactly how much longer this goes on? And don't be cheery either. My tailbone's not only tired. It's worn."

"You've been sitting in that saddle just about five hours, and from here we —"

"Correction. Just about five years. Not hours."

"Okay. And from here to camp at Haven Lake is just about an hour more."

"What do you mean, 'just about'? Is it more or is it less than an hour?"

"Depends. It may be a little more."

She was looking at her watch. "Frightful, I'd call it. And I'm chilly."

"We'll make good time. All downhill. You ready?"

"We can't just *stay* here, can we?"

"We could."

"Oh stop."

"There's impractical things about it."

"Most practical thing I can think of right now is a great big belt from a great big bottle."

"About an hour, you'll probably be having a deal like that. With the colonel. After you've shook him, riding into camp. It's going to shake him."

"It's shaking me, I must say."

He untied her warm jacket and helped her put it on before he boosted her into the saddle. They started down the

180

slope under shady spruce boughs still moist from yesterday's storm. She felt every jolt of Hemlock's pounding downhill gait.

The packs ahead swayed and scraped past the resiny blaze marks through the sunless forest down the winding trace. She had let herself sink into an aching torpor while time and trees went by, when the file of horses came to a halt. Her guide had stopped them. He was looking back, calling up to her, "Haven Lake!" She saw him point. "Down there."

"Jubilation," she said.

"What?"

"Skip it."

His hand went up to cup his ear, and he looked at her. Drooped on old Hemlock, she looked small and beat, up there under the trees. He got off his horse. He put down the reins, threw the lead rope across the branch of a sapling, and climbed through the brush up the side of the trail to where she sat.

"That blue water right down there, that's it," he said. "The cabin's not three quarters of a mile."

"Cabin?" She straightened her hat. "I should probably fix my face."

"I got to say this. Now's the time." He was looking up at her. "I've made this ride with lots of people. A lot of trips. When it comes to being a sport, you don't need any fixing, I don't think. None at all. Your face or anything else," he grinned.

"What jazz," she said. "Doll baby."

"Semper fi — why'n't you get in front of this outfit? Lead us in. I'll be following you close, don't worry. Just mosey down this trail out ahead like you did it every day. Ease right up to the cabin door and say boo. They'll think they're seeing things!"

181

"Seeing things is right."

Around the rise of the hillock by the horse pen, through the trees and over Hemlock's pricked-up ears, the day's last sunlight high on Chuckbox Mountain stood mirrored gold on the evening calm of the lake. She came to where she could see the gray logs, the weedy roof of the cabin in the cove. Woodsmoke climbed from the stovepipe. No other sign, no sound but a soft scuff of the hooves moving easily behind her, no movement ahead, greeted her as she rode under the trees toward the cabin. Then a horse nickered — and a startled hatless head appeared in the shadowy cabin door. She saw her father, looking perfectly disreputable, with a thick stubble of fierce gray whiskers on his face, standing dumfounded.

"I thought at least you might be camped in mountains," she sparkled, "not these foothills, darling!"

"Godamighty —" he stumbled coming to grab his daughter down from the saddle — "You vixen!"

10

The creel he carried for her was already heavy with trout. He put it down and dropped the landing net beside it on ferns growing in the shade of a little spruce as perfect as a Christmas tree.

"This is a place," he said to her, "where you can nearly

always find a few. Let's take a look. Then we can work along to where we tied the horses. By that time the colonel and Dad ought to be riding back this way."

Ripples of light from the water were shining up in her face when she handed him the flyrod. He held out his other hand to help her go stepping up the side of the big rock. It stood like a sentinel over a pool the stream made not far below the granite-choked outlet of Rainbow Lake.

They got to the big rock's outer edge, careful not to show their shadows, and looked down into the clear water.

"Urr!" he said. "See what I see?" He held his voice low, like a stalker's.

"What?"

"Under this side that bubbly riffle, deep down — see? Barely waving his tail —"

"I don't see —"

"Just parked, faced up-current, taking feed lazy as it comes drifting through — woop! See that? See him scare that middleweight? I'm king of this hole, he says. That rascal looks like the king of —"

"I do see! I do now! That's a *fish* like a dark shadow down there —" she whispered it — "more than one!"

"But the big one — you hold this rod here, like this! While we get it beefed up, uh? Lordy!"

He pulled down the yellow silk line from the rod tip and unstrung the sporty light leader; he replaced it with a tough one made for holding big steelheads, seven and a half feet of blackly green translucent heavy-test gut. He was grinning, happy.

"Hook that little beat-up Adams on your hatband, it's been hauling in the rainbows the whole afternoon," he said.

Working fast he straightened the wiry gut, soaped it, stuck the leader box back into his hip pocket, got out the fly book. "Crash gear," he said, "we're going for the crash

184

gear —" he found the right page — "this thing here is a number six. Flying caddis. Lunker special if I ever saw one. That old rainbow down there, that monster, I bet he's been to all the wars. He may not rise to anything at all, he may not."

He put the taper end of the gut in his mouth to soak it wetter and he went to the edge of the rock to look down again.

"Vishus zdill dthere," he said.

A movement of breeze made a most delicate high hum along the luster of the leader swaying up from his mouth to the rod tip she held over his head. In the silence they both heard the tiny humming while he tied on the big-hooked, hairy dryfly. He gave the knotting an extra turn; he pulled it very tight, testing to make certain.

When he released it, the new fly on the new leader jumped dancing out into the sunny air.

"Geared up," he said. "Take that monster, Champ."

"Not me. Honestly!"

"Why not? You're fishing, aren't you?"

"Oh yes. My special swifty beaching technique. Here —"

When she tried to give him the flyrod he held his hands behind his back. Her eyes came very close to his; the fly dancing around them in the breeze sailed in and snagged her sweater sleeve. He unhooked it carefully, giving it great attention, trying not to notice her closeness.

"Listen Dorothy," he said. "That fish is some fish. See if he'll rise."

In the bright light shining up from the water her eyes were more violet than blue. Her long eyelashes caught a faint gold in their darkness, like her hair. Her mouth was velvety scarlet.

"Just cast," he said.

"Cast where?"

"So it lands upstream from that riffle." He pointed. "The current'll swing the lure slow this way. Float it nice up there over the big boy's snoot. See?"

"You make me nervous, Coach," she sparkled. She took a step forward. He moved over on the rock to give her room.

"After you cast, drift it natural — but keep your slack in. It's not yanking that sets the hook, remember. Only the wrist flick. Just tightening that line the split second you can see him touch, feel him touch. Go ahead."

"Okay, Coach."

The airborne line shot out rather well, she thought. It shot back to shoot again, farther, on lengthening trips with the darting fly. When it shot out far enough, she rocked her right wrist forward and sent the fly down upon the water. It hit with a little plip beyond the riffle, nearly where she aimed, and it came drifting over the deep smooth trough where the big fish lay.

"Jerk it!" Hank said sharply.

The fly popped from the water and swung in the air. She turned at him.

"I couldn't see anything! And you told me never to jerk!"

"Excuse me. I meant to pull the fly out of the way, a lightweight was headed for it. You hook on any other fish and roil this hole, see, it'll spook grandpop right out of the country. You were doing very good. Looks like this fly does good! Try it again."

"Poo."

Her next cast went too far sideward. It came down on a granite snag, slid off into water where a curl of current catching the line's slack sunk the fly under.

"Try fishing it wet," he said. "Keep bringing it slow this way. See if anything happens."

Shady water of the pool below its surface looked like wavy green-brown glass; the fly's fluff made a pale spot in

186

it. Floating through a leaf-green shaft of underwater light, the paleness turned a sudden white. It slanted down to olive green and a dim indigo. Then the fly went drab in overhanging shadow by rusty brown and porphyry red of watery stone. No fish came.

She brought the fly in; it broke from the water with a dabbling drip.

"I guess wet's no good," he said. With his thumb and forefinger he squeezed water from the fly, then blew on it raising and drying the fluff.

"That cast was no good," she said. "It was filthy."

"Cast again. Dry like that first time."

"You cast."

"You're fishing. Fishing great all afternoon."

"And you're itching. You're sweating. Take the rod, Coach."

"Tell you what. You make three casts, then I make three. Turn about. How's that?"

"Why three? Take a turn now."

"Go on, make your third."

"Stinker. Here goes nothing," she said.

The fly fell short of where she aimed, to the left of the riffle. It floated dry, almost unmoving at the edge of twinkling sun glints, then bobbled sidling in an eddy toward a backwash from the current's side.

It seemed to happen, she thought, in a slowness of time that made it dreamlike, magic in its clarity. A gray green ghost shaped like a great bullet came in a satiny glide. It bent into an ascending turn. It flashed a coppery red along a dark swirl that curved up smooth and slid away in a spatter of plash taking the fly.

An unbid small cry wavering from her throat tore away time's slowness. The rod wrenched at her. The line suddenly alive and whining from the reel was too hot for her

187

fingers to hold. She saw the fish jump crashing water. It flailed upstream through the rocky strait; she felt a hard hand grab the rod handle from her and she heard the reel jerk silent.

She heard herself scream when he plunged.

Appalled she looked down at him lurching cross-water, saw him grab, slip, flounder, spring splashing out with his wet hat crooked on his head, the rod held high yet in his hard hand and the yellow shine of the line slanting out through the air. Stunned she watched him trot then hop unpausing from stone to stone and go from sight around a turn of tall boulder upstream, leaving her alone.

"Dahhh-t —" she heard his voice. It came to her calling with a sound of infinite remoteness, "the *nehh-t!* The lann-ding net! Brrr-ing thuh nehhh-t!" It echoed.

She grabbed it and the awkward weight of the loaded creel from under the tree and she started. Caught at the stream's rough rock narrows she had to turn back and find her way up a steep sidehill slope away from the water. It took time: hurrying she stumbled. Low brush snagged the net, made her stop to untangle it. The creel got heavier, slapping damp and fishy against her legs. She scraped through a thicket, scrambled past a rock pile over the brow of the slope, and saw him.

He stood at the lip of the lake on a strip of sand and sedge grass, gripping the flyrod yet. It was bent in a wag-gling arc. Yellow line slanted out from it to bright blue water.

She was relieved, irked, wordlessly out of breath when she got to the softness of the sand where he stood.

"Hey gal," he said in a kind of acknowledgment over his shoulder. His voice was husky dry, his hat was still awry on his head. He was busy.

188

She dropped the net and creel, swallowed hard and made the sound of "Oh —"

The line had swerved. The fish jumped, with a silver splash and flash of red. It jumped again. It seemed to reach up high to stand on its tail and shake at the hook. Then it slashed into the froth, jerking line, more line.

"Whilikers!" she breathed out.

"When he was fresh — he danced a jig —" he said, working.

"Hank you're a madman, you're a lovely idiot —"

"Still got my hat!"

The rod bent hard; the line veered cutting water on a wide sideward swing; it payed out with spurts of clacking from the reel. The rod quivered and eased. Line came in noiseless, slow.

"You musta *nailed* him — on —" he said.

"I can't bee-*lieve* it!"

"Nobody will. Unless — we land him — this thing's a brute, oh he's a beauty, he's nailed on."

She watched his bent fingers and tendinous grimy thumb grip and bring line. Over on his right hand its skinned little finger hooked out pressing at the button on the automatic reel. The spool turned in silence. The waxy yellow silk came feeding in upon it.

"You going to do me a favor?" he asked.

"What favor?"

"Play your fish —" he glanced turning sideward to grin at her. She saw the blood smeared on his forehead, the clot caking thick in his eyebrow.

"You're hurt!"

"I'm laughing!"

"I've a handkerchief I'll —"

"I want you to take over your rod. Will you? While I

wipe my own eye. That's to see good — when you and me land him?"

She felt her heart pounding and her hands holding the heaviness at the end of the slender tremulant line. She payed it out when it yanked insisting, she earnestly inched it in when it eased, sometimes almost floaty.

"Champ," he said, standing close at her back, watching every movement she made in handling the taut weight of the line.

"It's — exciting," she said, really excited.

With a soggy bandana from his soggy pants pocket he wiped itchy caking blood from his eyelid — and he had to grab the rod.

At the end of its strength the fish made a frantic run. It nearly emptied the reel. The violence of the flurry spent the last of the fish's gameness. The heavy pull went sluggish, weakening.

"He's tuckered. Take the rod, Dorothy."

"Do I have to?"

"You ease him in now, see? I'll net him. I hope."

"God. Let me get this glove on —" Her hands shook. She clutched the rod again and took the line into her scraped, aching, damp-gloved fingers.

"He's about done."

"He's — he weighs — a ton —"

"Slow — slow. Just keep bringing him. He's coming — ease now! Now reel in. Good. Keee-p him coming. Some more —"

Yellow line ended: dark leader came from the water. It brought a shifting glimmer of vague red and shadowy silver.

"I can't bee-*lieve* —" Her throat went tight. Her right wrist felt numbed.

He crouched under the arc of the rod. His left hand waited for the leader. His right hand readied the net. His

190

eyes measured at the scoop and pull his arm must make.

"Dorothy. Listen what you do now —" his voice sounded scratchy — "you hold the line firm and you back away from the water and — raise your rod tip *up* —"

The fish saw him.

There was a breath-taking flap and swift splash — beyond reach —

"Oh Hank *Hank* —"

"*Okay!*" The line had already quit speeding, its tug had already slacked. "Again now. Exactly like you done. Backing off. Raising the rod. *Now* — while he's this tired —"

Hank Spurling's hands trembled too.

The fish came, hauled half sideward. It kept coming. The leader came — he got it, drew it in, whipped the net out and scooped quick. He fell stumbling back with the great bending gleam of the fish and he bellowed, "Hod *dam* YEE!"

Both her hands clamped to the rod, she looked down round-eyed at the fish and the man.

The fish's tail thrashed at the ground with a furious popping; it slithered shiny free, copper-sided, from the knocked net and the man grabbed. His fingers rammed clutching into the gills. The fish made a loud rasping *goo-ack,* squeezed. The man pulled a knife from his belt. He punched the knife point into the big broad dark slick speckled top of the fish's head. It jerked in a racking throe and went quiet. At the exact center of the gaped mouth the hook was still set, embedded tight around the hard bone of the mandible. Sticking out from it were raveled remains of the fly. The man cut it from the bone and then from the knot on the leader. He carefully returned the wrecked lure to its page in the fly book. "Some souvenir," he said. He grinned then, looking up at her. "You know what you just done?"

"Nearly wet my pants!"

191

"What you just done, Dorothy kid, was hook and bring to net the biggest rainbow trout I ever seen caught in these mountains."

She set down the rod. Her unsteady hand brought a cigarette from her pocket. She lit it unsteadily and pulled off her glove. "Broke three fingernails. Gave myself a trauma."

He got up with the sand sticking to his damp clothes. "Wish I knew how long we were fighting this booger. You didn't happen to look at your watch, did you?"

"Look at my watch! Don't be insane!"

"It was a battle. Jeez. Proud to know you, Champ."

"I nearly died. Will you please take off that droop-poop hat? I want to see your forehead." She took his chin in her hand. "You do smell fishy. Bend down. It's a mean scrape over your eye. Did you fall, Hank?"

"Clown act in the circus! Clobbering out of that water, trying to hold the rod up."

She dipped her handkerchief in the lake and dabbed cleaning his forehead and eyelid while he stood holding his hat in his hand.

"We were a riot," she said. "Hold still. Ought to have a Band-Aid, a big one. Ick. Dorothy Florence Nightingale. Let me finish. The Battle of the Fish. And we won. Father will suffer a no-fooling trauma. When he sees our whale. How you feel, Punkin?"

"Gitting well."

"Aren't you cold, in those clammy clothes?"

"Nearly dry. If you want to warm up, rassle a fish."

"Hawready done that, haven't we?"

"We could call it a day. A great day, if you ask me. You want to head for the horses?"

"Let's just grab a cab. And go for a belt at Jack's."

At the foot of steep granite and dark timber they walked along the lake's wild edge.

192

She carried the slender flyrod. He carried the creel and net and the noble trout slung on the fork of a willow. They went moving through the last of sunlight, with blue shade lengthening in the Indian summer air.

It wasn't anything to describe with words in his own mind, it was a feeling, not a thought. It seemed to him like having all the good for once, everything to care about, come all together. And be there actually. So that he was in the middle of it knowing now, without thinking, it was so vivid and he was so alive that he would not forget a thing about any of it, for as long as he would live. Walking along with Dorothy Haskett in the Cloudrocks.

He wanted so much to keep it going on, the way it was, without anybody else in it, that he said nothing when he spotted the two familiar riders moving like dark dots at the far inlet end of the lake.

"Hank —" She stopped to rest, a little out of breath. She pointed with the springy flyrod. "What could cause that? All those trees and things broken over there? I noticed it at lunch."

"It was a slide. Ava-lanche. Snow and rock both."

"Oh."

"Scared the bejiggers out of me."

"How do you mean?"

"I was up here —"

"You saw it?"

"I heard it and felt the shake. I saw the cloud it raised. I was down at Haven."

"When was that?"

"March, last March. The whole slope went. It was sunny, just enough temperature change, started the thing some way."

"What were you doing? Why were you up here in snow?"

"I came up. To see the old place."

"Isn't it terribly hard to ride in snow?"

"I walked up. Snowshoes."

"Oh stop. You walked? How many people were with you?"

"The afternoon of the slide, an old trapper came. Mr. Claunch, he's the one that built the cabin at Haven. You ought to meet Mr. Claunch sometime. You ought to see this up here in wintertime. It's different."

"Brr. Walking up. Lost in a Christmas card."

"When that slide broke loose I was fishing. Pulling a brookie out of a hole in the ice. You ever ski?"

"No. But it sounds rather better. Those big ribbed sweaters. *Fondue* or something by the fireside, those tanned attractive Austrians — look! There's Father and Ingo!"

"Yep."

"I want to see his face — when I show him our fish."

"He'll turn green."

"Pea-green. What is it he's doing now, over there?"

"Working that rod from horseback — hey, he's really going! See that shiny fish flap past old Hemlock's ear, right into the creel? The colonel'll be feeling sharp."

"I'm feeling fairly sharp myself."

They started walking again. The last of the warming sun left the lake.

"It's been a day, Dorothy. I won't forget it. I wish you'd decide to go with us. The real high country. Like to see you catch a golden. Not leave us. Not leave the mountains yet."

"Old Dot on a campfire kick. Ghastly, isn't it?"

They were waiting by their horses and they had the big fish rigged handily behind a log when Royston and Ingo Spurling came riding through the trees.

Dottie gave them a burlesqued curtsy. "Hello, darlings. Fight any windmills lately?"

Royston reined and looked down at his daughter, at her

194

scuffed round-toed brogans, her wrinkled breeches, her tight sweater, her smile. "Windmills?"

"Thought you were Don Quixote. Riding along with those whiskers and that fishing pole."

"Rod," Royston said. "Are you the Cheshire cat? What's she been up to, Hank? And — what've you been doing in the water — what'd you do to your forehead?"

"Fishing a little," Hank grinned.

Royston looked at Dottie again. "Catch anything? Hank'll probably catch cold —"

"We fished like mad," Dottie said.

"No doubt. No doubt," Royston said. "Wish you had been with us."

"Colonel's got a four-pounder there in the creel, Hank," Ingo said. "A fighting fool, up on the Longstick."

"How big's a four-pounder?" Dottie asked.

"You'll see," Royston said. "When we get back to camp. Shall we start moving?"

"One moment," Dottie said. "Hank must help me on."

She came back from behind the log. The great trout swayed on the willow fork. She had to use both her hands to grip it. "You like?" she asked.

"*Yow!*" yelped Ingo.

"Gad," Royston said, blinking. "Who caught that?"

"Why Daddy Boy!"

"Hank! You wretch! You *caught* that!"

"Listen, Colonel!" The gray eyes were the merriest Royston had ever seen them. "Dorothy hooked it! And then she brought it to net! It's the truth, so help me."

"I'm defeated," Royston said. His delight showed in his eyes, it seemed to make his gray whiskers stick out sharper. "I'm bleeding. I'm dying, little Dottie Egypt! Dammit, Ingo — what's the record rainbow for Wyoming?"

"Eighteen and a half pounds."

Royston was off his horse, he was hefting the trout. "Hold it, Hank. Let me get out my de-liar." He pulled the compact spring-scale from a pocket and they hooked the fish on.

"A shade over — thirteen —" Royston said peering, a little sorrowfully. "My dear daughter. I have been fly fishing for fifty years. Man and boy. I have never landed a mountain rainbow like this. *Blast* you!"

"I thought you'd look greener, darling, I really did."

"I'm green to the interior of the pericardium. Also — I suspect there's more to this damnable fish story, including the lump on Hank's head, than I've heard about!"

The colonel heard about it, with embellishments, nearly all the way to Haven Lake. Sunlight was gone from the high face of Chuckbox Mountain when the horseback fishermen came into camp.

"Fenny's not here yet, I thought he'd be here," Ingo said. "Hope he hasn't spilled a pack, or anything. We need that grub."

"I'm plain pooped," Dottie said. "Can't quite recall how a hot tub might feel."

"Let me bring you some warm water to your tent," Hank said. "Soon's I turn out the horses and get a fire stirred."

"I'll have the stove popping in no time," Ingo said. "And tarp these fish. Fenny must've got a late start. Should be here." Ingo shouldered the two creels and lifted the big fish. "You ought to get this giant mounted up pretty on a plaque. I believe we could save it good enough. Try anyway. Nobody's going to believe this one. Without seeing it."

The Roystons started toward the cove where their tents were pitched side by side under the firs.

"Like a large stuffed trout, Dot? Carry it around with you, from place to place." Royston grinned.

196

"It's all I need! I might possibly accept a drink. If offered."

"How about a martini? Preserved for a Cloudrock occasion. Ingo!" Royston called. "Any snow left up there at our rock hollow? Martini snow?"

"Might scrape up a little. *Hey!* Here comes Fenny!"

"The U. S. Mail!" Fenwick yelled. He came leading his two loaded pack horses down the path toward the cabin. "The Jughead Express!"

"Little Beaver!" Dottie waved.

Fenwick tossed the lead rope to Hank, and ambled over to where the Roystons stood in front of their tents.

"Hello Fen. You look cheerful," Royston said. "How are things on the lower levels?"

"Not so bad, Colonel. You going back down the hill with me tomorrow, Dot?"

"Can't really say. Yet. The Sahib hasn't spoken."

"Huh?" Fenwick scratched his head. "I already made your plane reservations and everything, at Junction, like you said. For day after tomorrow. September sixth."

"Shall we worry, Beaver Boy? You just got here!"

"I'm only worrying if I got to stay here. That's all. Anyway, I brought the water colors Flynn gave me. Some box, and all sable brushes. Say, Colonel, he wrote to you. Here. And I got a letter for you, Dot. San Francisco."

"Any more for me?" Royston asked.

"Nothing."

"Thank you, Fen. Will you remind them over at the cabin that some warm water and a few lumps of snow are requested?"

"Yes sir. Brought chicken for dinner tonight. Mom killed and dressed her fryers."

Royston got out his glasses and sat down on a log by his

tent. His daughter sat by him while they read their letters to themselves. Dottie finished her reading first.

"How's mad old Cosmo Flynn," she asked. "And Chicago. City of horrors."

"Flynn's fine, I guess. Voluble as usual. I don't know about Chicago."

"Mr. Flynn was a bird."

"He's an artist. He's started on my pictures, he says."

"That idiot knows a deadly lot of Shakespeare. When he's stone."

"Who'd you hear from, Dot?"

"Cynthia."

"I thought so. And how is she?"

"Up to form. Care to read?"

"Not unless you'd like me to."

"Why not?" She handed him the blue sheets of notepaper, the remembered handwriting.

Dorothy dear —

I heard where you are in a most curious way — I think you could keep me better informed! Hulette Bent from Chicago happened to be here. I hadn't seen him in such a long while, he is really much more charming, when he wants to be, than I recalled and I had him to lunch. He told me about Robert vacationing in Wyoming and that the company plane flew you out to join him — need I say I was rather amazed!! But you've always been a startling one. I'm sure you must be quite an event for your father at that mountain lodge or whatever it is where he "roughs it." I believe you are on "sacred ground" and I do hope it is fascinating for you. And I hope you do receive this. I want to persuade you to come on to San Francisco to be with me this fall. Your Aunt Crash is anxious for me to travel with her to see for herself how the house in Fiesole fared during the war and I have promised *Isabel I shall be in Taos but I am delaying all until I have some idea what your latest plan may be, now summer is done. Are the Fessendens back? Could Crash and I tempt you with a short junket to Paris and Rome — we learn that accommodations* can *be had! I do hope that you are not seeing any more of that awful Ricci Pineda. Ever. People who* know *say monstrous things about him. You know that. You know how much I wish you would alight with me here. You're showing preference, darling,* for your father. *Please telephone and say you are coming. Farewell now.*

Lovingly,
Cynthia

"Dial zero for operator," Royston said. He handed back the letter.

"I love that word 'alight.' Sounds so gay."

"This preference you're showing, Dot. I like it."

"Who is Hulette Bent?"

"He's Executive Vice-president, Royston Machine Corporation."

"Oh. Poor dear. He's in trade."

"Actively in trade." The furrow deepened between Royston's gray eyebrows. "And hardly a poor dear —"

Royston saw Hank coming. He was hurrying up the trail from the cabin, carrying a bucket.

"We got hot water," Hank said. "But no snow. That last little patch melted."

"I had a friend once," Dottie said. "Always ordered warm gin with a hair in it."

Royston frowned. "We can do without that."

"We'll have snow when we ride up-country. Plenty there," Hank smiled at Dottie.

"You haven't done a thing about the forehead," she said.

199

"Let's forget it."

"You hold everything. Where is that stuff, Father?"

"You borrowed it."

"Don't you let him escape." She went to her tent.

"Hank," Royston quietly said while she was gone, "I haven't made up my mind but I might leave with Dot. I hate to, but I might. I'll discuss it with Ingo later this evening —"

"Leave?"

Royston saw the unmistakable stricken look in the gray eyes.

Dottie stepped from her tent where she had been rummaging. "After the battle, Mother," she sparkled at Hank. Royston watched her dab mercurochrome and rather ineptly stick on a wide Band-Aid. "Now Coach," she said, "if I'm to be tidy for this air-cooled martini bit, how about pouring some of that hot water in the Good Angel's wash pan? Dressing for dinner — clean shirt, no less. One of Ernest's enormously outdoorsy scratchy jobs."

Robert Royston sat on the log in the luminous twilight. Huley Bent in San Francisco, Royston thought, Huley Bent at lunch with Cynthia — that last part, it was a very unlikely thing, it was downright peculiar. And it could be made to fit a picture. He looked down at the electric flash lantern, at the bright yellow label on the unopened bottle of ready-mix martini on the log. He wished to God it was a telephone. To talk to Mullins. But Bent would never swing it, Royston told himself. Impossible picture, it was a morbidly absurd picture —

He really did not know, sitting with himself there in the mountains, deciding to thrust the absurdity from his mind, whether he felt older, or more foolish, or more unhappy than he should. He knew he felt tired. He looked over at his daughter. In a tight undershirt her young back was firm and splendid, bent over the wash basin on the sawed stump. She was rinsing soap from her face with a wash cloth. She was singing.

"Da-da-da duh son of a gun again —"

The blue-note words carried Royston's mind out upon another kind of prowl, uncomfortably:

"He keeps telling me
That I'm the lucky one again.
But I still have that rain,
Still have those tears,
    And those rocks in my heart."

He gazed as she dried her face and arms, hung her towel on a tent rope, peered into a glass, patted powder on her face, singing to that face,

"Suppose I didn't stay,
    Ran away,
    Wouldn't play —"

She stopped, applying lipstick deftly.

"Duh day-dee duh potion he would brew.
He'd follow me around,
Build me up, tear me down,
Till I'd be so bewildered
I wouldn't know what to do —

"Shirt, and the jacket," she said. "Then I'm ready." She stepped into her tent.

When she came walking toward him, Royston said, "It's some song."

"Song? What song?"

"The one you were singing."

"Oh that."

"Hank ever heard it?"

"I haven't the slightest — why?"

"I hope he doesn't."

"Not the way I sing it!"

"The way you sing it."

"Don't be cunning, Doll."

"Sit down, Dot." When she was seated beside him he said, "Maybe you and I would be wise to go down that hill about tomorrow."

"Leave?"

The exact word startled Royston a little. He saw a roused, not a stricken look in the very dark blue eyes.

"For one thing," he said, "I have a notion it might be wise for me to get back. Been up here three weeks." Royston hesitated. "I have another notion. You're being unwise. Again. It seems to me."

"I must say I'm not digging you. At all."

"Hank Spurling. Not the most relaxed young man you'll meet. He's fought a war. He's had the luck to get back. Right now he has the even better luck to know where he belongs. It gives him a way to live, a way to think, a way to be. He's a mountain fellow. All he has, is up here. Don't you be thoughtless about yourself, Dot. Or about him. Don't amuse yourself that way."

"You're being damned odd. I haven't done anything."

"I know it. Nothing serious. That's why we ought to cut it off. He's a good man, here in his mountains. Let him stay that way."

"You're quite serious, aren't you? You're weird!" She rose to her feet.

"Dot. This thing I'm trying to talk to you about." Royston stood up to face her. "This goes way back. This goes way ahead. This goes way beyond any Hank Spurling now or

202

next week or next year. Take an example. Look at it. Look at yourself: ten days ago — just that recently — you were involved with an oily scrub by the name of Ricci Something. It was no good and you knew it. So you ran. God knows you should have! It was the thing to do. You got away. As always, you had a place to run. But Dot. You can't count on it. Some day you might have to stay, not run. Nobody there to pick up the pieces but you —"

"Hey Dot!" Fenwick came leading the unloaded pack horses, on his way to the horse pen. "Some fish! It's the prize money, down at the Cloudrock Bar!"

He and the horses disappeared through the trees. Royston and his daughter stood uncomfortably looking at each other in the growing dusk.

"Colonel," she said. "Aren't you playing this whole bit on the heavy side?"

"Mrs. Haskett —" Royston hesitated — "let me make you certain of this: I'm with you. And for you. Always have been."

"Do you say that to your Viennese friend? Miss Bren?"

Royston felt as if he had been punched in the face.

"Sermons give me the horrors," Dottie said in the silence. "The horrors."

"Yes. There are horrors. And we hold still, sooner or later. And look them in the face."

Dottie pulled the cigarette pack from her shirt pocket, put a cigarette in her lips, offered one to her father. He took it, struck a match, and they lit up.

"Back to civilization," she said, inhaling deep. "Tomorrow. Not bad. At least we won't be trapped. Wonder how the westbound is, from Cow Corners. The Paris and Rome kick. Could be worth a whirl."

"Well." Royston's thumbnail broke the plastic seal around

203

the martini bottle's screw cap. "It might be worth something, Dot, to drink a toast together. Before any decision is final. The two of us."

Fenwick Spurling could see them clink their tin cups as he went by on the dim path, his chores done. He headed through the twilight's blueness toward the faint yellow glow of the cabin's open door. A few steps from it, his ear caught an emphatic tone in his father's voice. Fenwick stopped to listen.

"— I said. You take care of a guest up here, you never take a chance with their safety at any time. They never see you lose your temper. They never hear you cuss. You never drink with any of them unless you're asked. Some will treat you like a friend. Some will treat you like a flunky. Regardless, you don't never forget that you are hired out to them. And a main thing, hell's fire, I've said it and taught it to my boys ever since I worked for that goddamned stud horse Plunk Blakely and seen some stuff around camps, *don't* get to mooning around and for Christ's sake don't *never* get to fooling around with a female dude while you are in the mountains, it's poison I —"

"Knock it off," another voice said. "I heard it. And I've never touched her. Knock it off."

Whistling the Marine Corps Hymn, softly, Fenwick stepped into the door.

"Fenny!" Fenwick saw his father's scowl. "Where's Colonel and that Dorothy?"

"Taking another toddy for the body, over there in front of their tents."

"Go tell them to come eat this fried chicken."

"Okay."

He decided to say nothing else. He caught a look in his brother's eye.

204

Forty paces from the Roystons' tents, fewer
paces from an open cookfire, the tarpaulin half-shelter
pitched by the shore of Sundog Lake at desolate nightfall
was a stout specimen of camp craft. It was rigged on
stubby green spruce poles, stayed by lash ropes from the

packs. The slant of the canvas was staked and fastened so that its high edge, and the open side of the shelter it made, faced a big protecting boulder. A hot campfire burned against this rock and, like the back wall of a hearth, it reflected the fire's heat into the space enclosed under the sloped canvas. Toward its back where the headroom lowered, bedrolls were thrown to furnish rests for backs tired by a long day of riding; a pack cover spread down as a floor cloth helped to insulate those backs from some of the frosty damp in the hard ground. A hissing Coleman lantern added brightness to the fire's light. Shifts of wind drifted occasional wreaths of smoke under the canvas, stinging the eyes, yet in the night's cold at timberline the shelter was a warm and welcome place to be.

Supper was over. Hank gathered the emptied plates into a stack and started with them for the dishpan, over by the coals of the cookfire. He asked, "More coffee, anybody?"

"Bring the pot over handy," Ingo called.

"You consider that we would be on top the divide in something like two hours of riding," Royston said.

"Just the two of us, with no pack horses to fool with, and no poking along," Ingo said. "From up on top, I figure it would take another couple of hours, maybe less, down to those lakes. Depends on how we find we can work that snowfield and the talus on the other side."

"Eight hours horseback, over and back," Royston said. "At least eight hours."

"Well," Ingo said, "say we rode out of camp no later than six o'clock tomorrow morning. Be at those lakes — if we can get there at all — by eleven. Wet a line. Leave there no later than two. Get back here, with luck, just about dark."

"Rough day."

Hank came with the coffeepot. "More joe," he said. He filled Dottie's cup first.

206

"Another thing is weather," Ingo said. "I don't know how it will be by morning. Better, I hope. We can't go if it's bad. That divide is a mean place, any kind of storm. That's why I say I'd rather have Dorothy in a comfortable camp and why I want to leave both boys to take care of her tomorrow. If the weather was good and stayed good — even so, it would make quite a one-day trip to give Dorothy. And if the weather went sour while we were up there — I've spent myself some miserable times, laying out. It's a kind of a chance —"

"Ditched," Dottie said. "As usual. Left in the lurch."

"Not so much of a lurch," Royston said. "The ride tomorrow is a genuine lurch."

"My day's all planned. I'll sit by the fire and spin. Spin my wheels."

"We'll be sitting here with you if this weather doesn't ease."

"Anybody for pinochle?"

"Damn it, tomorrow's got to be good!" said Royston. "If I can't make it over there tomorrow, this outfit has got to head back, down the hill for home!" He gave Dottie's knee a pat.

"I'm as anxious to find out about those goldens as you are," Ingo said.

"Say Dorothy," Hank said. "Tomorrow instead of sitting around, I could pack lunches and we could ride up this Basin to the face of Ezekiel Glacier."

"Haven't faced a nice glacier for years."

"This time of year you'll see old snow a peculiar pink. Snow algae. I was telling you about glissading. You could have some fun."

"No skis," Fenwick said, staring comfortably into the fire.

"How about you, Fen?" Royston said. "You haven't said a word since supper."

"I guess three's a crowd. Most any way you pitch it," Fenwick said faintly smiling.

Dottie smiled too. "Darling! You *are* with us! The pink glacier crowd."

A flaw of wind stirred the canvas overhead, veered smoke into the shelter. Hank quit frowning at his brother, got up, kicked the unburnt end of a big wood chunk into the flame and the smoke changed.

"Fenny," Ingo said, rolling a cigarette. "Old Ezekiel ought to be queer enough of a subject, that spooky ice up there. How about you painting us a picture tomorrow? Let's see how you can use that coloring box Flynn give you."

Fenwick grunted. "I might."

"And I'll hold brushes for you!" Dottie said. "May I? There's art in our family too —" She paused just long enough for her father to notice it, and then was sorry. "My sister Isabel is an authority. She really is."

"Putting a water-color wash on, I've had it freeze to ice. Little bitty crystals on the paper," Fenwick said.

Ingo lit his cigarette. "Last time I stood on the divide, was with Merlin Claunch. You was in Australia, Hank. You never seen the place Colonel and me named Hardway Pass, what we're going to try tomorrow. Jings, it's a world all its own, that far up. Nothing but bare rock and you, and the Lord — He's right close sometimes the way the lightning cracks up there!"

"You religious, Ingo?" Dottie asked.

"Well, Mrs. Spurling tends to that mostly. She's an expert. I belong to the round church, myself."

"Sounds rather special."

"It's round enough to keep the Devil from getting me cornered."

Dottie laughed. Royston and the Spurlings, all of them,

208

had heard it before. "How was it that you happened to meet Mrs. Spurling, Ingo?"

"I always say it was pickles that done it. We met over an old Cook-Ezy brine vat deal."

"Isn't that a frightfully complicated way to meet a girl?"

"Seemed real natural."

"Was it fun?"

"I thought it was. Miss Emma Rutherford. Her hair was almost identical the color of yours, Dorothy. But dressed a pompadour style, like they did. Kind of high, lots of it. November, 1919. That was before the flappers come in."

"Where was this?"

"Denver, Colorado. They had a song, raggity-time, the first war. How you gonna keep 'em down on a farm, after they've seen Paree? I knew what they meant. When I saw home, Lincoln County, Wisconsin. People there were still trying to raise a potato crop. I knew all about that. Ever since I was big enough to hold a hoe by the handle. To make a long story short, my mother had a brother in Denver named Barney O. Whetmer. At that time he was regional sales manager for Cook-Ezy Wares. He give me a job. I traveled the territory for Cook-Ezy from Fort Collins as far as Ogden — say, Colonel, that was where I picked up 'Mormon Town.' A hat and gloves drummer give me the words. One night on a U.P. accommodation coach out of Medicine Bow. I sang a fair baritone, those days.

"Anyway. I happened to be in Denver to hit Uncle Barney for a raise. He told me so flat-out I didn't need one, that he said he'd buy dinner. At the old Brown Palace. We were standing in the lobby and here comes a fellow name of Edgar Fink, a real good Cook-Ezy customer, he had Fink's Fine Pickle Products.

"Fink introduced his wife. Then he introduced his brother Will Fink and his wife. Then he introduced Mrs.

209

Will Fink's niece. They were from Kansas City, out visiting the Edgar Finks. Uncle Barney invited them to dinner with us. He was a card. He kind of put on a little, about me over in France in the trenches, and he says 'Miss Rutherford, this Ingo here's what I'd call my Wild Man of Barney O., He's Just Come to Town!' It kind of went from there, with a laugh. It's how we met."

Dottie lit a cigarette, smiling. "Was it hectic?"

"It was less than two weeks, she was going back to a business college in Kansas City. And I didn't seem to get across to the Finks. I never did, to their dying day. Em was an orphan. The Finks didn't have children, they raised her like their own.

"The day before she was leaving, I bought a ring. We showed it to the Finks. *Uhh!* Never was any woman ever, with more spunk than Em! So Uncle Barney, he drove Em and me in his seven-passenger Haynes up to Boulder and a Baptist preacher tied the knot. Uncle Barney was game, he give me the raise, bless his heart."

"Creepers," Fenwick said. "Mom and you eloped. I never knew that."

"You never listened, Fenny. I guess your mother's had a call for all the spunk she could find. That knot is still tied."

"Ingo," Royston said. "What did Barney O. Whetmer say when you quit your job?"

"He thought I was crazy. I told him, I said, 'A job like this is just like going on paying rent. At the end of twenty years you haven't got a thing!' And he says, 'You're quitting and you haven't got a thing now either, but a wife' and I says, 'I got a lot more'n you think, I got sense enough to enjoy life, it's the only one I got. I'm figuring to try a job at the Diamond Slash Ranch, for a Pennsylvania man named Plunkett Blakely, I sold Cook-Ezy to, the finest de luxe dude hunting and fishing lodge in the State of Wyo-

210

ming, governors and senators go there. Why,' I says, 'people like that pay to stay there and I'm gonna get paid for it!' And Uncle Barney says, 'You know about as much Wyoming country as a hog knows side saddle. Talk about a *dude* dude wrangler! Your brains are leaking, Ingo.' 'I been around,' I told him. 'I'll learn. I'm a natural born rimfire brass-trimmed salesman and I'm going to be selling the big Cloudrock Mountains. Which is some product!' That's what I told him. He just shook his head. It's true to say that I never did sell the Cloudrock Mountains yet. They sold me."

"What I'd like to hear," Dottie said, "is what Mrs. Spurling thought about it. What did she have to say?"

"Oh," Ingo said. "It took her a while, to get used to it."

Hank went out into the dark. He came back with wood for the fire. "Clouds breaking," he said. "Moon's showing."

"Ingo," Royston said, "that early turn-out is getting closer every minute. I'm going to bed."

"I'm going to freeze," Dottie said. "Goose bumps all over, thinking of that canvas cocoon I have to crawl into. Might I order late breakfast? Six o'clock sounds creepy."

"Tomorrow you take it easy," Royston said. "For a change. I want to say you've been grand. You're rugged, Dot!"

"Correction. Squalid is the word for Dottie. When I think of confronting an odd little item like a skirt. Or a hairdresser. When I fondly recall just a simple example of ordinary plumbing! The word is delirious."

"Well, this time next week, you'll be in Lake Forest."

"The age of miracles, darling. In more ways than one."

The Roystons got up to go to their tents.

"How about us fixing you a hot rock special, for your feet tonight," Hank said. "If you want one."

211

"I want one," Dottie said. "For more than my feet."

"We'll fix a rock for you too, Colonel. How about your drinking water over there?"

"Need some for tooth brushing. General health."

Ingo sent Fenwick with icy water he dipped from the lake; he was back and already half asleep snug in his mummy bag under the half-shelter by the time his father and brother had finished fixing the hot rocks.

They worked with gloves on, by the light of the lantern, wrapping two fire-heated stones with layers of old newspapers Ingo dug from the bottom of a box pannier by the dead cookfire. They fastened the papers on tight, binding them around with lengths of cords from the same pannier.

Holding a package toasty hot in each hand, Hank walked into the chilly dark beyond the dim clump of dwarf spruce. Moving glows of dulled light and slant-angled shapes of shadows showed through the fabric of Dottie's closed tent. Royston was standing out in the dark, looking at the sky, when Hank came.

"Set those on my sleeping bag," Royston said, holding back the tent flap. "I'll take Dot's over to her in a minute." When Hank had put down his load Royston said, "The sky looks like anything might happen."

"It's hard to tell. This time of year," Hank said.

"We waited too long, I think. To come up here."

They stood together for a moment.

The clouds raced revealing then hiding a moon that waxed toward full. Snow-veined peaks rising from inky blacks stood pale against the veiled sky's pallor. Glimmers of the moon's vagrant silver touched at the lake. From beyond, a roar of falls blended with a cold northern sound of wind. Near at hand, the two tents stirred, billowing taut then sagging, rustling in the unquiet air.

"Hank," Royston said.

212

"Yes sir."

"During my absence from camp all day tomorrow — if this weather allows — you and your brother will be here with my daughter. I am leaving her here in full confidence. You will take the proper care of her."

"Well Colonel? — Certainly. Don't you depend on that?"

"I depend on you. That's what I'm doing, in the circumstances. Good night, Hank. See you at breakfast."

"Good night sir."

Hank walked away, toward the fire by the shelter, wondering exactly what Royston meant. And knowing, knowing very well with a kind of discomfort — and a kind of less honest pique — what Royston meant. Talking like a colonel. There wasn't anything out of line, what Royston had actually said, Hank Spurling had to admit to himself, it was just goddamned unnecessary.

"In the morning," Ingo said, pulling off his other boot, "I want you to get the horses yourself. Fenny'll do all the dirty dishes. I'll stir up breakfast, make the lunches. If it does look stormy, I'm not going to take no chances with Colonel. I'll just get set to go, and we'll see. Sorry you can't be going up there, Hank, this time." Ingo turned off the lantern.

"So am I," Hank said.

The white glow went dead on the lantern's mantles. The fire's yellow light flickered. Overhead the tarpaulin murmured and moved in the wind's sound.

"You and me will scout those lakes right, next summer," Ingo said. "The two of us."

"This trip we are hired out, uh?"

"Yeah, Hank. Good night."

His eyes were still open when he heard his father begin to snore. Fenwick turned in his mummy bag, gritting his teeth in his sleep.

213

Then Hank's mind drifted with his body's weariness. He shifted his hip to ease the faint stitch at the old place in his side. He slept uneasily.

It was the place where the lodgepole pines grew so thick, the gray shade place where the sky was gone. It was troubled with something very bad and he knew it. Then he knew the very bad thing about it was not the timber slope on the way to Haven. It was gone. The skeleton logs fallen gray to the ground, the skeleton trunks standing straight to gray nothing were not lodgepoles because they were coconut trees. It was Pavuvu the beach beyond the tents where he sobbed. No. It was the Canal again, not Pavuvu. The coconut trees were wrecked and stripped by gunfire, they were ruined. He could feel the hot BAR heavy in his hands. Then a log began to move, he remembered it, Guadalcanal. It crawled shadowy, the long gray quiet jungle crocodile. It went slow right past his boondockers and he watched. But he did not shoot. He could not. From the long line of patterned leathery knots and bumps on the crocodile's back stared the big eye on the quaker tree. It was a terrible thing to see it there. It slipped into the glassy water and swam away. Then he saw all the ships in Sealark Channel, beyond the Point toward Savo. Out upon the water there were ships as far as the eye could see and they were leaving and he ran calling through the trees. His foot knocked the big rustly dead coconut palm leaf from where it carefully covered the little mound on the ground. It was Dinker Rackley's face with the maggots working white in the swollen purple and he ran from it calling to the ships that were leaving him —

"Hank —" it was his father's voice. His father's hand gripped his shoulder.

"Godamighty!" Hank felt the cold air, the sweat on his face.

214

"You all right?" his father asked.

"Godamighty is right —" Fenwick's sleep-dried voice said.

Hank could see his father, sitting up in his sack.

"Musta dreamed —" Hank said. "I wake you?"

"I was half awake." Ingo rustled around and lit a match. "Ten minutes to five."

Hank cleared his throat and spit toward the ashes of the fire. "Horse time," he said.

He shivered pulling on his boots. When he stepped stiff-kneed from the shelter he saw the morning star, the cold cloudless sky. "It's clear," he called. His teeth chattered. He pulled his cold hat tight to his head in the breeze.

He went afoot in the dawn light, swinging a halter rope. Half a mile around the lake's nearly treeless edge, he heard in the blur of sound from the waterfall a dim *clink-clat* of the bell on Big Agnes; he spotted the horses, dark shapes on a frost-pale slope of grass, in the alpine meadow above the inlet's bog.

He headed back to camp riding bareback on Dorothy's gentle sorrel, with wet hobbles slung over his shoulder, driving the other four saddle horses before him toward the twist of smoke climbing from the cookfire. Over the lake, above sheer walls of granite deep in shadow, sunlight hit the airy white pinnacle of Cloudrock Peak. A thin snow plume blew from it, then misted away.

By gnarled larches at the edge of camp he bridled then saddled all five mounts. Their grassy breaths smoked. He left them tied and, while his father and the colonel had their breakfast and day grew in the blue above, he hacked pitchy firewood from a lightning-blasted stump he found on the hill.

Sun spangles were dancing on glacial-green waters when the two horsemen stepped into their stirrups. They left with

215

a leather-cased flyrod and folded landing net, with saddle-bags that bulged, with raincoats tied behind their cantles; they waved as the two brothers watched them jog away in the sunny cold. They went from sight behind a granite jut smoothed and scoured by ancient ice, toward the bare stone steeps of the windy passage dubbed Hardway nearly two thousand feet higher into the pale sky.

Morning grew to mid-morning in a thin shine of sun.

The washed pots, pans, plates, utensils were stacked in a pannier propped near the fire. The pitchy stump was entirely demolished and hauled down to the woodpile near the shelter. The three saddled horses tied to the larches were drowsing on their feet, when Dottie in saggy blue balbriggan pajamas waved from in front of her tent. She called cheerfully for water both hot and cold. The flaps of the tent's entrance were pulled shut and she did not appear when Hank delivered the buckets.

She came at last to the cookfire looking clean, fresh, well groomed even in her camp-stained clothes. Her presence carried a liveliness into the air, and a hint of scent strange to the tang of woodsmoke at chilly timberline.

"Gentlemen." She sparkled it. "Don't look now but we must be orphans."

Hank smiled. "They got off all right. By now they're probably over the divide."

"Heavens. I slept like a little angel."

"Looking pert," Fenwick said.

"Feeling pert, Beaver Boy." She patted him on the cheek.

"Feeling like bacon and eggs with the hot cakes?" Hank asked, poking at the fire.

"The works. Tomato juice right away."

They cleared and cleaned a box pannier for her to sit on while she ate and they sat with her, attentively, drinking coffee by the pleasant fire.

216

"Seems terribly undisciplined not having a colonel around! Bristling orders —" She lit her after-breakfast cigarette. "I hope we're not well organized — I see those horses saddled. Are we really going to toot around today?"

"Thought we might look at the glacier," Hank said, puffing his pipe. "It's about an hour from here, up the Basin. It's something you ought to see."

"Are you going to paint today?" Dottie smiled at Fenwick.

"I don't know. I'm way out of practice. But I might."

"Might I watch?"

"Um. What'll you give me if I do?"

"Inspiration, darling!"

"Yeh. Natch."

"Fen," she said. "What if I asked you to paint something up here just for me?"

"You wouldn't go for it."

"You mean I'm that dull?"

"I mean nobody, but nobody, goes much for what I do."

"Suppose I commissioned you. To do me a picture. The glacier — sort of mountain thing. Sort of memento bit. I would buy it."

"Buy it? Are you kidding?"

"Perfectly serious! Though I don't know your prices."

"Crr-ipes, does anybody! I'd have to paint it first. See if it was any good."

"If you like it and I can afford it — may I have it? Or am I asking you to be crassly commercial? As my sister Isabel is fond of saying —"

"Heck with that. You really not kidding me?"

"Won't you come off it, please?"

"Okay."

"I said inspiration, didn't I? How am I doing?"

"How am *I* doing, is the question."

She sparkled at him. "It's in your lap, maestro."

"When do we start?"

"Big rush?" Hank asked. He looked frankly unhappy with the turn of conversation. "Ought to clean up this griddle and stuff before we go. Square away the camp." He knocked his pipe on his boot heel. "I haven't fixed no lunches yet, to take."

"See what I see, up there behind Mount Felix and the big peak?" Fenwick asked.

"Been watching. Quite a while," Hank said. "I didn't want to notice it out loud."

"What's that?" Dottie asked.

"Clouds."

"What time is it, Dot?"

"This says ten past eleven."

"What if Dot and me took off for the glacier, Hank? You could find us —"

"Darn right I could find you. Don't worry about that."

"I mean — if I gotta deal with a landscape."

"How long's this deal going to take?"

"I don't know what I'm going to paint, see? So I don't know how long. Maybe forever."

"That's fairly long."

Dottie seemed to be enjoying it.

"You're liable to end up painting the inside of a cloud," Hank said.

"Hey, not a bad title, 'Inside of a Cloud,' " Fenwick said. "Not bad. 'Ezekiel in a Storm.' "

"Sounds like the Bible."

"You ready, Dot?"

"I'd have to change to boots, and things. Must we speed?"

218

"Got my paints and stuff all set! You want a water color, I'm in the groove."

"Could you go ahead, Fen? Could you rough it in? Whatever artists do. Then we'll come along with sandwiches. Inspiration by the ton — I could pose in the foreground if you like! Ezekiel's Nymph — in longies. Too bad the day's not warmer!"

"Um," Fenwick said. "No fooling, that's a funny haze the whole sky is getting. Kinda sick."

"I don't like it," Hank said.

"Mood. Old Ezekiel in a storm."

"If it storms — you can't paint. You can't see anything. I know what I'm talking about, if it storms."

"I can remember," Fenwick said, pointing to his forehead.

"I've heard Flynn say that," Hank said.

"What's wrong with that?" Fenwick said.

"Nothing, I guess. The ar-teests."

Fenwick studied the snowy crown of Cloudrock Peak against the threatening clouds. He gazed out at the milkish green water of Sundog Lake. It looked like curdled metal not quite congealed in a gray stone bowl. He glanced up at the chalked sky, the wan disk of the sun. "Phooey," he said. "Why stall? I'm going up the Basin."

"I'm telling you it's no use if that crud socks in! This is September. Use your head! Why don't you sketch something around camp? At least till we see how this sky's going to act —"

"Because today I'm gonna paint the genuine Ezekiel, is why. Winsor Newton and glacier juice. Right out of the old icebox, gritty. It's gonna cost you, Dot!"

He walked over to the half-shelter and reappeared carrying his torn slicker, with his paint box, sketch block and water cup slung in a knotted flour sack. He stepped jauntily up the slope to his black horse, tied the gear on his saddle, untied the reins and jumped on. He felt the eyes watching him; he turned toward them and grinned. "Hey Dot! Don't you inspire Hank —" Still grinning he disappeared beyond the boulders.

"I may cut his throat," Hank said.

"Little Beaver. The ar-teest," Dottie said.

It seemed to Hank that she was gone a long while after she left the fire and went toward her tent.

He washed her breakfast dishes. He scraped and wiped the black iron griddle cleaner than it had been in some time. He could not make up his mind, when everything was stowed, to start the sandwiches for the trip to the glacier.

The two saddled horses by the larches shifted their weights often, stamping their hoofs. Their ears moved a good deal.

Dusky cloud reached across the sun's face. Its raying silver went quenched. A gust of wind brought, then carried away, the roar of the falls like a sound of surf.

In the presence of the rocks, the sway of fir, the shake of willow, in the hum and whuff of wind-blown fire he saw her come walking like a fate to where he stood.

Mists like coiling smoke swallowed the peaks as he walked with her and she with him tremble-handed to the enclosure of her tent. A pelting rain fell thrashing at the fabric that hid them from the lowered sky.

She lay ravished in the yoke of her throbbed flesh and he lay spent; he lifted his face to look down at her. She gazed up devoured, at the devouring gray eyes, at the slack lips no longer straight, smeared a raddled red with the whetted whet of her own bruised open mouth.

"I had to, Dorothy. I love you, love you."

"Love me oh lovely Hank, I'm ready, so ready, I'm always ready."

220

They lost the patter and sigh and drum of the long cold rain above them. They heard only their own heaved breaths, the cries caught in their own rutting throats, the joined hammers of their own scalding bloods.

Icy hail struck with a rattling seethe upon the fabric over their heads and they heard it.

He lay stretched on his back almost drowsed with the wanton press of her limp nakedness upon him, her tangled sweat-sweet curls against the side of his jaw, in a corner of his slaked mouth, when the hand gripped the tent flap and moved it. He saw it, beyond the blurred edge of her bare shoulder. Pinned, helpless, he saw the face poke inquiring into the tent's door.

It was the face of Merlin Claunch under a dark hat whitened with sleet.

Merlin Claunch saw.

A gruff rumble like an animal sound escaped the storm-burned lips.

"Huhh! Uh-Haven —"

Dottie jerked turning to see and screamed.

The face of Merlin Claunch disappeared. The tent flap went closed with a scrape as Dottie scrambled untangling her legs to twist herself around.

"My God!" She sat bolt upright in the cold air. "What — who, who was *that?*"

"Merlin Claunch —" Hank said.

"What's the son of a bitch doing here?"

"I don't know what the son of a bitch is doing here. I got to see. See about that." He sat up beside her, reaching out for his skivvies in the muddle of mixed clothes on her duffel bag.

Shivering, with her hands over her breasts, Dottie lay down. Hank pulled the covers up on her. He saw the tears welled in her eyes. "Will he tell anybody?" she said.

221

"I don't know," Hank said.

In a quietness, with the hail stopped, with his hands fumbling, with his mind numb, he got dressed. He shoved his hat down on his roughed hair, leaned over and said, "Kiss me." She kissed him, with her eyes closed. "I love you," he said. He got to his feet, dizzy. "You're my woman —"

"I better get dressed," she said.

He left her.

Merlin Claunch stood in the sleety mist. He had stirred the cookfire half to life; the wood was damp and smoking.

The dark figure of Merlin Claunch looked unreal, standing silent in the gray mist, in the spits of snow, in the wreathing gray smoke. His old horse, wet, unmoving, looked unreal.

Merlin Claunch had nothing to say when Hank came to the smoke at the cookfire. It burst into flame with one licking yellow tongue. Merlin Claunch held his hands out over it.

The silence became intolerable to Hank Spurling.

"I didn't — expect you. Up here." It sounded foolish, worse than silence.

The small dark eyes in the massive wrinkled face regarded him.

Hank Spurling did not know his mouth was smeared scarlet on his gray face.

"Your mother sent me," Merlin Claunch said.

"What for?"

"Whur's Ruston?"

"On a ride. Why?"

"Whur's Ingo?"

"With him, over the divide. Why?"

"Better be gitting back."

222

"They're getting back."

"When's that?"

"About dark."

"Yeh. Bad day, on the divide."

"It started better."

"This morning heerd the ring of winter in the air."

Merlin Claunch unbuttoned a pocket and pulled a wrinkled white envelope from it. "I hailed this camp when I come. Loud. Nobody give me no answer. See? I honed to locate Ruston. See? Give him this."

Hank took the envelope. It was sealed. On its face his mother's neat writing was blurred with damp. It said: Deliver to Col. R. K. Royston — Urgent.

"She sent you with this?"

"I said I'd come."

"How'd you find us?"

"Fuh. I trailed you."

The small dark bear-like eyes looked straight at Hank's red mouth. The bronzed wrinkled face squinted to deeper wrinkles and turned to glance at a misty shape of sleet-covered tent.

"Now I'm going," Merlin Claunch said.

"Going? Where?"

"Back."

"This weather? Hey Mr. Claunch? You — you aren't staying?"

He was already mounting his old horse. "Not here, I'm not. Good-bye, Haven."

Hank watched him ride away.

223

12

In the dark below them they saw the far yellow dots, the twin fires, pinpoint beacons of cheer. They rode toward that cheer, feeling occasional flakes of snow touch and melt on their faces. The ghost luster from the shrouded moon and the scatter of snow pale in crannies on the slope gave dim shapes to the ground along the descending way.

224

The two horsemen found it an interminable way, winding down, farther down, into a void. They dismounted to walk down broken turns, steep pitches of loose rock, then mounted to ride again; the hooves of the patient horses went on scraping bare stone with small sharp sounds in the hushed air. Out ahead the dots of yellow fire were like illusions. They seemed to come no closer.

Down a ravine, across a pocket of scree, beyond the foot of a looming granite jut, the horsemen reached the first trees, thin huddles of runt alpine fir with tracings of snow caught in their boughs. Then the hooves moved with less patience, to the edge of the lake's blackness, to a sound of water lapping and the roar of falls. Around a knoll scraggy with brush the fires were no longer illusions. Shouts were answered. Cold, tired and glad the benighted horsemen came to camp.

"Hey, goldens?" a voice greeted.

"You damn right, *goldens!*"

"Goldens and weather! Plenty!"

They got stiffly down from their saddles; flecks of fine sleet tumbled around them in the fire's glow.

"Dot, my girl!" Royston hugged her.

"Hank — Fenny!" Ingo gave them both a happy slap on the back. "Dorothy! That daddy of yours — had himself a ride!"

"You all right, Dot?" Royston grinned. He stamped his numbed feet walking toward the cookfire. He smelled its cheer in his watery nose.

"We were worried," Dottie said, unsmiling.

"I'll say now, so was I. For a while — that hellatious hail, snow, gale! God! Old Ingo looked a little peaked himself!"

"Folks, this camp looks just as welcome as the flowers in May. Yee!" Ingo said. "Got some supper?"

225

"Figured venison chops, trapper's potatoes — we were waiting —"

"I'll take over, Hank. Maybe the colonel'll dig into a few goldens! The creel on his saddle's full. Fenny'll give me a hand here, if you'll mind the horses — those two poor devils, you better give them the last of that grain. And when you turn them out you better drive them a ways into that box at the inlet. So they'll get with the rest of the string. This weather's —"

"Yeah," Hank said.

His father watched him walk away with the grain sack, to the two horses standing drooped at the edge of the dark.

Dottie watched him too.

Royston blew his nose. "Fen!" he called. "Where are you?"

"Right here," Fenwick said.

"How'd you like to save a couple of lives? Here's my flashlight. There's a box in the corner of my tent. In that box there's one last bottle, bless it. Demerara one hundred and fifty-one proof. The Admiralty's best. Bring it."

"Socko," Fenwick said.

"Run!" Ingo told him.

Four figures, all tired, sat together under the half-shelter's protection and faced the good fire.

Royston felt the fire and the fiery rum bring a surge of ardor to his mind. "Day of fulfillment," he smiled. "With the trickiest of fresh water game fishes, those lovely rascals. Let's drink to the golden trout. The ones up there all by themselves. Innocent of the angler's hook. Living in fish heaven. Here's to them — I have to believe, speaking of heaven, I might have been there today myself. I thought of it, that hour at noon, just before it began to storm. I was an intruder in paradise. That happiest uncrowded corner

226

of it — where the heavenly waters are teeming, and a dry fly fisherman has his reward." Royston sipped again at the ardurous fire in his cup. "About this paradise: it's even harder to get back from the place, than it is to get up there. I'll testify under oath the portals are formidable! If you want to know what a mountain is, go up and take a look at the savage place where a mountain touches the sky."

"It's what scares horses," Ingo grinned. "Me too. We were lucky today."

Royston poured more rum and turned to his daughter. "How did you get along down here all day? You haven't told me."

"Not badly," Dottie said. "I slept most of the morning. We had some weather here too — ugh, Fenwick darling, add me some water to cut this hellish booze. It's scorching the main brace."

"Making my boots smoke," Fenwick said. "It'd be something, for skiing. Wham."

"Did you get up to the big glacier?" Royston asked.

"Fen braved it. Made a water-color sort of thing up there. It's quite good."

"It is? May we see it?"

"Sure," Fenwick said. "Dottie's bought it."

"Well hurrah —" Royston's puzzlement showed slightly.

"You bought it?" Ingo shoved back his hat and scratched his head. "Can you tell what it is? Does it look like just a bunch of lines and dabs?"

"I like it. 'Ezekiel in a Storm.' Sort of memento bit. Of the Cloudrock Mountains."

"Dig it out of that sack, Fenny!" Ingo drained his cup. "Before I go over and put those goldens on the griddle."

The figure of Hank Spurling appeared suddenly before the half-shelter.

"All set, wrangler?" His father smiled up at him. "We got a art exhibit."

"Colonel —" Hank said.

He could feel Dottie's eyes. They were fastened upon him. He glanced at her face, golden, flawless in the firelight. But he had to look at Royston —

"I went to take care of those horses. Before I got a chance to tell you. A message came for you."

"What do you mean, message?"

"Word from Mother down at Silvertip. Mr. Claunch brought it."

"Claunch?" asked Ingo.

Royston said nothing.

Hank held out the envelope. "What he brought."

Royston took it.

Ingo got to his feet, peering at Hank. "Merlin? Where is he?"

"He went back."

"Back? This weather? Way up here?"

"He went back."

"I didn't know the old geezer came —" Fenwick said.

"You were painting, the glacier."

"What'd he *say?*" Ingo pursued it. "Did you see him, Dorothy?"

"I was at my tent. He had gone. When I came here to the fire."

Ingo shook his head. "Not like Merlin. What time, Hank?"

"Middle of the afternoon. About an hour before Fenny came in. It stormed so bad I kept Dorothy in camp all day. I asked Mr. Claunch to stay —" Hank felt Dottie's eyes. "I thought he would. But he left."

Royston had gotten his glasses from a pocket and he had put them on. The last time he had used them he had tied a

228

fly on a leader to take a golden trout: he thought of that, in his reluctance to deal with whatever it was he held now in his hand. He tore the envelope open. Then he shifted his position, holding the unfolded paper at an angle to see by the light from the fire. He read to himself.

Silvertip, Saturday Sept. 7, 9 A.M.
Mr. Richard Mullins in Chicago has been trying for two days to call you on the phone. I told him I do not know exactly when you or your daughter either are coming down. Mr. Mullins insisted that he must contact you. Then he had the aviator at Green Junction fly a message to Haven Lake but he reports there is no sign of anybody camped there. I have no way to know where Ingo has taken your party now. I told Mr. Mullins this. He seemed very upset not to reach you. I told him I would do the best I could. Mr. Mullins wants you to know there will be an emergency meeting of share holders 2 P.M. *Monday September 9 and you must get there. It is about a Mr. Vent a bid for stock control. I had Mr. Mullins repeat that. I wrote it down as he told me, so I could get it exact. I am asking Mr. Claunch, the only one I know to do it, to find you in the mountains. I hope you and everyone in camp are well and that I am doing right sending this information at Mr. Mullins's request.*
Emma Spurling
Mr. Claunch could guide
you back immediately if
you wish him to —

Royston looked up, looked around, conscious of the silence and of the inquiring eyes.

By some impulse which he did not understand, then or later, he reached over and with no word, no change of expression, dropped the message into the fire. The paper

229

flamed instantly. Everyone watched it burn. Then it was gone.

"Will someone give me the exact date?" Royston calmly asked. "The day I thought I intruded in paradise."

"Today's the eighth," Fenwick said. "It's Sunday. A week from tomorrow I'm in Laramie. I keep track."

"Thank you," Royston said, peering at the place in the fire where the paper had been.

All that was left of it was in Royston's skull. Not an ash but a wound, he thought. A wound that might be serious. Was serious.

His mind grappled with a kind of numbness. I suspected it, his mind said to him. And you wouldn't quite believe it.

"Colonel — something bad?"

"Something bad —" Royston repeated, to himself not Ingo.

That Hulette Bent, his mind said, shaping a kind of rage in the name. Foolish, helpless rage.

"What is it? Daddy Boy?"

"A business matter. It's technical."

"Oh."

He turned to look squarely at his daughter sitting beside him. "You and I should have gone down the hill last week."

"This was your idea," Dottie said. "To stay."

"I know. And here we are. I made a mistake in judgment."

Her eyes would not quite meet his.

Ingo cleared his throat. "We better get some supper on the plates. Fenny, we'll see that picture there later. I need you and Hank both. Come on."

"Wait a minute," Royston said. "Wait."

Ingo looked down at Royston's face. It was like a gray-stubbled stiff mask peering at a flickering fire.

The mask spoke. "If I took Hank and I left with him at

230

first light tomorrow morning. And we rode all the way down. What time would we make it to a telephone in Silvertip?"

Ingo's eyebrows raised. Furrows creased across his forehead while his mind compassed such a question. "Uh uh —" he said. "No, Colonel. That's a devil of a ride from here. Right after such a rough day today you —"

"I didn't ask whether I should make the ride. I asked how long it would take. Give me the information."

The Adam's apple bobbled in Ingo's throat. "Uhn —" he said. "Fourteen — maybe thirteen hours, pounding — in the saddle. Look here, Colonel. Let me carry a message. Let me go for you."

"It wouldn't do. No message. I have to go. Tomorrow morning, five o'clock, two horses. Hank — you'll take me down the mountain. As fast as I can get there. Which won't be fast enough."

"You may be bucking snow."

"I presume this is not the first time people named Spurling have dealt with snow."

The furrows were deep across Ingo Spurling's forehead. "I got to say it, Colonel, unless it's an emergency you —"

"It's an emergency."

"And *just* a moment!" Dottie said. "What about me?"

"You'll be with Ingo. And Fenwick. They'll have the pack string, and the gear. To make you a decent camp tomorrow evening at Haven Lake. You will be in Green Junction the next day. With me."

"Sorry. I'm going with Hank and you."

Royston turned his stiff face at her. "There are enough difficulties. Already." He kept his voice very even. "Don't make more difficulties. Please."

"But I'm not staying behind."

The stiff mask fell away. "You will god damned well do

231

exactly what I tell you to do! *For once in your life!* And you won't discuss it! Is that clear?"

Her eyes flashed wide open at him. "Fairly clear! And god damned rude."

The stiff mask returned to Royston's face. His eyes went weary, and peered into the fire. He said nothing.

Ingo nudged Hank. He gave Fenwick's sleeve a quick tug. The three Spurlings moved to the cookfire.

Dorothy Royston Haskett got to her feet. She hurled her tin cup at the fire. It hit the rock behind the flame and bounced back. A soft little blue glow of high-proof rum afire flickered in the cup on the dark ground, then died. "I'm *boffing* tired of your *boffing* mountains, Colonel Royston!" she said. "And we won't discuss that!" She left him.

He sat there.

Colonel Royston. R. K. Royston. Robert Kendall Royston, founder. Royston Machine Corporation. Home offices Chicago, Cable Address Roymac. He once found a promising young man named Hulette Bent. Quite promising. He set Hulette Bent's feet upon the rock and ordered his goings. Robert Kendall Royston did it.

Not only that. Among this same Robert Kendall Royston's splendid accomplishments he sired a brat. A female brat apparently incapable of avoiding oestrus even at timberline.

Royston poured a heavy drink of rum into his cup and drank its fire.

Not much else to do about any of it, at the moment. Not much. No communication.

He could query Demerara at the moment. He could write an executive memo one hundred and fifty-one proof. Write it in the convenient heavenly waters.

Fool.

232

Royston felt his mind slip down, down. It wallowed in its own welter.

Alarmed, his mind reached up. It groped for a comfort of unassailable fact, of incontrovertible figure.

There was indeed a good thirty percent of RMC stock still in his own name. There was the approximate thirty percent owned by the Trust endowment of the Royston Foundation. Cynthia had the ten he gave her, damn her. Bent had got five, damn him. And the public, the small holders, altogether must own about twenty-five percent of all RMC's corporate shares.

So what are you worrying about?

Rich Mullins is plenty worried. He's sounding frantic. He's there, on the ground. While you couldn't bring yourself to believe it. While you fished. For the transplanted Kern River *salmo agua bonita* to hell and gone in the Cloudrock Mountains of Wyoming. That's where you are now.

Royston poured his cup full of rum.

Meet Jason Royston. His golden quest. Fish not fleece.

Fish in your creel and rum on your chin. Egg all over your face.

Hulette Bent had clearly found himself some very important outside money.

Even so, regardless of how much money and from where, there were not enough shares available on any market to get Hulette Bent any control of the works —

The incredible bastard might actually have wangled or bought the voting power of Cynthia's stock. The real stab. Not any decisive stab, just the real stab. Lovely Cynthia Gleaves Royston. Another splendid accomplishment. A life's work.

But the decisive stab, if there was one. There was only a

single place to look. All those shares the Trust owned. That was the woodpile Hulette Bent must be trying to stack. And that was and always had been a domain of the donor Robert Kendall Royston.

By tacit consent the tacit domain — hell, the donor had never been challenged to count up his votes, like a worried girl counting days on a calendar!

He took a big gulp of fire, and coughed.

Tacit. There was a word. Very fine financial and industrial adjective. The tacit bearfight.

How about that tacit memo you were going to write?

It's an aphorism. Not out of Poor Richard. Not out of Demerara either. It's from a hook inside an ancient rib cage. The only connive that's objectionable is the connive that's not your own.

That's tacit enough.

That's how you fight bears.

That's what you forgot.

No.

You didn't forget it, you didn't.

You simply neglected it.

No. Change that.

You stupidly neglected it.

Former President Royston. Like hell. Don't get mawkish. Have a tot of rum in the circumstances that is not mawkish that is medicinal.

Not medicinal only miserable miserable that daughter of mine and that dumb tough-muscled mountain boy getting involved all wrong and all bad and all my self-deceiving fault among my true accomplishments of self deception —

He could not remember much about trying to swallow any broiled golden trout so dearly won it stuck dry in the throat dry like chewed-up paper all the signed proxies in Hulette Bent's faithless hand it was sorely dry as the gall

234

under the old yoke hard yoke of the world and the flesh and he could not remember much about the trial of going to his bed on the ground except that he did know of Ingo Spurling's worried face bending down round-eyed solemn at him. Don't worry so hard Ingo we are both old but I am the one that is worried you see I am an intruder in mountains the heavenly waters are the immortal ice and that was all he said because he could not remotely describe to Ingo or to anyone else the tilt in his skull before it whirled down in a veer with the rum to nothingness.

13

A leaden dawn seemed not to grow. It stayed faint and grim, as if neither light of day nor snow of winter could decide to arrive. It felt wrong, Hank Spurling thought, just to climb on a horse and leave now. Leave Dorothy asleep yet in her tent, not see her, just leave her. It felt

236

wrong to turn his back on the peaks, leaving them now, wrapped in murk. It felt wrong to leave a half-dismantled camp with its work not done, every piece of gear so familiar to gather and take care of, with his father and Fenny starting to pack the panniers, the cookfire burning yet, the horses saddled waiting for loads. Just to leave now, it felt unfinished. It felt, for some wrong reason there in the leaden light, like good-bye forever.

Hank Spurling left it with a stiff-faced horseman riding at his heels, like conscience.

In a misty cold the two riders climbed from sight of Sundog Lake. They made their way through a weathered shatter of mother rock above timberline, up the twisting of a savage alpine glen where a meltwater torrent rumbled unseen under a clutter of jag-edged talus slabs. At the head of a rotten snowfield, leading their horses up the last steep and slippery fifty yards, they topped out into the windy desolation of Moraine Pass, far above Ezekiel Basin. Beyond the pass's granite saddle a wilderness of rounded boulders, strewn down an enormous glacial gouge, sloped toward remote clumps of spear-pointed spruce.

They rode in a wind sound, in a shadowless gray light, down the barren groove along the broken shoulder of Rampart Mountain. Flurries of fine-grain snow slanted in the wind. The riders came again to timber and wound through maimed stands of lopsided whitebark pines.

They glimpsed Sky Lake, slate dull under the shrouded face of Anvil Peak. They skirted the tawny grass bogs of Little Meadows Basin forlorn in wreaths of moving mists. Along the treeless foot of the black Quill Bluffs, snow changed to coarse sleet; myriad furry pellets of white ice struck bouncing on carbon-black stone under the nervous hooves of the hurrying, tiring horses.

Where a dim trace leading from Haven Lake met a dimmer trace leading down Possibles Canyon, in a windless cove under the glower of a cliff at the lower end of Big Native Lake, Hank Spurling stopped his horse and looked around.

"What time is it?"

"Twenty minutes to one," Royston said.

Both their voices were hoarse. They had not spoken for nearly three hours in the windy cold.

Hollow-bellied, stiff in the knees, Hank got off his horse and stood on the ground. "I'm going to build you a fire. Get warm for a few minutes. That coffee and those sandwiches —"

Royston got off. "Twenty to three," he said, looking out across the wind-ruffled water. "Chicago time. They've started the meeting."

"Sir? What meeting?"

"Nothing."

When the fire began to burn, Royston stood over it with his shoulders sagging, entirely withdrawn to himself, gazing down at the flame. Hank got the thermos and cups and lunch sack from a saddlebag. The horses cropped hungrily at the tall yellowed grass. Their breaths smoked.

"You better eat something. Here —" Hank said. "Colonel."

"I'm not hungry." Royston eased himself down, close by the fire, and sat slumped. "I want some of that coffee and I hope it's hot."

It smoked but it was not very hot.

"My throat's sore," Royston said.

"I notice, you're getting hoarse." Hank bit a big bite from a cold venison sandwich. He had to chew hard.

"Son of a bitching ride," Royston said. "I wish I had Hemlock."

238

"He's gitting pretty old, Dad figured old Hemlock — he had a rough day yesterday."

"Christ. So did I."

"About Hemlock, we figured this sorrel of Dorothy's was fresher today. To give you a surer ride."

"I'm a damned sight older than Hemlock." Royston took more coffee, and coughed.

"We're not going to Haven," Hank said in the quiet.

"Why aren't we?"

"We're going a short cut from here. Possibles Canyon is rough as a cob, but we can save an hour, maybe more. Right down through Blue Gap, then straight to Silvertip and the phone. That is, unless you want to go by our house."

"A telephone is what I want." Royston frowned and straightened up. "And I want something else. What's left of that rum. The bottle is in my saddlebag. The on side. Will you get it?"

Hank went over and got it for him.

Royston took a swig from the bottle. It made him cough; it watered his bloodshot eyes. *"Wuh!"* He coughed again. "You want some? Before I kill it?"

"No thanks. It don't agree with me."

Royston looked at him. Then he tipped up the bottle and killed it. "Jesus!" he said. He shuddered. He wiped his whiskery chin with the back of his hand and abruptly flung away the empty bottle. It hit a rock. The broken pieces of brown glass and the bright red and blue label lay on the ground in a thin dusting of snow like salt.

Hank looked over at it.

"Don't bother," Royston said. "The next glacier will take care of it. Till then, leave it. Nice little monument. Where R. K. Royston, former president Royston Machine Corporation, had a drink."

Hank looked at the haggard face.

"Hank."

"Yes sir."

"Some good advice."

"Sir?"

"Some advice. Some information. Straight. Tomorrow evening my daughter Dorothy will be leaving the state of Wyoming. I am sorry she came. I am glad she is leaving. I am furthermore god damned anxious for you to forget she was ever here!"

Royston saw the jaw muscles bulge clamping, he saw the look in the gray eyes and he said, "You're not in a position to get sore at me at this point. I ask you to listen to what I say. Carefully.

"Listen. By early next week my daughter Dorothy will have conveniently forgotten that she ever set foot in these mountains except, possibly, for some truncated ramble in her own *chic* jargon to casually amuse a friend. If she has a friend. She has many acquaintances. She has two former husbands. One of them, a nice boy, prominent family, plenty of money, divorced my daughter Dorothy in a suit with very unpleasant charges, four years ago. A second husband was, when last heard from, a Chief Boatswain's Mate serving a third hitch in the United States Navy. As far as I have been able to discover, he picked up my daughter Dorothy in the crowded lobby of a San Francisco hotel hardly a month after her first divorce. She got another divorce last March in Nevada. Since then — for one thing, she's allowed the attentions of a raffish glamour boy who's not only a gigolo son of a bitch I think but a blackmailer to boot. I know about Dorothy. I worry about her. And I am speaking to you about her. She's my daughter. I protect her however I can — I always have. I always will. She does indeed have qualities. They are not, God knows, the kind

240

to stir illusions in a responsible man like yourself. They could spell nothing but trouble to you. Then sorrow. My daughter costs an appalling lot of money and she's been miserably spoiled. A spectacular drawing power as a female is no blessing, believe me, it's a blight, it's made her irresponsible to herself. To everybody else. And her tastes are getting — I'll call them damned gamy! I'll call them no damned good. You stick to your mountains. Consider your luck. I'm telling you now because I see it. Don't mess yourself up. That's friendly and that's straight advice." Royston's bloodshot eyes drilled straight, hard, close into Hank's sullen eyes.

Mere resentment, even anger, could not quite endure Royston's eyes: they probed at the guilt Hank Spurling harbored. He looked away, to escape the probe.

"Now —" Royston coughed hard. "Get me the hell *out* of your mountains."

They came through Blue Gap in a cold rain, down the severe canyon of the tumbling white water creek, under somber pines to the rocky turn and the opening out, to the foothills of sage, to the gray flat, to the mown hayfields and willows by the Freefolk River and a road. In stormy twilight they followed the twin tracks toward the straggle of houses and the main stem of the drab town. A few electric lights showed from gloomy windows. One automobile rattled by, headlamps lit, splashing mud from a puddle.

Royston's legs nearly refused to support him when he got from the saddle. He had to catch himself and lean for a moment, unsteadily, against one of the porchway's peeled log columns in front of Rodemacher's store.

"The joint's locked up," Hank said, tying the horses.

Royston tried to focus his eyes on his watch in the dim light. The hands seemed to say nearly seven.

"I'll go around back and stir up old Max," Hank said.

241

Royston stood alone, it seemed for a long while, hearing the rain, too bitterly tired to think where Rich Mullins might be now, what Rich Mullins might know now. Nine o'clock Chicago time. Then he heard the door behind him click unlocking and he heard Rodemacher's voice, "Yes *sir*, Colonel Royston!"

"Good evening," Royston said. "I want to use your phone." He stepped into the bright light inside, and squinted. "Hank. While I put in this call I want you to take those poor damned nags to your place and turn them out. Get my suitcase. Put it in the truck. Then come right back here. Ready to take me to Green Junction." Royston turned to Rodemacher and walked with him toward the back of the store.

Hank went out to the two horses in the rainy dusk.

His mother heard him opening the gate. She called to him. Then she came hurrying from the kitchen door, with an old coat hooding her head and shoulders, with a lighted flashlight in her hand.

"What in the world? Where are the others?"

"Hi." He let her kiss his cheek. "Brought Royston down."

"Where is he?"

"Rodemacher's. Telephoning."

She walked with him toward the saddle shed. "Are you all right, Haven?"

"Royston's not so good."

Hank uncinched his horse and pulled off the wet saddle and hot wet blanket.

"That Mr. Mullins called twice today. It's something that's serious I think, for Colonel."

"He's clammed up. Never did say what it was about. Just said he had to bust himself gitting down here. We left before six this morning. From Ezekiel Basin." He got the other saddle and the bridles off.

242

"I know you must be dead, son! Both of you. And it was storming — looked like snow!"

"It didn't settle down to really storm. Thank God. I'm going to grain these horses, poor devils."

Em walked with him to the barn, then the feed trough, holding the light for him to portion the oats.

"Fenwick and your father, and Mr. Claunch and that Mrs. Haskett — when will they get here?"

"Tomorrow I hope."

"I'm glad Mr. Claunch is there. To help your father pull camp."

Hank slapped his horse on the shoulder and started walking toward the house. Em came along, shining the light.

"Old Claunch isn't with them," Hank said.

"Did he come down with you?"

"Nope."

"Where is he?"

"Home, I guess. By now."

"Do you mean he didn't stay, or offer to bring Colonel back?"

They went in the kitchen door.

"He brought your letter. Then he left."

"You asked him to stay and share the camp, didn't you?"

"Naturally."

"Haven, he carried that message as a favor. I don't understand why he didn't stay with you, this weather. He's such a strange old man. When did he find you?"

"Yesterday afternoon at Sundog Lake — look, I got to get Royston's suitcase. And take him to Junction."

"Junction? When?"

"Right now."

"I think that's awful. You look worn out!"

"You ought to see Royston."

243

"You're so tired your hands are trembly. Can't you rest a while? You want some coffee?"

"Royston's down there waiting. Is the truck okay?"

"Why don't I go with you? See if I can get Colonel to have some supper with us and spend the night here and get some rest. He could use your room —"

"I'll ask him myself — no use dragging you over there. I think he's lining up to go to Junction anyway. He's got something eating at him. He's on the prod. Let's get that suitcase."

Hank carried it out to the truck; his mother walked with him, worried.

"Haven. I'm praying things are all right. Those up in the mountains too. When you get back here, there'll be something good and hot for you to eat. I hope you'll just bring Colonel."

"Don't plan a thing until I show. And don't expect me until you see me."

When he pulled up in front of the porchway, he could see Royston waiting inside near the door. Max Rodemacher had brought him a cup of coffee. Royston saw the truck arrive; he put down the cup, thanked Rodemacher and came out the door.

"Head for Junction," Royston said. "Let's get there."

They left Silvertip with the headlights probing the rainy dark along the gravel road.

"I guess you got your phone call made," Hank finally said.

"To the contrary." Royston had to raise his voice in the rattling noise. "I didn't locate my man. Left word with the operator. To call me at that tourist court. Suppose I can't get a room there?"

"You ought to. Summer season's about gone."

"This morning I'd say it was completely gone —" Royston coughed and threw away his cigarette. "Damned things taste like hay." He coughed again.

The old windshield wiper worked by hand; Hank had to slow up and waggle the blade often. Braced on the jolting seat, Royston sank into a lurching, groggy tedium. The two riders finished their hard ride from Sundog Lake too tired and too preoccupied to hunt merely for things they might say.

It was still raining when they stopped under a poison glare of green neon at the Fontenelle Motor Court.

In the office the stout woman behind the desk clucked and declared she could hardly believe it was Mr. R. K. Royston.

"It is," he said. "Unfortunately. You have a room?"

"We do."

"Does it have a phone?"

"None of our rooms have a phone. The pay telephone's right there —" she pointed.

"Have you had a call for me this evening?"

"No indeedy. I'm remembering now — wasn't your daughter with you in the mountains? Such a fashionable-looking girl, and those airplane pilots and that man with red whiskers. They had a gay time! Is your daughter with you, Mr. Royston?"

"No," Royston said. "May I tell you that I'm expecting the long distance operator to call me here?"

"Hope we hear the phone. Where is your daughter now, Mr. Royston?"

Royston looked at her, wearily. "My daughter will be here tomorrow, I presume. Meanwhile —" he said. There was a distinct edge to his hoarse voice. "Meanwhile —" He reached into a hip pocket, brought out a billfold, took from it a twenty-dollar bill. "This," he said, fixing his eyes on the stout woman's big face, "is a tip. Your tip, madam. Might it help you hear the telephone ring? Do you suppose you might find someone to render me a little help this evening? To run an errand or to call me promptly to your phone? Do you suppose that might be arranged?"

The stout woman picked up the money. "Well now *Mister* Royston. We certainly will take care of you."

"Thank you," Royston said.

"Thank *you*," she said. "Now what was it special you wanted, sir? I'll get my nephew."

"Colonel," Hank said. He was frowning. "I'm standing by. Right here. That's what I'm for — to help."

"All right. Tell you what you do now. Go bring in that bag from the truck. The next thing you can do for me is to get in that truck. Drive home. Get yourself something to eat. Get in your own bed. And sleep. You're dead on your feet. So am I, so don't argue with me. I also want you to accept my thanks for getting me here, all this way. Now do as I say. You hear?"

"I'm not that tired, Colonel."

"Good night, Hank."

"What about tomorrow?"

"I'm afraid we'll live to see it."

"Is that right?" Hank said, still frowning.

He brought in the suitcase and set it down by the door.

"Hank — in the morning I'll call your mother at the store. Do something else for me. Have your mother get my bill all ready, so she can tell me, everything I owe you people for the trip. Another thing. When Ingo shows up tomorrow you tell him I want him to put Dot in that truck and I want *him* to drive her over here. She'll catch a plane with me." Royston turned away and started toward the pay telephone. "Good night, Hank. You remember what I told you."

246

Moving along the rainy road in the dark, Hank Spurling's mind moved on a treadmill. It belabored him, it asked him to think. And his mind took him nowhere, over and over again.

Dorothy.

Royston knew about it. I didn't tell him. Dorothy didn't tell him. But the old bird knew it, plain. He guessed it. And that speech at noon today, what he said about Dorothy. The stuff he was hinting about her. It couldn't be true. Well, it's his own daughter he is talking about. Suppose it is true —

His mind found something new on the treadmill.

The old fat dame Borchers at the Fontenelle. Talking about a gay time. With those pilots. With Flynn. Gay time was what she said. The hell with Flynn. The hell with those pilots. Dorothy wouldn't do anything like that.

Her father is lying about her, some. At least, some. He is trying to scare me off. He is trying to knock me off, I'm not good enough. Not one of those nice boys, prominent family, plenty of money. Not a big-mouth bull boatswain neither. Not a gigolo son of a bitch for sure, I wonder what it is exactly a gigolo does. With a woman.

Suppose some of it is true. Okay, even supposing it is all true. Suppose that. Suppose she has been around. Okay, what difference does it make? She is only perfect, that is all. And besides, this is different, this time, all different. I love her. She loves me, I have to think she must love me. She is leaving tomorrow —

The treadmill took his mind nowhere.

His mother was waiting by the door when he walked into the kitchen. He saw she had been reading Scripture; her opened Bible lay on the checkered oilcloth. She had set a place for him at the table.

"Here's some coffee, son," she said, pouring him a cup. "I wish you had persuaded Colonel to stay with us to-night."

"He had to get to Junction."

"I know you're just dead — you'll feel better with some supper. I'll have it on your plate in no time!"

"I'm not too hungry."

"Why, what's the matter? I thought you'd be starving."

"Right now I'd rather sleep than eat."

"You have to eat something. Here —" she put his plate before him.

"I'm bushed," he said.

"I worry about that old wound. Do you feel well, Haven? You never tell me."

"I told you. I'm bushed." He started eating.

"Did Colonel get in touch with Mr. Mullins?"

"No. He was trying, when I left the Fontenelle. He give that old lady Borchers a twenty-dollar bill for a tip, to call him to the phone."

"It must be that important —"

"Speaking of the do re mi, he wants you to have his bill all figured when he calls you in the morning."

"I'll get it ready, first thing. We do need that money, Haven."

"Royston's lousy with it."

"We don't know a more generous or a less stuck-up rich man. You mustn't talk as if you covet. It's not like you," she said. "Tell me, did that Mrs. Haskett get along all right in the mountains?"

"She got along okay."

"Fenwick said she was, when he came down. I made her a reservation with the airline, and I expected Fenwick to bring her back the next day. Then they didn't get here. What happened?"

248

"She decided to stay. And we kept Fenny to help, packing to the high country."

"Mrs. Haskett must have enjoyed herself. Staying so long."

"You know what? She caught the biggest rainbow I ever seen caught. Weighed thirteen pounds."

"She certainly didn't look like an outdoor woman to me."

"She did fine."

"Is that so?"

"Turned out very good."

"Well. I'm glad I was mistaken. I'm glad she wasn't any trouble. Up there in a men's camp."

"A gal like that, she has lived a different kind of life, different places, from what we have." Hank felt his mother's eyes. He put down his napkin, pushed back his chair from the table. "I hope you don't mind if I knock off about now. I guess I'm beat. I've got to fold."

"I want you to go to bed. You're exhausted. Hunting opens Monday and I haven't had a chance to tell you that those three men from Oklahoma are coming. Arriving Junction Sunday afternoon."

Hank got up from the table feeling a kink of pain dull in his side. "What a life," he said.

It was in a tone of voice his mother noticed.

He started toward his room.

"Son —"

"What?"

"I won't wake you in the morning. I want you to sleep."

"I'll sleep, don't worry."

"When you do get up I hope you'll feel like driving over to the Longstick to see if Mr. Claunch is all right. And to thank him again. It's on my mind. I can't think why he didn't ride in here on his way back, and let me know he found you."

"I'm going to ride up the ridge tomorrow morning."

"You are? Why?"

"Help Dad bring the outfit down." He walked away, to his room.

14

He was worried. It was long past noon and it
was snowing harder. Then the feeling of relief flooded into
him. A sound came first, a vague snow-muffled trampling,
a scrape of a pack against a tree, a faint pop of a broken

251

branch. In the swirl of snowflakes up the slope, his eyes found the flicks of movement he watched for: the outfit came, down the dimmed mazes through the lodgepole pines.

Fenwick rode the lead, sitting slumped in the saddle. Close behind him the pack string jounced in a motley file unroped and loose on the trail. Ingo followed, wearing a stained yellow slicker, swinging the knot end of a halter rope in his hand. At an interval behind Ingo the color of Dottie Haskett's jacket and old Hemlock's bay hide showed coming through the timber.

Halted by the side of the trail, watching, Hank thought Dorothy, Dorothy now, now I will be with you Dorothy. For a while now Dorothy. Her name itself allured his mind.

Fenwick's sagged straw hat was caked with snow. His voice sounded sharply clear in the snow's silence. "Don't tell me it's the Horse Marine," he said, riding by. The pack string came crowding him as if pursued by the big wet snowflakes thick in the air.

Ingo pulled out of the trail, stopped, peered at Hank.

He's got it in his mind too, Hank thought, he knows —

"What about Colonel?" The lines were deep in Ingo's tired face. "Trouble?"

Hank did not answer his father. "Hi there, Dorothy!" Hank said smiling.

"Don't hand me any jolly bit," she said. She brusquely rode by.

Hank's smile died. He stared at the back of her jacket, the back of her hat moving down the slope.

"You wait a minute, Hank," said his father. "I asked you. About Royston."

Hank pulled his eyes from downtrail, he tried to pull his mind back.

"He took off."

252

"What I want to know was he okay? Did he do all right?"

"He made the ride. On the prod. What about her?" Hank pointed, scowling.

"Yeah. What about her?"

"I was asking."

"And I already told you, Hank! A hell of a long time ago. So you figure it out — you ought to be able."

"Okay. I'll figure it out. You skip it."

"It'd be something to skip. I'll tell you something else, if you want to know. I'll be god *damned* glad to get the — the smart set — out of here." Ingo's roused eyes turned to glance downtrail. "And that god *damned* Pavuvu bronc you bought ain't worth cutting up for bear bait —" Ingo vented some of his feeling with a jab of his spurs.

Unmoving Hank watched his father jerk his horse plunging down through the trees to chouse the stragglers from the pack string, watched him use the knot end of a wet rope to whack at the lumbering Pavuvu's rump, watched him ride herding the file down, down beyond a tangle of deadfall. Then Hank was all alone again.

The gaunt boles of the pines stood in the quiet queerly witched with the snow of another winter gathering white at their gray feet.

Hank moved. He followed the niggardly small comfort of dirt-spattered horse tracks in the snow down the slope where Dorothy had gone. It was like a reprieve when she finally deigned to look back, to notice he was there.

"Go on moping," she said.

He closed the distance between them. "What'd you say?"

"You're reading me, Gus."

"I don't get it, Dorothy."

"You better get it. You left me. Do you get that?"

"You mean yesterday?"

253

"You hadn't the courtesy to wake me."

She did not look quite as perfect as usual, he thought. "That ride wasn't one for you to try. It was a tough one."

"Don't go into any jazz. You deserted me. Where's Father?"

"He's flying to Cheyenne. I guess."

"How nice of him. The dog."

Hank did not answer.

The horses worked through the tangled timber at the steep foot of the lodgepole slope. They came out upon a narrow spine of whitened ridge.

As if the morbid air presented the audible sound to match his morbid thought, noise drifted down in the snow's stillness, into Hank Spurling's bitter gloom. He looked up, with nothing to see but white flakes tumbling from dull gray. The noise went over, toward the peaks, throbbing, dimming.

"Took off without me," said Dorothy. "The jerks!"

"Four-engine job," Hank said, to be saying something to her. "Maybe from Salt Lake."

"Four engines and a cushion seat. That's for me, Gus."

"Too bad." There was an edge to his voice.

"In the pig's eye, too bad. What do you mean?"

It was a different Dorothy, not the real Dorothy, not the Dorothy in his mind, going away forever, already gone somehow, this cruel Dorothy. "I mean," Hank Spurling had to say to her now, "you taking off is too bad. Leaving Wyoming. Leaving —"

"Don't dazzle me. All caked with virgin snow. Leaving Wyoming! Has it come to that?"

"You're making it real tough."

"I must say you're making it easier."

They rode down, farther down, in the silence.

"Dorothy," he said to the back of her jacket.

254

"Dorothy here. God knows."

"I was going to say. When I came to meet you. We don't have to tail this pack outfit. I could show you down the hill. If you want to ride faster. Get to the house quicker."

"Why haven't you said so?"

"I didn't have a chance is why."

"Dear man, when do we start?"

"When you poke Hemlock." Hank gigged his horse and pulled out from the trail.

They rode down abreast of Ingo and Hank called, "We're going on — chopchop — to the house —" Ingo made a wave-off motion downtrail; they did not hear what he said. Fenwick whistled at them as they trotted out ahead, toward the aspens.

In the pallid light on the cloud-gripped ridge the aspens were a strange glory. Down twisting pitches of wooded slope blanched with snow, the horses' hooves stirred and trampled fallen leaves a color of fire.

Ashy sage smelled pungent in the wet and the ground was the brown of earth when he stopped to wait for her by the cairn at the foot of Quaker Ridge.

"Fast enough for you?" he asked.

"O my aching keester," she said, halting her horse by the cairn. "This is where we came in, I do declare. Small world, isn't it?"

"And two weeks is a long time."

"Isn't it?"

She turned in her saddle. For a moment she gazed up at the topless wall of mist that hid the Cloudrock Mountains. Still gazing up, she thumbed her nose. "That's *that*. Now," she said, "get me out of here. Dottie's been to your mountains. She's hawready done that."

He thought of nothing to say. Nothing that would help.

They crossed the Plew, they came across the haying field.

255

The truck stood empty, wet in the rain at the feed yard gate. Em Spurling did not appear.

"Ah me," Dottie said, dismounting in mud by the saddle shed. She dropped the reins from her hand. "You oaf," she said to Hemlock. "I can't say I'm sorry to lose touch with you." She pulled off her soggy gloves. For herself she untied her veteran leather handbag and took it, wet and battered, from the pommel of her saddle. "I suppose I might go into the house and flush the john. For excitement," she said.

Hank unsaddled, wondering what his mother and Dorothy might be saying to each other in the house. He racked the saddles, turned the horses out the pasture gate and with reluctance started for the kitchen door. He found no one when he walked in; he saw the note face up on the kitchen table.

> *Noon. Ingo: I'm walking so you will have the truck for Mrs. Haskett. Bring her by the store. Col. R. left word for her. Glad you are home!!!*

He heard footsteps in the silent house; Dottie appeared. "Civilization exists," she said. Then she noticed the paper he held in his hand. "I couldn't help seeing that," she said, "when I came in. So I read it."

"You want me to drive you over to town? I could fix you a little coffee here, it's on the stove. Or maybe you'd like to change your clothes or something. Whatever you say." An awkwardness, a hollowness possessed him, standing there by a kitchen stove, trying to say something, or not say something, to this Dorothy who had already left him. "You want to bathe or anything, I could light the hot water heater," he said.

"Oh stop. Let's have that word, whatever it is, from dear

256

Colonel R. The sooner the better, if you don't mind, and if you would please wag out my luggage I left here and speed me toward that airfield."

He loaded her bags in a corner of the truck bed next to the cab and covered them with a tarpaulin to keep the rain off. Standing on the truck, looking toward the mountains he could see the pack string moving down the foot of Quaker Ridge under the mist.

She was in the truck with him and he had the engine started when she said, "Oh hell I've left my handbag! I can't abandon the damned thing yet. The relic. The saddle-horn companion. It's in the bathroom." He went and got it and brought it to her. For the last time. Then she sat beside him on the old cab seat and they jolted along the muddy ruts the gray mile to Silvertip.

At the store Em Spurling's greeting was carefully cordial. "And where are Ingo and Fenwick?" she asked glancing at the porchway outside.

"Coming down the ridge," Hank said. "It was snowing up there, I brought Dorothy in. Ahead of the outfit."

"Oh," Em said.

Studying her son, she thought he looked very business-like. Mrs. Haskett looked a little distraught, not lustrous at all, in those soiled clothes, she looked as if she had been living by a campfire for a long time. And she was certainly not shining her eyes, that foolishness, on Haven now.

"You've had such a trip, Mrs. Haskett, and stormy weather too," Em said with less careful cordiality. "I wanted to tell you about your father, he called me on the phone this morning. He left word for you."

"I have word for him. I'm furious, the way he simply took off." Mrs. Haskett's scarlet mouth gave a small smile. "Like a goosed goose. And I'm out of cigarettes. Since yesterday. May I have Camels please?"

"Right over here. Your father wanted me to be sure and explain why he had to leave this morning," Em said.

"Could I have matches too?"

Hank pulled a match from his pocket, struck it with his thumbnail and held a light for her.

"He finally got in touch with Mr. Mullins," Em tried to go on.

Mrs. Haskett inhaled smoke deeply. "Who's Mr. Mullins?"

"Why, he's in business with your father in Chicago. He talked to him long distance. Your father thought it was very important. He wanted to wait for you, so you could fly home together, and then he had to leave without you."

"An ugly moment for him, I'm sure."

"One reason, the airlines man told him this storm threw the schedules off and the plane for the East might not be landing at Junction this evening, the field was closing in, he said —"

"Delightful news," Mrs. Haskett said.

"Another reason was, Colonel said he thought he was beginning to take down sick. He thought he must try to get home before he got worse. I'm worried about him. He was hiring that flyer at Junction. To take him to Cheyenne. He hoped to make a connection for Chicago and be home tonight by midnight. He sounded distressed to me. He had just about lost his voice."

"It would distress Father no end. Losing his voice."

"He wasn't forgetting to do things for you, mam. When you get to Junction you'll have a nice room at the Fontenelle. It's all taken care of, paid. He made you a reservation on the plane, when it comes in. He asked me to tell you he's left you a personal check in case you need it. The man at the airline desk has it and can cash it for you when you get there. And when you land in Denver you are to wire

258

Ernest. Let him know your flight and arrival time so there will be a car to meet you. I think that's everything. We will ship all your camp things with Colonel's, to Lake Forest. Unless you'd need to take anything along now."

"What I need is a bath. And soon!" Mrs. Haskett said. She smiled suddenly and pleasantly. "You really have been very kind. Thank you for all —" It startled Em; Mrs. Haskett's extended hand seemed even more startling. Em shook it — she saw Max Rodemacher and old Bill Clancy still standing by, waiting to speak to the colonel's daughter.

"You remember Mr. Rodemacher here and Mr. Clancy —" Em said.

"Well hello Miss Royston," Max said. "How did you find the Cloudrocks, mam?"

"Cloudy and rocky," she said.

"They git that way," said old Bill Clancy.

Starting toward the door Em found a chance to speak to her son.

"Our check from Colonel, he's left it with Mrs. Borchers."

"I'll get it."

"Get home early as you can. We'll save supper for you."

He heard Dorothy laughing now. At something old Clancy had said. Laughing again.

"— Inquire about her plane soon as you get there. Hope you can get her settled and come right back — oh, and something you'll be pleased about, Mr. Claunch came by, Haven. Rode in with his grub list. He's fine."

Hank turned to glance at his mother's face. "What'd he have to say?"

"I don't know a soul that says less. Do you? I did ask why he wouldn't share your camp. He just grumped, the way he does, and said he honed to kill meat on his way home —"

"— Why Mister Claaancy!" Dottie was saying, coming through the doorway. "That is not the way *I* heerd it! Ingo sings it —

Although she knows her book,
She's got that *meet*-me-later look,
That little Mormon down in Mormon Town —"

"*Good* heavens —" Em said.

"You ready?" Hank called, frowning, opening the truck's squeaky door in the rain. "Shall we go?"

It was the same road, every twist and turn of it.

And it was Dorothy again. The unaccountable Dorothy, all of a sudden the Dorothy he knew. Sitting there beside him, real. Not already gone at all. Still near.

But going. Lighting a new cigarette from the one she had been smoking, rolling down the window, flipping out the stub. On her way now. Leaving. On State Road 241 in drizzling rain.

"I suppose you have heard," she was saying, with a gaiety Hank Spurling thought callous and unbecoming to the occasion, "about the time old Melvin Barkenbooze and his wife both wearing snowshoes got treed by the moose?"

"Melvin Boozenbark," Hank said. "Clancy been giving you that cornball load."

"Must remember Melvin and his missus. Bug a formal dinner sometime."

It was the same road, every twist and turn of it. But it would not be the same again. The wheel of the truck felt to Hank Spurling like the wheel of a hearse. Carrying away a dream. Beyond the Freefolk River's farthest turn, to a grave.

They came to the straightness of the highway, to the smoothness, the quietness of the pavement. "Old Daniel

Boom. The stem-winding Wyoming trail blazer," she said to his profile.

"Name's Spurling. Not Gus either."

"He loves um. Then he leaves um. At Cow Corners."

He took his foot from the gas, and looked at her. "Just a minute, Dorothy. Get it straight. Who's leaving. You're getting on a plane to Chicago and I have got that straight already. That's the end of me."

"Not getting on a plane to Chicago, darling."

"What? You're not?"

"I'm not."

"How come you're not? Dorothy?"

"Mainly, I think Father needs discipline."

"You — you'll have to fill me in."

"Father left me. I leave Father."

The truck almost went off the road. "What are you going to do?"

"Take a plane, darling. Go West, old girl. Go West. That's a quote. From Abraham Lincoln."

"This is west."

"Wrong west. We've missed Sacramento Street somehow."

"What's Sacramento Street? You mind saying?"

"Dull. My mother's little pink home in the west. All Louis Quinze. At last report, that is."

"You talking about Frisco?"

"San Francisco. What time does a westbound depart Cow Corners?"

"I don't know what time. I was in Frisco once."

"San Francisco."

"They put us in trucks by the railroad yards and took us to a dock. We went aboard an old bucket named the *Willie Ward Burroughs*. Then we sailed, under the bridge. In fog. The Navy had anti-sub dirigibles with big squawking

261

bullhorns overhead for a while. Then they went back. That's all I saw of San Francisco."

"You saw enough."

"Then why are you going there?"

"Pillow to post, as they say. I may be going to Europe."

"Myself, I may get over to Dwindle. To see the sights."

"Sounds unattractive. About Europe, I've a mother and an aunt going soon. I may."

"You serious?"

"Certainly I'm serious."

"You drive me nuts. Europe."

"What is so mad about Europe?"

"I wouldn't know."

He drove in silence around the sweep of the sign-marked curve, over the rain-darkened rimrock of the Fontenelle Plateau; he wagged the blade of the windshield wiper and turned the headlights on.

"The field out there's socked in tight," he said. "Would you mind if I asked you something?"

"I might not mind."

"Would you mind letting me take you to dinner? There in town this evening."

"I think you're obligated. To take me to dinner."

"I bet you're hungry. Where'd you eat last?"

"Ingo built a fire, under a snowy rock. At that place where we had a can of beer. Ages ago."

"Chickaree Spring."

"A chickaree is a little brown squirrel," she said.

He braked the truck to a sharp stop on the side of the road and he said, "Kiss me, Dorothy."

She turned to him, pliant, avid, to let him have her opened mouth. For a long moment he held her, before she resisted, pushing him from her.

262

"No — Hank!" She held him away. "Drive this truck, dammit! I want a bath."

He thought there were tears in her eyes.

He could not be sure, with the truck grinding into gear again on the road. He could not be sure of anything but the baleful burden of desire, while Dorothy sat there going out of his life on a black line of wet asphalt, while he gripped the wheel so hard his fingers numbed, while he drove to old lady Borchers's tourist court under its lighted sign of poison green.

She was waiting in the office and she said, "You *have* been fishing in those mountains, haven't you! And I have a message. The airport called. That airplane to Denver is canceled this evening. I hope we can make you just real comfortable here until all this bad weather lets up."

"I am leaving for San Francisco. Not Denver."

"They said you were going to Denver."

"I do hate to fail them." She turned to Hank. "Might you find out on the phone or something, what sort of scheme they'd have for a spook going west?"

"Well all I know is what the airport man told me. You were going to Denver," said the stout lady behind the desk. "I wouldn't get on one of those airplanes for anything! The Union Pacific is good enough for me any time, and it stays right on this earth —"

"Hold it!" Dottie said. Hank had the phone book opened. "I'm tuning —" She turned to the stout lady. "Could there be a decent train from here to the west coast?"

"Decent? I'll have you to know that my husband before he passed was a railroad man! I love those old train whistles and always will, the mister had a special one he'd give for me, coming in off his run! Why, that westbound that's Number Twelve, it's such a lovely train now the war's

263

over, those streamline pullmans, fancy club car and bar
and all —"

"Mrs. — uh? —" Dottie asked.

"Borchers. Jewel Borchers."

"Mrs. Borchers. Could it be a whistle blowing now inside my bright little mind? Could you possibly be talking
about a same Union Pacific train that goes through Reno,
Nevada?"

"Goes right through Reno."

"Fantastic," said Dottie. "We are at the crux, the absolute
crux. What time does it come through Cow Corners?"

"Beg your pardon?"

"This town. Does it stop here?"

"Mam. Number Twelve arrives Green Junction eight-oh-
five in the evening. Departs eight-ten. Usually."

"Holy potato," said Dottie. "My luck must be changing."
She looked at her wrist watch. "Says five after six."

"It's twenty-five to seven."

"Been in the hills. — Hank old pal. How long does it
take to go out to that airport and back? From here?"

He looked at her, dismally. "Half hour, I guess."

"Would you be a doll? Would you run out there and
pick up that check your mother mentioned? I'll be trying to
scrub and change. Then you can take me to the train."

"Key-riste —" Hank said.

"If you'll just show me a room please, I can find the
tub myself. And Hank now if you will get high behind and
bring in the luggage darling."

At the airport desk the young fellow in the gray shirt
handed Hank the envelope marked "Mrs. D. R. Haskett."
"I've put her ticket in there too," he said. "She can turn it
in for refund."

"Ought to send it to her old man," Hank said, dry. "He's
in need."

264

"You know it! Anyway, I'm sorry this doggone weather's gone to work for another carrier. Sorry we had to cancel out this evening."

I am canceled out the rest of my life, Hank Spurling thought. Without her.

He sat alone in the rattling truck, mashing on the gas, driving toward the misted lights of Junction.

It couldn't happen to me, meeting her. Loving her. It did happen. It happened impossible unbelievable like getting back from the Pacific. Those four years I thought I couldn't live through, now these two weeks I can't ever get through living. Such a small amount of my life, two weeks, with nothing like it again, from here on. Without her. Remembering over and over. That Dorothy damn her. She blows up a storm. Everything she does. Crazy. Not so crazy. Crazy wonderful with her there in those mountains the old Cloudrocks. All washed up unless I do something. Do what you god damned fool she is getting on a train in less than an hour she is going away. So the rest of my life from here on I can remember the certain name having to remember Sundog O God think of forgetting love me Hank I am ready I am always ready a woman like that.

In the poison light his hand looked as green as a dead Jap's. He knocked with his dead-looking hand on the rainy door. He knocked again.

She was there. Not gone and he stepped into the warm light where she was, alive. Changed. Not belonging to any Cloudrock Mountains in any way but other heights, luring glittery, unmapped, unmeasured in Hank Spurling's brain. She stood on silken rounded legs high-heeled, taller, in a creamy smooth cling of dress, sparkling.

"Haven't got my face on yet —" unpowdered, untinted, her washed skin had a tanned glow and shine completely flawless — "and there's no hope whatever for this fright-

265

ening hair until it's had a do. But I'm in clean smalls, no less! See? Just zooty as all hell, I'd say."

He stood there looking at her and he said, "Jeez," and he shook his head.

He handed her the envelope. "The ticket was already made out. You can turn it in. For a refund."

She found her father's check and unfolded it to glance at the amount. "Oops," she said. "Might be worth a shake at old Reno, this might —"

She saw Hank's somber face and she laughed. "You know something? Our heavyweight madam from the office, I do believe she expected to find you in the shower with me, the old snoop. She came bringing something for you to take to Ingo. Father left it for him. Here —"

"Much obliged." He carefully put the sealed envelope into his pocket.

"All rich," she said smiling, turning to the clutter of cosmetics before the mirror. "All rich but Little Beaver. He called me on the phone, frantic."

"On the phone for what?"

"The water color, darling. I forgot it. I forgot to pay. Rash of me, becoming a patron of art. Nicked me for fifty bucks."

"You mean he phoned you from Silvertip about that?"

"Wants to mail the thing to me. And don't ever say I'm not honor bright —" she put down her powderpuff, found her billfold in the clutter on the dresser top. "My little ole folding mad money. Here. You're to deliver this." It was a fifty-dollar bill.

"That bum."

"He'll be looking for you!"

"Where's he going to ship the stinking picture?"

"Sacramento Street, darling. So rash of me, keeping art-

266

ists quiet. And my train leaves in thirty-five minutes. Will you close up my bags? I have got to do my face."

"What about these?" He pointed to her mountain camp clothes strewn on the floor, to the gaped leather handbag emptied and tossed in a corner.

"Burn the damned things. They're ghastly."

"Like hell. I'll get it all into your duffel, to ship back with your gear. So you'll have it." He paused. "For your next trip. To the Cloudrocks."

"Ha," she said, applying eye shadow. "Ha."

When all her luggage had been loaded on the truck, everything but the cosmetic case she was still using, he came in from the rain. She saw him in the mirror's reflection.

He stood so solemnly, she thought, watching her finish her face.

The blue note tune she hummed had found words; she was singing them to her face — then to his face — in the mirror, gaily.

> "He'd follow me around,
> Build me up, tear me down,
> Till I'd be so bewildered
> I wouldn't know what to do!
> Might as well give up the fight again.
> I know darned well he'll convince me
> That he's right again —
> When he sings that siren song,
> I just got to tag along
> With that ole devil called Love —"

"Dorothy —" his hand took her arm, turning her. She saw not his reflection but his face. "Marry me."

The very dark blue eyes opened very wide. "Marry you? Why?"

267

"Because you can't go away. Because I love you."

"You're — a sweet man, Hank. It wouldn't last."

"Make it last! Don't you see? It has to last! Nothing in your life will last if this doesn't last! Loving each other. We'd make it last. Till we died —"

"Don't ruin my mouth, Hank. Don't. I just finished it, don't smear it — please —"

"Dorothy, Dorothy Spurling, look at me. Will you marry me?"

"You're mad! When?"

It crashed into his anguish. When.

"Now. Marry me now." It was not anguish. It was joy. "Stay! Tomorrow morning, we'll go to the courthouse, you see? And I can get it all figured, a place for us to live, Silvertip, you and me together, and those old mountains —"

"Hank. Hank! Take your hands away. — Now. Listen to me. You're mad! So am I. That train leaves in twenty-five minutes. Let's get on with it." She began to gather the clutter of cosmetics into the case.

"You're not staying. You're leaving," he said.

"I said let's get on that train. Together."

It stunned Hank Spurling.

"Stay, Dorothy. Stay. Marry me here."

"Come to, Hank. I'm not a total lunatic. Can you think of anything I am less likely to do than to marry you and live in a wigwam?" She snapped the lid shut on the case. "Will you please hold my coat for me? And take me to that train?"

In torment he tried to tell her, he tried to tell himself, sitting by her on the truck seat in the dark, moving through a desolation of misty lights, by the red sign blinking EATS — "You see I can't leave, can't leave Wyoming now, not even a warning to my people, them depending on me. Me just shoving off. We got the first party of hunters coming

268

Monday! I couldn't leave anyway. Without money. The way it is now, I can't go. Any place at all."

"It was only a thought. And so mad! About money, I have a little."

"I haven't. I am way out of line. And I love you."

"And there's that train to old Reno!"

"Promise me. That you'll let me know where you are. I'll be there for you. Wait for me. I'll get some money. I'll quit here, the mountains and everything. And we'll be together, Dorothy, wherever you say. Only give me a little time."

"Old Daniel Boom! Really Boom, a-courtin' disaster. Wanting to marry up now with Dottie — you must throw my damn junk on that train!" She opened the truck door. "I must make them hold it." She jumped out and she ran across the station platform, her high heels tapping, toward a porter standing by his little step.

Hank did get all her luggage aboard.

"What about ticket?" he huffed.

"I'm wizard, with railroad conductors."

"That diner's closing, looks like."

"I'm thirsty, with club cars! Aren't you taking me to dinner?"

" 'Board, mam," the porter said. "We're leaving."

"You're not coming, Hank?"

"Kiss me."

She kissed him.

"You've got to get on, mam," the porter said.

"Good-bye, Hank," Dottie Haskett said.

"It's not. It's not good-bye — it's only —" The train was moving. The train carried her away and he stood there. Under the lighted bulbs on the station platform the painted sign still said: GREEN JUNCTION, ELEVATION 6778, UNION PACIFIC.

269

15

The nurse's starchy uniform rustled with a brisk sound in the room's silence.

"Here is Mr. Mullins to see you," the nurse said.

Robert Royston was not in the hospital bed, he was up and dressed, seated in a lounging chair by the window. He looked thin, sitting there. His hair looked whiter. His face looked older.

"Hello, Rich," he said.

Richard Mullins shook the thin hand and grinned saying, "This is great."

"Feels good. Seeing you from this angle. Instead of from that goddamned double damned bed!"

"You sound good. Like yourself."

"Profane. I'm making the noise to show vigor. I'm getting sprung from stir! Ernest is bringing a car."

"I just saw Doc, at lunch, at the club — he told me he's turning you loose today. So I thought I'd come by for a minute, Robert, to give a salute. I can say it: you've had us all scared. You've had a real rough go."

Beneath the bristly grizzled eyebrows Royston's eyes in their bony sockets looked somehow bigger and more piercing. "Fooled a few people, including myself," he said. "Blame it on the sulfa — and that carload of oxygen. Anyway, here I am. In a suit that doesn't fit me. And a shave and a haircut. Damned near as neat as if they were putting me in the box to bury me."

"You've got to take it easy for a while now. Take some time for yourself, Robert. And enjoy not being buried."

"You please tell him that again, Mr. Mullins!" the nurse said, rather too brightly.

Royston scowled. Still scowling he sighed, looking at the window, at the light from the smoky flatness of the sky.

"Now that I'm so comfortably not buried. Now that I'm enjoying myself," Royston said, "you could tell me a good deal." He poked with the toe of his shoe at a newspaper scattered by his feet. "RMC, for instance, closed at one sixty-nine and a quarter. New high."

"You noticed, less than two hundred shares."

271

"That big man still trying to buy. Or steal."

"That big man getting only little dabs. All the publicity —"

"Notoriety."

"Much better word. Everybody wants some RMC. While he's wanting more. There's very little he can get, at this point!"

Royston's eyes had turned toward the nurse, and she had noticed. "Angel," he addressed her. "I think you might watch for Ernest when he comes. Lead him down that long hall. He could get lost, trying to find this room."

"Oh? Why, yes. Yes of course," the nurse said.

Royston and Mullins both watched her go rustling out the door. She closed it behind her.

"Such a bright girl," Royston said. "Give me some word for a change, Rich. You've found the miscreant yet? Over in that trust department? That sold all those shares out from under me?"

"There's a crowd of red-faced bankers. Every one of them claiming they absolutely didn't know a thing was cooking! In the circumstances, I believe what they say. And they justify their transaction. They dug out, and showed to me, a transcript of a trustees' meeting in May, 27th of May, in which you verbally concurred, yourself, with their recommendation that at some favorable time — there's the kicker, 'favorable time' — the Milo P. Royston Foundation could well divest itself of a portion of its RMC stock, to diversify. The vagueness — was the calamity. The bank construed an unspecific recommendation, and your equally unspecific concurrence, as a specific instruction —"

"The bank made a bitter damned terrible mistake, if it was only a mistake!"

"Fully as horrible as it was honest. They admit that. In August, it so happened, came a very favorable offer from a

272

good New York house. The trust officers took action. They made a sound deal — that's strictly from the viewpoint of the trust administration — disposing of a little less than half the RMC shares held by the foundation. Jim Stanley himself, who is certainly no miscreant where you're concerned, and he wants to come by and see you soon, swears on a stack of Bibles that he could not and he did not know Romulus Tullman was behind the New York offer."

"You know as well as I do — you and I once spoke of it — that trade on the Exchange all summer indicated somebody was consistently nibbling RMC shares. Why was it Jim didn't inform me of the New York offer? For my opinion. Why didn't he ask me for an approval of the trust's action? Why didn't he?"

"You were away. He thought your approval was tacit."

"Tacit." The word came like corrosive acid from Royston's mouth. "By God. Tacit."

Mullins looked at him. "By the time I found it out — it was *fait accompli*. And that was when I started to burn wires. Trying to locate you, out fishing."

"Okay." The acid was still there. "Hard luck story. I went fishing. I caught pneumonia. I lost my job. Nobody's fault but mine. '*Huley Bent's Coup.*' As the snide bastards at *Time* called it. What a coup." Royston's acid-dry lips made a try at a smile. "For that matter, what a Huley Bent. Mortgaged to Romulus Tullman! Hulcy's LaSalle Street Romulus may have suckled a wolf briefly. He got most of his pap from the teats of a striped polecat."

"Might interest you to know, Robert, a policy was issued early in September insuring Chairman and President Bent's life in the amount of five million dollars."

"Enviable Huley. Write it on his grave: Brilliantly mortgaged. In death as in life."

"Whatever that man has in mind for himself —" Mullins

273

shook his head — "I thank God I'm your lawyer, not Hulette Bent's! Whatever contract he and Tullman have made with each other — it must be weird! — and whatever their holdings in RMC, I can hardly conceive of thinner ice than Bent goes skating on. He and Tullman have rigged control at RMC. But they don't own control, yet. At a stockholders' meeting, your voting shares combined with what the foundation still owns, with Mrs. Royston's holdings, can command a majority."

Royston's eyes were leveled into Mullins's face. "Any personal element there — is not up for discussion with me, at any time!"

"I by no means discuss it, or intend to."

"You're a friend of mine, Rich. And she is in Europe. And no friend of mine needs to point —"

A knock came on the door.

"I'll point to one thing. I'm your friend any way you take it —"

"I know it, Rich —"

The knocking was louder.

"Well, come in, damn it!" Royston called over his shoulder.

"Colonel Royston," the nurse's voice said, tentatively.

"What?"

"Mrs. Royston is here."

Royston turned. Mullins came to his feet, and stared.

From around the side of the pleated screen in front of the hospital room's door, Mrs. Royston appeared. Her carefully wrought blondeness was distinguished, impeccable, cool in a gray of tailored woolens and soft furs. Her aging eyes were cold.

Angry with the weakness in his legs, Royston got himself up from his chair. "Come in, Cynthia," his voice said.

274

Mullins glanced toward where he had left his hat.

Mrs. Royston swept forward with an effective poise, proffering her husband a gray-gloved hand. He accepted it.

Mullins moved toward his hat.

"You may remember Rich Mullins here —" Royston said, "Cynthia."

"How do you do?" she said.

Mullins had his hat in his hand. "I must be going." He bowed, slightly. He took the nurse by the arm firmly and he walked her around the screen, out of the room, and he closed the door.

Royston stood, feeling the frailty in his legs, facing his wife.

"You are up and about," she said to him.

"I'm going to Lake Forest. This afternoon."

"Robert. Don't make this so difficult for me."

"Cynthia. Please sit down. I would like to myself, if you don't mind."

"Are you all right?"

He did not answer for a moment, seated again, trying to adjust himself to his own fecklessness. "I suppose I may say this visitation is — not ordinary. I thought you — had gone abroad."

"Robert, you look so fragile! Ought I call Nurse?"

"Not unless you'd really prefer to have 'Nurse' with us."

"You make it so frightful, don't you? To cope! Now that I'm here."

"No frightfulness intended."

"It took great courage. To come. The greatest courage."

"I appreciate that."

"We are booked to London by air, then Rome. Crash is already in New York waiting. Meeting Dorothy there I *do* hope — while I — I've made this journey —" She was discomfited by the bigness of the eyes peering from the thinner, older face. "I've come. As a matter of principle! If you *would* care to hear."

"I'd care very much."

"I was in Taos with Isabel and René, so isolated! When I learned you were ill, René quite by chance reading a *New York Times*. We called Ernest, not knowing the hospital."

"Ernest told me. I got a letter from Isabel. And a phonograph album, of some kind, she sent."

"And my telegram? The flowers?"

"You were very kind."

"I think you could keep me informed, I had no idea you might be at death's door, it seemed so unlike you! Ernest did post me you were improving, then I had a call from Dorothy. That scamp was at Tahoe. And *dear* Crash, planning itinerary for ruined Tuscany and all the rest, wanting me in San Francisco. So I left Isabel and René in their primitive canyon — to alight a moment and look after so many things —

"Robert, my legal people had been asking for me. Those guardians of my poor little treasury. The elder Mr. Ott himself came. He was gruff with me. Insisting I should have sought his counsel. The man, Hulette Bent I mean, is power-mad, isn't he? — Oh this is all hideously difficult! Yet I felt duty-bound. A matter of principle, to come here, the whole way to Chicago. To let you know my feeling."

"What feeling, Cynthia?"

"Why, it's quite important, don't you see, Mr. Ott was unpleasantly clear. I'm to cancel that voting thing I granted. I'm to utterly renounce it."

Royston's eyes went shut, as if light hurt them.

"Don't you see why I came? The little voice of my vote. I'm to assign it properly to my husband, at the head of our corporation here."

276

Royston's eyes came open.

"Thank you, Cynthia," he said.

He wanted to say more, he might have said much, but there was a brisk knock on the door. "Must be Ernest," Royston said simply. "He'll be glad to see you here." Then Royston did say more. "Would you drive out with us, to the house, Cynthia? The old place —" The knocking on the door persisted, more briskly. "Come *in!*"

The door made a sound, opening. "Surprise," said a voice pleasantly, "we've come with Ernest, Colonel! It's Flynn and Hester Bren." They appeared from around the side of the opaque screen. They entered smiling; their smiles faded.

"Pardon —" Flynn said. "We didn't see the nurse, to ask. We just knocked —" he floundered.

"Mrs. Royston!" Ernest said, and realized it too late.

Hester Bren stood riveted, too far into the room to retreat.

Mrs. Royston in a chilled loftiness arose from her chair, gripping her furs.

"I beg your pardon," she said to Royston. He came to his feet unsteadily. "And you might beg mine! Flaunting that person — that —" a scorn pale in the cold eyes cut to Hester Bren's face, then again to Royston's — "that tatty Jewess of yours. Do keep her to yourself, please!" Mrs. Royston walked out of the smitten silence of the room. She walked away, down the hall. To London.

Royston let himself down into his chair. He brought a hand up to his forehead.

"Oh —" The sound came anguished. Hester Bren stood riveted yet, straight-backed, fighting tears. "I am sorry, Robert. Sorry, sorry."

Cosmo Flynn stood stunned as if a lightning bolt had melted his foolish feet to the floor.

277

Ernest withdrew. He went into the hall to lay hold of the ruddy nurse.

Royston sat in the chair by the window's unrelenting light, unmoving.

In the stillness Hester Bren moved to mend her dignity, her pride. She disposed of her tears with a handkerchief. She said, "Cozzzzmo Flynnnn — such a terrible thing — bringing me here! Take me away! Now!"

"It's my fault," Flynn found himself able to say. "But how could —"

"Right now, just get the hell out of here," Royston's voice grated the words. "If you don't mind."

He heard them, but he did not watch them go. Then he was alone with the pounding in his head, the weakness. He was alone with the hollow weakness, the weariness, standing on the empty porch in the dark in the rain in front of the store in the desolate town in Wyoming.

"Ernest!"

Ernest's harried face appeared around the side of the pleated screen. "Sir?"

"I want you to find that goddamned nurse. Where is she?"

"Here, sir. Waiting."

"You tell her not to speak to me. Just have her show you my suitcase. It's packed, ready somewhere. Get me squared with the front office of this *abattoir*. Then get me my overcoat and my hat. And get me the hell OUT. Before I find any more goddamned sympathetic friends and family around here!"

It seemed to Royston a very long walk to the elevator. The elevator seemed very slow in arriving, very slow, tomb-like, in descending; the hall seemed very long and complicated, to the steps, to the wide glass door. It seemed to Royston strange, dramatic, to stand once more in the un-

278

roofed open with nothing but a hat between his head and the sky. Ernest helped him into the tonneau, put a robe over his tired legs. He felt the unaccustomed rawness and good freshness of the air; he tucked the woolen muffler a little higher around his throat. Then Ernest got in front and drove.

Somehow Robert Royston had emerged, he thought — he had come out on the other side, the far side, of an oxygen tent. The car carried him away, alive yet. He moved along the windowed faces of the streets. High above the oil-stained asphalt where he moved, tall brick and stone in snaggled piles stood like teeth bared at the smoky sun.

He saw the lake, an abrupt emptiness at the city's edge, an outreaching bluish calm of watery quiet flat in November's slanting sunlight. He moved, in an engined sweep of smoothness through the Parkway's trees. Their branches had a few dried leaves clinging yet against the sky before they fell.

Belmont, Sheridan Road, clattery Howard Street unchanged; the turn, into Evanston's prim traffic, the stop lights and beyond, the narrow cove with the stiff-sparred little jostled crowd of winter-tied boats; Wilmette, Hubbard Woods, Kenilworth, Glencoe all familiar; the long drive went curving, straightening again, with expensive shrubberies and prosperous melancholies of household architectures, past frost-slain gardens and leaves fallen dead on hushed lawns.

"Ernest," Royston said, oppressed, suddenly too silent on the other side of an oxygen tent, "stop. Let me get in front. It's too hard to talk, from back here."

He felt only a little less oppressed seated by the driver. "How's the house, Ernest? Did that heating unit need any repair?"

"It seems satisfactory, sir."

279

"I haven't set foot in the place since the thirteenth of August. It was summer, then."

"Now it's autumn again. Nearly winter, isn't it? I think you'll find the house in order," Ernest said. "Nothing changed. Almost nothing, I should say. I had better tell you, sir. There are two new pictures hanging, in oils."

"How's that?"

"A quite large one, in the library now. One not quite so large, in your bedroom upstairs."

"You mean Flynn? You mean he's been out there, prowling around, putting up pictures?"

"The fellow pushes a bit. I think I must explain. I think I should. About this afternoon." Ernest's eyes paid scrupulous attention to the road, leaving Highland Park. "How it occurred. It was an arrangement, I regret to say. You had told me, if you will recall, I could allow Mr. Flynn the house whenever he came. Yesterday, he came with paintings. They were attached to the outside of a taxicab. With knotted cords. Miss ah-Bren came with him. Inside the taxicab. They rather took over, sir! I must say I found no reason to object, in fact, I rather entered into it all. To my eye, the pictures seemed wizard, quite like good views of Alps. In any event it was to be a surprise. For your homecoming. As I was taking Mr. Flynn and Miss Bren to the North Shore station for a train back to town late yesterday afternoon, a suggestion came from Mr. Flynn, he's a genial sort. Quite unwisely I agreed to drive them this afternoon to the hospital — and then, perhaps, if you wished — Miss Bren considered it might be cheering to you, bit of friendly company, the two of them, on your drive home. I was to attend to some tea. When we arrived. A bit of jolliness with the pictures, after your illness. It was meant well. I am enormously sorry, sir."

280

"So am I, Ernest."

They drove through mauve shadows under bare elms, by a long brick wall with a line of sycamores and oaks, to the maples still mantled with a hardiness of dusky autumn red, and the dark green ivy by the gate.

They turned in, moving up the rise along the graveled drive between the pines, across the lawn beyond the clipped hedge to the gray stone house with the steep slate roof on the gardened terrace above the edge of the lake's great emptiness. The door opened before Ernest could ring the bell. Fat Frieda in white uniform opened it, smiling. Her husband Walt, the gardener, wearing one of Royston's old shaggy Harris jackets, appeared. Royston shook their hands.

He walked into his house and stood in the hall with his feet again upon its black and white floor of *checquy* marble, by the familiar pedestal of mahogany and the looming glint of Norman steel panoply. The suit of armor stood very empty, the house stood very quiet. Robert Royston stood very weary while Ernest took his coat and hat.

The lights in the library were all on; Frieda had prepared a tea table there. Royston walked in, to drop himself deep into the ease of a leather reading chair. Before he reached it — he saw. The Rungius painting of a grizzly bear had been moved to the alcove by the library door. Replacing the bear, filling the central space of the paneled big wall, flanked at either hand by long ranges of books, there was something else. Shaken, Royston sat down — he sat a saddle on top of Blue Gap Ridge. He looked out upon the Cloudrock Mountains.

They stood in their primal cleanliness, in their aerial radiance above the snow slopes and slashed ravines at their feet. Their heights had a luminous pallor, of sheer

281

stone and flinty ice, ribbed with angled shadows of a vivid blue. They were quiet.

Royston sat with them.

I change, Royston heard his mind say, gazing. They do not. I move. They do not. I die. They do not. I am glad I saw them. I am glad I stopped, to look at them. I am glad I went back, to see them. While I could see with these eyes, Royston's mind said, for eyes are very great, neither lasting as stone, nor immortal as ice.

In the weakness of his body, in the weariness of his mind, in the loneliness of mountains, in the silence of an empty house, Royston was suddenly ashamed of his eyes. They had tears.

"Colonel Royston," Ernest said, "might I bring you tea? Frieda has made scones, and crumpets too."

"Ernest, thank Frieda, will you? I think I won't have any tea. I'll tell you what you could do for me. You could go to the cellar and you could see if there is one of those smaller bottles of the good Pol Roger, or the Piper Brut. And chill it. And bring it. And light the fire here in the fireplace for me. I'm looking at the mountains here, Ernest."

"You like them, sir? Mr. Flynn thought they looked well placed there."

"It's probably not important, whether I like them. There they are. They don't change, as we do. They only feel different to us, viewed from the other side of an oxygen tent."

"Oh?" Ernest said.

Royston sat with the Cloudrock Mountains over his shoulder, with the crystal stem of a glass cool between his fingers, with the flame and sound of fire on the hearth before him.

"Today a letter came," Ernest said, "I believe from those mountains." He offered it on a tray. The old cut of the trout on the envelope had not changed, it only looked worn.

282

Dear Colonel Royston:

Hope you are getting along and better every day. We have one more party of hunters coming then it is quits till next year. The season was big, easy antelope and good elk quite a bit of snow and cold weather put them in low country early this year. I got one of my people, fellow from Shrevport a moose the biggest ever in those Freefolk bogs above Possibles. Trophy head. Finely got all your camp gear and tackle and etc. crated and shipped, hope it come thru all oK, sent xpress collect. Sorry I was so long doing it but have been working my old tail off with the hunters and one thing another. Hank soreheaded and not worth shooting about half the time lately talking about getting a high pay job some place and leaving the Cloudrocks entirely but we all got our troubles I guess. He will come back to his sences, like we all do. Those Goldens came down in such good shape I Indian-smoked them for you to eat, I figured we had such h —— getting such good fish you would enjoy a few with scrambbled egg for breakfast. Hope you got the package oK, and think of good camps. With warmest personall regards till the end of time your friend

Gratefully,

Ingo Spurling

Ernest cleared the unused tea table.

"Ernest," Royston said. "Did some smoked trout from Silvertip get delivered here?"

"Yes, sir."

"I don't want them. Throw them away."

"Oh I did, sir. They arrived high."

Ernest brought another table, set with plain white napery. He used it to serve Royston a light supper, from a menu suggested by his doctor.

Royston ate resolutely, less from appetite than from

duty to his servants who were glad he was home. When he had finished, he asked for a cigar. He asked for a touch more wine from the bottle sitting angled in the beaded ice bucket by the table.

The cigar went out, half smoked. The pale wine, with a few tiny sets of bubbles in broken lines issuing from the goblet's crystal toward the air, sat undisturbed near his unmoving hand. The fire in the hearth danced slower figures. Royston half dozed.

Some undertone of the flame's sound in the silence snagged half-dreamed at his half-relinquished consciousness. In the fire's whispering a tin cup clacked thrown against a rock again, a dented cup fell on shadowy ground. A blue thin glow of high-proof rum afire flickered from it.

Ernest stood near the library door, under the dim shape of the bear. Royston was awake from his doze. "I'm going to bed," he said. He cleared his throat. "I didn't think I'd be so tired."

"I'll go up the stairs with you, Colonel Royston," Ernest said. "To see if there may be anything you'd want. You'll find your strength, not all in a day."

Royston had forgotten there was another painting to view. Lighted with dramatic effectiveness, it confronted him as he walked into his room.

A storm sky's malign grandeur invested the jagged peaks' crestline. An unseen sun through ragged mist struck silver down the steeps into the awesome cirque. Gray stone cupped a lake. Its water was milky, glacial green. Its shape, by a few timberline trees, was unmistakable. Cosmo Flynn had unknowingly and unfortunately painted for Robert Royston, of all the possible subject matter in the Cloudrock Mountains, the baleful image of Sundog Lake.

"Ernest —" Royston said, in a somber exhaustion. "Get that thing down. Get it out of here. Right now. Tomorrow you tell Flynn to come take it away. I don't want to see it again!"

"I'm sorry you don't like it, sir."

"A little too much mountain, to sleep with," Royston said.

16

"The day the eagle craps, what we called it in the Corps, Svensen," Hank said. He tried to focus his eyes in the swayed brightness, the jangled babble of the crowded room. "Pay day, see? The day the eagle craps. Lend me a twenty, Svensen."

"Killer my boy," Svensen answered. "We looking for you."

286

"The eagle crapped, Svensen." Blues and scarlets of Svensen's big ski sweater made a jumpy dazzle in Hank's eyes; Svensen grinned at him from two overlapping mouths with twice as many gold teeth as Svensen had. "So he crapped, Svensen. He crapped out. Lend me a ten."

"Lots of crap, uh?" said Svensen. He glanced past Hank, toward the eroded stone face of the dice man standing at his solemn station by the green-topped crap table. The man wagged the stony face, very slightly, at Svensen. The eyes in the face described a journey, from Hank Spurling to the street door; the man's thumb made a small motion toward the door, amplifying the suggestion his eyes had made.

"Come on, Killer. We taking off."

"Hell with that. I need dough."

"Outside now is down to twenty below. We catch a good ride in Rusty's car, uh? You and me."

"Goddammit, Svensen! Lend me a five."

"Listen, Killer. We make another run, this steilhang! We both get rich. But later. Not tonight," Svensen said. "Now we yust go home — hey — Rusty! Sepp!"

"Sven the Svensen," Rusty Devrin said. He eased through the rim of the roulette crowd. "And Killer Spurling, himself." There was an executive assurance in Devrin's voice, in his smile. "The gloomiest man in Ketchum, old Killer! The terror of Canyon Run." He measured his employee's unsteadiness, his evident truculence, with a quick precision. "Let's give Lady Luck a chance to powder her nose, Spurling."

"I never met the babe." Hank glowered at the dice man.

"I don't know her too well myself," Devrin said. "They say she's a dream. And tomorrow's a day." He smiled, just enough. "A thousand sitzmarks in the snow. Let's go get ready for them, *Herren* Professors." He casually took Hank by the arm. Svensen and Sepp Schreck closed in on

287

the other side. "These local dice leave shitzmarks. The hell with them —" The casual hand on Hank's tensed arm already had him headed for the door.

"Key-riste —" Hank breathed, unable to decide upon any target.

A kind of momentum supplied by his three companions put him into the back seat of Devrin's parked car. The engine started finally, the dull blow and smell of the heater came on. Then the car moved; the chains clinked on the pavement's pack of dirtied ice. The headlights' shine moved on the frozen muck up the length of the street to the turn and the empty road tracked through rounded drifts of starlit snow.

Buried in the dim joggle of the car's progress, in the muffled clittering of the chains along the crusty cold, Hank Spurling suffered a hopelessness, a helplessness. In revulsion he shut his eyes. The joggle swung off into a sickening spin behind his eyes. He opened them desperately alone with himself.

He heard Sepp's voice, from far away in the front seat. "Dot singing tomato is built. Vot's her name, Boss, you said? Dot dame's name?"

"Piddipum." Devrin's voice came from greater distance. "Piddipum Dawson."

"Goofy."

"They claim her feet make a noise like that, running down a hall."

"Pitti-poom. Zounds like more dun feet."

Svensen's voice came from closer. "Lots of camber! Yeesus!"

"Such cases, ve umploy Appenzell trindletail teknik."

"Not endorsed by F.I.S.," said Devrin. "But we do have Piddipum booked at the Lodge. She's going to work with the combo."

288

"I'm sick," Hank said, to himself but they heard him. Devrin looked back. "Hold it, Killer. If you get out here you'll frostbite the trindletail."

They took a familiar curve that led along the line of planted spruce and the fence, turned sharp left, slowed through the parking area, passed the bare trees, entered the bottleneck behind the sprawl of the Inn. Devrin nosed his car into a waiting space close by the side of a rustic outbuilding hunched deep in snow, lit with a lonely light.

Hank stooped dizzy from the car door, stood for a moment reeling at the snowbank that edged the shoveled walkway. Then he heaved, straining, furious, sick. He got himself straightened up, with a pull of pain kinked in his side; the bitter cold prickled at the clammy sweat on his forehead.

"Better, uh?" Svensen stood by. "Now for the sack."

They walked the heated corridor past dark cubicles where most of the inmates lay asleep, to their own narrow clutter of room. Svensen switched on their light. Hank with a grave preoccupation eased himself prone upon his bunk. Flat on his back, fully dressed, he shut his eyes, he shut away the world, the world's trouble and his defeat.

Svensen was pulling off his shoes when Rusty Devrin stuck his head in the doorway. He looked over at Hank, and said to Svensen, "There's some coffee in the office. How about it?" Svensen stuck his feet into shaggy slippers and walked along the creaky boards of the corridor to a larger room crowded with an old desk and lines of scuffed benches. Sepp Schreck had three coffee cups lined up by the hotplate on the little table in the corner near the bulletin board.

Devrin closed the door. A vague smell of sweatered sweat, damped wool, boiled coffee, ski wax — a curious lingering odor of professional athletic experience shared,

289

judged, enjoyed — lived in the male air of the plain wooden, boot-scarred room.

"Let's talk about your roommate a minute, Svensen," Devrin said. "I want to find out more about the guy. He got a snootful."

"First time I ever see it! Give me sugar, Sepp."

"It's his business. And part mine too. Did he lose all his pay check?"

"I figure that is why he take on such load, Rusty."

"I don't care for those gambling dumps in Ketchum as a place for getting plastered. Any instructor that works for me keeps his nose clean around here, and I thought Spurling knew it. He was all cocked to throw a punch and get jammed real good. I saw Marine types, winding up, in the Pacific during the war. The Gyrenes. Spurling damn near had tonight what they used to call the two-thousand-yard stare. They usually got it holding a knife in their hand. Yet the fact is, one of the reasons I took on Spurling is because he was a Marine with a Navy Cross. He looked steady. What's he got chewing on him, Sven?"

"*I Guds navn —*" Svensen shrugged. "Everybody got something, uh?"

Sepp grinned. "First ding alvays, Boss. *Cherchez la femme.* Spurling provly catch shooting pains off dose Norshki pin-opps Svensen got over his bonk."

"I don't see Spurling catting much."

"He don't play," Svensen said. "Quiet guy."

"What I notice," Devrin said, "is how he hits that post office. Every noon. Every evening. Who does he do all the big glum writing to? Sitting at night over there in the Inn."

"He don't say."

"He got any photos around, he stares at?"

"I never see any."

"Must be a dame. Who does he hear from?"

290

"He don't say. Maybe nobody. Only yust once in the while from his mother. From Wyooming."

"He got dose blues. By U.S. Mail," Sepp said. "May be dot Dear Johann. Tonight is taking de cure, could be."

"He better get cured. And get on the ball," Devrin said. "Or I'll let him go."

"Maybe on guy like Killer, what he done in war still bother him," Svensen said. "You see him in shower bath. You know frigging Yapanese put hole in that boy's belly, uh? He dreams plenty rough at nights, sometime. You take last night. He wake up crying, uh? 'Son-dawk!' It sounds like. Crazy. 'Sondawk!' Then he get up. Smoke his pipe."

" 'We're the First Battalion Seventh Marines of the famous First Mar Div —' I've listened. In APA 49." Devrin shook his head. "Tell me, Sepp. With that novice class lately, how has Spurling been doing? Your opinion."

"So so. Horst unt dot Ekstein is more shmooth, vif bonnies on Dollar. You ask. I shpeak only as old kanone, Boss. Shpurling is goot poy. Pet too tenzed opp."

"He'll be in form tomorrow. Creeping out into the winter wonderland. Could be just the lad to analyze the Appenzell nose plow, by demonstration, for the advanced hangover class. Have you seen that Hollywood bird, Bassett Jackling, ski?"

"I vill only answer, Boss, does Pittipoom ski? Vould she ski? Hif so I vould like to haf reassignment, prifate instroction, plizz!"

"I'm just reassigning myself. See you guys in the morning."

Svensen stopped by the bathroom, then went to his cubicle. "Hey Killer," he said. "You going to sleep all night in your shoes, uh?" He stirred Hank up, helped him to undress, put his covers over him. Then Sven Svensen peeled to

291

his red flannels, turned out the light, got into his bunk, sighed in the darkness, and snored soon.

The light of day and the trouble of the world arrived in a harshly short time to Hank Spurling. He awoke in sounds of raucous awakenings around him, with aches as if he had lain unmoving in chains. He got from his bunk unable to recall how he had gotten to it, but able to recall well enough a presence of folly, defeat, which his mind housed thick in the ache of his skull.

Sullen in the dormitory's morning racket and horseplay, he grappled in a clouded bitterness with the pains of washing, shaving, combing, dressing somehow to take a quailing body and leaden mind into toils the day demanded. The bowl of hot repugnant oatmeal and cream, the black coffee he managed to swallow, did not brace him. They only pointed his weakness, armed more heavily the throb in his head.

He had signed the breakfast chit at the cashier's stand and he had come grimly and alone through the cafeteria door inside the Inn, his ski boots clonking on the tile, when a finger tapped his shoulder. He turned.

"Spurling. How do you feel?" Rusty Devrin had on his big sunglasses under the bill of his smart tweed cap.

"I feel okay —" the voice belied it.

"That's good. You'll see it in a minute on the board, but I wanted to tell you myself, beforehand. I'm asking Ekstein to take over your bunnies this morning."

"How come?" A jab of new worry joined the throb in his head. "Something wrong? The way I been handling it?"

"Routine change. I'm taking you off Dollar. Putting you on Baldy — you ought not to mind that. For the time being, you're available to give individual instruction, as booked. And whenever you're not occupied, I'm putting you to give Andy a hand with Ski Patrol. He'll have enough for you to do! But this morning — you've got a lady from Detroit. She says her stemming to the left is dreamy. She wants to know how to turn right. And she's all yours. One other thing. The reason I wanted to pass the word to you myself. I hired you to be on the ball at all times here at the Valley. Stay on the ball! I'm sure you will." He walked away, toward the Sports Desk.

When Hank Spurling got on his parka and stocking cap and gloves and headed out into the crackling sharpness of the sunny cold, many figures moved with long sleek boards slanted on their shoulders and slim poles in their mittened hands; many breaths smoked in silvery puffs; many blunt-toed boots crunched squeaky snow. Out ahead on the valleyside's tilt the chairs were in motion on the lift up Dollar. Distant figures like gay stick-men moved tiny black on the slope's whiteness, already released into the day's first swoops and glidings. Over the snow cornice on the Opera House roof, far beyond and high above the brown Lodge's icicled face, stood blue-misted timber and white runs slicing down from where Baldy's crest touched at the sky.

On the trampled open space facing a wing of the Lodge, where classes gathered, Devrin was busy. He called Hank over, introduced him to the lady from Detroit. Hank did not quite hear her name, a Mrs. Something. She was trim, in dark green pants and hooded parka of quilted brown nylon. She smiled. Hank, not successfully smiling, stowed her skis and poles with his in the long rack on the side of one of the waiting big yellow buses. Its seats were filled, its aisle jammed, when Hank and his student got aboard.

The close air, the heat, the press of the winter-bundled crowd and especially its jolly banter were swaying punishments to Hank's head. He got his snow goggles from his pocket and put them on; his fuzzed brain and hollow-feeling legs were in wobbly need of the bracing cold air when

293

the bus stopped and the door came open at last by the ticket cage at the foot of the lift on River Run.

The crowd piled out in good humor, drew their pairs of skis and poles clattering from the jumbled rack, bought lift tickets, knelt briefly snapping bindings to eager feet, hurried with the odd racking jog of skiers at a walk, to the queue where airy chairs came taking their turn on slim stilted cable, to swing away unpausing, up the first section of Baldy's beckoning slopes.

The Mrs. Something was named Francene, she told him, fastening her bindings. She had skied in Quebec, she said. "I'm Hank, plain Hank," he said. "We will start down easy, from this first lift. Now while River Run is not full of schuss-bums and — we will sort of see how you do."

Sort of see how I do, he thought.

He sat the chair behind her, sailing through cold and shady silence up the slot of the timber-sided ravine. Empty chairs came easing by, passing him on their noiseless way down; his feet attached to the swingy lengths of his skis on their noiseless way up dangled in empty air over the pale linework of tracks made by skis neither so noiseless nor so spiritless, on their way down. Abruptly, as if he had awakened from sleep, his skis came touching down and slid with him away from the chair, toward his student standing braced between her poles, smiling at him.

"It's a relief," she said, "that your name's Hank. Not Hannes. Or Rudi. Or Bisch or anything so Arlberg-y! I'm not a bit fancy, on these lovely boards."

"Well. I bet you're real good," Hank said, pulling himself together. "You've skied this run, along here, before?"

"Yesterday afternoon, my first time. I came out by myself to see. I was afraid to go any higher than here and — I didn't do well, at all. I thought I'd surely not forget that exact shift of weight on a stem turn — but I have! I'm do-

294

ing something silly, I don't know quite what. So here I am, with an expert. Isn't it a gorgeous, gorgeous day?"

He gulped. "I guess we — better start with snow plows," he said. "Let's see your best ones, with crouch and lift, linked smooth. I'll go down a little ways and wait for you, and watch. Then we'll talk about it, starting simple, sort of go from there. Give me those snow plows nice," he said over his shoulder, "plenty of traverse and not fast, just smooth and even —" he shoved off easy, showing her.

The cold air's biting tonic, the morning sparkle of the slope, then the sweet and swift sorcery of skis, moved in on him. A tingle arrived from underfoot. A faint glow came seeping through his skis. The glow spread, it climbed up into him, invading the darkness inside his heart. It even denied the ache inside his skull. The world very suddenly was the slope of snow: it was his, and it was enough.

His student caught on. She felt the glow. By the third trip down, she was making stem turns with creditable correctness, and a childlike gladness, to the right as to the left of the fall line. Before straightening to schuss out the end of the run, she neatly linked five flowing turns and Hank yelped a cheer; then he poured on speed and passed her, jumping a few moguls and weaving swingy playful turns. Near the foot of the lift, with the run eked out to its limit he leaned into a sharp stop christie — his turn tossed a gallant, satisfying, showy, snowy plume. Stone still, watching, he waited for her arrival. He felt the grin on his face.

"You got it now!" he said to her. "Simple?"

She was grinning too, a little out of breath. "I wish I could do what *you* do! How were my turns?"

"They felt right, didn't they? Just watching your timing. That crouch, lift, *then* the rotation with the weight going into the uphill ski *after* it's already stemmed! What you were doing before was being too anxious to shove that

295

weight into your uphill ski. So you stiffened your lower knee and leaned *in* toward the slope, and kerplop!"

"I honestly do think I've got it whipped — I hope —" she laughed. "I'm so grateful to you! And you know something? My watch says quarter to one. I'm hungry! Aren't you?"

"I might be a little hungry, come to think of it."

Come to think of a lot of things, he thought, not grinning.

"Where do you usually eat lunch?" she asked. "I'm so new here."

"Oh I eat all my meals at what they call the Continental Buffet — that means plain cafeteria — at the Inn. Teaching staff gets a chow ticket there. There's a bus going, every so often. If we go back, what would you like to do about this afternoon? Would you want some more lesson?"

"I'd love some more lesson, if you're not engaged."

"I'm not engaged. I sure am not — say, Francene —" his thought, his utterance surprised him — "they have some lunch up at the Round House. That's at the top of the middle lift up there. How about it? We could eat and then you could cut your first tracks down the Sunnyside Run, all the way to the Coldsprings bus stop. How about that? For an afternoon."

"My heavens," she said. "You think I'm ready?"

"Sure you are. I'd tell you if you weren't."

They took the lift.

It is a queer day, he thought, riding an airborne chair again. It is a hell of a day. It is a hell of a queer day for me. I don't feel so bad! I feel like a boil has busted. It is the first day since I got here that I say to hell with the post office, to hell with it, to hell with it. It is the first day since I got here that I don't feel like some hopeless trouble was gnawing away my — heart. Yeah, my heart. Chump. It is the

296

first day I ever spent with such a stinking hangover. No money at all. No future of any kind. And I never skied so easy! Feeling it right. It is the first day since the tenth day of September, five lousy months, that I really don't give a good goddam, whether I hear from that goddam Dorothy. Because I never will. It is the first day I feel like I am waking up. And this morning I wished I wouldn't. I didn't think I could.

Another chair carried him, lifting him in steady smoothness up the timbered side of Exhibition Run. Two skiers came swinging narrow christies down the white trough. One laughed. Skis made their whispering, passing softly, fading into the quiet.

On a sudden impulse Hank ungloved both his hands. Bare-fingered he unzipped his parka, reached down his sweater neck, got into his left shirt pocket, located what he wanted, brought it from the pocket — a postcard wrinkled and worn dog's-eared. He looked at the Place de la Concorde, the French stamp, the blurry November postmark, the writing for the last time. Darling Daniel. Wish you were here. Is Old Ezekiel still in a Storm? Dauntless Dottie. Carefully he tore the postcard to bits and he sowed the bits below, a few at a time. They fell like gray flakes far down through the air and lost themselves scattered on the sunny snow. Then he gloved his cold fingers, and lifted the tips of his skis.

It was like one of those good moments when packs were all lashed, when horses and riders stepped out moving toward a promise of heights ahead. There was a quiet fadeless elation in looking up.

Perched high in Baldy's timber, the Round House was a pleasant aerie. The sunlit side of its open porch held an almost somnolent warmth for skiers after a morning of exertion along the slopes. Hank and his student carried their

297

lunch trays to the outdoors and sat on a board bench at a trestle table in the sun, not far from where they had parked their skis.

The sense of newly found, unspoken comfort in Hank's mind blended with an afterglow of exhilaration his body had vouched during the morning. The exhilaration had been shared with the healthy and not unattractive woman seated at his side; it brought the two of them together. It flavored the ease they found now in each other's company.

"You married, Hank?" she asked.

A little of the comfort took flight. "No. I'm not married."

"So many young war veterans are settling down now with families. You haven't found the girl yet?"

"I guess not. How'd you know I was a vet?"

"Mr. Devrin told me this morning. He said you were a Marine. With an outstanding record in the Pacific. The war still seems very close to me. My husband was killed in Hürtgen Forest."

Hank glanced at her face, in silence.

"He taught me to ski — I mean, he tried to teach me." She smiled. "I kept up with him a good deal better, I think, when we were duck shooting. Or fishing, summers in Canada. He learned to ski at Dartmouth. Class of '33."

"I got a crazy kid brother, he's talking about going to Dartmouth. Next year, he says. My mother wrote to me that he is getting some kind of scholarship there, someway. From the Royston Foundation. He's an artist, paints pictures, modernistic. But he's not too bad a skier. He's on the team at Wyoming University."

"A family of skiers."

"I guess you could say, all but my mother. I had another brother, he was tops, any kind of sports. Including mountaineering. He was killed in a paratroop drop over Holland. Hundred-and-First Division."

298

She shook her head, and did not speak.

"He spent his last leave rock climbing in the Welsh hills. He won the downhill here at the valley, before the war. His name was Rut, Rutherford Spurling. Quite a guy."

"Hank. What does a ski instructor do when the snow melts?"

"I haven't had much experience, on that. He louses around mainly waiting for next winter, uh? Ski bum."

"Where do you live in summer? Here?"

"I live over in Wyoming. Or did live there."

"Is that where your people live?"

"Silvertip, Wyoming. A wide place on a gravel road."

"Do your people have a ranch? Something like that?"

"A real small place, just some hay for the horses. At the foot of the mountains. Cloudrock Mountains. My dad's a mountain outfitter, and guide, there. Has been, more than twenty-five years."

Her alert eyes, gazing at his face, showed her interest. "The Cloudrock Mountains. Al — my husband — knew about them. We had friends that used to talk about going to Wyoming, hunting and fishing both. The old fur trader Ezekiel Williams's domain. And wilderness yet, they say! Even the name sounds grand: Cloudrock."

"I was born in the Cloudrocks."

"And how you love them. I see that."

"I — was pretty glad to see them, last March. After the Pacific."

"And you'll be pretty glad to see them again, when the snow melts here. Won't you?"

"Yeah."

"You must run awfully short of time."

"What do you mean by that?"

"For instance, if I'm thinking the same Cloudrocks. Fishing, the summer. Hunting, the fall. Skiing, the winter. Only

299

leaves the spring, to do that lousing around, refitting! How lucky does a man get, Hank?"

"I guess he can have the luck, sometimes. When he's not doped off!" His straight mouth smiled. "Like I was — last night, that is. You must've noticed I started derned slow, this morning! Those hickory sticks we got, they're a fair cure, aren't they? For what ails ya."

She laughed. "I didn't notice anything very slow." He struck a match and held it for her cigarette. "Could you be referring, by any long arm of coincidence, to the effects of hot buttered rums?"

He grinned. "I think I got caught in Ketchum last night. As I remember. Clobbered in Ketchum." He filled his pipe and lit it.

The warm strip of sunlight on the porch was narrower. They sat in a mild silence, gazing past the porch rail, far out over the dark timber, across the shining bowl of the valley, to the crystal sharpness of Sawtooth Mountain ridges steep and white against the sky.

"Well, I liked this lunch. Just sitting here," Hank said. "You about ready to gear up again? We'll do a touch of work here on Round House Slope, for a while. Kind of mean work. So you'll think I'm a real tough teacher. I want to see you do controlled side slips, and be sure of your stopping turns, before we burn down that slope. Sunnyside has a couple of little places where I want you to have confidence. One, they call Niagara — we're going to work it out easy, beforehand. Actually now, I think you're about ready to take on the stem christies — it's just the same, only you don't stem the uphill ski — and I bet you something, Francene. I bet you in a few days you'll be pointing them downhill right from the top of Baldy."

It was an afternoon to outmatch the morning, and it did.

300

Shade came reaching out blue across Sunnyside's ravine; the late sun's dazzle showed only in slanted patches between the trees when the two skiers turned to the right at the lower edge of the Round House Slope and shoved off down the long tilt of their run. At the head of a narrowing steepness he called for her to stop; he showed her exactly how to slip with speed controlled to the foot of the tricky passage — she came with only one quick spill, laughing. Farther down the deepening blue, sorcery awaited them.

It moved along the silky snow, it spoke in the sing of the air. Begot by its own downsweeping glide, it transmuted earth's fettering gravity to a pull of poetry, alive.

It filled them and they moved with it knowing the ease not the effort of poetry's making. It drew them down the dips, over the swells, around the turns of the way. At the widened jointure of a steeper ravine, high Broadway Run, four skiers came racing in skimming swings. All six skiers homebound flew softly streaming wakes of whispery powder, down a last schuss, to a leveling outrun, smooth on the meadow's evening blue cold.

Crisply cutting around, alongside, as she came to her stop, Hank grinned at her again.

"Oh —" she said. She looked back, as if she might glimpse the sorcery returning to its high place. "It's glorious."

"It's what skiing is about," he said.

"My ankles are going to be killing me, by tomorrow," she said while he knelt unfastening her bindings. "I think I'll be falling in pieces."

"You'll be pounding the slopes!"

They caught the last bus from the Coldspring station; they sat side by side feeling tired, good, quiet all the way to where the bus stopped on the driveway in front of the Inn.

"You stay at the Inn or the Lodge?" he asked when he had pulled her skis and poles from the rack.

"The Inn," she said. "Where do you live?"

"Back of the Inn. Instructors got a bachelor dorm. Snake farm. What about tomorrow, Francene? We going to work out again together?"

"I'd love to, but — you see, I may be able to afford staying a little longer, if I don't spend too much on private lessons —"

He looked disappointed. "I see. Hope you can stay! Look. Why don't you, tomorrow, practice real good on what you did today? Get it plenty sharp and then maybe, if you'd like to, in a day or so you could ask for me, and we could hit those christies?"

"Let's do that!" They started down the squeaky white walk with their skis on their shoulders. "I hope I will be seeing you," she said. "I would like to hear a good deal more about those Cloudrock Mountains. Especially —"

"— That's easy. How about us eating in the cafeteria tonight?"

"Love it! Possibly I could keep you from getting caught in Ketchum."

"That's easy too! That's for sure! I have to check in at Instructors' Meeting, then I'll clean up and I'll give you a buzz, the lobby there in the Inn. Say about six-thirty? You might care to take on a brew, or something worse, before we chow — maybe we could bend an ear at those yodeling jokers, in that so-called always popular Ram Room. You think?"

"Can't wait," she said.

He was all soaped up in the shower, he was actually humming a tune, fairly close to "Across the Wide Missouri," when he heard his name yelled from down the corridor — "Hey Spurling! *Telly*-phone!"

302

He yelled back, sticking his head from the stall. "In the shower! Git the message!" He went on with the tune in the hot water's steaming.

At the room, Sven Svensen was changing his shirt. He gave a grin at Hank coming barefooted through the door with the towel around his lanky middle.

"The coome-back kid," Svensen said.

"I'm just smokestackin'."

"This morning, the ghoost. *Gode Gud,* you was yust color like *firnschnee!* Now rosy pink. Getting phones from the lonesome *pikene!*"

"Lonesome what? Is it that bad, Svensen?"

"Nice voice, no name. Wants to meet Mister Spurling at lobby of Lodge."

"Lodge?"

"It's what she say. Lobby of Lodge."

"I had a date with her over here! Son of a gun, it means dough, that Lodge life. I'm ruptured."

"You don't look too bad, ruptured."

"Goddam, I'm still livin'! Last night what a slob. The original stoop."

"Ho the voice of aquavit! That crazy Appenzeller Sepp, he say this evening after meeting, he tell me he think it done you oak-kay. He seen you by Round House. You look different. Cheerful."

"Broke as hell, don't give a damn, skiing good — it's a funny thing."

"You yust clean the soot from the flue, Killer my boy. Wot's her name?"

"Whose name?"

"The girl. *Den piken!*"

"I haven't got a girl. This is my private student today. From Detroit. And this here, is my Sunday shirt."

"Old Killer. I lend you a ten, if you need it."

303

"Svensen my old Norshki pal."

The cold was deep and still, the snow glowed blue, in the dark outside. Through the blue-laden trees across the drive the lights of the Lodge had a golden shine. He walked briskly, planning how he would suggest a return to the Inn for dinner. He stood for a moment alone on the Lodge's lighted porch, unbuttoned his topcoat casually, turned his collar down smooth, touched his tie, and walked in the door.

Francene was not in the lobby, he did not see her. He strolled slowly, past the columns, into the lounge, then glanced inquiring at the scattered chairs in front of the great hearth's open fire.

"Doll baby," a voice behind him said. "Golly!"

It was Dottie.

17

The storming of the wind awoke him. It came in gusts rattling at the window sash, and mourned with eddied murmurings, until another gust came swelling, crying the death of night.

He lay very still behind the shut lids of his eyes in the dark safekeeping of the bed. The warmth of her rounded nakedness deep in sleep pressed against the yielded ease, the drowsed comfort, of his own nakedness. He opened his eyes in the gray of day's coming, then closed them again in the sound of the wind, the boding wind. It whirled and tumbled and hurled itself through dawn's high space outside and he lay still, for a while yet, in the cloaked nest of the effortless bed. Only his mind moved. He tried to hold it motionless, but it moved, awake.

She is here with her bottom curved sweet to my belly she is my own now in this bed, he told himself. All of her. Everything she has brought to me. Every smooth nakedness of her. On her, inside her, it is mine. Right now this minute mine. How long, mine?

Until death do you part, what the old geezer said as if he did not believe it. The old geezer with the eyes, the book, the fountain pen. The honorable district judge. Swintee County, Idaho.

This is what I wanted. This is what I thought about hungry, what I imagined so long. And she wanted this, she said she did. How else can I think of it, she would not have come back to me all of a sudden there at the Valley if this was not what she wanted. So this is what I want. Of course it is. I have it now.

What is it, that I have?

Her.

Be honest. What else, besides her?

I am honest. Nothing else besides her. That is all, the way it is. That is everything. That is enough, isn't it?

Before now, I did not have anything.

Yes I did. I had myself. Now I do not. Now I am not mine. She has me. And I — I have her. What love is: I have her: she has me. My lawfully wedded wife.

With something on her mind that she will not tell me. I thought so the night she got to the Valley, and there she

306

was. I could feel it. I can feel it more now a week later for
sure she is not exactly Dorothy. Not natural. Not blowing
up a storm that great way she did those days in the mountains.

Dorothy Spurling. No home. No prospects. With husband
number three and a used car he bought with her money
at Twin Falls, Idaho. For a quiet footloose honeymoon
she says. On the quiet backroads of the West she says.
Away from it all. Mr. and Mrs. Haven Spurling.

No, I do not have all of her. I was wrong about it, thinking what I have. I do not have what is on her mind, I do
not have the way she thinks of things. That part will come
later. It has to. Because when you love somebody you understand them. Don't you. You have to understand them
if you love them, isn't that right? You love her and that is
plenty for now. Today.

Today going to Silvertip. It will not be easy.

He opened his eyes. It was light enough to see the stains
on the warped wallboard ceiling. It was light enough to see
the walls were dull green, the curtains by the little window
had red dots. It was light enough to see the opened top of
Dorothy's suitcase, and the clutter on the top of the cheap
wooden dresser, and the pink bedspread. It was light
enough to see a piece of colorless sky outside in the bad
wind and the corrugated iron roof on the Chevrolet Garage
of Wapiti Pass, Wyoming.

"Wake?" she said to him, moving.

"Dorothy Spurling," he said.

"Umm," she said. She started to turn. "Ouch!" She sat
up. "What *is*—" They both jerked, pushing back the
covers to look. "It hurt!"

It lay in a wrinkle of the sheet, by her hip. Hank reached
down and got it. "Your wedding ring," he said. "Slipped off."

307

She eased back down, pulled up the covers, snugged herself against him.

"So derned big for your finger." He held it up, out of the covers, to look at it. "I'm sorry it is. It's only until I can get you a real nice one."

"You better put it back on. This one," she said. She held her hand up over him and he slipped the ring on her finger. She turned her hand, looking up at it. Inlaid in the smooth dark tortoise shell were the little silver letters: *s a m o a* USMC *1942*.

"Those native people that made them, they would get the silver from New Zealand shillings," he said. "Some ring. To use for a wedding. The only ring I ever owned, though. I always kept it. The Pacific. Now it's yours. Such as it is."

"What's Samoa like, darling?"

"I never was there. I went straight to the Canal. This belonged to a Seventh Marine that was on Samoa. He got two rings, he got a native to make them for him. He give me a chance to buy one, it was down in Melbourne, one time when he was hard up. He kept the other. Name was Vogle. My buddy. But I am going to get you a lot better ring. When I can."

"This is my wedding ring, this one." She put her hand under the covers, out of sight. "Dottie's all married up. Day before yesterday. Remember? You married her."

"I did?"

"Punkin. So we don't have a thing to do now."

"But this."

"Things like this."

"You like this?"

"Mad about it."

"So am I. About this."

"Darling. My mouth's icky. Should brush teeth?"

308

"No. Too cold."

"So right! What are you doing now?"

"This."

"You're so act-ive!"

Her watch said twenty-five minutes to ten when she latched it on her wrist and they were finally ready for breakfast.

"Hanky Boy," she said to him standing with the room key in his hand. "My Hanky Boy. We do make music, now. Really, don't we? My God!"

"I think I better kiss you. Before we go out into that bad wind," he said. She let his hand touch, move at smoothness curving, ungirdled, soft. She let his hand stay.

"Oh dear."

Her watch said twenty-five minutes after ten when they walked into the dining room side of the Knotty Pine Tavern on the snow-crusted main stem of Wapiti Pass, and sat down at a table for breakfast.

Their eyes had the look, the softed glassiness, bespeaking the loins, throbbed loins, each other's loins. Their mouths had the look. Scarlet edges on her lips went imprecise, gone faintly stretched and blurred with a mouth's late imprecise uses; his dried lips were less thin, less straight, carrying yet their late slaking.

"First may I have a Bloody Mary," she said, partly to Hank, partly to the waitress.

The waitress already had the picture. She got it. "Sorry, mam. The bar has no vodka. We could make you one with gin."

"Ug. Bring me a martini, double. No olive."

"Yes mam. And you, sir?"

"Tomato juice. Just tomato juice."

"Hanky," she said when the waitress had gone. "Hanky, it's honeymoon. Isn't it? I do need a little belt. After the

way you — unbelt me. Darling." She scratched across the top of his hand with a long scarlet fingernail.

"Wouldn't it be dreamy," she said when her drink was nearly gone, "what a life! Just belted. Then unbelted by my Hanky. Forever."

"I'm saving my strength," he said.

"I unbelt so easy, don't I? I've always thought I do. Don't you think I do?"

"You do."

"Ping! And I come unbelted. Just talking about it, Hanky!"

"I haven't started on you yet."

"Oh yes you have!"

They ate looking much at each other; they looked very little through the plate glass at the main street icy and the sky thin gray and the wind blustering.

"Dorothy. We got a day ahead of us."

"I know. On the phone, what time did you tell them? That we'd arrive."

"Late afternoon."

"Do we *have* to go?"

"We both told them we would."

"We couldn't change our mind?"

"No. We wouldn't want to."

"Do we *have* to stay there tonight?"

"I guess we could go on to Junction. But we ought to stay. Mother fixing up the room, and everything. For us to stay. She took it calm, about us. So did Dad."

"Calm. Before the storm!" She frowned.

"We ought to tell your father, I keep saying."

"You'll be sorry. And my mother — but she's in Lausanne."

"I'm the one to tell your father. I ought to do it, let him know it, Dorothy."

310

"No, no! Not yet."

"Why? We've done right. I want him to know it."

"He will raise pure hell with us, Hank."

"Sound like you're afraid."

"So what? Do you suppose he knows it already? Do you suppose he's found out?"

"So what if he has! Anything to be ashamed of, marrying me?"

"Anything to be ashamed of, marrying you! God *no,* Hank Spurling!" She looked at him. "Don't you see that? It might be the other way, Hank Spurling."

"What way?"

"To be ashamed. You might be the one."

"Tell me something. I got to ask you, looking right at you. Are you running from something?"

"Yes."

"What? Tell me what, Dorothy. What are you running from?"

"From myself. It's why I ran to you."

"Well." His eyes left hers.

"Is that awful? Do you think it is?"

"Well. I don't know. You better stand with yourself." His eyes came back to hers. "Because if you run now, you'd have to run from me. And I won't let you get away, Dorothy Spurling. See?"

"I — hope you're right."

"So we'll go see my folks today. Like we should. And we'll call your father on the phone, or write to him, or something, like we should. Then we'll figure it from there. What we'll do. You and me. Together."

She lit a cigarette and they sat at the table saying nothing.

"Maybe it would help," he said, "if we called your father from Silvertip. With my folks there, and everything. Maybe he would take it better."

"Nothing will help. And finally you won't love me enough."

"You don't think I will? Why?"

"You're a sweet man, Hank. That's why."

"Look, Dorothy. This kind of stuff — this kind of talk — why don't we get going on something else? Let's go get the car gassed up. And load up, and hit the road. The sun's coming out. And it's almost noon."

"It looks so grim."

"Tomorrow we can head for Steamboat Springs."

"Gad. I think I'll just sit here, Hank. While you get the car checked. If you don't mind."

"Okay. Then I'll pick you up. And we'll go pack at the room and check out."

"You have money for the gas?"

"I got enough."

"I'll pay the breakfast, while you're gone."

He could smell liquor on her breath, it was strong, when she got into the front seat by him and they drove up the street to the motel. They walked into their room and closed the door against the cold.

"Bongo," she said, looking at the room's disarray. "What a mess." She dropped off her fur coat. "It's so cold, out there!" She sat down on the side of the rumpled bed. "Where do we ever begin?"

"I'll close up my suitcase, then help you with yours," he said.

"Hello," she said when he came carrying his kit from the cubbyhole bathroom. Her shoes were off. She lay back, propped on the bed pillows, smiling. A pint bottle of bourbon, uncapped, sat on the bed table near her arm.

"Where'd that come from?" he frowned.

"The Knotty Pine Tavern. Honeymoon. Honey honey-

312

moon. Did you see this bruise on my thigh, darling? Look. Look at it."

The afternoon shade was a cold blue on the snow along the highway, beneath the pines and wintery thickets down the serpentine canyon of frozen Wapiti Creek. Bundled in her coat she sat close at his side, lulled with the blend of sound from the engine's hum, the steady sing of tire chains, the vague blow of the heater near her feet.

"Feel exhausted," she said to him. "Depressed."

He turned to glance at her. "Those belts, you call them. They were a bum idea."

"Don't be critical. You weren't feeling badly, yourself. You were feeling lovely. Naughty. Don't say you weren't."

He said nothing.

"Honeymoon. What we're here for, isn't it? What *else* are we here for? Old Hanky the Zonker. In old Wyoming. Zonks me."

"I wish you hadn't got tight."

"Not. Not very. Not stoned. Just exhausted. Depressed. Could anything be more mournful, I ask you really, than the great open spaces? Just tooting along through the boon-docks. The great open spaces, they're frightening, Hank. A frightening bore. Wonder if there's any radio. In Greenland's icy mountains." She reached forward, turned one of the knobs on the dash.

A voice emerged from the popple and scratch of the static, "— Democratic nominee for president. A White House spokesman said Truman had 'no comment' to make on Hannegan's speech —"

"Poot," she commented, turning the dial knob. Its turning brought silence, then a fuzzed wash of sound with words: "— point west of Cheyenne. The airliner, though reporting no trouble in flight at three-seventeen A.M. —"

313

"And *why* is there never anything but yakyak —" she said, reaching forward —

"Hold that," Hank said.

"— overdue, may be downed in the Cloudrock Mountains, one of the most inaccessible winter areas in the nation. — And on the international front: Warsaw. Józef Cyrankiewicz, Socialist leader, today was given a mandate to form —"

"Knock that," Hank said.

"Want music, please. Need music."

"You hear what it said? The Cloudrocks."

She turned the knob to silence. "Been there. No plumbing. No place for girls. Airplanes either."

"Up there —" he shook his head — "something like that happening. I hope it didn't."

"*I* want music. Something pleasant. Please."

It was nearly dusk; the dark-tracked highway cut straight between the snow fences, the humped drifts of empty white, toward the lonely town of Dwindle on the Fontenelle Plateau. A radio cowboy had finished a lament with his guitar. Dorothy Royston Alton Haskett Spurling with her head propped against the seat back, uncomfortably, had dozed.

Issuing from the little screened grille in the dash, the voice was crisp. "A rift in murky cloud over Wyoming's high Cloudrock Peak this afternoon briefly disclosed wreckage assumed to be that of the Transcontinent Airways airliner missing since before dawn today. Scars and scattered debris, according to a search plane pilot, were sighted on a snowy mountainside below the summit of Wyoming's most formidable peak. Alerted air search craft await weather conditions which will allow confirmation and positive identification and location of the reported wreckage.

314

Civil Aeronautics officials late today state that heavy snow-storms frequent in Wyoming's high Rockies might effectually bury a crashed aircraft until spring. They state that extreme ruggedness of winter mountain terrain in the isolated Cloudrock area can severely impede ground search or rescue operations at this time of year. The westbound airliner, carrying twenty-nine passengers and crew of four, was last heard from at three-seventeen A.M. today, reporting normal flight on instruments in solid overcast at an altitude reading of twelve thousand five hundred feet, on course over Grimes Gap, Wyoming, a position approximately thirty air miles southeast of Cloudrock Peak. Prominent on the missing plane's passenger list is the name of Robert K. Royston, noted Chicago industri —"

Dorothy Spurling sat straight up. Both her hands covered her mouth. A cry came crowding up her throat, out between her fingers, into the air. Gripping her shoulder with one hand, Hank Spurling jammed the car to a stop.

"— and founder of the Milo P. Royston Foundation," the voice said crisply. "Royston was booked to San Francisco on the missing Transcontinent airliner. Yesterday in San Francisco, the wealthy Royston's daughter —" her body tensed rigid: Hank turned, taking both her arms tight in his hands: he held her — "Mrs. Dorothy Royston Haskett —"

"Oh no Hank Hank Hank —"

"— news when her name appeared in testimony at a public hearing of a coroner's report and police evidence relating to the suicide death of Osbert 'Slick' Dodgens, famed band leader, jazz trumpeter and, according to police, known user of narcotics. Testimony mentioned the socially prominent Mrs. Haskett as being escorted by Dodgens for a part of the evening previous to his dawn suicide leap from

315

the sixth floor window of a San Francisco apartment hotel on January 30. — Now to Washington, for today's news at the nation's capital —"

He released her arms. He reached over, turned the knob, silenced the voice. The car engine's whir, the car heater's hum, had both gone dead: a nightmare stillness hung in the air. From behind the two hands covering all her face, she made no sound. Her shoulders moved with a steady, small, dreadful shaking.

He stared through the windshield at the empty road. He sat there. He touched his lips with his tongue. He shut his dry mouth. He swallowed, clamping his jaws. He commanded his head to turn on his neck, to look again at whatever he might have to see there in the silence beside him.

He saw the glister of wetness spilled from between the fingers hiding the face.

He felt his mind fight for a word, to somehow locate, to somehow encompass, to somehow name its calamity. His tongue shaped what his mind found and he said, "Dorothy." He said it again, "Dorothy." Sitting there, not trying to touch her. Only trying to reach her, only trying to reach himself. With something not silence. Something not wrong. Something not alone.

"Two things. Now," he said. "There's two things."

Her shoulders quit their shaking. He could hear her breathing through her mouth, behind her hands.

"One thing," he said, "is your dad. I am going up there. Tomorrow. To find him. And I will find him. You hear me?"

"Yes."

"Before I go, there is the other thing. Whatever it is. About you. I would like to know it. Before I see your dad."

Her shoulders shook again. When they had stopped, she said, "Don't look at me. You hear me? Don't look at me.

316

Find my handkerchief. It's in my bag. And don't be righteous."

He handed her the handkerchief. "I'm not righteous. I'm your husband."

"I'll skip that," she said and blew her nose.

"I won't skip it," he said. He touched at the ignition key, it was still on, and he stepped on the starter. The engine began running, the heater hummed again.

"Dwindle's about five miles," he said. "Silvertip's fourteen from there." He turned on the lights, put the car into gear. It moved along the road in the growing dark.

Out on the gloaming plain were the first awakening lights of Dwindle.

"Hank."

"Yes."

"Do you think this is real?"

"Do I think what?"

"Do you think it might not be true? Can you think that voice — wasn't real? That it did not happen. That we will wake up. That it will be all right. Because it didn't happen and it is not real?"

"It's real."

"Yes, I know it is. I killed him —" She started crying again.

"You killed *who?*"

"My father. He is dead! Because of me." She covered her face.

"Listen here! An airplane crash — a thing like that — it happens, or it doesn't happen. You didn't cause it, you couldn't. Not you. It crashed for some other reason. Not you."

"He got on that plane. Because of me. Now he is dead."

"You don't know that. You're not sure of that —"

"I'm sure. I caused it."

317

"He may still be alive. You don't know."

"Why can't I be dead instead of Daddy Boy dead — dead —"

"Keep control of yourself. Hear me? Keep control. Going to pieces out here on the road won't do no good. You hear me?"

He slowed the car at the sign on the edge of Dwindle. Passing the shine of a filling station's floodlit pumps, he had a glimpse of her face strained, puff-eyed with fallen tears. The streets of Dwindle seemed emptied. A traffic light seemed long, long in changing from silent red to silent green. While the car stood still on the street's dirty snow, suspended in a dimness of winter's evening dark, she drew a cigarette from the pack in her handbag, pushed the lighter on the shadowy dash. When it clicked she drew its orange glow from its socket, lighted the cigarette. He heard her inhale.

Beyond the last of Dwindle, he turned the car from the highway to a narrower snow-plowed track. It led toward the valley of the frozen Freefolk through a lifeless dark and quiet to the foot of the Cloudrock Mountains. The tip of her cigarette made a dot of tiny fire in the awaiting dark, in the awaiting quiet.

"I will tell you this much," he heard her voice say.

He waited, for what she would tell.

"I always lie, some. Don't I?"

"No. I don't think you do." He tried to see her face. "And not now, you wouldn't."

"Why wouldn't I? I always have."

"No. You would let me have the truth. If you told me anything now. It would be true."

"This is true," she said. "I do not know anything at all about how or about why that vile man jumped from a window. I knew him in New York, yes. I saw him once in

318

San Francisco, that night. At a horrible café. I was there with unspeakable people, yes. The minute I got in the taxi alone with him I knew he was not on fu, like New York. He was on something else, hideous, mad — I managed to jump from the cab at a stop light, when I realized. I ran, I hid in a drugstore telephone booth, I was petrified and I finally got another cab. That was all there was, with him. I will tell you this much more. I felt so hideous, I felt I shouldn't face my aunt, I felt I couldn't, if she asked me anything. I had my own key to my mother's and I went there and I spent that night there in that empty place and I saw all those letters you had written me, I found them, I read them, there alone that night at my mother's. The next day I saw the headline in the paper, the suicide, and I left San Francisco to find you, Hank Spurling. I told my aunt I was going to Santa Barbara. I know perfectly well that an unspeakable person, unspeakable, wanted money to keep my name out of it, and oh my God so perfectly tragic that my father found it out and was on his way to do something about it, he *must* have been, he always did, but this time I was terribly afraid to tell him and don't ask me any more because I can't stand it and I have not lied to you, Hank Spurling, I have only ruined your life."

"I will decide that," he heard himself saying.

She was crying again.

The headlights' beam reached ahead tracing the ice-crusted tracks through starless dark. The slender snow poles set as winter markers along the road's buried flanks glowed transient dashes of ghostly shine as the car found its way along the desolate grades and twists, along the wordless miles, of the snow-plowed cut.

A far point of misted yellow light appeared, disappeared, appeared again a little brighter, nearer. Another light like it showed, then another, steady.

"Silvertip," he said.

"I can't face them, Hank. I can't face anyone."

"You can do what you have to do. All of us will do all we can —"

"You despise me. I know you do."

"I don't despise you, Dorothy. Let me tell you something. When you love somebody, you try to understand. So you can help each other."

They crossed the Freefolk's bridge. They came to the shapes of leafless trees, a few houses, the square faces of buildings on a snow-banked street. They passed the light of Tom Piggott's garage, Rodemacher's, the Cloudrock Bar; they found the dark turn, the rough track along the empty field. Through the line of brush along the Plew, they slowed over the planking across the creek.

Lights were shining at the Spurling house. The old truck was parked at the feed yard. Two other cars stood darkly by the front gate.

"Somebody here," Hank said.

He put the two cars in his headlights' glare before he drew up to turn and park. One car was a mud-spattered, nondescript sedan. The other was an unworn and sturdy panel truck by no means nondescript. It had a tall, heavy, official radio antenna. It had pale marks of stenciled lettering and official symbol small on its side door. It had a federal government license plate.

Hank pulled in stopping, turned off the lights and the engine. Through the sudden dark silence there by the front fence came a muffled rasp of radio noise, a voice speaking briefly in coded numerals, a murmurous scratch of loudspeaker reply and closed silence: the antenna was at work: an operator sat, in a barely visible glow of light, busy behind the pale stencilings on the dark door.

"Oh my God, God, God —" she said whispering.

320

"What's the matter?"

"It's police, isn't it?"

Yellow light reached from the opening door of the house. A silhouetted figure came out the door, closed it, walked toward them, bobbling a flashlight.

"Hank?" The figure came closer. "That you, Hank?"

"Yes, Dad."

Ingo snapped off the flashlight and stepped to the driver's side of the car. He saw his son. He saw his son's wife hunched down with her hands covering her face.

"You have heard," Ingo said. "What they say has happened."

"Yes," Hank said.

"We been expecting you to get here. Quite a while."

"Who's in there? What's this radio car?"

"Federal aviation people. Department of Commerce. A CAB man, he is in the house, he has come all the way from Denver. Claude Nagle brought them, he showed them up here from Junction, few minutes ago. About going up, Hank. The mountain."

She sat listening, her face uncovered. Ingo saw her face. He walked around to her side of the car, and opened the door. "Poor kid," he said, looking at her. "You come in the house. We will do everything we can. The best we can. You come on."

She got out of the car, stiffly, numbly. Holding her fur coat wrapped tight around her, she walked between the two men along the tracked snow to the door, into the glare of the light, past the two strangers risen from their parlor chairs. She felt their eyes, in the silence. She turned, she saw Em Spurling kiss her son, in the silence.

Dorothy Spurling saw Em Spurling's face, in the silence. Dorothy Spurling felt both her hands gripped in both of Em Spurling's hands. Dorothy Spurling saw two, only two,

hard-fought tears, one from each eye, well and spill down Em Spurling's cheeks.

"Would you like to go to your room? It's fixed clean for you and Haven. Would you feel better, going there?" Em asked her.

"I would like to go there. Awhile," she said. "If I wouldn't be alone. I would rather be — not alone."

She went with Em to the bedroom.

Hank and his father brought the baggage in from the car.

"Mr. Gannion —" Ingo said. "You will want to talk to my son here. This is Mr. Gannion, Hank. From Denver. And I guess you know Claude Nagle from Junction."

"Seen him the morning he got back from the Army," Claude Nagle said. "I told Gannion, I says to him, if they was anybody could get up to the big wreck, you and your old daddy would know the way!"

Controlling himself, Hank turned from Claude Nagle to look at the big man in the clean new outdoor clothes and high laced boots.

"Have you got the word for sure, Mr. Gannion? Is it true, Cloudrock Peak?"

"Only one thing is certain. The plane is down," Gannion said. "We never raised anything from it after three-seventeen A.M. It had fuel to fly until approximately six-fifty. We're forced to assume the plane is down somewhere between Grimes Gap and our next check point which is Elk Park station. At three-forty this afternoon one of the Air Force search pilots working a grid northwest of Grimes Gap says he saw what's left of Flight 909 smacked on the side of the big peak, a little under thirteen thousand feet. He got only a quickie. Cloud closed on it, and he had to come in without another look. He could be wrong! But he's an old hand, flew 38s in Italy. He could be right too. So we're

322

praying to God for decent weather up there tomorrow morning. As soon as it's light enough for search — We got something tough on our hands —" Gannion shook his head. "Transcontinent's division head will be out here by morning. So will a postal guy, there's air mail up on that mountain. My boss will probably show from Washington. We will get every kind of equipment, every conceivable facility we can, for the job. And quick. Transcontinent is talking about alpine experts, mountain climbers, arctic specialists, whatever it takes — too bad there isn't a chopper made that could handle that altitude, or that stinking weather! Whoever gets up there, it will be the hard way. That's why I didn't wait, that's why I came up here tonight. I want some men who know the country, who know what it would take, to get there. And quick."

"I've been giving Mr. Gannion an idy," Ingo said. He pointed to the wall behind Hank.

Hank turned to look. In the stress of his arrival, he had not noticed, he had not seen; it shook him. "Where'd that come from?" he asked his father.

"Flynn. He sent it all framed up, a present."

Under the stormy peaks, gray stone cupped a milky glacial lake. Its shape, by a few timberline trees, was unmistakable.

"I been trying to show Mr. Gannion, if it's on the big peak, this is the only way to get up to it —" Ingo had explained the Ezekiel Basin's head and he was moving his finger on traverses up West Shoulder Mountain along the side of the Ezekiel Glacier when Em Spurling and Dorothy came quietly into the room, to the warmth of the fire in the hearth.

Dorothy saw the painting. She stood there, looking.

"Mr. Flynn sent it to us," Em said to her, standing by her, looking. "He's a wonderful artist. Did you meet Mr.

Cosmo Flynn? I can't remember, last summer, if you met him."

"I met him."

"We had a letter from him, only last week," Em said. "He has a bride, he wrote to tell us. They live in an old house back in Connecticut. He married a lady named Miss Hester Bren, I believe that was it, he met her in Chicago —"

Something, Em saw, had caused Dorothy to cry.

Em took her by the arm. She did not know what else to do, standing there. "Dorothy —" Em said. She did not know what else to say.

"Could I have — coffee — there, in the kitchen," Dorothy said, wiping at her eyes.

Hank watched them go through the kitchen door, then brought his mind back to what Gannion was saying —

"— needn't worry about any heavy back packs or carrying problems. That's one thing at least we can take care of. Absolutely all the supply stuff, and any gear or equipment you want for the job, can be delivered by air drop. The main thing is to get competent mountain people up there on the ground as soon as humanly possible, so we can know the situation. A larger party, for the real work, can follow later."

"My wife's father is up there. He has been a friend of this family for a long time," Hank said. He looked at Ingo. "I've already said that I am going. With my dad, here. We're ready. And there is an old trapper, a man named Claunch, Merlin Claunch. Knows these mountains. Like the palm of his hand. You tell us where that plane is down. Wherever it is. We'll get there."

"I want you to get back too," Gannion said.

324

18

Up the white tilt of the peak's giant face loomed a jag of bare rock, fissured and snow-veined. Bent around the jag, in the slope of its harsh bed, the Ezekiel Glacier slept under a blanket of new powder snow. Along the blanket's rumpled edge, three men labored in a snowshoe trudge.

325

Over them, over their smallness, their slowness, clouds flew like scarves tattering gray to hide blue patches of uncertain sky, shredding gray to mantle an uncertain sun.

The clouds lapped their flying edges, thickening.

A pale scud swept down enwinding in a shroud the glacier's blanketed ice. Into the shroud's quiet, thick whirls of snowflakes tumbled. The three men drew together, for the solace of each other's visible presence.

Standing still they rested, gaining their breath, shifting their weight on their snowshoes to ease their ankles and knees, leaning a little on their propped ice axes. They stared out, through the dark amber panes of their big goggles, viewing the contents of the world closed to an arm's length in the blinding swirl of snowflakes touching, caking on each other's dark caps, dark shoulders, dark rucksacks.

Ingo Spurling felt the need of voice, the need of sharing more than vaguely visible presence in the void of nothingness roundabout, above, below.

"White-out," he said aloud.

Hank Spurling devoted himself to a slight rearrangement of the mountaineer's coil of rope over his left shoulder. He said nothing.

Merlin Claunch squinted up into the void, his lips pulled back in an ungrinning grin, his teeth bared to the snowflakes.

"Better let up. Pretty soon," Ingo said. His anxiety showed. He realized it. He was sorry he let it show.

But he felt strange. Standing in nothing. Higher than Hardway Pass. Much higher. He felt mountain strange. Not giddy. Not sick. Strange.

He thought about camp. He thought about it, not seeing anything, yet seeing camp sharp and clear in his mind, too sharp and clear, everything about it.

326

Down there. Some place down there. That way. Toward the fine tent lashed in the lee of the split granite, toward the spread of bright orange canvas the fliers could spot from the air — not now they couldn't, not now. Toward the stove that worked, hot, toward the two iron drums of gasoline, toward the half a ton of grub, boxes, cans, sacks, toward the double arctic real eider sleeping bags, toward the battery lanterns, the signal smoke flares, the skis, the rope, toward all the stuff including a busted radio, toward everything aviators and a whole winter army could think of, for a camp. Down there. In a white-out.

"We will wait, awhile," Claunch said.

"Not too long," Ingo said.

"I didn't mean too long."

They waited.

Stick to your mountains Hank Spurling, was what he said. Squatting by that fire. Handing me the word. Consider your luck, was what he said. Don't mess yourself up. Forget her. She'll forget you quick. Maybe she would have forgotten me. She didn't. Seems queer to remember it now, he said to me, get me the hell out of your mountains, he actually said that to me. Different from now, key-riste! Get me out of your mountains —

"Hank."

"What?"

"On that watch Gannion give you. What time does it say?"

He managed to read it between the glove top and the snow-flecked knitted cuff he hooked back from his wrist. "Nearly eleven. Ten to eleven."

"Four hours from camp," Ingo said.

"Less, going down."

"In this? And from here on up —" It was a bad question without being asked; Ingo abandoned it. He looked at

327

Merlin Claunch. "I wish to the Lord God we had been able to spot the place exact, through these glasses. So we would know. How it stands."

"Never seen through such fine glasses," Claunch said. "But they don't look through weather. Or around a rock."

They waited.

"I wish to the Lord God we knew more about it than is marked with a red X on a government map," Ingo said.

Hank looked at his father. The snow was caked on his cap down to the rubber rim of his goggles. "We do know. We're nearly there."

"If we were there — we wouldn't know."

"This might stop, you know."

"This might not stop."

"It might not."

They waited.

The need of utterance pressed hard upon Ingo Spurling waiting. Flecks of flying white in white stung his cheeks, his nose, his opened lips. "The higher we come," he said. "The more I keep on thinking it."

"Thinking what?"

Dark-goggled faces peered at him from the void.

"About him."

"About who?"

"Royston."

"Ruston ain't alive, Ingo. Couldn't be. Not now."

"I don't mean about that. I mean about him being here. Now. Don't you see? It wasn't other mountains! It was these. The ones he knew. The ones that knew him. See? And it is not other people going up to find him. It's us. Nobody else. Us! Just accident, you say? I don't know, the higher up we get. Calling it just accident. Don't quite fill the bill. Not in my mind."

328

The dark-goggled faces peered intently, too intently, from whiteness, from silence.

"You both think I got flimflams. Up here."

Mouths in the goggled faces said nothing.

"Well, I haven't. But it's strange, all right. Isn't it?"

The pairs of eyes gazed obscurely at him from behind their amber darkness.

"It kind of reminds me —" Ingo called upon his own mouth to perform a smile — "of old Senator Pycheley. The last time he came. 'Ingo,' he'd say, holding a drink. 'All the good men are dead and I am not feeling so well myself.' "

Merlin Claunch felt it, he felt it. Now. He brushed the back of his dark mitten, like a bearpaw, across the frost caked in the heavy stubble under his nose. He spoke. "We better start back."

"Back to camp," Ingo said after a silence.

"While we can."

"While we can," Ingo said.

"Mr. Claunch. What's the matter?" Hank said it through clamped teeth. "I thought we were making this push to get where we said we would go."

"Not today. It changed. Luck ain't here. I'm feeling it go. A man don't fool with mountains, Haven."

Merlin Claunch took a hitch at his rucksack straps, and stuck his paw through the sliding strap on the shaft of his ice ax. Then he turned, he headed down. He did not think how to go into the white void, he only knew. He went knowing subtly by the pitch of his snowshoes feeling slope under him, and by something more important, built inside his skull. It felt the way to go: he followed. Ingo Spurling stepped close in his tracks. Hank Spurling stood still, awhile, in the fade paleness of nothing. Inside of a cloud.

Oh Hank don't go don't go I don't want you to try to go up there. What good will it do now what good will it do

for you to go. I don't want you to leave me here alone because I can't stand this I can't stand any of it trapped here in this place without you my God don't leave me alone alone now come back Hank *come back.*

Haven son my prayers will be right there with you and your father all the time you are gone. O set me up upon the rock that is higher than I. The Bible verse you knew when you were a little boy Haven remember He that keepeth thee will not sleep.

His heart, his feet moved in sudden fear to find and follow ghost marks of snowshoe tracks filling and blurring with swirling white. He stepped swinging paces, down, farther down. Straining, he found the sure shape of his father's swaying back faint in the curtain of the void.

A lambent light flickered the paleness overhead.

A thin flare of hurrying silver swooped, passed over, melted. In queer suddenness snowflakes no longer fell: three men snowshoeing down a sidehill slope were sharp-edged in each other's sight. A great and swift radiance of torn white above them brought a flick, then a beam, of incredible blue. A cut of shine flashed down. The sun stood revealed, magic in clear sky. Iced breath of wind stirred through the shine, down the savage groove of the glacier. Mist furled and folded away from the white deeps of Ezekiel Basin.

The three men looked down at it. They looked around. They looked again up the long blanketed bed of ice to the bare jag of snow-veined stone on the unchanged face of Cloudrock Peak in sunny dazzle against vagrant wisps of dissolving cloud.

Mountain strange.

They looked at each other, unspeaking. In small slow file they moved following their own tracks, the overlapped big webbed leaf-shaped marks of snowshoes to where they

330

faded, to where they were gone from the glitter underfoot and the snowshoes made their patterned line up and up powder marked only by the wind.

They came even with the dark stone jag on the other side of the glacier's snow-buried bed; Hank stopped. The two men behind him stopped. They all stood breathing hard, sweating, looking now across the blanketed ice toward the tall tooth of rock and the build of the slope above it.

"About here?" Hank said.

"Un. Slaunchways. Upwards and acrost."

"Yeah."

"We better rope."

He slipped the coil from his shoulder, tossed out the twists, found the rope's middle. He helped his father put a proper middleman's knot around his waist.

"Rut used to do this," his father said.

"Rut taught me."

Hank tied on, with a bowline on a bight. He checked out Claunch's bowline at the other end of the line.

"Who's leading the rope?" Hank asked. He picked up his ax.

"You are."

They stepped out roped, with plenty of interval, with the slack in their hands, upslope diagonally across the buried, hummocked, ancient ice. Ingo, then Claunch, stepped with a meticulous gingerliness in Hank's proven tracks. Hank stopped once on the winding way, to probe ahead with his ax at a suspicious wale and hollow of powder. It was firm. They came gladly into the violet blue shade around the up-hill shoulder of the dark tooth. Hank reached out and touched with his glove the frost-gritted bareness of stone.

Up a sharp slot of corn snow, then wind-packed hard-crust, they came again into the stab of the sun's white dazzle; they stopped to unrope. The hump of the slope out

331

ahead hid the face of the peak farther up. High to the left of where they stood, up the steepening of the twisted ice bed, they saw the hanging edge of the awesome *bergschrund,* indigo-shadowed crevasse no blasts of snow could fill or bridge.

Hank got the smoothed, bound coil of rope again over his shoulder. In tense and unspoken urgency now, the file of three men plodded rightward, climbing along a glare of greater and emptier highness, stopping often, worried with the looseness of glittery deep powder underfoot.

Revealed above the easing crest of the hump ahead, first they saw a thick cornice of snow wind-scoured against the sky. Next they saw a granite face of scarp below the cornice. They climbed toward it seeing how the granite footed down to wall the back edge of a cupped shelf tilted on the mountainside; they saw how the shelf's outer edge over its broken stone rim plunged in the sheer drop of the Steeple crags, to the floor of the Ezekiel Basin.

A sing of wind in barren silence, a sound muffled through knitted wool over the three men's ears, oddly exaltation, oddly dread, whispered a high mountain strangeness.

They arrived in the wind's sing over the rise. On a high lip of the cupped shelf they stood together seeing with expectant and yet unprepared eyes a scatter of alien metal torn apart and nearly entombed in a white tilt of snow.

A hundred paces away the nearest and the least shattered piece was the aftermost portion of the fuselage, ripped away and fallen far from the rest. The rudder's soft aluminum shine leaned askew over the buried taper of the tail and the split crumple of fins.

Ingo Spurling with trembling hands pushed his goggles above his eyes and drew the Navy binoculars from the black case under his arm.

332

The farthest piece, up near the foot of the granite, sharp in the glasses' focus, was a fire-blackened and buckled wreck of severed wing. A knob of outboard engine nacelle, with one bent propeller blade, stuck up from its edge. Chunks and twists of jagged metal less identifiably shaped, dark in mounded whiteness, lay strewn on the slope from the far slab of the burned wing to the wry glint of the near rudder. Scar trails of the shorn pieces' tumblings, pits of their lodgings afire, were still faintly grooved and pocked down the pitch of the tilted shelf.

That was all.

Ingo handed the glasses to Hank.

There was not anything about it that the sound of the wind could not say better.

"We got here," Ingo said. "That is all the good it done." He wiped his ungoggled eyes with the ungloved back of his hand. "He might've been asleep in his seat. At the time. And never woke up." Ingo filled the wind's sound with words. "Snow covered him over. It covered them all."

Hank spoke. "You want to take a look through the glasses, Mr. Claunch? Here —"

Claunch did not reach out to take them.

"No," he said. "I see it, Haven. We won't find the dead. Even saying we could, what good would it do? There is nobody can find them now. July will find them." Claunch lifted his hand like a bearpaw, pointing, gazing out across the Ezekiel Basin, to its rim. "Moraine Pass," he said. "I have stood in it. Summertime. Clear weather. I have looked at where we are standing now. This bench here has a rocky swale carrying meltwater from the top. Summertime. There is a dab of green shows along the swale. Barely green, highest on Cloudrock. It is all right, being buried here, I believe."

The wind's sound went on, alone.

"Not a thing three live men can do here now," Claunch said.

"There is one thing," Hank said. "It won't take ten minutes to do. Then we'll start back. Gannion will want to know if we saw inside the tail section. The part that didn't burn. Shall we go and take a look?"

"You think we ought to, Hank?"

"Somebody ought to."

"Maybe —" Ingo said, wishing it were not so.

"I don't hone for it," Claunch said.

"That's okay. I don't either," Hank said. "But I don't mind." He slipped the rucksack from his shoulders, set it down on the coil of rope, picked up his ax, slung it on his wrist. "No use of your going too. I'll be right back."

He moved carefully into the cupping of the white tilt, down into the summertime swale. The winter tomb of Robert Royston, of many. July will find them.

The wind's sound said.

Another sound came joining the wind.

His eyes found the winged dot that brought the sound. The dot grew to a silver shape with a highlight of sun sharp on its metal nose: its sound enlarged. The sound beat down, steady, louder. It utterly destroyed the wind's weak sound in a thrusting, drumming roar.

Hank looked up at it. He waved.

Over the wind-scoured cornice against the blue the silver shape banked, turned. In its turn all its slim wing flashed for an instant of flight a diamond shine of high sun. Then it came back, smooth silver, lower over the cupped tilt. It waggled its cobalt-shadowed wings overhead, banked circling again, then flew away carrying its sound into the silence of blue over Ezekiel Basin.

He walked again in the wind's sound.

It spotted us, it saw us, it will go back with the word all

334

right and she will know. Dorothy will know. We got here. She will know I will soon be with her. She will know I'll be there, she will know. I will be with you again as soon as I can make it now Dorothy. I will bet by tomorrow the mountain troop will be getting to the Basin, I will bet I may be seeing Sepp Schreck that Appenzeller, I may be seeing Sven Svensen my old Norshki pal I owe him ten bucks —

Under the angled loom of the cracked rudder he scraped with his ax's blade at the crusted drift choking the torn metal mouth of the cave in the snow. It was hard to see in. He knocked loose a chunk of white: it fell away from the blue fabric back of a twisted seat chair. Beyond was dusky cold, snowy dim. He pushed his goggles back on his cap. He leaned into the dim. Powder slid from a touch of his ax's spike. It slid from an arm in cloth like a stained sack; grainy snow spilled from gray flesh, a woman's head of hair, a face, black blood caked a nose — he stepped back. He stepped into the sun's clean and living dazzle, looked up, and saw the cornice fall. He had one showshoe off, he had the binding loosed on the other, when the thunder shook.

He was running out upon the tilt, thrashing knee deep, when the monster slipping caught him sideward. The white blind monster grabbed him, threw him, swallowed him.

He had time flailing he had time ice needling terror sharp in his lungs O he had time when you don't care is when *they don't get you* but I care now I care *I care*.

Then in tearing shatter whitelighted as the sun he did not care.

On the lip of the tilt Ingo Spurling and Merlin Claunch cared hugging at snow in eyeless whip of whiteslashing wind, in roaring tremble of whitehurled cloud boiling the sky.

335

They cared, shivering, their bodies jerked with shivering, in the quiet, the dead quiet, over the swath of the slide marked down the tilt, scarred over the edge, with the plane taken, with Hank gone.

Gone his father cried in his heart, my son gone. Gone and his rope and his rucksack lying dark here with me in grains of snow thin as dust.

Ingo Spurling cried aloud with Merlin Claunch in the sun dazzle on the marked snow. They carried Hank Spurling's rope and rucksack to camp, to the tent by the split granite, in the luminous grieving light of dusk.

The silver plane of noontime had dropped a pack, a bright orange bundle on the snow, by the ice edge of Sundog Lake.

They found it in the morning's light; they went together to bring it into camp. They found the crayoned words written black on the bright orange near its grommeted lashing. Hank Darling. I've just seen you. You waved to me from down there on the snow. Hurry back. I love you. Hurry back. Dottie.

"Merlin. The mountains had already lost him."

"Now you see, Ingo. They claimed him before he got away."